NOW THEY LAY ME DOWN TO REST

Hodgie's Story

by Connie L. Aiken and Thomas M. Aiken

- HODGIES HOPE -

#seesomethingsaysomething

DORRANCE
PUBLISHING CO
EST. 1920
PITTSBURGH, PENNSYLVANIA 15238

The contents of this work, including, but not limited to, the accuracy of events, people, and places depicted; opinions expressed; permission to use previously published materials included; and any advice given or actions advocated are solely the responsibility of the author, who assumes all liability for said work and indemnifies the publisher against any claims stemming from publication of the work.

All Rights Reserved
Copyright © 2022 by Connie L. Aiken and Thomas M. Aiken

No part of this book may be reproduced or transmitted, downloaded, distributed, reverse engineered, or stored in or introduced into any information storage and retrieval system, in any form or by any means, including photocopying and recording, whether electronic or mechanical, now known or hereinafter invented without permission in writing from the publisher.

Dorrance Publishing Co
585 Alpha Drive
Suite 103
Pittsburgh, PA 15238
Visit our website at *www.dorrancebookstore.com*

ISBN: 979-8-8860-4218-4
eISBN: 979-8-8860-4871-1

Now They Lay me Down to Rest
Hodgie's Story

DISCLAIMER: This book contains graphic content that could be disturbing to some readers.

This book was written by Connie L. Aiken and Thomas M. Aiken.

It was written from the perspective of Connie, but there will be some sentences and some chapters directly from Tom

CREDITS AND PERMISSIONS:

We need to give credit to:
The Post Star Newspaper, Glens Falls, NY
The Pember Library, Granville, NY

Table of Contents

Chapter 1 - Every Child Needs To "Feel" Loved 1
Chapter 2 - The Big Apple 11
Chapter 3 – Brotherhood, Disillusioned, Resentment.......... 17
Chapter 4 – A Prosecutor's Request 21
Chapter 5 – An Impossible Start............................... 29
Chapter 6 – Where Were You 22 Years Ago.? 43
Chapter 7 – The Voice Of Evil 75
Chapter 8 – Doc, The Tooth Fairy, And Manner Of Death...... 93
Chapter 9 - They Seemed To Wear Troubled Expressions 103
Chapter 10 – Hey, Jo Ann 137
Chapter 11 - 911 151
Chapter 12 - The Chicken Bone................................. 171
Chapter 13 – Acquittal 175
Chapter 14 - Unmarked Grave 183
Chapter 15 - Forensic Soup.................................... 195
Chapter 16 - A Mother's Worst Nightmare 211
Chapter 17 – Time Out... 251
Chapter 18 – Battered Child Syndrome (The Trial) 257
Chapter 19 – The Closing...................................... 265
Chapter 20 - Avenging Angel 299
Chapter 21 – Closure 309
Chapter 22 – The Forgotten.................................... 317
Chapter 23 – True Reflections Of A Police Investigator 337
Chapter 24 – My Life 355

Foreword

New York State Trooper Tom Aiken has written an important investigative report exposing how child abuse cases were mismanaged in the 1970s that continues today. Medical examiners now investigate more than 1,700 child abuse deaths each year. The great majority of the deaths occur after repeated injuries over time and could be prevented with appropriate intervention. The death of two-year-old Hodgie White in 1972 could have been prevented.

During the 1970s, and now, traumatic child abuse complaints were primarily investigated by social workers in child protective services, not by police. This was, perhaps, a remnant of the concept that children were the property of the parents, and that all child injuries were assumed to be accidental. The social services goal was to keep the family together. The children the medical examiners saw, then, and often now, were unintended sacrifices on the altar of family preservation. So, it was with Hodgie.

When I began as a New York City medical examiner in the 1960s, I could easily get information from Child Protective Services as to whether there had been previous reports of abuse of the child whose death I was investigating. Such information was helpful in distinguishing whether fatal injuries were from an accidental cause or followed repeated inflicted traumas. I would get a quick response. Many of the deaths did have histories of prior abuse reports without appropriate actions taken to protect the child. The reports proved sufficiently embarrassing so that CPS made all reports confidential, even from the medical examiner's office. Reports of abuse considered unreliable by CPS were expunged.

Hodgie died from a blow to his abdomen by his father that ruptured his stomach. There had been previous reports by neighbors to CPS who saw his father beat him, who saw repeated bruising on his body, who secretly gave him food because he searched through garbage for something to eat. Social services hid this information from the prosecutor when Hodgie died which prevented him from bringing murder charges. Years later Aiken was able to obtain the CPS complaints concerning Hodgie and also information relative to physical and sexual abuse by the father of other siblings.

In 1995, 23 years after Hodgie died, Aiken's cold case investigation led to the conviction of the father for murder.

Aiken has brought Hodgie's painful and hidden death to life. Hodgie's story resonates today and demands that changes be made when issues of child abuse arise:

- Injuring a child is a crime and police should be directly involved in the investigation;
- Confidentiality laws must be changed so that treating physicians, police and medical examiners are aware of prior reports of injuries;
- Prior reports of abuse should not be expunged but should remain available for appropriate evaluation and reevaluation.
- Listen to the child.
- Listen to what the child says.
- Listen to the bruises.
- Protect the child.

Michael M. Baden, M.D.
Former Chief Medical Examiner,
New York City
Former Chief Forensic Pathologist,
New York State Police
28 March 2022

Dr. Michael Baden
World famous, world-renowned forensic pathologist

Michael M. Baden (born July 27, 1934) is an American physician and board-certified forensic pathologist known for his work investigating high-profile deaths and as the host of HBO's *Autopsy*.[2] Baden was the chief medical examiner of the City of New York from 1978 to 1979. He was also chairman of the House Select Committee on Assassinations' Forensic Pathology Panel that investigated the assassination of John F. Kennedy. Baden's independent autopsy findings are often in conflict with the local authorities' opinions. ~ Wikipedia 2022

His most notable case are:

    JFK Assassination
    OJ Simpson
    Martin Luther King
    Michael Brown
    George Floyd

- Jeffrey Epstein
- Phil Spector
- Aaron Hernandez
- Marybeth Tinning

He is a frequent contributor on Fox National News, CNN, MSNBC and other major networks.

Foreword

As Americans, engrained in our collective national consciousness are the faces of certain famous murdered children. We all remember with sadness the photos of Jon Benet Ramsey, Etan Patz, Adam Walsh and so many others—all smiling to the camera without knowing the terrible fate that awaited them. These children were experiencing the happiest of childhoods until killed in manners most foul.

Nearly thirty years ago, in 1994, as a prosecutor in Upstate New York, I brushed off the dust of an old investigative file for a sociopath by the name of David Pope, opened the file and saw the autopsy photograph of the two-year-old Howard White, called "Hodgie." It was a photograph just as unforgettable as that of Jon Benet, Etan and the others, but the face of Hodgie White was not smiling. The bruised body of Hodgie White was laid out on an autopsy table with his eyes staring forward, expressing a combination of fear, pain, and wonder as to why he was treated so savagely, why no one seemed to care, why his life could not be spared. They were the eyes of a two-year-old whose short life was filled with pain and sadness. Unlike Jon Benet, Etan and Adam, whose short lives were filled with happiness, the short life of Hodgie was filled with abuse which went unpunished for 22 years from 1972 until 1995, when his killer was tried and convicted by a jury and sent to prison.

No child should live the life that Hodgie lived. Our hope is always that no child in our great country is subjected to such abuse. This story is a cautionary tale to social workers, police, prosecutors, and society at large to listen to the voices of the abused so that you will be spared the experience of looking into the eyes of an abused child laid out on an autopsy table because no one who heard his cries for help took action.

Robert Winn
Washington County District Attorney, Retired
Prosecutor of the David Pope Case

Dedication

This book is dedicated to Howard James "Hodgie" White. A little boy that never experienced an ounce of love from a mother, father, or the professional people tasked with protecting and saving children. A little boy who suffered abuse, beatings, torture, and starvation that an ordinary person could never imagine. May we all collectively pray for his heavenly life to be everything and more than we could wish for.

This book is also dedicated to Michael Paul Pope, a survivor, and his siblings whom all suffered an unimaginable life at the hands of an evil monster and a mother who failed them all.

This book is also dedicated to each and every survivor of child abuse, both physical and sexual. May they heal knowing there are people who truly love and care about them.

Finally, this book is dedicated to our six (6) children. They have all sacrificed for so many years living a life where death, destruction, and evil has kept their father away for too many hours, days, and years.

"We would like to thank our granddaughter Tessa Dean Rose for her insight and vision."

Chapter 1
Every Child Needs to "Feel" Loved

I want to tell you about a little girl I know. She lived at 25A, Kenworthy Avenue, in Glens Falls, New York, a small town in Upstate New York where the Adirondacks begin. As far back as she can remember, she was only 5 and ½ years old and having her baby sister placed into her arms. The innocence and the naivety of a just approaching 6-year-old girl that thought her mother was going to be bringing home a baby girl that would resemble her baby dolls. Her innocence of what it was going to be like was completely different. The "doll" they brought home looked like a wrinkly old man that cried a lot and didn't smell so great. Almost immediately, though, she fell in love with this little girl, who was my baby sister. As much as I tried, I can't remember anything of my childhood before having her placed in my arms. Despite my initial reaction, I felt an overwhelming sense of love and I wanted her to feel that because even then, I never really truly knew what it was like to "feel" loved myself. My motherly instinct was so strong and even at such a young age, I knew my parents were not able to give her what she needed.

My older brother was an unruly boy, just 7 and ½, and all he wanted to do was to get into mischief. I never realized until later in life the enormity of the responsibility. It just came naturally. As I found out, motherly instinct does not come so natural to everyone. I didn't know what to call it at the time. Now I know my childhood was a very unstable, dysfunctional mess. This was mixed with mental illness, alcoholism, and selfishness. I had just barely started kindergarten when my sister was placed into my arms that October. I was just a baby myself. I should have been having someone reading me nursery rhymes, instead of me singing her lullabies. Understanding between the different cries, because she was hungry or because she smelled bad. I also realized that she cried for no reason at all, or maybe because she needed a mother and not a "baby" sister.

When I was able to get myself up and ready for school and actually attend, children in kindergarten in the early 70s still actually took naps. When my head hit the nap mat, I fell into a very deep sleep knowing I did not have to worry about my baby sister. I remember the sweetness of Mrs. Shoemaker's voice and her hand caressing my face telling me it was snack time as she tried to arouse me from a deep sleep. I would try to open my eyes from being dead tired. I know now it was from the enormous responsibility of caring for an infant and from the hunger pangs I learned to live with.

You see, when she would tell me it was snack time, I knew just like breakfast and lunch there might not be dinner at home. I learned at a young age how to cope with that grumbling in my tummy and going off to school in the morning never knowing what, if anything, I could find. We had one hour to walk home for lunch. One of my coping skills to take my mind off that rumbling in my tummy was to play games. So, "Skip to my Lou, my darling," hopping the railroad tracks and not stepping on any cracks to break my mother's back, only to find her (Bettie Lou) still in bed. I would quickly check on my baby sister and usually I could find some bread and possibly peanut butter if I was lucky, or a margarine sandwich would do. Most of the time, it was not even fresh bread. It was from the Friehoffer's discount store. So off I would go, skipping to my Lou, my darling, crossing the railroad tracks, not stepping on any cracks to break my mother's back, and before I knew it, the hour was up and I was back with Mrs. Shoemaker. I loved being there and seeing her smiling face, her beautiful red hair, and just knowing I could be a little girl. Then I was back to skipping my Lou, my darling, crossing the railroad tracks, not stepping on any cracks and breaking my mother's back, only to get home around 3:00 P.M. and she would sometimes still be in bed. Of course, he, meaning my father (Jerry), was never around. There was never anyone to welcome me home or to check my homework, so I would make my way up the stairs and down the hall and grab my baby doll out of bed and the dolls I used to play with were hardly ever touched again. She, meaning my mother, would go from the bed to the black recliner. Rarely, but on some occasions, she would throw some things together and call it a meal. Most of the time it was just find what you could if there was even anything to find.

Somehow, before I knew it, kindergarten came to an end and my baby doll didn't just lay there anymore. She was just as much responsibility, just in a different way. Her cries were different. She wanted to get up and she wanted to play. She wanted to get out of that bedroom where the drapes were drawn and it was pitch black and you couldn't tell if it was day or night. Summer mornings, knowing which friends were outside playing by the sounds of their voices and laughter, as my brother and I were belted in by our wrists to the headboard. She didn't know what to do with us all summer long. She could pacify my baby doll by tossing her a bottle or plugging her with a pacifier until Connie got home from kindergarten. My mischievous brother would somehow get himself undone and run down and grab something to eat and bring it back up and we gobbled it as quick as we could. He would pretend to be still belted in. If he was caught, he would get the belt. Year after year it was the same thing. Through the years, the dysfunction continued. My father became more dependent on alcohol and running around, if you know what I mean, and was rarely seen. If he did show up, he would come home smelling like cheap perfume, stale barroom smoke, and booze. This was a smell I will never forget. To this day it turns my stomach. Everyone knows that smell that lingers from a barroom door, but I never realized that was where that smell came from. It was just the normal smell of my father. You know that smell of a newborn baby that nobody can ever seem to get enough of? It was quite the opposite. The smell that came from my daddy turned my stomach. The screaming and fighting would start, while he laid on the couch snoring in a drunken stupor, promising not to do it again. But of course, it happened again. It was a pattern all through my childhood. The years went on and before you knew it, it was escalating to being awakened in the middle of the night by her to have me call every barroom in town looking for him. Only to hear a bar maid yelling, "Jerry, it's your kid on the phone again." You would either hear a dial tone or him saying, "What's up, babe?" Then off we would go again in the middle of the night. We would get to the barroom at last call and if his truck was there, we were sent in to get him. The fighting pattern would begin again. She did not even have a driver's license, driving the wrong way on one-way roads, with a shotgun on the backseat floor. With one whore in particular, she was going to use that shotgun on. That was the beginning of the end.

We were becoming too old to control and my brother's mischievousness escalated to small minor crimes, including stealing. He wasn't the same little boy I knew. Drinking and smoking pot, she couldn't control him anymore. She couldn't keep him tied to the bed. It got to the point where he would just wander. Because of the sleepless nights, the embarrassment of not having clothes or even clean clothes, every year I fell behind more and more academically. Wishing I could be more like the other girls in my class. Coming to school with a lunch pail full of food, cute clothes, and then talking about the birthday parties because you see I never wanted anyone to know what was happening inside of 25A Kenworthy Avenue. There were no birthday parties. There were no sleepovers. When I realized everyone wasn't living like I was I became resentful of the responsibility of raising my sister. My love for her never changed, I just wanted to be like the other girls. Not cooking and cleaning and caring for a little girl, not a baby anymore. The more I fell behind academically, the more I felt useless, confused, and angry. No one knew it because I always hid it behind my bright blue eyes and my beautiful smile. I had one spot in particular under an old tree where I would sit and that is where I learned that speaking to God would give me a sense of peace. I also learned it didn't matter where I was, I could always turn to God and I always knew he would be there. I would ask him to forgive me for my bitterness toward my sister. I wanted to be her sister and not her mother. I felt like I was juggling all sorts of emotions trying to be a mother, but yet dying to just be a sister.

As the dysfunction continued, the only escape we ever had was spending time with my grandmother up on Lake Sunnyside Road, which was known as the country then. She never had much. She came from a very poor beginning where her father walked out and she was left to raise her brothers while her mother worked to make ends meet. She had a glimmer of hope when she fell madly in love with my grandpa and he fell madly in love with her. I know this from the times she would take us for the weekends and we would lay in her pullout hide-a-bed watching TV, adjusting the rabbit ears after a long day of swimming, making biscuits with the berries we picked in her garden, and getting all cozy. Wow, getting all cuddled up and cozy! She would have me read her love letters from my grandpa, who passed away at 51 from a fatal heart attack. My grandmother and grandfather worked very hard from the moment they were married. When he came home from WWII while serving the United States in the Army as a cook, they worked day and night to open up what would become a popular diner in downtown Glens Falls, New York. I learned through my grandmother that you didn't have to have much money to have a loving and happy home. It hardly cost anything to make berry biscuits and green bean potato soup. I hated to go back to Kenworthy Avenue but I knew my grandmother had to work. Her dreams were crushed when my grandfather died at such a young age, when they had dreamt of peaceful days on Lake Sunnyside and doing some traveling. It all finally came to an end once and for all, when I, as a very mature 13-year-old, gave my mother her final ultimatum. It was either to divorce Jerry and start over, or I was going to turn them in for neglecting us. I knew things were getting out of control when on one of our nighttime patrols to find Jerry, my mother was pulled over and the police confiscated the hunting rifle. It was just time. My mother's newfound freedom was like she became a hormonal teenager hopping from man to man. It didn't take Jerry long to move one of his girlfriends in to Kenworthy Avenue. Before I knew it, Bettie Lou was moving my baby doll into the middle of nowhere and having her call a stranger "Daddy." I begged my grandmother to take me. It was still dysfunctional, just in a different way. I was a teenage girl worrying myself sick over whether my sister was being taken care of only to find out she ran away in the middle of the night in the middle of nowhere in the pitch dark. My grandmother worked Monday through Friday. There wasn't much supervision because she never got home until going on midnight. No one ever cared whether I got an A or an F.

Somehow my baby doll ended up with Jerry and his new wife and she was neglected worse than ever. She was left from morning until night to fend for herself at a horse farm, never knowing if or when anyone would ever come to pick her up. This is where her love for horses began. Eventually as my grandmother approached retirement, she knew she had to protect my baby sister. She brought her home to us only for me to realize she wasn't a baby anymore. My mother bounced from man to man and my father was ordered to pay only $4.00 per each for my sister and I. $8.00 a week. Less than a $10 bill. Somehow my grandmother managed. That's when I realized my father didn't really have a conscience. My sister and I together were not even worth a $10 bill. We were forced to grow up before our time.

When I was having my first baby at the young age of 18, I was bouncing from an abusive relationship back to the safe haven of my grandmother. My sister was dating an older boy and it wasn't before she became pregnant with her first son. I found myself back with my son's father in a small town named Whitehall, New York, near the Vermont border. I was determined to make things work. Not having a driver's license, I would walk a few miles to work at a local pizza shop and usually getting a ride home from a girlfriend. He became insanely controlling and abusive to the point that I came home from work one night with a rifle pointed at my head. As I stood there in the dark, not knowing if he was going to pull the trigger or not, all I could think of was my infant son growing up without his momma and hearing the voices of Whitehall girls echoing in my head, saying to me many times, "Hey, Connie, you have to get out of here or you are going to be the next **Jo Ann**." I never knew this Jo Ann and only heard rumors from the girls in town about a madman being so insanely jealous that he shot this young girl, a young mother herself, and how he murdered her in broad daylight on the streets of Whitehall. I never forgot what these girls told me or the desperation in their voices while knowing the abuse I was enduring. I don't know why he didn't pull the trigger or if he was just trying to scare me for the next time, I might not be so lucky.

I worked the evening shift and by the time I got done closing up the pizza shop, it would never be before 11:00 P.M. by the time I made it home. It wasn't long before he went into a deep sleep and I knew I was not going to end up like the girl they talked about. Trying not to startle my baby boy, I bundled him into a blanket and I called the police. I never looked back. Only to look over my shoulder to get a quick glance of his cute nursery. Somehow word got back to Trooper Aiken from one of the local police officers, telling him about what had occurred. Although they never did arrest my son's father that night, I was just thankful to have escaped knowing my son was safe. How ironic that years later I realized they never did arrest the man who took Jo Ann's life when he had been stalking and abusing her prior to her brutal death. It seemed like a blur. I am not sure if it was that night or the next morning, but Trooper Aiken called to make sure I was okay and to find out how my baby boy was. We talked about getting together and meeting up for dinner. I did not know that someday I would be the wife of a police officer and married to the New York State Police.

During his dinner break, we met at a small restaurant while he was on duty only to have him called out just as the meal was being served. That became the norm. One case led to another to another and to another. We were two determined people bound to make it work, which turned into now as I sit here writing this book, just shy of our 38th wedding anniversary. Six children later and many, many cases with some so horrific that it made it hard to sleep at night and some that scarred us both for life.

I first met Trooper Aiken when I was a struggling young mom of a 9-month-old baby boy and he was fresh out of the State Police academy. I was waiting tables at a pizza place in Whitehall, New York, and he came in on his break for what he later would tell me was the worst pizza he ever had! I was still in an abusive relationship with my son's father. The attraction was instant...!! Like we both knew we were meant to be together...!!! As strange as it seems, we just knew. The more he came in for breaks, the more we realized we had the same hopes and dreams for the future. To say the least, we were very attracted to one another for many reasons, not just physically, but I never met anyone so handsome in a uniform, who thought family was the most important thing in the world. In my world that was never the case. He acted like I was the most beautiful girl in the world...! We began a relationship and I was moving into a place of my own. Things happened very fast. I was very apprehensive for Tom and my Little Wayne to meet for the first time. In the short nine months of his life he had seen a lot of violence between his father and I. I don't know what brought this abusive side out in his father. I never saw any signs of this until I became pregnant. Being a young mother from a very dysfunctional childhood, I knew I wanted better for my son and my strong motherly instinct to protect him was the most important thing in my world. I didn't want to introduce him to another man and have this happen again. I had never been able to trust any man in my life so this was a very confusing and heart-wrenching time for me. He pulled up in a shiny new red truck smelling very nice and looking very handsome and it was love at first sight. Not just for me, but for my son and soon-to-be-husband.

Things continued to move forward quickly and Tom was being transferred to Fonda, NY. He didn't want to move on without us so we planned our wedding and started our family. We were excited to start our family together. One night, I surprised my husband with what we would now call the most beautiful circle we ever saw. A positive pregnancy test and a baby boy would soon be born named Jason Thomas Aiken. Tom burned both ends building his career and nurturing his growing family. Soon we found ourselves back in our hometown of Fort Ann, New York, and buying our first home together, only to be surprised that we would soon be parents again. Just barely a year and a half apart, our other precious baby boy was born just before Christmas in 1987. Aaron Michael Aiken now completed our family, or so we thought!

Connie Lynn 5 years old

Tammie Lee "Baby Doll"

Chapter 2
The Big Apple

I was a young mom of three very active boys. My husband was determined to climb the ladder, determined not to just collect a paycheck, but to make a difference. 1989 turned out to be a very hectic, confusing, and troubling year for our family. Tom was working patrol on the New York State Northway when he was summoned into his zone headquarters. Not having a clue what he did wrong, he immediately drove there and was handed a gas mask and a large wooden riot baton, told to call his family and advise them to pack a bag for a week that would be collected from our home by Troopers and sent up north, and immediately went into a State Police car with three other Troopers and started what would normally be a two-hour drive up north to an Indian reservation. This drive took less than an hour as the Troop "B" Headquarters communication kept asking them to expedite. Tom had heard stories about the reservation and gambling raids up there and he has seen the many slot machines taken into evidence, but he never knew what a true reservation was. He had images of majestic and proud Indians and an area that would match their pride and culture. In that car, one of four State Police cars holding 15 State Troopers and driving at rates of speed you could not even imagine, Tom's head was spinning as much as the scenery. By the end of the summer of 1989 all of these images were gone and from the stories he told, their pride and great culture was gone too. He told of many that were drunks and on welfare and said you could not tell where the reservation began or ended if not for the state signs indicating so. He told of an entire summer full of harrowing challenges in which he truly thought many times over he was going to be seriously injured or killed. He talked of confrontations between the New York State Police and Indians that had more weapons than the State Police because there was no control between the two country borders. He talked of the many State Police and FBI SWAT teams rotating in all summer and the frightening confrontations that all could have ended tragically. One confrontation he talked about occurred on a bridge and the first line of State Troopers and Indians were literally so close in a staring contest that their noses appeared to be touching. During this confrontation, the State Police charged through the line to arrest the Indian with a megaphone on a Federal Arrest Warrant just received from the US Attorney's office and all hell breaking loose. This is where he understood what they meant in his training when they said you could not swing a baton in a crowded environment and all you could do is push and jab with it as he and others tried to get to a seriously injured Trooper that was on the ground and being continuously beaten and stomped. This Trooper ended up being a State Police Captain and he was seriously injured and missed many months of work.

 Finally, the summer ended and we as a family had another work and family issue to address. He was being promoted after only 5 and a half short years in being offered a position into the New York State Police Bureau of Criminal Investigation (BCI). This meant a transfer to the Big Apple which ended up being a very long grueling almost 2 years. As part of the promotion to Investigator he was transferred to NYC to a drug task force unit, while I stayed behind caring for and raising our three sons. Daddy would work long hours M-F in the city and make the trip home every weekend to spend time with his family. I really don't know how he did it all...!! He was also working on his degree. We would all get in as much love as we could, and send him back to the city for another long week. I soon realized this was a very dangerous job. I will never forget my sister-in-law's call telling me that Tom was involved in a horrific shooting in a drug bust gone bad. All I could whisper was "Is he ok...?" She said physically yes, but his partner and classmate from the academy was shot and killed. I can tell you now that I felt enormous guilt that it wasn't my husband. Still to this day, I see how this haunts my husband and when he came home that night, he was forever changed...! Crippling fear. The Big Apple was forever tarnished and never considered the same. It felt like a rotten apple, wondering if we had made a big mistake. Sending him back that Sunday was one of the hardest things I ever had to do, even after surviving my childhood I realized things could be much worse. It was like holding your breath until this grueling assignment was finally over. As bad as this was, it was the beginning of a long journey of healing for me and for my husband after seeing such a horrific thing and knowing he had a job to do and had just begun his long assignment in the Rotten Apple. I felt like I was suffocating and holding my breath and still feeling enormous guilt that it was Joey and not my husband, which would leave my boys without a daddy. Trying to hold it together for the sake of our sons, we tried to move forward but it was a very long, stressful, frightening year and a half. I always wondered if we would ever see him again. There were a lot of long sleepless nights of worry. Not to mention our boys missed their daddy, and the financial strain. We were trying to pay a mortgage and rent for the cheapest apartment for Tom to have a bed to sleep in located in Harlem that we could afford. We sent him back each week with leftovers from the weekend with a can a soup, a loaf of bread for grilled cheese, a coupon for one fast food night and one night his highlight of the week in the city was to get a homecooked meal at his sister's place in Queens, New York. Tom's sister and brother-in-law learned the city very well. They were both agents of the Federal Bureau of Investigation (FBI) and that is how she learned so quickly of the horrendous shooting Tom was involved in. The city in the late 80s, early 90s was not a place you wanted to live much less work such a dangerous job. Late at night when he would get back to his apartment that he shared with three other guys on the 19th floor and I could always hear police sirens and even gunfire..! Not something you want to hear before going to bed at night. I never wanted to let Tom know how much his stories or cases bothered me because I wanted him to be able to vent and to let him get things off his chest. It made the days very long caring for three active boys. It would take me hours to fall asleep as he would start snoring on the other end of the phone. The Big Apple was not like it is today, but it actually is now reverting back to the way it was in the late 80s to early 90s. It was like a warzone until Mayor Giuliani was elected into office in 1994 and changed New York City into the beautiful city it became again. They were involved in many dangerous cases. This was a very high-level Federal Drug Task force that conducted long-term Title III wiretap cases against the major drug cartels including the Columbian, Mexican, Dominican and other major ones. This was a very intense position and we both agonized if this was really worth it after Tom lost his friend, Academy roommate, and partner, Joseph Aversa, in a brutal buy / bust operation in which two other New York City detectives were shot and left permanently disabled. The depth of losing a "brother" whose brutal murder is felt as raw today as it was on March 5th, 1990. Tom telling me the details of having to run into the middle of this frightful horrendous shootout left me with more sleepless nights that I could ever detail in this book.

Drugs were running rampant in the city at this time. While I was tucking our three boys in bed, my husband was fighting the war on drugs. He would tell me about how in China Town they were doing surveillance and there were Chinese drug and gang wars going on all through China Town. It was not unusual to have fully automatic gun battles on the streets in broad daylight. It's hard to believe that they actually had a street in the borough of Brooklyn where marked uniformed police cars were not allowed to drive down or answer calls on. When and if a call for service came in for that street, multiple cars or a SWAT team were sent in. From where we grew up in the Adirondacks, only a few hours from the city, this was unheard of...! This was a whole new world and hard to believe it was still part of New York State. It was like a warzone...! This assignment was taking a toll on all of us. The three boys missed their daddy, I missed my husband, and when he came home on the weekends it was so busy trying to get things caught up around the house that we were having some hard times in our marriage with so much stress. Somehow, finally, we made it through the long agonizing assignment. Somehow, someway we survived mentally and physically to welcome home a man who was forever changed.

Joseph Aversa – NYSP Academy Photo   Thomas Aiken – NYSP Academy Photo

JOSEPH T. AVERSA - DETF - MARCH 5, 1990

On March 5, 1990, at 3:35 p.m., Investigator Joseph Aversa, age 31, was fatally wounded and two New York City Police Department detectives were shot in an exchange of gunfire with an armed assailant who attempted to rob one of the officers during a narcotics operation. Investigator Aversa, a member of the New York City Drug Enforcement Task Force (DETF), was engaged in a "buy-bust" operation which involved the purchase of a large quantity of cocaine.

Investigator Aversa was a six-year veteran of the New York State Police at the time of his death.

NYSP Honor Wall- Fallen Troopers – Joey Aversa

Chapter 3

Brotherhood, Disillusioned, Resentment

Investigator Aiken was so happy to be out of the drug warzone. He was now stationed in the Albany area for the next year. We were all so happy to have him home every night. They were still long days with over an hour drive on each end of his shift. Just knowing he was home in our bed every night was enough for me. The boys were growing quickly and starting school, and life seemed to be getting back to normal. Although I could see stress building over time, and for the first time Tom would not talk much. The next transfer was to the Wilton station (Saratoga Springs, New York). More stress seemed to be building. He was then transferred to Queensbury and had an office in the Granville barracks. By then we had built our first home just down Route 40 from the Granville station. You would think life would be wonderful, but we were both disillusioned. One day over one of the simplest things, Tom had a meltdown. It came pouring out about the pressure from some coworkers on the job being resentful of his promotion and they tried many ways to make his life a living hell and ruin his reputation. After surviving his partner's death in the concrete jungle to come home to this treatment, I thought he was going to have a nervous breakdown…! His heart was broken believing that becoming a New

York State Police Officer was a brotherhood that had your back, not stab you in the back. The tainted rumors flying around from county to county caused the newly elected District Attorney Robert Winn to request that Tom not be assigned to his county. This is how their relationship started. Lo and behold it was the head of the clique that hurt my husband the most in the future backstabbing lies, that stood up to the District Attorney and told him that he was not going to dictate where our personnel were assigned. This was only because it was a pissing match and no one was going to dictate to him where his investigators were assigned. At this same time, Rob Winn had a full unit of criminal investigators working in his office. District Attorney Winn had a written contract between his office and the Washington County child protective service unit that all child abuse hotline reports would be investigated by his investigators.

After months of Rob observing Tom's talented investigative skills from afar, including how victims were treated, and his detailed confessions, he knew he made a bad judgment call letting himself get caught up in the vicious rumors. He and Tom started changing the way these cases were investigated and prosecuted. They started getting plea bargains of 2-6 years, 3-9 years, and 5-15 years. By the time these two were done working together, they had plea bargains on child abuse cases starting at 20-25 years in state prison. This model did not go unnoticed. Other counties started some of these same concepts. District Attorney Robert Winn decided to rip up the contract in place between CPS & his Investigators in his office and went as far as to request the director of CPS to have all child abuse cases referred to Tom. This was the beginning of an impressive working relationship where cases that would normally result in the sentencing of criminals to a slap on the wrist developed into sentences that they set the bar for other counties and other prosecutors to follow with lengthy plea bargains. It wasn't until he got his first promotion to Investigator and back to our hometown that I saw a different side of his police work. He had a way of getting the most perverted, evil pedophiles to confess. He investigated many different crimes but I could see where his heart was, it was to help the innocent victims against the evil bullies that would threaten these children to the point where they had no voice. Experiencing the bullying in his own brotherhood gave him a glimpse of the powerlessness that these children felt. Especially when most of these children had no one who cared, not even their mothers.

The backstabbing was minor compared to what would continue when Tom was again promoted to Senior Investigator, when certain ones in this clique resented Tom being promoted before others. Again, this promotion did not come easy. He commuted to Albany, New York, for over an hour each way every day. The long drive started again, but we were so thankful he was home every night. At least he was home nightly. This position was at the State Police Headquarters and he worked for the Internal Affairs Division for the next two years. The rumors were flying about such ludicrous allegations of District Attorney Robert Winn calling the Superintendent to get him promoted before others that were on the job for much longer than he had been. This brotherhood that my husband took so seriously was weighing very heavily on him and the malicious backstabbing to get others promoted or later transferred back home before him almost led to another almost nervous breakdown over the most minute things that wouldn't have bothered him before. It felt like Post-Traumatic Stress. Climbing the ladder was literally not as easy as it appeared. He kept his emotions in check while on duty, but behind closed doors he was a wreck. He was determined to keep his morals intact despite his disillusion about right and wrong. They were on a power struggle because their power was in their numbers and they had friends near the top of the organization. My husband was never one to back down, especially when it comes to bullying. Even against men you thought were part of your brotherhood. The resentment set in when he was out on an assignment in the field and he could feel the knife in his back, the rumors swirling, and the lies spreading. I don't think they ever met anyone like my husband. He finally took the time to examine the situation. This wasn't the brotherhood he expected and he was no longer disillusioned and he finally let the resentment go when he approached Superintendent Bennett as he was coming in the door. He was actually a man of good character himself and made Tom the promise that this deceitful plan that they plotted for nearly two years would not take place, not on his watch. This allowed Tom to let go of the enormous resentment and again focus on what really mattered. Their plan was to get the other Seniors to step ahead of Tom and move forward towards home and leave him behind all the while laughing behind his back. As the Superintendent promised, this did not happen.

Chapter 4
A Prosecutor's Request

Tom and Rob Winn's unique relationship picked up right where it left off. There was no more awkwardness and there were no more trust issues. The trust was now 100 percent between the two of them. What one didn't think of, the other did. Two men who had very dry senses of humor, big hearts, and a passion for justice. The relationship that certainly started on the wrong foot. The trust and the crimes they worked day and night on started before Tom was promoted and did his assignment at Internal Affairs. Some of the high-profile cases that led to my husband's promotion to Senior Investigator which included the unsolved murder case from the 1970s that led to the death of little Hodgie. A name we will never forget. A boy we both eventually came to know from the inside out. This was the David Pope murder case. The gap in time led them both for the desire and the exhilaration they both felt when the magic of convictions came that our area had rarely ever seen before was sparked again. These cases that led to my husband's promotion where he never missed crossing a "t" or dotting an "i" and Rob's passion in the courtroom was so professional and well done. A working relationship the county had never seen before and probably never will again. So many cases, too many to mention. The ones that led to the promotion, the publicity residents in the area being mesmerized by the convictions after convictions and the sentencing that should be the norm and not the exception. There was one case in particular that was always weighing on Rob's mind. One from his hometown of Granville, New York, where everyone knew your name, and a poor boy from the longhouses who was murdered by the cold-hearted vicious murderer David Pope. This little tot not even three years old, and how his mother's boyfriend David seemed to get away with murder for over 20 years. The main cases that led to Rob's decision to finally approach Investigator Aiken in August of 1994 were Colin Murphy, the three Gutkaiss brothers and an unrelated female baby-sitter, Gary Colvin, Robert Mercado, Tania Ladd, Jason Shephard, and Zind Nutting. These were such unique cases that hit on many different types of major crimes that Rob knew it was time for justice for little Howard "Hodgie" White. The other cases that stood out, and let's start with the Colin Murphys of the world. The ones that will do anything for a high, even taking a hammer to the head of a 17-year-old pregnant girl, a 7-year-old girl, and her mother. A scene that took place on a hot Sunday in August of 1993. A day my husband will always remember. There was always one case after another, but this one was one that would keep him away for days on end. Just when you thought you could let your guard down and just spend a day helping your sister and brother-in-law clear the land to build their future home. A sister who was finally back in the area who suffered her entire childhood and her entire adulthood with a rare lung disease. She happened to marry a man whose career in the Air Force of the United States of America that led them away from our home town to deployments around the world. Tom was overjoyed to spend that Sunday clearing trees until he was dead tired, but was so elated for future family gatherings with a sister he was told as a young child that would never live out of her teens. Only to arrive home and have his pager going crazy while trying to take a quick shower. The buzzing wouldn't quit. He knew by that constant buzz that something wasn't right. He quickly jumped out still dripping and realized there was a case that would cause him not to see his family for at least a few days. While I was downstairs waiting for him to come have a cup of coffee with me, only to see him fully dressed and rushing out the door. What they knew so far was this was a well-known drug dealer in the area where he and his girlfriend were major drug dealers. While he was serving his weekends in jail, the rule was, no sales while he was away. This gave the drug-dealing mother's younger sister a false sense of security when she went to her sister's place believing her sister could help her when she needed her the most at the beginning of her labor. A young girl naïve enough to not realize the dangers that were to lie before her when she was told earlier in the day to go home and make sure she had someone to get her back to the hospital when needed. Not realizing she would never make it there alive. She knew her older sister and niece would be alone for the weekend and she was anxious about becoming a new mom and excited to bond with her sister.

No one really knows what happened that Saturday night except for Colin Murphy. What we do know is that a horrific murder and two assaults that were so malicious, no one knew how her sister and her 7-year-old niece managed to survive. A crazed drug addict breaking all the rules of a drug dealer's laws used both ends of a hammer in a violent outrage when he realized he wasn't going to get his fix. Leaving all three with smashed skulls, not expecting a one of them to live. All he could think about was his next fix. None of the girls were discovered until Sunday afternoon when family members were concerned knowing this 17-year-old was about to give birth. When help arrived, they had no hope that any of them would survive. This girl was kept alive long enough for them to deliver her baby by Cesarean section while they worked frantically to save the 7-year-old niece who survived her horrific injuries only to live with the agony of being paralyzed the rest of her life on her left side. While in the other operating room, they were able to save the little girl's drug-dealing mother. A young mother who never got a chance to meet or raise her child while her sister did and while she should have known better and protected them from a crime that should have never taken place. The "mother" or any kind of mother knows that there is a risk involved with that kind of drug dealing. She will now have to live with the fact that her sister is gone, a child was born that will never know his mother, and every time she looks at her daughter, she will be reminded of the choices she made and the predicament she put them in. This horrific crime led to a very long investigation with a long list of drug addict suspects and was an eye opener to everyone working the case as to how bad the cocaine and crack epidemic had affected our entire area. Finally, after long days and nights and after extensive work by many police investigators, they were determined to hold the person responsible for these assaults by building an airtight case while in reality they could have pinned this on 3 or 4 good suspects. They did this by letting the evidence lead them to the responsible person instead of making the evidence fit any one suspect. This led Colin to being convicted of 2nd-degree murder and two 2nd-degree attempted murder charges and a state prison sentence of 75 years to life. He will not be eligible for parole until at least 2069.

Within the next few years before my husband's next promotion, he was involved in many cases. A case that led to the area public being glued to their newspapers and televisions involved three brothers and a babysitter who allowed it and participated in the horrendous sexual abuse of young boys in their care. Unfortunately, one of the brothers was acquitted, but two of the brothers and the babysitter all got very lengthy prison sentences. One brother received a sentence of 21 and 1/3 years to 64 years, the other brother was sentenced to 8 and 1/3 to 25 years and the babysitter was sentenced to 29 and 2/3 years to 69 years. This led us to another sexual predator in the area, a middle school janitor, who was sentenced to 8 and 1/3 to 25 years on a plea bargain for sexually abusing young children. While there were many predators and many DWI cases with too many to mention, one DWI case seemed to stick out the most in our memory. This involved an innocent family on their way from Vermont to the Albany Airport on a foggy night with the excitement of a vacation they would never make it to because of the actions of an 18-year-old female drunken driver who was not only way over the limit, but had worked a long night prior with no sleep on that foggy night. She took the lives of two innocent people. It was one of the first cases in the area that stood out because my husband applied for and obtained a court order to draw her blood immediately following the deadly crash. Many people in her hometown had mixed emotions because of her age and she was from a well-known family, but she was convicted after trial and sentenced to jail. She chose to get behind the wheel that night and take the lives of innocent people just driving in the middle of the night to the airport. This led to Robert Winn, District Attorney of Washington County, New York, asking my husband if he thought there was any chance of reopening a 22-year-old unsolved murder of a little boy from his hometown of Granville, New York. They discussed this for many hours and both made a commitment knowing this was going to be an extremely difficult and a very lengthy investigation. He asked my husband if he was up to the task.

That night my husband came home and we went for one of our usual long walks where we would discuss what had happened during the day in both of our lives, which led to my husband explaining what Rob had approached him with that day. I remember thinking NO! How much more, how many more cases, how much more time away from our family, and not being compensated extra financially? This was just about the time he began getting overtime pay. We all know police officers do not join this profession to become wealthy. Once my motherly instincts kicked in, I knew this little boy needed justice and I knew the man that could do this.

On August 19th, the day after, Tom anxiously met Rob in his office. This was a day Rob seemed to have been planning and thinking about for a very long time. While handing him over what little he had on the decades-old long tortuous murder of a baby boy, like a boy in a candy store drooling and knowing the sweet victory and how much faith he had in my husband. As he handed over this little bit that he had, he apologized that there were no new leads. Rob had such faith after working with Tom and was mesmerized by his ability to put a case together without much at all. Rob knew this was a huge gamble politically as his position is an elected position. He felt it in his bones that they could accomplish what needed to be completed. My husband had never heard of the name David Pope prior to this in his lifetime. This was a crime that happened when Tom was just a 10-year-old boy, doing all the things a 10-year-old boy should be doing. He was playing little league, going on family vacations, shooting hoops against his grandfather's garage, all while not having to worry about all the evils in the world. A family that was a working-class family living on a father's paycheck and always having his mom home. He and his four siblings were not overindulged, but they never went to bed hungry. There was a stability that you could not put a price tag on. Myself, witnessing this when we were newly married, reinforced what my grandmother had always instilled in me. You didn't have to have a lot of money to have a good life. Not far from Hudson Falls, New York, which was their primary residence, they had a small camp in Fort Ann, New York, on Hadlock Pond, not really a pond but actually a small lake at the foothills of the Adirondack Mountains. They spent every summer there as a family. It was a modest camp that my husband's father had built with scrap wood before Tom was born, on a piece of land lovingly deeded to them from his mom's grandfather. My father-in-law was a family man through and through, and knew quality was more valuable than quantity. This was instilled in all of the Aiken children. A modest camp they all grew to love and cherish. Not a care in the world at 10 years old except for how big of a fish he could catch that day. They literally had a dinner bell you could hear all the way down to the lake, and Tom ran home anxious to show his parents his catch of the day. His only real worry in the world was knowing he better go to the bathroom before sunset and hoping he did not have to walk out to the outhouse in the dark. Never realizing that a few short towns over just shy of the Vermont border, little boys Robert and his younger brother Howard "Hodgie" White were not getting the same love, care, and attention. The norm for Tom growing up. Lo and behold 22 years later, 32 years young, he would come to know every gory detail of poor Howard White's short life.

Again, Rob found himself apologizing for what little he had to go on. Rob informed Tom that this case involved a boy who never got justice. Rob knew that if the case was put together right, David Pope would be charged with 2nd murder, not like the fiasco that happened in 1972. Rob informed Tom that David Pope was currently in the Washington County Jail on charges not related to Hodgie's death and that he had personally spoken with Hodgie's mother and she told him that she was not totally honest back in the 70s. They talked about where to begin and before you knew it, a whole day was gone. Tom came home that night with his head spinning, not knowing quite where to begin. The enormity of being asked to open a cold case and never having experience with a case like this before. He mulled it over all night long and hit the ground running, knowing he had to meet up and join with the detective of Granville, Frank Hunt, who has become a lifelong friend. A friend, not a member of the State Police, but was a brother through and through. A man that had your back and would never think of stabbing you in the back. Frank also grew up in the small town of Granville and heard rumors of this case from the past. Everyone knew the name. Frank had anxiously agreed to join forces and do whatever he could to get justice. He was also never paid extra to take over a grueling case, working from sunup to sundown and not realizing that there were going to be days way beyond sundown which included missing some special family events. The jurisdiction of this investigation was technically still with the Granville Police Department so Tom and Rob agreed that working with Frank Hunt was where they needed to begin. Going on what little they had, they formed a game plan and both made a pact to let the challenge begin.

Robert Winn

Thomas Aiken

Frank Hunt

Chapter 5

An Impossible Start

Now we would like to introduce you to Howard James White, 10/29/1969, "Hodgie."

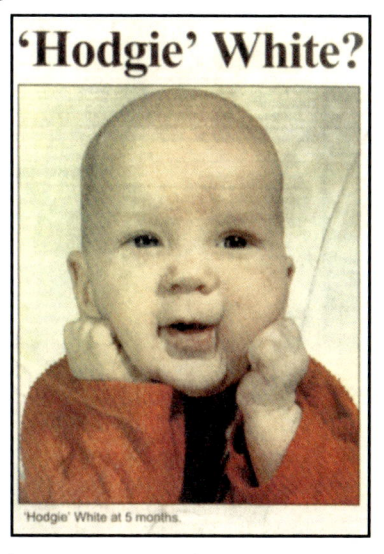

'Hodgie' White?

'Hodgie' White at 5 months.

This is one of the pictures we have never been able to get out of our minds. With the other pictures to come, you will soon realize why.

As we contemplated writing this book, we feel it is time now to let him out of our safekeeping where we have kept him in the back of our minds and in our hearts, where we hope this book and his story will not be in vain and hopefully keep another tragic story like this from becoming real. The life and story of Hodgie will not be in vain. We have moved many times since 1994, and he has moved with us along our journey and was safely kept. After over 100 interviews, we both realized that this little boy had nothing to look forward to. The mundane life of foraging for food from garbage cans in the neighborhood and knowing as a little tot, the fear and the fright he felt that if he got caught, he would get the steel-toed boots of his mother's boyfriend to his emaciated back end. From the time of his mom became involved with David Pope, you will see why we have kept him safely guarded. We both felt this in 1994 while my husband was working on this case, a strong connection to this little boy who never had the unconditional love and protection which should be the norm for every child. As you look at this picture of an adorable infant, you will come to realize what can happen to a child when they are introduced to the wrong person. A vicious murder that took place in the early 70s when Mae White began an official relationship with the evil David Pope, as we have come to know him. As I was researching for this book, and doing many telephone interviews myself, I came to realize after talking to Hodgie's mother, Mae, that the deep motherly instinct that I have is not felt the same way. I knew this, but hearing it from her own mouth caused me to feel very sick to my stomach with knowing the hardest part of this book is yet to come, this was very hard to swallow. Some say she was bouncing from her husband Robert White to David. Hodgie had an older brother, Robert White. He was a year and a half older and not as much of a target as Hodgie because Robbie had learned to shy away and hide. Therefore, Hodgie became more of a target. Some say that certain children are more targeted for abuse than their siblings. Some would also say that the rumors were driving David crazy because he wasn't sure if Hodgie was his biological son or not. This brought out the violence people knew David was capable of. As we learned through the years, he had severely abused all of their children. This is the image of what Hodgie looked like to my husband and had in his mind when he started the investigation. As he would find out, he was unrecognizable and certainly did not look like the same 5-month-old boy in the picture above.

Naively, as the investigation began, Frank Hunt went to his Granville Police Department, to search for any and all records or files maintained on the David Pope case. They were both stunned to find hardly anything. Knowing very well this was a homicide investigation, especially involving a young child. They knew that there should have been a lot more than the scant bit that they found. Having it echoing in Tom's head of Rob's apology for not having more to offer. Their next step would be to go to the Glens Falls Hospital to get any records pertaining to Hodgie. They bypassed the Emma Laing Stevens Hospital where Hodgie was rushed to that night by two devoted ambulance drivers, because both Tom and Frank knew the Emma Laing Stevens Hospital was closed and all of their records were transferred to the Glens Falls Hospital where the original autopsy took place. This was anything but your normal homicide investigation conducted by the New York State Police. Any homicide investigation would normally be run by a lead desk with many investigators assigned. On that August morning, not knowing what lay ahead of them with the obstacles in the way, it seemed like an impossible feat. The impossible start began that mid-August morning when they arrived at the Glens Falls Hospital in a small city in Upstate New York where my husband and I were both born. A hospital we knew very well. They approached the people working in the morgue that morning, a morgue that Tom was very familiar with and where he attended many autopsies. As they discussed why they were there, the pathology staff referred him to the pathologist that performed the 1972 autopsy on Howard White. This was Dr. Walter Stern. Dr. Walter Stern's wife unfortunately let them know that he and the other attending pathologist, Dr. R.H Stokes, were both deceased. After speaking with Mrs. Stern, they were informed by the pathology department that these doctors had a third person in the morgue while this autopsy was performed on Hodgie. They said the morgue attendant's name was Julius Bennett. Tom and Frank went to the records department and spoke with a woman named Debra Manell. As they introduced themselves to her, they requested any and all medical records pertaining to the death and autopsy of Howard White from 1972. They talked to this woman and related the sad and tragic reason they were there for, and explained how David Pope got away with this for 22 years. They also asked Debra Manell if she could help them locate the attendant, Julius Bennett, because the two doctors performing the autopsy were now deceased. She could not find any records at first, but asked them to give her some time to look deeper because records going back that far were sometimes not in their computerized files. She also requested that they obtain a subpoena to cover her search and the turning over of any records. Tom's first inkling that something didn't seem right came when he heard there were two attending pathologists and also an attendant for Hodgie's autopsy. Usually it is only a pathologist and an assistant. On Tom's way home that day, he contacted Rob to let him know that they felt they were striking out, saying they still had hope that Debra Manell was going to do everything she could, so they would wait and see where that led to. Tom also requested the Grand Jury subpoena from Rob's office.

The first night coming home from the hospital, I remember Tom calling me and hearing it in his voice, telling me that this seemed impossible. A defeated look on his face and his slumped shoulders as he walked through the door that night. I could hear it in his voice, but to see it on his face was difficult! The highs and lows of this job were not easy on either one of us. As he walked through the door, he learned to decompartmentalize from the horrors of his job he dealt with on a daily basis, and to keep it separated from family, as his three active boys would come running and jumping on their daddy, ready to play. Your normal little boys wanting to play with their daddy, not having any idea as to what their father had seen on any given day. Anything just to get his attention. Tom learning that this was important for his own mental wellbeing as he tried to enjoy playing with his boys. It is a fine line between going home after a long shift and knowing that you need to nurture your own children. He knew this, it was just difficult to switch gears. It also became therapeutic for him that you don't even realize you are doing. Only to have the third strike come a few days later. Debra Manell called Tom and informed them that the attendant was also deceased. With this impossible start, she gave them a glimmer of hope that she would do everything she could, even going into the musty, dark, and dirty dungeon archives of the hospital, to search for any and all records. This is the part of the hospital where records go after a certain amount of years. Hospitals, including the Glens Falls Hospital, electronically filed and saved all hospital records many years ago, but these records predate that time. As we have learned while writing this, only approximately 1% of all cold cases get solved. This one really did feel like it would not get solved and had an impossible start. That is when they decided while waiting for Debra's call, they began the first of many interviews. It was only a short couple of weeks that they knew they had to have everything to present to New York State Police Forensic Pathologist Dr. Michael Baden. Many of you know of him, from his long history of world-famous cases, HBO series, and has written many successful books. They anxiously waited daily for her call because they knew without these records, this could hamper the success of this initial consultation. The clock was ticking, the presentation was quickly approaching.

STATE OF NEW YORK
COUNTY COURT   COUNTY OF WASHINGTON

In the Matter of the
Grand Jury Investigation
Concerning the Death of   Subpoena Duces Tecum
Howard White, an Infant

To: Glens Falls Hospital
     Pathology Department
     Park Street
     Glens Falls, New York   12801

     WE COMMAND YOU, that all business and excuses being laid aside you appear and attend before the Grand Jury of Washington County at a session to be held in and for the County of Washington at the Courthouse located on Upper Broadway, Fort Edward, New York on September 9, 1994 at 7:00 p.m., to testify and give evidence in a certain criminal prosecution now pending undetermined in the said court on the part of the People of the State of New York, and to bring with you and produce at the time and place aforesaid, now in your custody and control and in particular, all records pertaining to the autopsy done by Walter Stern on Howard White, infant son of Mae and Robert White, Date of Death being September 11, 1972.

     For a failure to attend, you will be deemed guilty of a contempt of court, and liable to pay all loss and damage sustained thereby to the party aggrieved, and forfeit $50.00 in addition thereto.

Dated: August 24, 1994

                                                Robert M. Winn, Esq.
                                                District Attorney of Washington
                                                County
                                                383 Upper Broadway
                                                Fort Edward, New York   12839
                                                (518) 746-2525

Now They Lay me Down to Rest

1972 Granville Police Department Files

```
Dr. Lynch records:
 1. 3-16-71   contusions forehead
 2. 5-1-72    stomach pains
 3. 8-28-72   lacerations right eye brow
 4. 9-11-72   died
```

```
RESCUE SQUAD
1. Davies and Flower


1. Received call at 9:05pm
2. David Pope had child in his arms when ambulance arrived at residence of Pope
3. Davies attended child while Flower drove to hospital.  Child was breathing
   with short gasps.  When ambulance reached Main Street child stopped
   breathing and eyes rolled back in head.  Davies applied mouth to mouth
   and the child was put on oxygen at the hospital.  Nurse Bates could find
   no pulse.
```

Connie L. Aiken and Thomas M. Aiken

Now They Lay me Down to Rest

```
9-11-72 Monday 9:15PM

Received call from Dr. Glennon of suspicious death of a child at hospital.

Arrived at hospital and found Howard James White, dob 10-29-69 dead.
Looked body over and found cuts on the chin. There were numerous bruises
all over the body. This includes the arms and legs and backsides as well
as the head. The childs stomach seemed bloated.

Mother, Mae Pope dob 7-26-49   STATED:

The child complained of stomach aches all week.  Noticed it acted sick
at supper time. Took to bed and when it moaned took it out of bed.
Child couldn't stand and fell. Husband picked child up and called rescue
squad.

The boy is very inactive. Seems to desire to be alone. Walks very slowly.
Won't or can't talk much. Cries a great deal. Usually cries when anyone
comes near him. Cries when it has to go to bathroom.

Boy has had diarrhea all week. All children have. Ate a large supper.
Three plates of potatoes, gravy and canned meat and desert of cake.

Boy fell down outside stairs last wednesday and cut his eye. Took to Lynch
and he advised stitches. Didn't get this done.

Had baby to doctors in May or June with same stomach pains. Doctor said
to cut down on baby's food.

Child has been in foster homes four times. Got back the last time in Jan 72

The childs father is Robert White of Whitehall. Lives with his mother
Oliver White. Husband last saw kids in January. Pays $25 every two weeks.
Doesn't pay very often.

Have four children: 1. Robert age 4, 2. Howard age 3, 3. David Jr. age 1,
and Edward Michael age 2 months. David treats all four kids fine. Plays
with them and does not misuse in any way. Robert White acted indifferent
to his two kids.

David Pope dob 9-8-45  STATES:

I went into boys room around 9pm and he was gasping. I stood him up and he
staggered. I saw his eyes were real big. Took him down stairs and called
rescue squad. Was something like this two months ago but not as bad.
His stomach was hard also but his eyes were not as big. I cut his food down
like Dr. Lynch said but after a couple of weeks he looked thin so I let him
have all he wanted. The boy was a heavy eater and ate more than I did or
the four year old did. The boy fell down the stairs today at about 4:30pm/
Fell about five steps and got up and looked alright. His stomach has
been bothering him two or three months.
```

GRANVILLE POLICE DEPARTMENT

Subject: Howard White
Address: Long Houses
Type of Complaint: Child Abuse
Number: C

Victim: Howard White
Address: Long Houses
Date, Rec'd: 9/3/72
Time: 11:15 PM
By Whom: [illegible]

Complainant: Gladys Barker
Address: Long Houses

FACTS OF COMPLAINT: (Criminal) Called to long houses by Gladys Barker. She complained that the infant Howard White was being physically abused by David Pope. She stated that she baby sitted for the Popes quite often and had seen Pope beat Howard with a board which had a nail in the end of it. She also stated that once when Pope got mad at Howard he took him by his feet and dunked his head in a container of water and held his head under until the boy turned blue. She also stated that one day Pope came home from work & little Howard was playing in the yard Pope started kicking him with he big boots for no reason. She said they hardly ever fed him because she saw him taking bones away from the dog and eating them like he hadn't eat before. I went to see Dr. Glennon to see if he could do anything he stated he could do nothing & we had to go to

ACTION RECOMMENDED: social services

Assigned to: Sweet
Date: 9/4/72
Time:

Action Taken and Disposition:

Physical description of subject necessary in all criminal cases (Use reverse side.)

DESCRIPTION OF SUBJECT

Age: approx 2
DOB:
Sex: M
Color: W
Height:
Weight:
Build:
Complexion:
Hair:
Eyes:
Glasses:
Scars or Marks:
Accent:
Dress:

Final Classification:
Loss:
Recovered:
Closed Date Initials:

Keith
Gladys states that boy looks in bad shape.
Joel

Dulcolax® bisacodyl NF

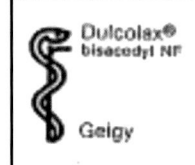

Geigy

October 6, 1972

Enclosed please find a copy of post mortem examination on Howard White.

M.J. Lynch, M.D.

---

1. Starvation
2. Multiple Bruises
3. Puncture Scalp — top of head
4. Blood clot Beneath Skin
5. Swelling of the Brain — Cause?
6. meningitis? cause
7. puncture - recent
8. Food + Gastric Juice in abdomen
9. Fracture Rib - R Kidney Region
10. ? ?
11. Liver - Starvation or alcoholism
12. Blood + fluid in chest cavity.
    (Could be from attempts at Cardiac Bsearch
13. Bleeding in L. Kidney injury
14. Bleeding into supporting outside layer of intestine injury
    or Starvation caused Blood-clotting defect

Connie L. Aiken and Thomas M. Aiken

```
ACCUSATORY INSTRUMENT
COMPLAINT – GENERAL C.P.L. 100.15     FORM NO. 256     Chas. R. Houghtaling, Publisher, Albany, N.Y.
```

STATE OF NEW YORK : COUNTY OF ____Washington____
(TOWN) (VILLAGE) COURT : (TOWN) (VILLAGE) OF ____Granville____

People of the State of New York
-vs-
David Pope
                          Defendant

ACCUSATORY INSTRUMENT
COMPLAINT – GENERAL

I, May F. ~~Pope~~ White _____, residing at
12 Park St. Granville, N. Y. _____, by this information makes written accusation as follows:

That ____David Pope____, on the 28th day of ____December____, 19 72, in the ____Village____ of ____Granville____, County of ____Washington____, New York, did commit the offense of ____Harassment____

a (mi~~sdemeanor~~) (violation) in violation of Section ____240.25____ of the ____Penal____ Law of the State of New York, in that (s)he did, at the aforesaid time and place*

Count One: Did with intent to harass and annoy and alarm another person; strike the complainant in the face with his fist.

The facts upon which this information is based are as follows:
At complainants apartment at 12 Parkstt. in the Village of Granville, David Pope struck complainant in the face with his fist and slapped complainant and threatened to kill her if she left him and tryed to take her little boys, David J. Pope Jr., age 17 months and Edward Michael Pope, age 5 months with her.
David Pope said to complainant that he would kill her just like his Brother, William Pope had killed his wife, Jo Ann, if complainant took the Boys.

~~These~~
These facts mentioned in this complaint are the truth to the best of my knowledge.

Signed ____May F. White____
Witness _____

Now They Lay me Down to Rest

Connie L. Aiken and Thomas M. Aiken

```
NYSIIS-2 14/701        STATE OF NEW YORK - EXECUTIVE DEPARTMENT          Do not write in this space.
(Arrest)                IDENTIFICATION AND INTELLIGENCE SYSTEM
                              ALBANY, NEW YORK 12203
```

34. Name(s) and ID Number(s) of Associates

44-57-25
Chief of Police
Police Department
Granville, N. Y. 1283

35. Description of Crime
120.20-did duck child under water until blue
120.00-strike some 3 yr old with board with nails causing bleeding

36. Occupation: Quarry worker   37. Wt. 155   38. Color of Hair: brown

39. Physical Marks & Oddities
Curly hair - tatoo back of right hand
MAE-right forearm DEE ELLIE DP-right
bicep-broken heart --left forearm snake
around knife heart on left shoulder
SHARP FEATURES pointed nose

40. Additional Information
William Williams Jr. Police Justice
2 North Street Granville, NY
12832

INSTRUCTIONS

Leave all shaded areas blank.
Enter dates as month/day/year, e.g. 11-29-67.
When rolling fingerprints, disregard the dotted box in lower right corner.

1. NYSIIS No. — Formerly DCI Number.
6. Nickname — Enter any identifier, except versions of person's name, usually descriptive, e.g., Baldy, Shorty, Butch, Fatso.
7. Alias and/or Maiden Name — Enter any alias. An alias is a complete name in which the given and/or surname is different than those entered above.
9. Racial Appearance — Check the racial category which best describes the person's appearance: White if Caucasoid, Negroid if Negro, and Mongoloid if Oriental or American Indian. Classify as White persons those of mixed ancestry who are definitely not Negroid or Mongoloid.
10. Skin Tone — Check the skin tone category which best describes the individual's complexion in relation to his racial appearance. For example, classify white persons with olive or swarthy complexion as Dark Skin Tone, and classify light-colored Negroes in the Negroid Category as Light Skin Tone.
13. Place of Birth — If not U.S.A., enter city and country.
16. Agency Ident. Number — Enter your identification number assigned to this individual.
25. Date of Crime — If more than one, use space in Item 40.
26. Place of Crime — If more than one, use space in Item 40.
28. Facsimile Control Number — Enter when facsimile transmission is used.
30. Charge(s) — Enter all charges with most serious first, as set forth in the NYSIIS Charge Code Manuals. If more space is necessary, enter in Item 40.
   Law — Enter law abbreviation. For example
   PL — Penal Law   CCP — Code of Crim. Proced.
   PHL — Public Health Law VTL — Vehicle & Traffic Law
   Section Number — Enter Section Number.

Subsection Number — Enter number found after dash in Section Number.
Class — Enter class of crime, A, B, C, D, E, or U — Unclassified.
Offense Category — Enter letter as follows:
   F — Felony   V — Violation
   M — Misdemeanor   I — Infraction
Attempted Code — Enter letter as follows:
   A — Attempted Crime   O — Actual Crime
Name of Offense — Enter name of crime for which individual is charged, such as Fraud, Assault or Larceny.
Degree — Enter degree of crime, if applicable.
31. Contributor — Enter name of agency if different than Arresting Agency.
32. Court of Arraignment — Enter Court name and City, Town or Village. Enter name of Justice of Peace or Police Justice and mailing address in Item 40.
   NYC — Enter court name including part of court and borough. For example, Criminal Court, Part 1A, Queens.
34. Name(s) and ID Number(s) of Associates — Enter name(s) and ID Number(s) if known, of persons arrested with or involved with the arrestee in the commission of the offense for which the fingerprint card is submitted.
35. Description of Crime — Describe the criminal act for which this individual was arrested.
39. Physical Marks & Oddities — Enter any amputations, deformities, visible scars, marks or tattoos.
40. Additional Information — Enter any miscellaneous information which may be helpful.
   Refer to the original entry whenever an item is carried over to Item 40, e.g., Item 25, Date of Crime -11- -67.

Chapter 6
Where Were You 22 Years Ago?

As we now dig into the actual investigation, we believe it is important to outline what happened to Hodgie and how this case came about. Last chapter, you saw a photo of Hodgie taken at approximately 5 months old. From the time that picture was taken, until Hodgie succumbed to the final fatal blow, Hodgie was beaten, starved, and tortured every day of his life by David Pope. Because no one was ever held accountable, David Pope and Mae White did get married and they did have 5 additional children together. The abuse of these five living children is earth shattering and will hurt you to your soul. Imagine what it did to each of them as you continue reading. David Pope not only got away with murder with entire communities knowing this and watching, he also spread true fear and evil that scared witnesses, doctors, family members, and an entire community to their inner cores. This fear was real and justified. There was nothing David Pope was not capable of. While in the process of writing this book, I made several phone calls to Mae. She is no longer going by the name of Pope. She has returned to her maiden name. After several phone calls that lasted sometimes a couple of hours each, I was surprised that she would even talk to me, but with the first phone call she was reluctant. I had told her that the book would be written one way or another, with or without her, and I wanted her side of the story. At some point during our lengthy conversations, she seemed to act as if I was her friend. I wasn't sure if she was being manipulative or I have come to realize, if it was about her, she could talk all day. Yet, she still could not remember the date her son died. She went as far as sending me a friend request on Facebook. I wanted to believe, or should I say I was trying to wrap my mind around, whether she was truly a battered woman. I wanted her so bad to convince me that she was a battered woman. We had been working on this book at least 7 years. Going back to my first phone call, I could not wrap my mind around the fact that a mother would not protect her children. She had to have been a battered woman. This was swirling around in my mind. I wanted her, no, I needed her, to convince me she was a battered woman. The more I talked to her, the more she convinced me that she was not a truly battered woman. The more I talked to her, she remembered everything if it pertained to her, but not when it pertained to her children. She remembered right down to every detail about herself, but did not remember or was very selective and passé when it came to details of her children and this entire investigation. With all the statements I read prior to making that first phone call to her, people were saying she should have been in a cell next to him and that she was self-absorbed and allowed her children to be tortured. The longer the conversation went on, I referred to my notes and I was actually sick to my stomach after the third time of asking her and her mumbling, she was very loud and clear that she married David Pope because she loved him. I knew, and not only with a sick stomach, I was full of rage not only for Hodgie, but for all of the forgotten children in this dysfunctional family. I lost my cool for a moment because I knew that by befriending her, she was going to tell me more, but she acted like a scolded child when I could not help myself by yelling out, "HOW COULD YOU MARRY A MAN WHO YOU KNEW MURDERED YOUR CHILD? MARRY A MAN THAT TORTURED YOUR CHILDREN AND FORCED THE STATE OF MASSACHU-SETTS TO REMOVE THREE OTHER CHILDREN OF YOURS

PERMANENTLY?" How could you do that? She had a clever way of backpedaling to not accept blame by always becoming a victim. That convinced me that she was not a true battered woman.

As my husband learned through numerous statements and by interviewing her, he was trying to tell me and explain this because with all the cases he had done, he had seen true battered woman. I had to learn for myself, which made this book take on a whole new meaning: "Justice for Hodgie." As my husband went through the investigation, as we went through the interviews and statements to write this book, it wasn't only a couple people's opinions that Mae should have been in a cell right next to David Pope. She did not go to bed hungry every night like her children. She would even go as far as to give her leftover shrimp to her pet skunk in front of her drooling children. This is an example how she never saw, or heard, or remembered, details of her children's lives. She was part of the torment. She may not have physically abused them, but she was sure ready to tattle on them to David Pope when he came home from work fully knowing what was coming to them. She might as well as have been the physical abuser. There are many statements from her children showing they agonized and wondered why their mother wasn't helping them and protecting them and why she was actually tormenting them in her own ways. They learned as adults as we have heard in many statements, they were actually victimized by her as much as by their own physical abuser. They actually articulated to us that they held more resentment and venom to her for her inaction and not protecting them as they did to David Pope.

As these kids grew up to be adults and could look back on their past and try to learn from it, I realized they were thinking and feeling the same as I was. You look to your mom for unconditional love and protection and know they would lay their life down to save yours. A mother not protecting their young is rare. It is not natural. That is when it becomes the fine, fine line between a true battered woman and Mae. This is just my opinion after knowing everything there is to know about this case. I truly wanted to be convinced that there was a reason why this mom would not protect her children and she looked the other way. When a mom is asked what was the date your child died and she couldn't even tell me. She nonchalantly and with sort of a giggle told me that it had been so long ago she did not really remember. The same type of nervous giggle she used when she told me how much she loved David Pope and that was why she married him. I knew before I asked the question when her child died. We had already titled a chapter "911." She never even made the correlation between 911 and September 11th. It was like she didn't care. If it wasn't about her, it did not matter. That date is the remembrance of a tragedy to every American. It wasn't that she was that uneducated, she just did not care enough to remember the date her son died. Was murdered. She further convinced me, this book was being written for justice for Hodgie. He will not be forgotten. Me, an actual stranger who cared more about this child than she ever did, will never forget the date he died. He had a purpose.

While Tom and Frank waited to hear back from the Glens Falls Hospital, they did not wait on the investigation. They hit the road running. 10-16-hour days were their new normal for many weeks to come. Tom used a notebook and started listing the names of possible witnesses or people that needed interviewing from the back of the notebook, and he wrote notes starting from the front. As a new possible name popped up from leads or other interviews, it was written down and not checked off until completed. This was his own type of system. For many years I have seen all these notebooks, but only he knew what this system meant. This notebook happened to be very thick. Where do you start on a 22-year-old case with no new leads? They started with the first names provided to them and multiplied names until they concluded with over 100 interviews and leads by the time it was ready for a Grand Jury presentation. They interviewed neighbors, relatives, babysitters, social workers, doctors, ambulance drivers, and anyone that had pieces of the puzzle to put together. Each of these people shared what they had, but the most important interviews came later, the ones that actually lived through it. The living children of David and Mae Pope. You will learn more about some these children and the anguish they endured in their own words in an upcoming chapter about these forgotten children. Some of the children were not able to be found, and therefore access to all of the children was not possible. Three of the children were taken by the state of Massachusetts and never to be found. One suffered severe brain damage from all of the abuse and he was not able to provide a statement or testimony. That leaves us with three out of the 7 total. One was dead, one suffered brain damage preventing him from helping, and two were taken away and were never located even with the best efforts. Two boys and one girl. These three were able to provide the dirty details behind closed doors, and the screams that echoed through the night. What it was like to live day to day with David Pope while their momma looked the other way. What we want you to understand is the different types of abuse that each and every child went through. With only one daughter, she did suffer some of the physical abuse and beatings, but not as severe as the boys. Her most severe abuse was sexual. She was controlled in a different way. Psychologically and sexually. As far back as she could remember going back to grade school. Treating her like she was his wife now, seeming to make Mae jealous. Jealous of her own daughter. When you are a victim and sexually violated, it controls you in a different manner. This caused a lot of bitterness and resentment from her brothers because she was treated differently. This was another example of the mind-control games David Pope played. He wanted the boys to hate their sister. This was another form of abuse. She knew, even at a young age how wrong it was, but by the love and attention he put on her, and witnessing the severe abuse he did against the boys, she knew if she did not allow her father to have his way with her, she would trade off the sexual abuse for the physical abuse.

As Tom and Frank continued to interview all of these witnesses, they kept hearing from all walks of life that had anything to do with these children, the same phrase over and over again. "Where were you 22 years ago?" The other statement that was repeated to them so many times which gave them a picture in their minds of what these people witnessed as they described that little Hodgie looked like someone you would see on a television commercial seeking donations for starving children. They described his skin hanging off his bones, totally emaciated, unkempt, with a large distended stomach. They referred to it as what they saw from the commercials of Ethiopian children because that was being televised at that time period of the early 70s. No one ever brushed this child's teeth, no one ever brushed his hair, no one ever wiped his nose. No one ever cared for him. The most disturbing thing they described was witnessing his disproportionately large distended stomach, but yet gaunt face and emaciated body with it. It was a vision they could not get out of their minds. The other thing they kept hearing over and over was that when all of these people described what they witnessed, they described it as if they were seeing it from a day or two ago, and not 22 years ago. It was still that fresh in their minds after all of these years. Once that they kept hearing these things over and over from so many different people, they knew what they meant from the phrase, "Where were you 22 years ago?" They were in disbelief that the person responsible for the visions in their mind they could never get rid of, that someone was actually going to pay for it. They all knew that person was David Pope.

As the years went on, David Pope was losing some of his fear factor tactics and control. Although they did have some fear of this vicious maniac, Tom and Frank kept trying to assure each one that with all of their help, they were going to finally hold him accountable, charge him, and get a conviction. They came across very confident to each of them and this helped allow them to provide more and more information. Tom and Frank were very convincing and this helped to bring more and more people together to work as a team to hold him accountable. This meant that David Pope could not single out any one individual person, because eventually there were over 100 interviews and statements taken. Although he was in jail at the time, the fear was as real of him getting out as is was in 1973.

The true reality of this case and the torture to Hodgie come from firsthand accounts of relatives, neighbors, and others that were around to actually witness this in person. Their direct words from statements taken from the 1994 investigation are chilling, but needed to fully grasp the severity of this abuse. These words include firsthand accounts of neighbors so distraught over the emaciation of a little 2-year-old boy, but yet so justifiably fearful of a monster's rath, that they would intentionally burn food and cookies to justify throwing them out, but carefully placing them on the top of their garbage on the porch knowing Hodgie and Robbie would come by foraging for anything like starving animals. The one statement that haunts Tom to this day and actually brings tears to his eyes when mentioning it at lectures comes from one neighbor that took the time and expense to put a doggie door into their entrance door knowing that Hodgie and Robbie would crawl through to get food from their refrigerator. All this when they had no pets.

These will now be included in excerpts from many, many statements Tom and Frank took.

Babysitter Statements:

Patricia Dodge Perry lived in the long houses next to Carol Baker and Harold Burch. She stated, *"Gladys and I tried many times to get the welfare people to help Hodgie and Robert because David Pope would beat them kids. I have never been in their apartment, but I have seen David kick and beat Hodgie with his hands. I have seen David beat Hodgie many times with his hands and he did it so hard that it would knock Hodgie off his feet. I have seen David kick Hodgie all the way home on 2 occasions, each time kicking him so hard that he would fly up in the air. One time was when I was feeding Hodgie* crackers and David came over and grabbed the crackers and threw them and yanked Hodgie and kicked him all the way home. Hodgie and the kids looked starved and he was nothing but skin and bones with a large stomach. One time that I left food out for the dogs and we heard a noise and saw Hodgie and Robbie on our porch eating this scrap food."

Carol F. Baker lived in the long houses with her husband and two daughters. She stated, *"I can remember an incident when I saw the two white boys digging through the garbage cans and picking food out and eating it. There was an occasion where Howard was over to my place on the porch eating something and Dave Pope came over and took the food from him and threw it on the ground and then grabbed Howard and threw him off the porch. David kicked that boy in the rear end all the way home with steel-toed boots on."*

Linda Geraldine Bates was a teacher's aide and bus driver for the head start in Granville. *"To this day I remember Robbie and Howard White because when I went there for a home visit for head start, I have never seen a child in worse shape than Howard was in. He was skin and bones and looked like a poster child for the starving kids you see on TV. This home visit was standard because Robbie was going into head start and when we got back to the office we told our supervisors about this boy and that we wanted to report him to get him help. Back then they said that it would be a few days before Social Services could do anything and I am not sure if anyone got to report it because I heard that the boy died within days of our visit."*

Ambulance Driver

Robert Lewis Flower was a member of the Granville Rescue squad and his statement included so much about the night Hodgie died, we will include it all. "22 years ago I was a member of the Granville rescue squad and I responded to a call at the longhouses with Bud Davies for a call of a boy *with difficulty breathing. I drove and when we got to the apartment of David Pope and Mae White, David brought the small boy out and he gave him to Bud and said that the boy was acting like he was dying. It only took us less than a minute or two to get to the longhouses and when we got the boy we immediately left for the hospital. David Pope asked us to go to the Rutland Hospital, but I said no, that we were going to the Granville Hospital which was only a couple of minutes away. I do remember Bud saying that the boy was breathing a little bit when we left, but he stopped breathing before we got to the hospital and bud started mouth to mouth breathing. Dr. Glennon and a nurse worked on the boy for several minutes and during this time David stuck his head in a couple of times and asked if he was dead. Neither David nor Mae showed much concern at all. The boy died at the hospital and Dr. Glennon asked us a few questions. I remember this boy was very skinny with a distended stomach. Bud and I both felt that David and Mae waited until the last 5 minutes of this boy's life before they called for help. I was with the rescue squad for 8 years and this boy was the only child that I ever took to the hospital that died. The facts surrounding this boy's death have stuck in my mind very clearly ever since because we did everything we could do very quickly and he still died and because I had a son that age myself."* Ask yourself a question. Why did David Pope ask them to go to the Rutland Hospital about 40 minutes away when the Granville hospital was only a couple of minutes away? Also, what a small world we live in. Robert's son Duane grew up to be a teacher and he taught our 3 boys at the Hartford Central School and they always said Duane was their favorite teach ever.

Loving Foster Mom

Paulette Sheldon provided the following excerpts from her written statement about being a foster parent to Hodgie and Robbie. *"Sometime around the end of 1970, my husband at the time, Richard Drinkwine, and I were foster parents to Robert and Hodgie White, the children of Mae Kelley. When Dave would be talking with Robert and Hodgie, he would ask them if they wanted a punch in the eye or something of that nature. The boys, when they were first brought to our home by Social Services, had bruises and welts all over their bodies, but mostly around their head area. Social Services explained to me that Mae and Dave claimed the bruises are from the boys falling all the time, but for the 6 weeks that I had them, they would play as normal children and run around but did not seem clumsy. Hodgie was very energetic and had a happy, bright personality and smiled lot. I would like to add that the boys had black eyes and bruised faces."*

RELATIVES OF MAE AND DAVID

Kathy Louise Bishop is the sister of Mae Pope. She stated, *"I never stayed around David much because I couldn't stand him and he was mean so therefore I don't have any firsthand knowledge of him hitting the kids but I have seen the kids with bumps, bruises, and cuts all the time. Mae and David kept saying that the kids fell a lot. Hodgie was very skinny with a distended stomach and looked like he was starved. When the kids came to my mother's house, they ate like they were never fed. I mainly remember Hodgie in the casket and he was covered with bruises on every exposed part of his body including his face, hands, and arms."*

Lena Mae David was David Pope's aunt and helped raise him. She lived next door to Mae and David. She stated, *"I am David Pope's aunt and have known him all of his life. David started abusing Robert and Howard from the time they started living with him. I have seen David kick, punch, slap, club with sticks, throw him around, and much more to Hodgie. One time David was mad because the neighbors were feeding Hodgie crackers and he grabbed Hodgie and threw him off the porch and then kicked Hodgie all the* way home. He kicked Hodgie so hard that Hodgie flew off the ground and he did this all the way home. David treated all of his kids this way and I have seen him abuse them in ways that people would not even be able to imagine. I am afraid to give this statement because I am very afraid that David will get out of jail and come and kill me for telling the truth about all of this. I also heard David threaten Mae that he would kill her like his brother killed his girlfriend, and he even would tell her that he would do better than his brother did. The night Hodgie died, I remember that David and Mae came over to our apartment after dinner. They stayed until late and then went home and just a few minutes later Mae came over and told me that I had to call the ambulance because Hodgie was dying. I called the ambulance and they told me to have someone outside to flag them down. My husband Ed went out and came in later and said that he saw David walk by carrying Hodgie and he told me that I would never see Hodgie again because he heard the death rattle coming from Hodgie. I have seen Hodgie and all of the kids with bruises and cuts all the time. Hodgie always had a bump and a black-and-blue in the center of his forehead from all of David's beatings. I have seen David punch Hodgie in the head and stomach a lot. He would hit Hodgie and the kids so hard that it would knock them right off their feet. David and Mae did not have much food for the kids. I have seen David and Mae eating steak at the table and they would only be feeding the kids macaroni with no cheese. The boys were very skinny and Hodgie had a very large stomach. He looked like one of those kids from Africa that are starved. I also remember that at Hodgie's funeral, neither David or Mae shed a tear at all."

Rose Mary St. Louis was a sister to David Pope. She cooperated with the investigation and even tried to wear a body wire and engage her brother in conversation at the Washington County Jail, but he smelled a rat and called her out. She also lived next to David and Mae in Granville and in her statement she stated the following: "*I am David Pope's sister and I am going to be describing the physical abuse I observed that*

David inflicted on his girlfriend's son, Howard White. I have seen David hit Hodgie in the head and stomach with his fists on many occasions. I have seen David kick Hodgie with his boots and thrown him down the stairs. I have seen Hodgie whipped by David with an antenna cord on his bare legs and butt. David would hit Hodgie for any reason at all that made him mad, like wetting his pants or anything. Hodgie would always have black-and-blue bruises all over and cuts. Hodgie always appeared to have a bad bump or egg on his forehead from being punched. They never fed Hodgie much and he appeared malnourished. A lot of times David and Mae would buy steaks and eat it and give the food left over to the dogs while feeding the kids bread and water or nothing. Hodgie was sent to bed many times with no food at all. Hodgie was very skinny, just skin and bones and his stomach was swelled out terribly. When Hodgie came to my apartment, I would feed him and he would eat as if he never ate before. I remember bringing Hodgie to the Granville Hospital for a cracked rib or something and I was told that he fell down the stairs.

"*When DJ was about 2-2.5 years old, I visited Mae and David where they lived in Massachusetts and I saw that DJ was missing 2 teeth and DJ told me that Daddy hit him in the mouth with a hammer. One time when I was visiting with David and Mae shortly after Hodgie's death, I asked David how Hodgie died and he said it was from a chicken bone and I asked him if it wasn't from some of the beatings and David said no, that nobody could prove anything.*"

Lori Ann Beayon provided a short statement because she could not remember much and she was not around that much, so I will include her entire statement here. "*David Pope is my brother-in-law and I have spent summers with him and my sister Mae in Massachusetts. I remember that when Robbie was very small, David used to beat on him and he beat on him more than his own kids because Robbie wasn't his kid. I have seen Dave hit Robbie very hard with his fists. Dave used to tell us that if we didn't like what there was to eat, then we couldn't eat anything and we would have to go* hungry. I know that his kids were very afraid of David because I was afraid of him. Even Mae was very afraid of David and he used to threaten and beat her. This is all I remember because it was a long time ago and I wasn't very old." It should be noted that Hodgie was not included by her because by the time David and Mae were in Massachusetts, Hodgie had already been murdered and David had already been through the first trial. You would think he would have known better and not harmed any more children, but instead, he was emboldened because he got away with Hodgie's murder.

William Edward Parker was the son of William Parker that murdered Joann Zageski. This made him a nephew to David Pope and he witnessed so much because he lived with David Pope and the kids for 3 years. He stated, *"I don't remember Hodgie very well, but I have seen him abuse all of his other kids worse than you can imagine. I have seen David pound both Michael and Kevin with his hands and boots. I have seen David hit the kids with belts, throw wrenches and hammers and one day he had Kevin make him a cup of coffee and he didn't like the coffee so he threw the coffee in Kevin's face and then threw the cup and hit him in the face. I have seen David beat and abuse the kids so bad because I lived with them for 3 years on Pine Hill Road. David would beat on the kids every day from the time he got up until he went to bed and it was worse when he was drinking. I have seen David lock the kids in the basement from 7 A.M. until late at night and this would especially happen to Michael. I once threatened Dave that I was going to the police about all of this abuse and David put a gun to my head and threatened to kill me and I know that he would do it. David would kick the crap out of the kids all the times with steel-toed boots and pointed boots. One time I was sitting in the house on Pine Hill Road and Nellie came downstairs and he raised her shirt exposing her chest and he said look at this, she's growing titties. Another time about 3 years ago I was up to Sonny Tanners Quarry on Switch Road in West Pawlet and Nellie showed up at the end of the day and Dave started making out with Nellie and feeling up her breasts and walked away with his hand on her butt."*

Patricia Mae Longley is the daughter of William Pope and niece of William's brother David Pope. William killed JoAnn Zageski in August of 1972, just about three weeks before David Pope delivered the fatal hit or kick to Hodgie on September 11, 1972. *"My father who is William E. Pope Sr. died in August of 1972, but while he was alive my father always kept me away from Dave. I never understood why my father kept me away from Dave until one night when my family was at Dave and Mae's house eating supper. I was only six or seven years old at the time but this incident has always stuck in my mind. We were at the supper table and Hodgie (Howard) did something wrong and Dave slapped Hodgie in the head with an open hand. The force behind the slap sent Hodgie and the chair he was sitting in over backwards and Hodgie did a couple of somersaults. Shortly after my father's death, Hodgie died. I can remember hearing Hodgie died by choking on a chicken bone.*

"It was after my father's death when I became a victim of Dave's abuse. Dave has punched, slapped, pushed, shoved and verbally abused me. I can remember an incident at my grandmother's house on Water Street in the Village of Granville when I was 12 years old, Dave got mad at me because I gave him a cup of coffee in a cup, he claimed was dirty. Dave jumped up out of the chair he was sitting in and punched me in the face. I fell back into the wall causing my shoulder to go through the wall. I still have a scar on my left shoulder from that day."

Charlotte Ruth James is David Pope's cousin. She said, *"I used to visit my mother, Lena David, and David's mother, Nellie Pope, a lot and they both lived in the longhouses next to David. I have seen David physically abuse all of his kids except Nellie. I have seen David kick the kids, hit them with his fists, swat them and knock them right down to the ground. I have seen David kick Hodgie all the way from Harold Burch's place to his house just because they fed Hodgie crackers. He would kick Hodgie so hard that he would come off the ground. Hodgie was covered with cuts and bruises most of the time. Hodgie had an egg that was black and blue on his forehead a lot. Hodgie was skinny with a big stomach and looked like one of those starved kids on TV. After Hodgie died, Mae and David were selling things to make money and a shirt that I bought with other clothes had been Hodgie's shirt and it was covered with blood and had not even been washed. I remember at Hodgie's funeral that David acted like it was someone he didn't know and he did not feel bad."*

Michael Gene Bushman knew David Pope most of his life and at one time his sister was married to David's brother William, the other murderer. He stated, *"I have seen David beat Kevin and Michael many times. He would pick them up by the head of their hair and beat on them. He would punch and kick them and he even stopped him a few times from beating them."* He then described David Pope's relationship with his own daughter Nellie. *"Nellie had a wedding band on and David was holding her ass like a boyfriend/girlfriend thing. There were too many times I saw David be nasty and mean and beat on his kids to describe."*

Alice Marie Yates is related to David Pope and has known him all of her life. David is her stepmother's brother. She lived in the long-houses in Granville with her step-grandmother Nellie Pope (David's mother) and Rose Cook (Rose St. Louis – sister to David Pope). *"The winter before Hodgie died, the welfare people had Rose and I take care of Robert and Hodgie because they didn't want to put them in foster care but they wanted to remove them from David and Mae because they weren't taking care of them right. The last four months of Hodgie's life, I wasn't around much because I lived in Rutland, VT. But before this I have seen David shake, slap, hit, kick, and hit with belts and paddles on both Robert and Hodgie. I have seen him hit both of them so hard that he would knock the little boys right off their feet. He used to kick these boys very hard with steel-toed boots. Like I said, Robert and Hodgie were always covered with bumps, bruises and cuts but one I remember* the most was a 4"-wide red welt across Robbie's entire back that looked like he had been hit with a board, but David and Mae both said he fell off a porch and hit the railing. Mae and David made excuses all the time for the kids' bruises by saying that they fell a lot. Hodgie always seemed to have a black-and-blue bump in the center of his forehead, but David and Mae kept saying that he kept falling on the coffee table."

    Bonnie Regina Wilson was married to George Hurlburt, David Pope's half-brother. *"I remember once when Eddie was a couple of years old and he wet his pants and he was eating cereal at the kitchen table and David got mad at him slammed his face into the bowl of milk. He did this really hard and then took him into the bathroom and I heard Eddie screaming."* It should be noted that Eddie was one of two children removed permanently by the State of Massachusetts at a very young age. *"Kevin was about 13 years old and David got mad at him and hit Kevin with a fireplace poker. I remember that David locked Kevin in the basement from morning until night. I remember that Hodgie was a very cute boy and looked like he was starved."*

Neighbor and Witnesses

Bonnie Sue Rist lived in the long houses with her mother Carol Baker and her sister Audrey Baker Gaulin. When she was 9-10 years old, she saw and heard the abuse. *"Even though they lived a ways from our apartment, I could hear the boys screaming from being hit or abused. The only time I remember seeing David Pope abuse Hodgie was once when we fed him crackers and sandwiches on our porch and David came over and grabbed Hodgie by one arm and threw him off the porch and kicked him all the way home."*

    Mary Ann Webster lived on Water Street in Granville around this time and was not around the Pope's much so therefore did not see a lot of the abuse. She did say, *"Neither one of us saw David beat Hodgie because we were not around that much, but we have seen Hodgie covered with black* and blues. One I saw him naked, standing in the sink getting a bath, and he had lots of bruises on him. Hodgie was very skinny and looked like an Ethiopian kid with a large stomach. I remember that if Dave was mad at Hodgie, Hodgie would be too scared to cry and he would shake uncontrollably."

Linda Jean Wideawake was the sister to babysitter Gladys Barker. She lived across from Mae and David Pope. *"I have seen David Pope slap Hodgie's head very hard and I have seen him boot Hodgie all the way into the house one night. I worked a lot so therefore I did not see David or Mae a lot. I have seen David Pope pick Hodgie up by the arm in an abusive way. What gets me most is that I heard Hodgie crying and screaming so much at night and he would cry that he was hungry also. One time Hodgie came to my house and drank ketchup right out of the bottle. Hodgie was always hungry and he was very thin with a big stomach. I have seen a lot of bruises and cuts on Hodgie and he was very withdrawn and didn't talk much."*

Lionel Chamberlain described a time he and his wife took Kevin and Michael Pope to the 1976 Granville Bicentennial Parade. *"Dave asked us how the kids behaved and I told Dave there was no problems, they were good. Dave got mad at the boys and started smacking them around, punching and slapping them wherever he could hit them. Dave was mad and telling the children if they could behave for someone else, why couldn't they behave for him. This does not include the other times I have seen Dave Pope punch and slap his kids."*

Harold John Burch and his wife Carol Baker lived in the longhouses and Carol was David Pope's cousin. *"I have seen David abuse Hodgie 2 or 3 different times. I have seen him punch Hodgie for no reason and knocked him right off his feet. I have seen him kick Hodgie with steel-toed boots. Most of the times that I saw Hodgie, he had black-and-blue marks all over him and Mae just kept saying that he fell down and hurt himself. One day I was feeding Hodgie peanut butter sandwich and crackers and David came over and grabbed the food out of Hodgie's hand and threw it saying that if he wanted*

Hodgie to have something to eat, then he would give it to him. Hodgie always appeared undernourished and at least twice Carol and I both saw him and his brother eating food out of our garbage cans. I tried reporting this at least twice to Social Services and they came to David's house but never talked to us and they never did anything to help Hodgie."

Audrey Lynn Gaulin lived then in the longhouses with her mother Carol Baker and her sister Bonnie. *"I have seen David kick Hodgie with steel-toed boots and punch Hodgie, knocking him right off his feet. Hodgie always appeared undernourished and he would sneak out and grab food that we had set out for animals or garbage. One day Hodgie came over and we were feeding him crackers and sandwiches and David came over and grabbed Hodgie by the arm and threw him off the porch and kicked him all the way home. Hodgie was always covered with bruises from head to toe."*

Tammy Lynn Christian grew up on Pine Street in Granville, next door to the Pope family. She and her brother Michael Bushman were friends with Nellie, Kevin, and Michael Pope. She stated, *"When asked to describe their father David Pope, he was very loud, vulgar, mean, and always after the kids. He would physically and mentally abuse his kids. He would always belittle them and tell them that they were no good, stupid and wouldn't amount to anything. They were always afraid of him and always cowered away from him. I saw him abuse all the kids. I saw him once kick Kevin with steel-toed boots all the way into the house. I've seen him punch the kids causing black eyes, bloody noses, and bloody lips. I saw him hit the kids with a paddle, but he would mainly kick and punch them. I saw him lock Kevin up in the basement all day and sometimes all night with no food or water. I don't remember a day going by that he didn't abuse the kids. I remember one night that my mother babysat Michael and his face was all cut up and he only would say that he fell down the stairs. I have seen him touch Nellie in sexual ways. I have seen him put his hands up her dress, in her pants, and in her blouse and pajamas. Dave Pope has also touched me back then and he would touch me inside of my clothes the same way. David would always eat good food like steak and other meats and the kids would be lucky to get macaroni and butter and sometimes peanut butter and jelly."*

Joeann Webster provided a statement in 1972 when Hodgie died and she provided a second one during this investigation in 1994. She stated, *"I don't remember seeing David Pope beat on Howard because I wasn't around them much, but I do remember that almost every time I saw Howard, he was covered with black-and-blue marks, bruises and cuts. Howard always appeared malnourished and he would eat anything that anyone would offer him. I remember him one time eating ketchup right out of a bottle. I tried calling Social Services one time to report this abuse, but they later lied and said I never called."*

Barbara Snody was a woman that lived in Clemons, about 30-40 minutes from Granville, and she befriended Michael Pope. She stated, *"I have known Michael Pope since he was 14 years old. I met him and his family because they lived in the same trailer park as us on Ottenburgh Road in the Town of Dresden. Michael was the son of Mae and David Pope. Michael learned to trust me and he would tell me that he was hungry so I would give him food. One time while our family was swimming with their family, I noticed that David Pope would act like boyfriend and girlfriend with his daughter Nellie. He would hold hands with her in the water, dry her off from head to toe including her crotch area and breasts, and he would help her get dressed. I did not like what I saw so I talked with Michael about this and he started telling me that his father and sister were having sex and that his father would abuse him and that there was no food in the house.*

"Michael started staying overnight at my house because he had no bed at home and both he and his mother told me that his mother and father slept in the same bed with his sister Nellie. When Michael would go up to his house to do chores, there were many times that he would come down to my house crying. One time Michael came running to my house with clips to his gun and bullets

because he was afraid that his father was going to kill him. Michael has come to my house many times with bloody noses, black eyes, busted lips, crying, and telling me that he was afraid that his father was going to kill him."

WIFE OF DAVID POPE

The mother, Mae Evelyn Kelley, of Robbie, Hodgie, David Jr., Eddie, Kevin, Nellie, and Michael, was interviewed with a detailed statement obtained from her. As you read the excerpts of her statement, remember, this is coming from her and as bad as it seems reading it, Mae always minimized the abuse and her ability to protect her own children. "*Hodgie and Robert were first taken away from me when Hodgie was around a year old and they were taken away because the people from Social Services said that both boys were being abused. David started abusing the kids when I first moved in with him, but it got worse when we lived in the longhouses and continued on through all of the kids. David hit and kicked and abused all of the kids, but it seemed that he was even meaner and more vicious to Robert and Hodgie. David has an explosive temper and it would not take much to set him off, it seemed that the smaller things the kids did would make him even madder than the bigger things. David would not only physically abuse the kids, but he would send them to bed with no supper. I have seen David hit, punch, kick, and even hold Hodgie under a tub of water. David has hit the kids with a belt, boards, shovels, antenna wire, a hammer, other tools, hoses, and oars. David has caused broken noses, teeth knocked out, bruises, cuts, and many scars. I have seen David hold one of the kids under a running faucet. Once when we lived in Massachusetts, David whipped Robert with a belt because he was mad at him over schoolwork and his whipping caused many bruises and welts and I went into the bedroom to try to stop him but he made me get out and he threatened me. David drew a bathtub full of cold water and put Robert in the bathtub to try to get rid of the marks because someone told him that this would get rid of the marks, but it did not work and the neighbors turned us into welfare and the kids were taken away. I thought that I was a good mother, but I could not stop all of these beatings because David would threaten me. David has also beaten on me many times and I was very afraid of the threats he made. Hodgie died on September 11, 1972, when we lived in the longhouses in Granville. David had been beating and kicking Hodgie and Robert a lot that summer. Social service workers had been to our house when they were called by neighbors. The day Hodgie died we had a chicken dinner around four o'clock. People have said that Hodgie died from a chicken bone, but that was not possible because I always cut the meat from the bones before the kids got them, no matter what meat we were eating. After dinner that night I did my dishes and the kids went out to play and David and I went over to David's uncle until about 7:00 P.M. when it was time for the kids to go to bed. At some point when the kids were out playing, one of the other kids said that Hodgie was doing something wrong so David went over to discipline him and he took him into the house, but I don't know what he did. I put the kids to bed around 7:00 P.M. I just remember that after dinner Hodgie went upstairs to go to the bathroom and he fell down the stairs. I heard him fall and I went to see if he was okay and his color was not right. Hodgie had looked like he was sick all day anyways and acted as if he did not feel good. I do remember that the day before Hodgie died, David kicked and punched Hodgie a lot, but I can't remember what that was for because there were so many of these times. After we put the kids to bed around 7:00 P.M. the night Hodgie died, David and I went up to bed around 9:00 P.M. We were in bed with the lights off and I heard moaning and groaning and I went in and it was Hodgie and he told me that he did not feel good and that his stomach hurt. I went downstairs and got him a glass of ginger ale. Hodgie did not want this, he wanted a glass of water and David went and got the water, I think, I know one of us got the water* and gave it to Hodgie. Hodgie drank some water and his eyes got real big and he did not look good and I said that we should call the rescue squad, but David said that we shouldn't because of the bruises. Someone called the rescue squad and they came and took Hodgie. Dave and I went to the hospital and they were working on Hodgie and Dave looked in and asked the people if Hodgie was dead. The doctor came out and said that Hodgie did not make it and they asked me about Hodgie's bruises and I don't know what I said but I did not tell them that David did it to Hodgie because David always made me lie to cover up the bruises that he did to all the kids. Over the years, David would not let me visit Hodgie's grave and he would not let me put flowers on his grave because he said that it was stupid and a waste of money. I have been told that our kids would eat out of garbage cans, but I have never seen this and I always tried to have food for them. David would send them to bed without dinner, but I would try to get them up and feed them. One time I remember that Dave and I were eating steak and he got mad at the kids and took all of their steak and fed it to the dogs. He then made the kids go to bed without eating. I have also seen David knock out DJ's two front teeth with a hammer in Massachusetts.

"His Aunt Lena David and even his mother told him to stop beating on Hodgie and the kids, but he still did not stop. Many people have tried to tell David to stop beating the kids, but David usually told people to mind their own business. I also remember that the night Hodgie died and we were calling for the rescue squad, Hodgie was throwing up and it was greenish-yellow like phlegm." How alarming is it that a 2-year-old boy was smart enough to know that ginger ale would hurt his stomach even more and he wanted water instead. Imagine ginger ale going into his stomach when you see what his stomach looked like. Even on his deathbed with only minutes left to live and as much agony as this 2-year-old boy was in, he still knew ginger ale was not good for him.

Only Daughter of Mae and David:

Nellie Mae Younger is the only daughter to Mae and David Pope. Over the years, she and sometimes her mother would go to police agencies and report being sexually abused and raped by her dad starting from a very young age. Each time, she would back out and refuse to cooperate before an arrest was made, because she was that afraid of her father. It wasn't until she got a full-time boyfriend and left her parents' house when she came forward to the Washington County District Attorney's Office and fully cooperated. The investigators in the District Attorney's office did this investigation including a controlled telephone call she made to her father and he admitted most of what he did to her. He was arrested and put in jail, and this led to District Attorney Robert Winn requesting Tom to reopen the 1972 murder of Hodgie with no new evidence. Nellie provided a statement in which she states the following:

"I can remember my father abusing us kids physically meaning punching, slapping and kicking. He used to like to stomp us with his foot in the ribs. My father, David Pope, used to physically abuse all of us kids. The boys Robert, Kevin, and Michael. DJ and Eddie I don't even remember, but he used to abuse them more than me. I remember one night when my father put boxing gloves on and had Robert put a pair on and my father punched Robert really bad in the face and stomach. My father did this because he was mad at Robert because he went to a baseball game without permission. After it was over, Robert had a sore stomach which still bothers him today, and one of his eyes were bleeding and swelled shut.

"I have seen my father make Kevin eat cigarettes and sit down cellar in the dark, and I seen my father hit Kevin with a boat ore on the bare buttocks. My father has done the same thing with Michael too. I can remember a night when he made Michael sleep in the cellar one night. One day my father got mad at me because he found a cigarette butt in the toilet and he thought I had

put it there when in fact Kevin had done it. My father grabbed me by the hair and pulled me out of a chair, threw me to the floor and stomped me in the chest and stomach and when he was done stomping me he dragged me to the bathroom and made me pick the cigarette butt out of the toilet with my hand and throw it away in the wastepaper basket. These are just a few incidents over the years. There are many more involving my father punching or stomping one of my brothers. The abuse just wasn't with us kids, I can remember when my father came home one night and wanted a kiss from my mother. When my mother did not give him one, he grabbed a wooden coffee table and slammed it over my mother's head causing it to break. My mother got dizzy and her head was bleeding.

"The Washington County District Attorney's investigators are investigating the incidents of sexual abuse my father has done to me over the years. My father did tell me that if I ever reported him for that, he would kill me. To this day, I'm still afraid of my father and in my mind I feel if he got out of jail today he would try to kill me. I would now like to talk about some crimes my father made Michael and I be involved with on several occasions. My father would steal gas from area gas stations and convenience stores. The way we would steal the gas is my father would pump the gas and then he would make Michael or I go in and buy a loaf of bread or milk or something and not pay for the gas. On a couple of occasions, Michael paid for the gas after my father told him not to. My father did not hit him but would yell and be mean to him. There were times when my father used to make me steal food along with him from area grocery stores. We would put mostly meat inside our jackets under our arms and then not pay for it. My father had me do this every day for about a year. Sometime around November 1992, my brother Michael broke into our neighbor's house on Warren Road in Hartford, NY." Tom actually was assigned that burglary case and solved it when doing this case. It turned out that the boy in this house was younger than Michael, but they became friends and Michael made the mistake of telling his father about this boy's piggy bank in his bedroom. David Pope threatened Michael and forced him to break into his bedroom window and steal the piggy bank. He told Michael exactly what to wear and how to walk the wood line to prevent being seen. When David ordered Mike to break into this house a second time, Michael refused to do this to his friend again and ran away from home.

We have saved the most damning and terrifying statements for the end of this chapter. Statements from the two that survived, but never truly lived. The only two that could truly bring to life the torture, beatings, starvation, loveless, and unprotected life of a child living with an evil monster. Hodgie died. Robbie cannot provide this information because of his tortured mental state. David and Eddie were adopted out after tremendous abuse and hopefully saved. Nellie's was different. Kevin and Michael lived every day with no love, no protection, beatings, torture, starvations, and injury.

The following come directly from Kevin Pope's 1994 statement: *I, Kevin Pope, am 20 years old and I'm currently residing with my mother Mae Kelley. I'm now going to describe for Detective Hunt and Inv. Thomas Aiken the abuse my brothers and sister and myself have suffered over the years at the hands of my father David Pope. The abuse started when I was very young. I can remember an incident that occurred at my Uncle Jimmy Tanner's house on Aiken Road in Granville when I was 10 years old. My father bought a BB gun for me for my birthday, and I had the BB gun at Jimmy's house that day. I was shooting the BB gun and I had hit my brother and my cousin Jody with BBs. My father got mad at me, and he took the BB gun and he shot me in the leg with it and told me he was going to teach me a lesson. After he shot me in the leg with a BB, he took the BB gun and smashed it over the top of my head causing the handle of the gun to break. I suffered a laceration to the head from that. This is one of the many incidents where my father has severely beaten me or struck me* with something. There have been times when my father has struck me with pitchforks in the buttocks causing puncture wounds, boat oars, belts, boards, rubber hoses, tools, dishes, car parts, and mostly with his fists and feet. My father would most generally hit me and us kids with anything he could get his hands on. For most of my life I have had to walk around bruised or scarred from the abuse of my father. I have missing teeth from an incident when I was 13 years old, my father punched and kicked me repeatedly because I got in trouble in school. I have a scar on my left ring finger from where my father hit me with a running chainsaw. I was not the only one of us children my father beat up. My father beat on Michael, Nellie, and Robert. I don't remember my brothers DJ and Eddie because they were taken away when I was young. I remember Robert getting beat by my father once and he beat him real bad, causing cuts and swollen shut eyes. That is the only beating I remember Robert getting but I was not around much plus Robert did not live with us much either. I believe I have an ulcer and I throw up blook periodically. My stomach has bothered me for as long as I can remember. I can't say what has caused this condition, but I can say all the times my father has hit and kicked me in the stomach has not helped in any. I can remember times when my father for punishment would get me up in the morning and feed me breakfast and then make me spend the day in the basement. He would not let me come out until he went to bed at about nine or ten o'clock at night and in most cases, I would not get something to eat. This would start at six o'clock in the morning and would happen quite often. There were times my father would make me spend all day outside until he came home from work, without nothing to eat, because he did not trust me in the house.

The following come directly from Michael Pope's 1994 statement. *My parents are David and Mae Pope and David is now in jail because he had sex with my sister for the last 12 or 13 years that I know. I am now going to tell the truth about everything that I know my father did wrong, and about all of the abuse that my father did to me and my brothers. My father would steal gas from the IGA in Hartford, Stewarts in Granville, Poultney, Whitehall, and Fairhaven, Chapman's Store in Middle Granville, and there may even be other places that I don't remember right now. I was with him for all of the above places as well as my sister Nellie. My father or I would pump the gas and he would make Nellie go in and buy usually ½-gallon of milk or a soda or bread and she would not pay for the gas. This would happen 2 or 3 times a week for one or two years, and sometimes it would happen twice in the same day. I will now tell you about how my father has abused me and my brothers all of my life. I was born in Massachusetts and I was the youngest child. I don't remember my brothers Edward, David or Robert because they were taken away before I was born. I have met Robert about 6 years ago when he came back to live with us, but he then moved back to Massachusetts. I was beaten almost every day of my life that I lived in the same house as my father. He would beat me for different things, sometimes just for saying yes and sometimes just for saying no. Sometimes just because I didn't speak loud enough for him to hear me. He would beat me for any reason at all, most of them very dumb or small things. The main way he would beat me is with his hands and fists and if I fell down, he would stomp on my repeatedly. He would punch me anywhere on my body, my face, stomach, chest, anywhere. He would hit me with shovels, boards, guns, oars, hoses, chains, tools, belts, dishes, electrical wiring, parts of a car, and anything he could get his hands on when he got mad. I have had cuts, bruises, broken nose, and scars. I have a scar over my left eye from when my father hit me with his fist. Once when my father was trying to teach me to tie my shoes, he got mad at me and he had a glass of iced tea or Kool-Aid and he slapped me with this glass causing it to break and cut my ear. Because my father has punched and kicked my stomach so much during my life, there were times that I couldn't take much pressure on my stomach and I couldn't swim underwater at all because I would not be able to breathe. Now, since I haven't been beaten in a couple of years, I can now swim underwater, but I still can't take too much pressure, but it has subsided a lot. I have had a lot of cut lips and black eyes, and twice my father broke my nose from hitting me with a shovel and a 2 x 4 board. There was a time that my family lived on Ottenburg Road in Clemons and I got in trouble at school and my father was mad at me and he told me that if I ever got in trouble again that he would kill me and I was so afraid of him doing this that I took my clip and shells from my .22 rifle and gave them to Barbara Snoody to keep so that I did not get shot. I have been taken out of the house three times by Social Services and once when I was young and lived in Massachusetts. These were all because of my father beating me, but I would always go back. I have tried going to the police a couple of times, but my father would lie about my injuries and there was no proof. My mother would never beat us and her punishment would be to threaten us with "Wait until your father gets home."*

The excerpts of statements above in no way include most of the statements taken or the abuse witnessed. The entire case and all the interviews conducted, statements obtained, and evidence collected would be so voluminous that it would take up multiple books. The 12-16-hour days 5-6 days a week for so many weeks took away a lot of our family time, but it was a necessary evil. Tom knew how hard it is to convince a jury on easy or normal cases, but to know how much work had to be done from an exhumation to new autopsy because the death certificate had to read homicide to move forward, and how much overwhelming evidence must be presented in the form of witness testimony to overcome the fact that no one could testify to seeing the final fatal strike, much less who delivered it. Tom worked hard to gain the trust of the many, many witnesses to overcome a fear that ran through every one of them. Witnesses who saw David Pope face a first trial and walk away a free man and continue to abuse so many after witnessing him murder Hodgie. Their fear of David was real and their fear of another acquittal in court was valid. Tom felt like he was on trial at times. Still, the most common phrase he heard from so many witnesses was "Where were you 22 years ago?" Almost word for word from so many because they knew his passion was to hold David Pope accountable was strong and they saw he had no fear to face him down and to go right at him. He had no fear of David Pope for himself. His family, yes, but he has gone too many places and gone after too much evil to fear the likes of someone who abuses primarily children and women. They trusted Tom. They trusted his words when he promised to hold David Pope accountable and that they would be successful. Where was Tom 22 years ago? He was playing little league, playing basketball, hunting with his father and brother, and doing all the things that every 10-year-old boy should be able to experience. The love of a family. The protection of a mom and dad. Playing and laughing with friends. He never lacked for a meal.

Tom around 1972

Now They Lay me Down to Rest

Mae Kelly Pope

Chapter 7
The Voice of Evil

Tom has investigated some of the worse and most evil people that walk amongst us. The type of people that would keep you from sleeping at night if you knew about them or what they have done to victims. The day came early in his investigation where he knew an interview of David Pope must be attempted. Enough interviews, statements, and details were obtained that he knew the time was right. When Tom teaches interview and interrogation, he emphasizes that the devil is in the detail. The most tedious and minute details are what force most people to open up about crimes that are unspeakable. The more details he can gather prior to this crucial interview, the better his chance in obtaining a confession. In his career, the estimate of his confession rate is 80% or more. These are mainly major cases. Homicides and unimaginable child abuse cases. He has been challenged many times in his career when going after heinous people that this person or that person would never talk to him at all, much less confess. Almost all did. He won many if not all of these challenges. They all told him David Pope would be no different. David Pope was currently sitting in the Washington County Jail on very serious charges of Rape and Sodomy. Charges that could have meant spending a good part of his remaining life in prison if convicted. Why would he now talk about an investigation that could take the rest of his free life away…? Allegations that

Pope tried so hard to hide and cover up since Hodgie's death among many other people involved that also tried to bury this or sweep it under the rug. He also knew that the victim in that case set him up by confronting him over the phone with a controlled telephone call. He made many admissions on that phone call. He knew this led him to being incarcerated. He then told those investigators to pound salt when they attempted to interview him. Why would David Pope now talk to the police on such a serious investigation…? Why would Tom believe that Pope would talk to him…? Was Tom that pompous to believe he could get him to talk and make any admissions…? David Pope did agree to talk to Tom and Frank. David Pope did make admissions and provide incriminating information. He did talk about his relationship with Hodgie and Robbie and how he felt guilty about causing Hodgie's death. How did this happen…? Tom also knows that success to interviews and admissions also relies on the first approach. The phrase you get more with honey than vinegar is very true with interrogations. To have an 80% confession rate, Tom has many tried and true techniques to get into the mind of evil people. David Pope was no different. The first hurdle was getting Pope to even talk to him. Tom was very honest with him about not talking to him about anything he was currently in jail for. He even told him that if he (Tom) did ask him any questions about the current charges, he was free to get up and walk out. Honesty with suspects is extremely important. I don't know all of Tom's techniques and nor would I share the ones I know, but Tom can get into the psyche of very bad people. He can get grown men to admit having sex with young children with no known witnesses. I have had Tom tell me about how he would do this time after time in 30 years with the New York State Police. That was why he was so successful in these cases. Did David Pope give a full confession…? No. He did provide a 5-page statement that was very important and useful in the investigation and prosecution of David Pope. There was a legal problem Tom was dealing with when he interviewed David Pope in that small scary interview room in the middle of an old jail. Alone with Frank Hunt in a small room with a very dangerous man. An evil man. The law in New York State was literally changing right at that moment and Tom knew it. Prior to this change, you could interview a suspect in jail on unrelated charges as long as they were provided with their Miranda rights. With the changing law, this was now not permitted as long as they were in jail on any charges. This became a major appeal issue that Rob Winn had to answer many times.

When the interview process was completed and the written statement finalized, but before signing, Tom read the statement to Pope and he did not like some of the wording so he changed them. One of the changes was the wording of feeling guilty about causing Hodgie's death to feeling heavyhearted. He said it made him sound bad. It was his statement, so this like a few other things was changed before David Pope would sign it. All the statements Pope made that he refused to keep in his written statement were written down by Tom and preserved on an oral statement report. All of these statements, even though not in his written statement, could still be used against Pope at trial. The only difference is that Tom would have to recite them by memory to the jury instead of just reading off his statement. When the statement was completed, Tom had another technique he perfected. He would then bring out a tape recorder and read the statement one final time to Pope, this time into the tape recorder, with Pope acknowledging that everything in the statement is true. This taped reading included the Miranda Warning and questions to Pope to defeat any suppression hearing issues. These would include the signing of the Miranda Warning by Pope to stating that he heard everything very well with no difficulty and that everything in the statement was correct by him. To anyone hearing the tape recording produced with David Pope's own voice, they would know they are listening to the voice of evil. They can hear it from his own mouth. The contempt for law and people coming out loud and clear.

On the same date as David Pope was interviewed, August 26, 1994, his sister Rose St. Louis agreed to wear a body wire and confront her brother at the Washington County Jail. She signed the waiver and was then prepped by Tom and Frank with proper questions to ask. Her brother David Pope suspected that she was wearing a recording device and confronted her directly on that many times during this 45-minute conversation in a jail visiting room. She denied it, but Pope was very guarded and did not make any incriminating statements. She kept telling him that she needed to know what to say and what not to say and he kept accusing her of working against him. He kept stating she was sent there by the District Attorney. With all this paranoia, Pope did not make true admissions, but everything he says adds the necessary pieces to the overall puzzle. Pope knew that his sister knew just about everything he had done to Hodgie and all of his kids. He was very leery of her. The other person that knew everything was Mae. Rose was not going to be a partner in crime. She saw all the injustices over the years. She knew what he was like as a boy, as an adult, and as an abuser.

On August 28, 1994, Michael Pope agreed to wear a body wire and confront his father David Pope at the Washington County Jail. Michael knew firsthand all about his father and the abuse. Mike was also very confused as he wanted to cooperate and he wanted to hold his father accountable for all that he had done, but he also wanted to have a relationship with his father for the first time in his life. He then had a 30-minute conversation with him about many things including that the State Police wanted to interview him about his father's involvement with Hodgie's death. David Pope again suspected he was being set up and again he was very guarded. Pope told his son he was not afraid of this investigation. Michael also kept confronting his father about the burglary he made him commit to the young boy that lived next door to them. Pope told his son that he (Michael) was the one that knew the money was there. He was still manipulating his son. Pope told his son that he could not help the police with the death investigation of Hodgie because he wasn't alive when that happened. Pope asked Michael if his mother ever hit him or the kids and Michael told him no. Pope then said he did not think she did and that is what he told the investigators that interviewed him. David Pope kept accusing Michael of helping the police and that he was trying to help them hang him. Anyone listening to this taped confrontation and the one with his sister Rose can quickly realize they are listening to the "TRUE VOICE OF EVIL..!"

There was a funny story occurring when this interview was taking place. Frank Hunt's wife was due to give birth to their middle child at any moment. She kept paging Frank and during the callback she was very upset with him for not coming home and taking her to the hospital. He kept promising her he was just about done. A promise made many times until that interview was completed. A dedicated family man who did not want to miss the birth of his child, but he and Tom were right on the edge of their seat knowing that as long as they could continue this interview, they were close to getting Pope to hang himself. Just one sentence, one word, or one phrase away. One more promise to get there on time. When this interview was started, they never imagined this was the day she would go into labor. An interview they needed so badly, they need all their concentration on it. Their adrenaline was kicking in, but walking that fine line between the importance of a crucial interview versus the role of a husband and father. This is not an interview you can walk away from. Not a job you can always drop everything and leave when needed at home. This line of work is not easily intertwined with a family life as many birthdays, holidays, and special events are sometimes forfeited. Then they quickly packed up all of their equipment and threw it in the car and as Frank said, it was the fastest drive by far he ever was involved in going from Salem, New York, to Granville, New York. This crazy ride was on a back country road, not an interstate, and with every twist and turn, Frank was saying his prayers that he would at least get to make it to his wife and new daughter. When he finally did make it to his frazzled wife, he did not have time to think, he needed to transition from detective to father and daddy. You would have to know Frank to understand how he talks. His words were, "That crazy-ass bastard was going to kill me before I go to meet my daughter for the first time. It was the craziest ride I ever took!" Frank Hunt did make it back home just in time to drive his wife to the hospital and he did get to participate in his middle child's birth. I can say from talking to Frank many times, he did not have any time to spare.

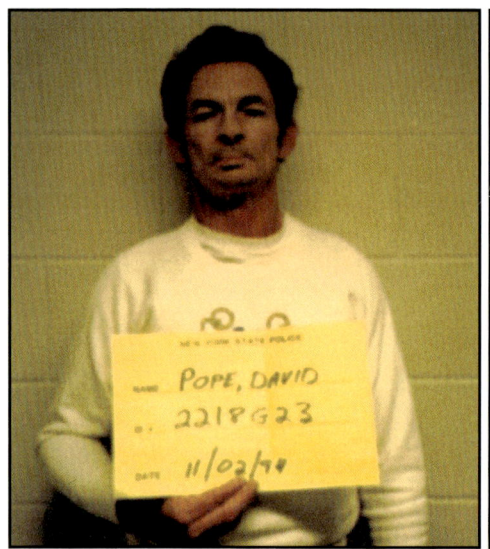

David Pope Arrest Photo   David Pope Court Photo

Now They Lay me Down to Rest

Statement of David Pope

GENL. 19 6/85

STATEMENT

STATE OF NEW YORK
COUNTY OF Washington
Village of Salem

PAGE ONE OF 5 PAGES
DATED: 08/26/94

I, David James Pope Sr., AGE 48, BORN ON 09/08/45
AND RESIDING AT 433 Vaughn Rd Hudson Falls, NY
HAVE BEEN ADVISED BY Investigator Thomas M. Aiken Detective Frank Hunt,
OF THE New York State Police / Granville Police Dept. OF THE FOLLOWING:

I HAVE THE RIGHT TO REMAIN SILENT, AND I DO NOT HAVE TO MAKE ANY STATEMENT IF I DON'T WANT TO.

IF I GIVE UP THAT RIGHT, ANYTHING I DO SAY CAN AND WILL BE USED AGAINST ME IN A COURT OF LAW.

I HAVE THE RIGHT TO HAVE A LAWYER PRESENT BEFORE MAKING ANY STATEMENT OR AT ANY TIME DURING THIS STATEMENT.

IF I SHOULD DECIDE I DO WANT A LAWYER, AND I CANNOT AFFORD TO HIRE ONE, A LAWYER WILL BE APPOINTED FOR ME FREE OF CHARGE AND I MAY HAVE THAT LAWYER PRESENT BEFORE MAKING ANY STATEMENT.

I ALSO UNDERSTAND THAT I HAVE THE RIGHT TO STOP AT ANY TIME DURING THIS STATEMENT AND REMAIN SILENT AND HAVE A LAWYER PRESENT.

I FULLY UNDERSTAND THESE RIGHTS, AND AT THIS TIME I AGREE TO GIVE UP MY RIGHTS AND MAKE THE FOLLOWING STATEMENT:

I AM AT THE WASHINGTON COUNTY JAIL TALKING TO INVESTIGATOR THOMAS AIKEN & DETECTIVE FRANK HUNT ABOUT THE TIME MY THEN GIRLFRIEND'S CHILD DIED. MY GIRLFRIEND THEN WAS MAC WHITE & I LATER MARRIED HER. THE CHILD'S NAME WAS HOWARD WHITE, BUT EVERYONE CALLED HIM HODGIE. AT THE TIME HE DIED WE LIVED IN THE LONGHOUSES & MAC'S SON ROBERT LIVED WITH US AND OUR TWO CHILDREN DAVID JR & EDWARD. HODGIE WAS NOT QUITE 3 YEARS OLD WHEN HE DIED IN SEPTEMBER OF 1972. HODGIE HAD NO MEDICAL PROBLEMS THAT I KNOW OF, BUT MAC TOLD ME THAT WHEN HE WAS BORN, FORCEPTS USED CAUSED A MARK IN THE CENTER OF HIS FOREHEAD & MAC SAID THAT IT WOULD GO

Connie L. Aiken and Thomas M. Aiken

GENL. 19A 6/85 STATEMENT CONTINUATION SHEET   PAGE 2 OF 5 PAGES

NAME: David James Pope, SR   DATE 08/26/94

away in time, but he never lived long enough for it to go away. This mark would get black & blue at times & it would swell up at times & it seemed that any time Hodgie got bumped that he got bumped in that spot because it was always there. It seemed to me that it was a birthmark, but from what I know about birthmarks, this was not a birthmark. I only know what Mac told me about the forceps. I believe in July, just before Hodgie died, Mac took Hodgie to Dr. Lynch's office for a checkup & Dr. Lynch was not concerned about Hodgie's large stomach & told us that it was just because of overeating. Hodgie was a very skinny boy, but had a large stomach & had no medical problems that I know about. Mac was not a very good mother at all, but she was not abusive & I don't believe that she ever hit any of the kids & just threatened that "I will tell your father when he gets home." That was her biggest punishment. Mac was not aggressive with punishment at all, Not like me because I was more aggressive with punishment. The long houses we lived in had about 6 apartments in each (2) & the living room & kitchen area was downstairs & the bedrooms & bathrooms were upstairs. The apartments would share a common stairway going upstairs. The day Hodgie died, September 11, 1972, I think that I was helping Charlie Tanner build his house & I came home & we ate around 4:00 PM & I don't remember what we ate, but based on what I was told about Hodgie having a chicken bone in his stomach, he must have ate chicken. Anytime that our kids ate any meat, Mac would always cut the meat

82

Now They Lay me Down to Rest

> STATEMENT CONTINUATION SHEET PAGE 5 OF 5 PAGES
> NAME: David James Pope Sr.   DATE: 08/26/94
>
> away from the bones before giving it to the kids, so therefore I don't know how he could have swallowed a chicken bone. After dinner I went to visit Ed & Lonn David & they lived two apartments away & I believe that Hodgie went with me & then came home on his own before me. When I went home, the kids were already upstairs in bed. The kids always went to bed at 7:00pm. Mac & I went upstairs to go to bed around 9pm & as we were going into our room, we could hear Hodgie making a commotion & when I went in to his room he was standing up in his crib & he asked for a glass of water. I got him a glass of water & he took a couple of sips & I then told Mac to call for an ambulance because something was wrong with him & his eyes were very big & his stomach was very hard. Mac said that she couldn't because of all the bruises on Hodgie & I told her to call anyway & she did. The ambulance came & they took Hodgie to the hospital & we went too, but Hodgie died quickly at the hospital. I don't remember what was said at the hospital. Later on that year I was arrested for abusing Hodgie, but I was found not guilty after a grand jury trial. One of the defenses used was that we had animals & that Hodgie could have gotten a bone from one of them, but I can't swear to it because I don't know. People have told me that Hodgie ate out of garbage cans, but I can't say so because I don't remember seeing him do this but I think any kid will grab food like potato chips that they see on the ground or in a garbage can. All I can say

GENL. 19A 6/85
STATEMENT CONTINUATION SHEET   PAGE 4 OF 5 PAGES
NAME: David James Pope Sr   DATE 07/26/94

That I did not hit him (Hodgie) with a board with nails like I was charged with, but if Hodgie was in this tub of water it was because he was getting water poured over him for a bath. I don't believe this tub would have been big enough for me to submerge him in like they charged me. I was aggressive with my punishment & my sister told me that I hit Hodgie with an antenna cord & I am not saying that I didn't because it sounds like something I might do, I have put my boots to his backside & I have slapped on his Hodgie causing him to fall off his feet. I remember Mae telling me that Hodgie fell a lot, but I don't remember seeing him fall much. Mae told me that the night Hodgie died & I was over visiting Ed & Lena, that Hodgie fell 3 or 4 steps down the stairs. At some time after Hodgie died, We moved to Massachusetts & the kids were taken away from us twice. The first time was when Robert was taken away & I hit him a few times causing marks on his back because he wouldn't do his schoolwork for me at home. I was mad because he came home with a paper that he did in school & when I asked him to do it for me, he couldn't do it. He was taken away for about a month. A couple of years after this all the kids were taken away because Kevin fell out of a tree & cut the back of his ear & they accused me of abusing him. Back when Robert was taken away, welfare made me go to a psychologist & I saw him once a week. During one of these visits I told the psychologist that I felt heavy hearted

Now They Lay me Down to Rest

```
GENL. 19A 6/85         STATEMENT CONTINUATION SHEET     PAGE 5 OF 5 PAGES
NAME: David James Pope SR                               DATE 08/26/94
```

That my punishment may have had something to do with Hodgie's death but Mac said that she didn't believe I punished Hodgie around the time of his death so the counselor felt comfortable with that & said he wouldn't have to report it. He felt comfortable with that but I am not sure if I feel comfortable with it. I never did believe that Hodgie died from swallowing a chicken bone. I am not sure what caused Hodgie's death but he could have died because of the fall down the stairs but I do have a very heavy heart about what happened because I did love Hodgie & I still do love him. I have been read this statement by Inv. Aiken and everything is the truth now as I remember it.

I have been advised by Inv. Aiken that it is a crime in New York State to knowingly make a false written statement.

Statement of: David J. Pope 1:22 PM

Witness: Inv. Thomas M. A.

Witness: Det. JE____ a #103

Oral Statement Report

Date: August 26, 1994

Time: 11:13AM to 2:00PM

Place: Washington County Sheriff's Department

Person Making Statement: David James Pope Sr. DOB-09/08/45

Person Receiving Statement: Investigator Thomas M. Aiken
Detective Frank E. Hunt Jr.

Statement(s):

During the interview prior to writing the statement, David Pope made the following admissions which were not included in the written statement:

-David Pope stated that he used to babysit for all the kids a lot of the nights because Mae was spending all the grocery money at Bingo.

-David Pope stated that he treated the boys a lot differently than Nellie becuase she was his pet. He also stated that he did not like Robert because he blamed Robert for them losing D.J. and Eddie and because Robert was not his child. He also did not like Howard as much because he wasn't his child, but he said that there was a time that he did think Howard was his child, but someone straightened him out so that he knew Howard was not his child.

After the written statement was completed, David Pope made the following admissions during continued conversations with Inv. Aiken and Det. Hunt:

-David Pope stated that he knew that Hodgie died from being abused. He further stated that Hodgie's bruises must have made it look like he was kicked and abused the length of a football field.

-David Pope stated over and over again that Mae did not hit or abuse any of the kids. When David was told that Hodgie died from abuse which caused his stomach to rupture and that someone had to cause this abuse and he was asked who could have possibly caused this abuse if he didn't, David had no answers for this and couldn't even provide one name of someone that could have done this to Hodgie. David said that no one could have done this abuse to Hodgie because Hodgie was always with him. David just said that he hopes that we arrest the right "guy".

-David Pope admitted causing some of Hodgie's bruises when he was told that most of his former neighbors were telling of seeing Hodgie with bruises all the time. He stated that he does feel guilty about kicking and hitting Hodgie so hard and that there was no reason for a grown man like him to hit a boy that size like he did.

While reading the statement back to David Pope, he wanted to change the word guilty to heavy hearted on the bottom of page 4 because he did not like the way it sounded. During the conversation before reducing David's statement to writing, David did state that he felt guilty that his punishment may have had something to do with Hodgie's death.

Oral statement report – David Pope

Now They Lay me Down to Rest

Letter / Notice – Attorney Valerie Zahn

VALERIE HUGHES ZAHN
ATTORNEY AND COUNSELOR AT LAW
POST OFFICE BOX 126 – ROUTE 22
MIDDLE GRANVILLE, NEW YORK 12849

(518) 642-2415

September 6, 1994

Investigator Tom Aiken   Investigator Frank Hunt
New York State Police   Granville Police Dept.
P.O. Box 130   Main Street
North Granville, New York 12854 Granville, New York 12832

Robert Winn, D.A.
383 Braodway
Ft. Edward, New York 12828

                Re: David J. Pope.
                D.O.B. 9-8-45
                Further Demand to Produce.

Dear Mr. Winn, Mr. Aiken and Mr. Hunt:

    Please be advised that D.A. Winn knew I represented David Pope as I was at his arraignment.

    Yet Investigator Aiken of the State Police and Investigator Hunt of the Granville Village Police went to Salem and interrogated my client without my consent or knowledge. This is totally unethical.

    Furthermore, it is my understanding that they have a copy of an autopsy report that was performed on his son, Howard, 22 years ago. I demand a copy of that report and I shall further demand the suppression of the statement he gave to Investigator Aiken and Investigator Hunt.

    Next, I have learned that David Pope did not receive notice of the Grand Jury Hearing concerning Nellie Pope until after the close of business on the 12th of August, 1994 and will be bringing a motion to suppress that indictment and allow him to testify before the Grand Jury since he was denied that right.

    To the best of my knowledge both Judge Berke and Judge Hemmett have recused themselves from Peo. V Pope on the charges of incest and sodomy.

    Until a Judge is appointed my client is incarcerated without judicial recourse.

Page 2 of 2
Re: Peo. V David Pope

 Kindly reply as soon as possible and comply with the demand to produce all current police reports, documents and records dealing with Mr. Pope including charges brought or are being considered.

Very truly yours,

Valerie Hughes Zahn

Valerie Hughes Zahn, Esq.

Encl. Daivd Pope's Authorization.

CC: David Pope.

VHZ/clr

Now They Lay me Down to Rest

FORM 101

Authorization for Record Request

TO: Robert Winn, D.A.
Investigator Tom Aiken
Investigator Frank Hunt

DATED: September 2, 1994

RE: David Pope
D.O.B. 09-08-45

Permission is hereby granted to my Attorney(X) Valerie Hughes Zahn, Esq., P.O. Box 126 - Rt. 22, Middle Granville, New York 12849

or authorized representative to obtain copy/copies of the

HOSPITAL	☐	POLICE	☒	
MEDICAL	☐	SCHOOL	☐	
PHYSICIAN	☐	WAGE/SALARY	☐	

Soc. Sec. No. 052-36-1141

OTHER/REMARKS:

record(s) and all such information relating to the same.

..................................[L.S.]
David Pope

STATE OF New York
} ss.
COUNTY OF Washington

On this 2nd day of September 19 94, before me personally appeared David Pope to me known and known to me to be the individual described in and who executed the foregoing instrument; and who duly acknowledged to me that he executed the same for the purposes therein contained.

In Witness Whereof I hereunto set my hand.

....
Commissioner of the Superior Court
Notary Public

CONNIE L. AIKEN AND THOMAS M. AIKEN

STATE OF NEW YORK
COUNTY OF ___Washington___
___Village___ of ___Granville___

DATE: ___August 26, 1994___

TELEPHONE INTERCEPT AUTHORIZATION

I, The undersigned, do hereby grant and give permission to ___Investigator Thomas M. Aiken___, and other members of the New York State Police, and to members of the Granville Police Department, to eavesdrop upon, listen to, overhear and report all conversations telephonic and otherwise pertaining to myself and all other subjects with whom I may be conversing, and to install whatever mechanical devices or technical equipment on my person or in whatever vehicle I may be riding in or building or place I may be in that is necessary to obtain certain conversations. This authorization is granted in connection with a criminal investigation that is being conducted by members of the New York State Police, and I further understand that this authorization does not exclude me from criminal liability and that all conversations obtained may be used against myself and others in any criminal action deemed necessary. This authorization shall take effect on ___August 26, 1994___ and it shall expire on ___September 20, 1994___ *.

Signed: ___Rose M. St Louis___
Print Name: ___Rose M. ST Louis___
Dated: ___Aug 26, 1994___

WITNESSED BY: ___Inv Thomas M A___
___Det. JE Farr Ph. #103___

*not to exceed 30 days

Telephone Intercept Authorization – Rose St. Louis

Now They Lay me Down to Rest

STATE OF NEW YORK
COUNTY OF Washington
Village   of   Granville

DATE: August 28, 1994

TELEPHONE INTERCEPT AUTHORIZATION

    I, The undersigned, do hereby grant and give permission to Investigator Thomas M. Aiken and Detective Frank Hunt, and other members of the New York State Police and the Granville Police Department, to eavesdrop upon, listen to, overhear and report all conversations telephonic and otherwise pertaining to myself and all other subjects with whom I may be conversing, and to install whatever mechanical devices or technical equipment on my person or in whatever vehicle I may be riding in or building or place I may be in that is necessary to obtain certain conversations. This authorization is granted in connection with a criminal investigation that is being conducted by members of the New York State Police, and I further understand that this authorization does not exclude me from criminal liability and that all conversations obtained may be used against myself and others in any criminal action deemed necessary. This authorization shall take effect on 08/28/94 and it shall expire on 09/20/94 *.

Signed: *Michael P Pope*

Print Name: *Michael P Pope*

Dated: *August 28, 1994*

WITNESSED BY: *Inv. Thomas M A*
Det. F E Hunt.   Barbara J Snoddy

*not to exceed 30 days

Telephone Intercept Authorization – Michael Pope

Chapter 8

Dog, the Tooth Fairy, and Manner of Death

Tom knew that to move forward with the prosecution of David Pope, and also to finish all the pieces of this investigative puzzle, a forensic partnership was a must. With his position in such an elite agency, the New York State Police, he had access to two of the best in the world. He knew that to move forward with a homicide investigation and prosecution, they must have a death certificate with an accurate cause of death and a manner of death that was amended to read by homicide.

As we reflect back on this case while writing, we looked back on it as a blessing. Not that everyone doesn't deserve the best, but Hodgie was actually a poor boy from the longhouses who was forgotten until 22 years later. Having a world renowned team examining every aspect of his death and new autopsy. One was Dr. Michael Baden. He is a world-famous, world-renowned Forensic Pathologist. Dr. Baden has worked on many major cases in the country and the world that you could think of. He worked on and consulted on investigations in the deaths of JFK, Martin Luther King, and the Czar Nicholas of Russia. He has worked on the OJ Simpson case as well as the case that initiated the BLM movement. The Michael Brown case in Ferguson, Missouri. People don't know that the family of Michael Brown hired him to oversee and consult on the autopsy of their son. The two most recent and very famous cases he worked on were Jeffrey Epstein and George Floyd. He had a very successful HBO show that ran for a long time on forensic autopsy cases. He worked on the Marybeth Tinning case in Schenectady County, NY. She was a mother who had 9 children die mysteriously, with the first 8 being recorded mostly as SIDS deaths. It wasn't until the 9th child died that Dr. Baden was brought in and she was convicted of murder. She was sentenced to 20 years to life in prison because of the expertise of Dr. Baden. Doc Baden wrote a book on this case: "Unnatural Death. Confessions of a Medical Examiner." Everyone deserves to have that final examination conducted by such a competent and knowledgeable medical examiner, but not all get it. During the investigation, you realized how fortunate Tom and Hodgie were to have this man that has these names and cases attached to him, that it was like putting your child in loving hands and protection. The names like JFK, Martin Luther King, OJ Simpson, Elvis Presley and thousands of others are well known to most living people, but Hodgie's name is not. There must be a reason Hodgie was included with these famous names and cases. At the end of this book, we want everyone to know the name of Hodgie and associate it with Dr. Baden and his famous cases. Hodgie was just as important as these names and his lesson to the world is to help other victims of child abuse and maltreatment. His mission through his short tortuous life is to bring awareness to just one person, one first responder, one teacher, one medical professional, or to any other person dealing with children to prevent or report any abuse of a child. To help just one child from his lesson is a living legacy to an unloved child.

Dr. Lowell Levine was a codirector with Dr. Michael Baden of the New York State Police Medico Legal Investigation Unit in the Forensic Science Center in Albany, NY. He worked on many famous cases and worked with the federal government to help identify military POWs' and MIAs' remains that were uncovered. His most famous case was testimony in the Ted Bundy case. Ted Bundy was a very famous serial murderer with movies made about his crimes. His charm and good looks allowed him to fool and lure victims. Dr. Levine is a forensic odontologist specializing in bite marks. The use of bite mark evidence is being challenged more and more in the legal world of criminal justice, but there was no doubt with Ted Bundy because he had a very unique set of teeth. A photograph of Dr. Lowell Levine testifying in the Ted Bundy case is included at the end of this chapter.

To start this process and request a consultation with these world-famous doctors, Tom had to submit a memorandum. His memorandum was submitted on August 19, 1994, and titled "REQUEST FOR CONSULTATION." In this memo, he requested a consultation with a panel of experts from the New York State Police to review his case, State Police Queensbury case 94-389. He wrote to them that this was a case involving the death of a then 2-year-old child on September 11, 1972, with the death stemming from continuous child abuse leading to chemical peritonitis. Yes, you see the connection, September 11th. Yes, we are aware that the September 11th we now know had not happened yet. This memorandum was sent on the day after opening this investigation and Tom and Frank were only at the beginning of their investigation and digging into the horrors caused by David Pope. Tom and Frank worked so hard and devoted so many hours every day until this initial consultation which occurred on September 2nd at the Forensic Science Center in Albany, New York. At this meeting were Tom and Frank, District Attorney Robert Winn, Assistant District Attorney Nancy Lynn Ferinni, Dr. Barbara Wolfe, and others.

In a stroke of good luck, the wonderful records clerk at the Glens Falls Hospital who went above and beyond to find any and all records struck gold and called Tom on September 1st and said that she found all the files, specimens, and research of Dr. Walter Stern. When Tom received this call, they felt hope for Hodgie. When they picked these up, it proved to be a major turning point. The abuse, heard so graphic from the statements taken already from witnesses, relatives, and the surviving victims themselves, told Tom and Frank how horrible this abuse was, but seeing the complete autopsy done with specimens, research and especially graphic photographs truly brought to life the unimaginable continuing abuse this little 2-year-old boy suffered his entire short life. These photographs showed a map of fresh, healing, and mostly healed bruises, abrasions, punctures, and starvation that was not from just one day, but obviously a pattern of continuing child abuse and torture. Tom and Frank went to the hospital and retrieved the following:

- Records obtained from the Glens Falls Hospital
    1. 86 Glass Slides labeled A72-149
    2. 55 Paraffin Blocks labeled A72-149
    3. 9 Kodachrome transparencies (slides) labeled A72-149
    4. Medical records and research by Dr. Walter Stern

All of these items of evidence were brought to the consultation meeting on September 2nd and they were turned over to Dr. Baden. Tom and Frank were also able to share dozens and dozens of interviews already conducted as well as some of the original Granville Police records and Social Service records from 1972. They had also conducted the interview of David Pope on August 26th, so that 5-page statement and the cassette recordings of his statement with his voice and consternation evident, and the two jailhouse confrontations by his sister and son were also shared and turned over to them. All of the items we picked up from the work of Dr. Stern became very crucial to the success of Dr. Baden. He was able to further examine the specimens preserved in the glass slides and paraffin blocks. The medical research was indicative of what Dr. Stern was seeing firsthand. Our specialty units were able to turn the 9 Kodachrome transparencies into actual film negatives and great quality photographs. These are the photographs you will see in a future chapter which will leave no doubt as to the condition of little Hodgie on the day of his death. They will leave no doubt as to the magnitude of starvation, emaciation, torture, and severe abuse that little boy suffered every day of his short-lived and unloved life. He knew nothing but abuse.

That evening, Tom came home and the look on his face was different. It was with hope. He was excited to take our nightly walk and tell me everything and how they were finally seeing some hope. Not only with the proof and evidence coming together, but it was the look on Dr. Michael Baden's face that there might be justice after all for Hodgie. As much as people don't realize the highs and lows of this job and how it affects you, they truly do affect you and they truly do come home with Tom as much as he tries to check it at the door. The frustrations of knowing that some cases were off limits to discuss due to confidentiality and they were trapped in his head and heart still to this day can't talk about. I knew and respected that there were some cases he could not discuss and I observed the torment he went through almost on a daily basis. Normal marriages and families cannot understand the daily toll and affect this takes on major case investigators. This is why there is such a high rate of suicide in the police world. Especially the types of cases Tom was working on. This was a case he could discuss with me. Some nights when things were not going too well, we felt we could feel every step. This night, the walk ended before we even knew it. Tom coming home after that consultation and telling me about the entire experience. He felt for the first time that all of their work to this day and all of the evidence was finally coming together and major pieces of this investigative puzzle were coming together. He described watching Doctors Baden and Levine discussing the statements taken and comparing them to the findings from the 1972 autopsy and seeing the magic and excitement coming alive in them, world experts, that this was a case that needed to be heard. Tom and Frank handed them a case that was very detailed and very complete for only a few weeks of 12-14-hour days of gathering so many statements, files, reports, and now these unbelievable medical records. Putting these cases together and knowing the need to win for the safety of the victims becomes a sort of an addiction. He is extremely competitive by nature, but his desire to always win in criminal cases can take its toll. It literally makes you feel it deep in your heart. For the first time, Tom was starting to see hope and justice for Hodgie coming.

At the end of this crucial consultation, Doctors Michael Baden and Lowell Levine both agreed. They must exhume the body of Hodgie and conduct a new autopsy. Tom asked them about the condition of Hodgie's body they might see and Dr. Baden told him it could look very similar to when he was buried. This was dependent on how well he was embalmed and whether or not water or critters were allowed to gain access to his body. The way your brain tries to protect itself is to imagine that this little boy will appear before you as a little boy, in body and soul trying to show them what needed to be seen. This was the image that Tom kept until the day the exhumation was to occur. Tom, Frank, and District Attorney Winn all felt very good when leaving this initial meeting. Rob went back and quickly started his work on an official exhumation application and order to present to the Supreme Court Judge. Tom and Frank went back and hit the road running with many, many more interviews and investigative tasks. This investigation was now well underway.

NOW THEY LAY ME DOWN TO REST

Dr. Michael Baden

Dr. Lowell Levine

Dr. Levine testifying in Ted Bundy Case

CONNIE L. AIKEN AND THOMAS M. AIKEN

NEW YORK STATE POLICE

MEMORANDUM

Troop G Station SP Queensbury
Date August 19, 1994

To: Major Lloyd R. Wilson, Troop Commander, Troop G

From: Investigator Thomas M. Aiken

Subject: REQUEST FOR CONSULTATION

        Member is respectfully requesting a consultation with a panel of experts from the New York State Police regarding SP Queensbury case 94-389 which involved the 1972 death of a then 3 year old boy in the Village of Granville. This request comes pursuant to a telephone conversation with Captain Timothy McAuliffe on 08/19/94 in which this member requested said consultation. A tentative date and time of September 02, 1994 at 9:30AM was set up for this consultation meeting at Division Headquarters with this member and Detective Frank Hunt of the Granville Police Department scheduled to present the facts of this death. Washington County District Attorney Robert Winn will be present and this consultation meeting will be used to develop leads for use in this investigation.

        The victim in this case was Howard James White with a date of birth of 10/29/69 and the date of his death was 09/11/72. This investigation centers around suspected continuing child abuse (physical) with the death stemming from suspected abuse which inflamed a current medical condition of Peritonitis.

Memorandum – Request for Consultation

Now They Lay me Down to Rest

Department of Pathology
GLENS FALLS HOSPITAL
Glens Falls, NY 12801
(518) XXXXXXXX 761-3900
FAX: (518) XXXXXXXX 761-3998

Jayant R. Paranjpe, M.D.
Medical Director
(518) 792-3700

Carl F. Rueckert
Laboratory Operations Manager (SBCL)

Sang Chul Nam, M.D.
Woong Man Lee, M.D.
Kathleen M. Shaheen, M.D.
Otelo G. Solis, M.D.

RE: WHITE, HOWARD
A-72-149

THE BELOW MENTIONED MATERIALS HAVE BEEN SUBPOENAED BY WASHINGTON COUNTY DISTRICT ATTORNEY, ROBERT M. WINN (SUBPOENA RECEIVED BY DR. SANG CHUL NAM FROM INVESTIGATOR THOMAS M. AIKEN, NEW YORK STATE POLICE, ON 8-24-94 AT 1:35 p.m.), FOR FURTHER (GRAND JURY) INVESTIGATION.

MATERIALS RELEASED:
** -86 GLASS SLIDES LABELED A72-149
 * -55 PARAFFIN BLOCKS LABELED A72-149
   -9 KODACHROME TRANSPARENCIES LABELED A72-149

ALSO, PHOTOCOPIES OF THE FOLLOWING:
-POST-STAR NEWSPAPER ARTICLE DATED THURSDAY, MARCH 22, 1973
-3 PAGES FROM (?)6TH EDITION "ANDERSON TEXT OF PATHOLOGY"
-4 PAGES FROM "LEGAL MEDICINE PATHOLOGY AND TOXICOLOGY", SECOND EDITION
-WORKSHEETS/NOTES CONSISTING OF 10 PAGES
-FINAL AUTOPSY REPORT CONSISTING OF 8 PAGES
-1 LETTER DATED MARCH 12, 1973 TO WALTER R. STERN, M.D. FROM GORDOM M. HEMMETT JR.
-1 LETTER DATED MARCH 21, 1973, FROM HERMON BENJAMIN, WASHINGTON COUNT TREASURER, TO WALTER R. STERN, M.D.

AS OF THIS DATE (8-31-94), THESE ARE ALL THE MATERIALS CONCERNING CASE A-72-149, HOWARD WHITE, THAT CAN BE LOCATED AT THE GLENS FALLS HOSPITA DEPARTMENT OF PATHOLOGY.

SANG CHUL NAM, M.D., ASS'T DIRECTOR

THE ABOVE MATERIALS ARE PICKED UP BY: _____
AGENCY (& BADGE #): New York State Police 1512
DATE AND TIME PICKED UP: 09/01/94 3:55pm
MATERIALS RELEASED BY: _____ 9-1-94
Department of Pathology

*Blocks 7,46,47,48,49 cannot be accounted for at this time.
**1 slide was labeled "A73 149" and was found filed with this case. Probably was mislabeled; we are including it anyway.

Autopsy File Receipt – 1994

CONNIE L. AIKEN AND THOMAS M. AIKEN

VILLAGE OF GRANVILLE
NEW YORK, 12832

THIS IS TO CERTIFY THAT THE FOREGOING is a true copy of a record on file in the OFFICE OF THE VILLAGE CLERK, VILLAGE OF GRANVILLE, NEW YORK.
IN WITNESS WHEREOF, THIS CERTIFICATE HAS BEEN DULY SIGNED AND SEALED BY THE VILLAGE CLERK, VILLAGE OF GRANVILLE, NY

DATE: *August 19, 1994*

Elizabeth M. Truso
ELIZABETH M. TRUSO
VILLAGE CLERK

Copy of First Death Certificate 1972

Chapter 9

They Seemed to Wear Troubled Expressions

Now that you have read the previous chapters, we are going to bring you all the way back to the early 1970s. This is important in the fact that this is what Tom had to do as part of the investigation to gather all of this information from Social Services, doctors, hospitals, foster parents, school personnel, and others to understand what happened in 1972 and how this system failed Hodgie and his slightly older brother Robbie who happened to survive. As they gathered information on this case and Hodgie, it also told the story of Robbie. What we want you to know in this chapter is that after Tom's 30-year career and observing many child abuse cases and deaths, we are in no way trying to discredit the importance of social workers. We believe there are many conscientious, caring, and hardworking social workers. As we go through life, most people know and hear that social workers are overworked with too many caseloads, and have a high rate of burnout. Even back then as Tom started to go through all of the paperwork / evidence pertaining to Hodgie's case, it wasn't just a failure of social workers, it was a failure of the whole system. What we feel makes this case unique is not only the fact he lost his life, but it was because of the first lie which led to the first coverup. We believe that he was just one of the forgotten. A poor boy from the longhouses. The first lie that we will expose will be after you read the letter from the District Attorney to the Commissioner of Social Services dated November 26, 1973, you will see this led to the second lie which snowballed into the massive coverup. This was 14 months after the death of Hodgie. His letter to the Commissioner was so on point because he knew this was much more than an assault charge he filed in the spring of 1973. We feel that you must first read this entire 7-page letter to help you understand that as Tom was gathering the files from all the involved departments that there was such a massive coverup going on. The lack of a proper homicide investigation in 1972, and Social Service workers and the family physician / coroner lying and covering things up after the death and also at the spring of 1973 trial, left Tom shaking his head in bewilderment and frustration. It motivated him ever more. This letter from District Attorney Philip A. Berke to Commissioner Donald Reynolds stated:

> *Dear Commissioner Reynolds:*
>
> *I have examined the above case file concerning the records involving Howard James White, who as you know died on September 11, 1972, under very suspicious circumstances.*
> *I was shocked at reading the notes in the file made by Miss Margaret Wunder and Mrs. Anita Sarchioto. Throughout the file there are references to constant complaints being made to both Mrs. Sarchioto and Miss Wunder concerning the abuse of Howard James White.*
> *On February 11, 1971, according to the records, Mrs. Sarchioto had indicated to Mrs. White and David Pope that she had received a complaint from Mrs. Tobin, Whitehall Town Welfare Officer, that Robert and Howard had bruises and Howard had black-and-blue marks on his face and that he had been punched in the face. Mrs. Sarchioto relates that her observation indicated that Howard had "bluish bruises*

in the middle of his forehead, a black-and-blue mark on the right side of the face near his mouth and a bruise that looked like a 1 ¼ cut covered with dry blood near the corner of his left eye." Mrs. Sarchioto states that Mrs. White stated that the bruises resulted from a fall by Howard. The file states: *"Worker is not sure Howie's bruises were from a fall as his mother states. It does not seem that he could have three such bruises on both sides of his face from a fall from a chair. Worker also noted that both boys seemed subdued."*

On March 17, 1971, Dr. John Glennon noted that Howard had an old contusion to his forehead with a fresh injury.

On March 23, 1971, Mrs. Kelley, mother of Mrs. Mae White, contacted Miss Wunder to advise that a high school girl had indicated to her that David Pope beat up Robert and that she had seen Mrs. White and Mr. Pope abuse the children many times.

On March 26, 1971, Mr. White, father of Howard, came to see Mrs. Sarchioto and told her that Mrs. Mae White had left Mr. Pope and told him she had gotten mad at Mr. Pope *"because he had been pounding the children."*

The file indicates that on just about every occasion Mrs. Sarchioto visited the home, Howard White had either bumps or bruises on his forehead.

On August 17, 1971, Mrs. Sarchioto noticed that Howard had a bruise on the side of his forehead. On September 23, 1971, Mrs. Sarchioto noticed on her visit that Howard had a small red spot on his cheek.

Throughout the file, Mr. White, father of Howard, was constantly complaining that both of his sons were being abused.

On November 12, 1971, Mrs. Kelley and Mr. White came to see Mrs. Sarchioto to complain about Mr. Pope mistreating the boys and indicated a neighbor had seen Mr. Pope hit the boys. On that day, Mrs. Kelley advised Mrs. Sarchioto that Kathy Touchette saw Mr. Pope mistreat the boys while she lived in their home.

On November 16, 1971, Mrs. Sarchioto took a statement from Miss Touchette indicating the following: "Mr. Pope slapped them with the back of his hand across the chest, knocking them across the room. This occurred almost daily. When Howard wet the bed, Mr. Pope spanked his bare buttocks until they were black and blue. One night, the adults were drinking and they gave Robert beer. Robert refused to drink it all, vomited and was sent to bed. Howard was given beer, apple wine and sloe gin. He got drunk and fell on the floor, getting black-and-blue marks, and was sent to bed. When Mr. Pope mistreats the children, Mrs. White does not object or say anything."

At no time was I advised by the Department of Social Services about a statement being taken from Miss Touchette, nor was I given a copy of same. Nor had I been advised that your file contained a history of complaints about mistreatments by Mr. Pope of Howard and Robert White.

On November 18, 1971, Robert and Howard were taken to the foster home of Mrs. Sweeney and "there was a bruise on Howard's back that resembled a mark made by a belt or stick," which is related in the note of November 22, 1971.

On July 21, 1972, a neighbor, Mr. Harold Burch, was so upset with the mistreatment of Howard that he went directly to the office and made a complaint that Howard had been abused the prior night. Mrs. Sarchioto testified at the trial, at page 22 of the transcript, a copy of which you have, that she went to the Pope home "in response to a phone call from Mr. Burch." She further testified that she observed no scratches or any recent injury on Howard's buttocks. Yet the notes of July 21, 1972, indicate that Mrs. Sarchioto observed bruises which were gray in several spots.

I have previously indicated to you that I was completely amazed at the hostile attitude shown to me by Miss Wunder and Mrs. Sarchioto at the trial. Gladys Barker had testified that she had reported the incident concerning Mr. Pope holding Howard's head in a bathtub under water and the incident charging Mr. Pope with striking Howard in the rear end with a board with nails protruding from it, to the Department of Social Services, but Miss Wunder indicated that it was impossible for these telephone calls to have been made because there was no entry in the file. She further testified that all telephone calls get through to the case worker and she took the position not that no calls were made to her knowledge, which I stated at the trial I assumed she meant to say, but that absolutely no telephone calls were made at all. Miss Wunder refused to acknowledge that is was even possible that Gladys Barker could have reported the incidents to the Department of Social Services in July of 1972. Mrs. Josephine Jurnak, who was the operator of Jurnak's Store, advised me on March 27, 1973, that she distinctly remembers Gladys Barker coming in to her store and asking for the telephone directory in order to find the Welfare number to report these incidents. Moreover, on January 30, 1973, Mrs. Sarchioto personally advised me by telephone that Miss Barker did report something about both incidents to the Department of Social Services.

The case file indicates that on September 5, 1972, Gladys Barker called and complained about David Pope abusing Howard. On September 6, 1972, Mrs. Sarchioto observed that Howard had a cut on his face over his right eye, which was about ¾" long and that the eye was black and blue. She further noticed that Howard and Robert stood in one spot in the kitchen, not moving during the visit, and it did not seem this was an ordinary thing for children that age to do.

On September 18, 1972, the records indicate that Mrs. Sarchioto indicated to Mrs. Kelley that the death of Howard was accidental. At that time, I had not even secured an autopsy report, and I am quite amazed as to how Mrs. Sarchioto reached her conclusions, since I still do not feel that the death was accidental.

Furthermore, what amazes me is that no action was taken by the Department of Social Services to initiate neglect proceedings until David Pope was arrested on November 17,

1972, and the notes indicated it was decided to institute such a proceeding on November 20, 1972, and on December 6, 1972, a petition was finally signed and the children were not taken out of the home until January 12, 1973.

The records indicate that on December 28, 1972, Mrs. White advised Mrs. Sarchioto that on Christmas Day David Pope slapped and hit her and that she is considering leaving him.

What amazes me even more is that on January 23, 1973, the records indicate that Mrs. Sarchioto advised Attorney Gordon Hemmett that Gladys Barker had called not to report the incident concerning Howard being struck with a board with nails in it, but to report that there was no food in the house. This contradicts the notes of September 5, 1972, which indicate that Miss Barker not only indicated there was no food in the house but claimed that Howard was being abused by Mr. Pope.

The file indicates that on March 16, 1973, Mrs. Mae White advised Mrs. Sarchioto that she wanted to withdraw the charges which she had made against Mr. Pope in December of 1972 and that she had talked to both Judge William Williams and I and (Typo on Doctor and sentence), according to Mrs. White, was being given a hard time concerning the withdrawal of her complaint. I have no objection to Mrs. Sarchioto quoting Mae White in the file but I do object to the following statements: "Worker remarked that she seemed to be getting the runaround and that she should attempt to clear up this matter by withdrawing the complaint and having the withdrawal accepted." If Mrs. Sarchioto had taken the time to contact me, she would have found that the facts were different than those related to her by Mrs. White. I do feel if Mrs. Sarchioto makes conclusionary comments like the aforesaid in other files that this can cause the District Attorney's Office many problems in prosecuting cases in the future. I do feel that Mrs. Sarchioto couldn't care less and her attitude is definitely anti-police, and I believe you and I know the reason why. I do feel it is your responsibility to set the policy straight on this matter.

As indicated, the children have been out of the Pope home since January 12, 1973, which would seem to indicate that the Department of Social Services seems to accept the fact that the children should not be in the home.

I have spent considerable time going over this file and I would strongly suggest that you do so, since the conduct of both Mrs. Sarchioto and Miss Wunder in ignoring the constant complaints of abuse of Howard and Robert is shocking indeed. On various occasions, it appears that Mrs. Sarchioto would indicate to Mrs. White and Mr. Pope that unless they treated the children better that Mr. White would take them back to Family Court. This obviously left the matter to Mr. White rather than the Department of Social Services taking action itself.

It appears clear that you haven't had the opportunity to read the file and I would suggest that you do so, since you may want to take some kind of disciplinary action against Miss Wunder and Mrs. Sarchioto. I do understand that Miss Wunder's department has been independent from the rest of the department, but I do also understand you intend to control this part of your department to make certain that their conduct is proper and that all abuse complaints are investigated and the necessary action taken. As Attorney McLenithan will advise you, throughout the police investigation, we have consistently cooperated with your department and given them statements which were taken from various witnesses, as well as a copy of the autopsy report and other information. On the other hand, no information was supplied to me and, as you know, I was told that I must go to Court to get a subpoena to examine this file. I am sure you are well aware of the fact that to prosecute a child abuse case is very difficult and is almost impossible without the cooperation of your department. I would, therefore, expect and assume that in the future you will make sure that Miss Wunder and Mrs. Sarchioto, if they still remain with your department, and any other members of your department, cooperate with both the police and my office.

I am sure that you are upset and concerned with the death of Howard White and wish to take appropriate actions so that members of your department will not allow a situation to exist so that this may happen again, and so that members of your department will not in the future feel, as obviously they did in this case, that they are on trial rather than the person actually involved. It is by no means my intention to in any way become involved with the way your department is run. However, I would strongly urge that you exert a stronger control over Miss Wunder's department and become familiar with the results of their investigation and complaints filed with members of this department.

I am returning the above case file to you.

Very truly yours,

Philip A. Berke
District Attorney

As we presented to you numerous statements from the reopening of this case in Chapter 6, statements from concerned neighbors, concerned relatives, babysitters, and others, many of these concerns were brought to the attention of the social workers. Some of the accusations were investigated and some were completely ignored and later covered up because as they stated, "Their hours were Monday – Friday from 9:00 A.M. to 5:00 P.M." These witnesses who Tom took statements from could hear the screams because living in the longhouses in 1972, you did not have air conditioning and windows were open on hot summer nights. Some of the neighbors and some of the family members actually did make calls and reports where they knew David was not mentally well and had a great fear of him. What's remarkable is he and his brother William had so many in this small town fearful because of the violent murder of a teenage girl. These adults and young teenage babysitters even had the guts to speak out on these kids' behalf because it was such severe abuse. Imagine what these little boys endured during the winter months when the windows were closed!! It was too cold to go out through the neighborhood and rummage for food. Even burnt toast would satisfy that gnawing hunger pang in their stomachs. When the neighbors witnessed that these boys would gobble up a piece of burnt toast, they all began to intentionally throw away burnt toast and other foods. Because the failure of the system and the neighbors witnessing them to be returned, they did not want the boys to have to actually dig through the garbage. They wanted to make it easier for the scant and emaciated toddlers to grab the food and not have to take time rummaging through the cans, so they would intentionally leave "thrown out" food on top of the garbage in these cans. They knew time was not their friend because if David caught them eating, they would get the boots, and these were not average boots, these were quarry worker steel-toed boots. The neighbors also had justified fears if caught intentionally feeding these kids as they all wanted to do. You just couldn't look the other way and we really don't know how the mother did, how the doctors did, and how the CPS workers did. The mother could have intentionally found times to sneak her kids food, not to have them running the neighborhood and looking like the starved children from what you had seen from commercials of starving African children. This didn't happen overnight. Your tummy does not become distended like that without months of starvation. She could have found opportunities to feed her children, hug her children, kiss her children, give them baths when David wasn't home so the fear of them being dunked underwater until they turned blue, but she chose not to. We have learned that she would come home with bags of snacks and eat them in front of these emotionally, physically starved children. How do you learn to trust anyone when the State would return them to this environment? What does this do to a toddler's brain? To a toddler's body and organs. To a toddler's thymus gland which we had to educate ourselves from the first autopsy where this was documented and highlighted. As you will come to find out, a normal thymus gland will naturally start shrinking during the teenage years, but in Hodgie's 1972 autopsy, it was very evident to the pathologist that Hodgie's Thymus gland, which is actually an organ, was diminished from severe abuse and emotional trauma. The true study of the thymus gland and its function only began in earnest starting in the 1960s. As our research showed us, the Thymus gland is at its largest and heaviest during the ages of birth through 30. The normal weight should be 20-28 g for his age. Hodgie's was 2.5 g. That tells us it was not just physical abuse. What we learned from studying the first autopsy was how diminished his thymus gland was. If Mom showed love and care to these boys, Hodgie wouldn't have had such atrophy to his thymus gland. Our research has shown that the thymus gland will regenerate like the liver, by releasing the happy hormone cortisol. Imagine it regenerating without thought, while placed in the foster care home. We can only imagine what happened to their little minds and thymus glands when they were returned, by the people who should have cared and protected them. What we want you to understand is the importance how important it was for the pathologist to document the atrophy of his thymus gland. The purpose of the thymus gland is to create a healthy immune system and to release the hormone of cortisol. Mom played as much of a role as David Pope. The failure of the system was so frustrating to see them taken away, but then returned soon thereafter. The abuse would then pick up right where it left off. When they would be returned to the hellish nightmare they endured, can you imagine the confusion going through these little boys' minds? They had every need met only to be returned and have it start all over again. Social workers did not come out to every call, every knock on their door, and even when one man was brave enough to go directly to their office and demand that something be done to protect these children. These children would periodically be taken out of their custody and placed in foster care, but briefly, only to be returned to their hell. As the investigation in the 1990s uncovered of homes these children would be placed in, these little boys got a little glimpse of what it felt like to have your basic needs met and to eat without being beaten for eating out of garbage cans. They were given baths without being dunked underwater until they turned blue and gasping for a lifesaving breath. Everything they endured in that hellhole was their basic need for survival and everything was twisted. Baths became torture, rummaging through neighbors' trash for food, being left food in a dog dish by neighbors in hopes that the sinister David Pope never caught wind of this. Like where neighbors installed doggy doors so the boys could go in and eat. Having foster moms show the true meaning of what a mom should have been. Rocking them, reading nursery rhymes, bathing them, giving hugs and kisses, and going to bed with their tummies full and clean clothing. They seemed to thrive for these short periods. These foster moms indicated that neither boy seemed aggressive. From notes of the police and Social Service workers, it appears that Hodgie and Robbie were removed to the state custody and placed into foster care 4 times. The last time they were placed back into the custody of David and Mae was in January of 1972, 9 months before his fatal injury and death. This placement back into their custody was a death sentence for Hodgie.

The average person knows instinctively that this type of abuse is so damning to a child's development, but yet the average person does not know the relevance of a pathologist highlighting abuse through the examination of a thymus gland. The overwhelming question we have as well as those involved in this case is this: If there was enough evidence of physical and emotional abuse to remove these kids to foster care 4 times, then why were the mother and father never arrested after hearing and seeing all the abuse documented in 1971 through Hodgie's death? Tom had heard numerous times, along with "Where were you 22 years ago?" but by what they observed in this case showed that there was something different about mom. None of them thought she was a battered woman. In a quote attributed directly to Mae Pope talking to Social Service workers, Mae stated she had no intention of reuniting with her husband, but she hoped she would soon be free to marry Pope. She played a huge role from her lack of caring. From doing many cases before this, Tom knew that there were many battered woman, but this seemed different. As the investigation was going, Tom heard almost as frequently as where were you 22 years ago, that Mae should have been in a cell right beside David Pope and rotting in hell for what happened to her son. We have come to know the surviving 7th child of Mae Pope who is now in his 40s that the importance a mother plays in a battered environment affects the child even more than the physical abuse. He could put that into words for us where Hodgie could not.

These following statements are excerpts from Social Services files, reports, and narratives from their investigations of Mae and David during the time leading up to Hodgie's death:

"Mr. Pope was present at all times every visit made."

"Robert looked thin and pale."

"An anonymous complaint that Mr. Pope had been seen abusing the children, Mrs. White stated again they had been suffering from another cold."

"They had numerous marks on their faces, large bump and bruise located on the center of his forehead, small cut on the corner of his left eye."

"Both children were quite subdued and seemed to wear troubled expressions."

"Robert was lying on a cot in the combination kitchen-living room area. He had a bruise on the left side of his face and appeared to be to be shaking or quivering. It was not possible to determine whether he was frightened or shivering but he wore what seemed to be a painful expression. The boy did not move at all during visit."

"Mrs. White explained that both children had fallen again and that Dr. White (mistake – Lynch) examined Howard yesterday.

Worker immediately telephoned the doctor. He described Howard's bump as a hematoma. When asked if he thought there was a possibility of abuse, he answered he had no definite feeling one way or the other."

"Worker attempted to persuade client to bring the children in to see Dr. Glennon that afternoon. Mr. Pope refused! He stated they would wait until Dr. Lynch was available." ***Note – *Dr. Lynch was the family doctor and coroner who failed to properly fill out the death certificate knowing they had been seen in his office for the following: 3-16-71 contusions forehead; 5-1-72 stomach pains; 8-28-72 lacerations right eye brow; 9-11-72 died. These were directly from his records. He saw him 14 days before his death with more injuries, lacerations, and punctures than can be documented in this paragraph. He also made up the story about the chicken bone.*

In most of the Social Service workers reports, they frequently stated that they boys always seemed quite subdued and stated that they seemed to "rarely utter a sound," they heard that the boys seemed to always fall down a lot from chairs and stairs. In a report, it states that the client's mother, Beatrice Kelley, "people have seen the children and observed bruises on their faces." Social workers did respond and had witnessed bruises on the left side of Robert's face and again mentioned that he seemed to be shaking and wore a very painful expression. They also noted several times that the boys were laying in the cots and did not move at all during their visits. During this visit, Howard's bump on his forehead was then covered with a new bruise. The mother stated that both of the children had fallen again. The judge did order them to be placed into the custody of the State. In one of their reports, they identified the children as being in need of protection. In another report they stated that Mr. Pope's presence in the household was considered everything but heathy.

In Mae Kelley's quotes to the police on the night of Hodgie's death, she stated, "He seems to desire to be alone. Walks very slowly. Won't or can't talk much. Cries a great deal. Cries when anyone comes near him. Cries when he has to go to the bathroom."

You tell me how these children could be covered with bruises, always seeming to be subdued, quivering and shaking, always suffering from a cold, always falling down staircases or out of chairs, how they could wear troubled expressions, shaking and wearing painful expressions, and many other obvious signs of children in need of protection, exactly how these children could be returned to these monsters and neither David or Mae charged and held accountable. How come in 1972, no one ever spoke to the neighbors?

District Attorney Philip Berke was so frustrated with the lack of police resources, the lack of forensic analysis, the lying and covering up from the Social Service workers and coroner that he wrote many letters to State commissioners and legislature members. One of those letters is attached to this chapter. This case became an impetus for the modern-day mandated child abuse hotline in place for New York and laid the framework for proper training of Social Service workers across the state and proper investigations coming from this training.

Now They Lay me Down to Rest

Page 1 of Letter from D.A. Berke to Commissioner Reynolds

November 26, 1973

Honorable Donald Reynolds, Commissioner
Washington County Department of Social Services
Church Street
Granville, New York

    Re: Hoard James White - Case No. 2801

Dear Commissioner Reynolds:

I have examined the above case file concerning the records involving Howard James White, who as you know died on September 11, 1972 under very suspicious circumstances.

I was shocked at reading the notes in the file made by Miss Margaret Wunder and Mrs. Anith Sarchioto. Throughout the file there are references to constant complaints being made to both Mrs. Sarchioto and Miss Wunder concerning the abuse of Howard James White.

On February 11, 1971, according to the records, Mrs. Sarchioto had indicated to Mrs. White and David Pope that she had received a complaint from Mrs. Tobin, Whitehall Town Welfare Officer, that Robert and Howard had bruises and Howard had black and blue marks on his face and that he had been punched in the face. Mrs. Sarchioto relates that her observation indicated that Howard had "bluish bruises in the middle of his forehead, a black and blue mark on the right side of the face near his mouth and a bruise that looked like a 1¼" cut covered with dry blood near the corner of his left eye." Mrs. Sarchioto states that Mrs. White stated that the bruises resulted from a fall by Howard. The file states "Worker is not sure Howdy's bruises were from a fall as his mother states. It does not seem that he could have three such bruises on both sides of his face from a fall from a chair. Worker also noted that both boys seemed subdued."

Wash. Co. Dept. Social Services   -2-   November 26, 1973

On March 17, 1971, Dr. John Glennon noted that Howard had an old contusion to his forehead with a fresh injury.

On March 23, 1971, Mrs. Kelley, mother of Mrs. Mae White, contacted Miss Wunder to advise that a high school girl had indicated to her that David Pope beat up Robert and that she had seen Mrs. White and Mr. Pope abuse the children many times.

On March 26, 1971, Mr. White, father of Howard, came to see Mrs. Sarchioto and told her that Mrs. Mae White had left Mr. Pope and told him she had gotten mad at Mr. Pope "because he had been pounding the children."

The file indicates that on just about every occasion Mrs. Sarchioto visited the home, Howard White had either bumps or bruises on his forehead.

On August 17, 1971, Mrs. Sarchioto noticed that Howard had a bruise on the side of his forehead. On September 23, 1971, Mrs. Sarchioto noticed on her visit that Howard had a small red spot on his cheek.

Throughout the file, Mr. White, father of Howard, was constantly complaining that both of his sons were being abused.

On November 12, 1971, Mrs. Kelley and Mr. White came to see Mrs. Sarchioto to complain about Mr. Pope mistreating the boys and indicated a neighbor had seen Mr. Pope hit the boys. On that day, Mrs. Kelley advised Mrs. Sarchioto that Kathy Touchette saw Mr. Pope mistreat the boys while she lived in their home.

On November 16, 1971, Mrs. Sarchioto took a statement from Miss Touchette indicating the following: " Mr. Pope slapped them with the back of his hand across the chest, knocking them across the room. This occurred almost daily. When Howard wet the bed, Mr. Pope spanked his bare buttocks until they were black and blue. One

Wash.Co. Dept. Social Services   -3-   November 26, 1973

night, the adults were drinking and they gave Robert beer. Robert refused to drink it all, vomited and was sent to bed. Howard was given beer, apple wine and sloe gin. He got drunk and fell on the floor, getting black and blue marks, and was sent to bed. When Mr. Pope mistreats the children, Mrs. White does not object or say anything."

At no time was I advised by the Department of Social Services about a statement being taken from Miss Touchette, nor was I given a copy of same. Nor had I been advised that your file contained a history of complaints about mistreatment by Mr. Pope of Howard and Robert White.

On November 18, 1971, Robert and Howard were taken to the foster home of Mrs. Swezey and "there was a bruise on Howard's back that resembled a mark made by a belt or stick", which is related in the note of November 22, 1971.

On July 21, 1972, a neighbor, Mr. Harold Burch, was so upset with the mistreatment of Howard that he went directly to the office and made a complaint that Howard had been abused the prior night. Mrs. Sarchioto testified at the trial, at page 22 of the transcript, a copy of which you have, that she went to the Pope home "in response to a 'phone call from Mr. Burch." She further testified that she observed no scratches or any recent injury on Howard's buttocks. Yet the notes of July 21, 1972, indicate that Mrs. Sarchioto observed bruises which were gray in several spots.

I have previously indicated to you that I was completely amazed at the hostile attitude shown to me by Miss Wunder and Mrs. Sarchioto at the trial. Gladys Barker had testified that she had reported the incident concerning Mr. Pope holding Howard's head in a bathtub under water and the incident charging Mr. Pope with striking Howard in the rear end with a board with nails protruding from it, to the Department of Social Services, but Miss Wunder indicated that it was impossible for these telephone calls to have been made because

Wash.Co. Dept. Social Services   -4-   November 26, 1973

there was no entry in the file. She further testified that all
telephone calls get through to the case worker, and she took the
position not that no calls were made to her knowledge, which I
stated at the trial I assumed she meant to say, but that absolutely
no telephone calls were made at all. Miss Wunder refused to
acknowledge that it was even possible that Gladys Barker could have
reported the incidents to the Department of Social Services. Mrs.
Sarchioto also testified at the trial that there were no calls
made by Gladys Barker to the Department of Social Services in July
of 1972. Mrs. Josephine Jurnak, who was the operator of Jurnak's
Store, advised me on March 27, 1973 that she distinctly remembers
Gladys Barker coming in to her store and asking for the telephone
directory in order to find the Welfare number to report these
incidents. Moreover, on January 30, 1973, Mrs. Sarchioto personally
advised me by telephone that Miss Barker did report something about
both incidents to the Department of Social Services.

The case file indicates that on September 5, 1972, Gladys Barker
called and complained about David Pope abusing Howard. On
September 6, 1972, Mrs. Sarchioto observed that Howard had a cut on
his face over his right eye, which was about 3/4" long and that
the eye was black and blue. She further noticed that Howard and
Robert stood in one spot in the kitchen, not moving during the visit,
and it did not seem this was an ordinary thing for children that age
to do.

On September 18, 1972, the records indicate that Mrs. Sarchioto
indicated to Mrs. Kelley that the death of Howard was accidental.
At that time, I had not even secured an autopsy report, and I am
quite amazed as to how Mrs. Sarchioto reached her conclusions, since
I still do not feel that the death was accidental.

Furthermore, what amazes me is that no action was taken by the
Department of Social Services to institute neglect proceedings until

Now They Lay me Down to Rest

Wash. Co. Dept. Social Services   -5-   November 26, 1973

David Pope was arrested on November 17, 1972 and the notes indicated it was decided to institute such a proceeding on November 20, 1972, and on December 6, 1972 a petition was finally signed and the children were not taken out of the home until January 12, 1973.

The records indicate that on December 28, 1972, Mrs. White advised Mrs. Sarchioto that on Christmas day David Pope slapped and hit her and that she is considering leaving him.

What amazes me even more is that on January 23, 1973, the records indicate that Mrs. Sarchioto advised Attorney Gordon Bennett that Gladys Barker had called not to report the incident concerning Howard being struck with a board with nails in it, but to report that there was no food in the house. This contradicts the notes of September 5, 1972, which indicate that Miss Barker not only indicated there was no food in the house but claimed that Howard was being abused by Mr. Pope.

The file indicates that on March 16, 1973, Mrs. Mae White advised Mrs. Sarchioto that she wanted to withdraw the charges which she had made against Mr. Pope in December of 1972 and that she had talked to both Judge William Williams and I and, according to Mrs. White, was being given a hard time concerning the withdrawal of her complaint. I have no objection to Mrs. Sarchioto quoting Mae White in the file but I do object to the following statement:- "Worker remarked that she seemed to be getting the runaround and that she should attempt to clear up this matter by withdrawing the complaint and having the withdrawal accepted." If Mrs. Sarchioto had taken the time to contact me, she would have found that the facts were different than those related to her by Mrs. White. I do feel that if Mrs. Sarchioto makes conclusionary comments like the aforesaid in other files, that this can cause the District Attorney's Office many problems in prosecuting cases in the future. I do feel that Mrs. Sarchioto could care less and her attitude is definitely anti-police, and I believe you and I know the reason why. I do feel it is your responsibility to set the policy straight on this matter.

Wash.Co. Dept. Public Welfare   -6-   November 26, 1973

As indicated, the children have been out of the Pope home since January 12, 1973, which would seem to indicate that the Department of Social Services seems to accept the fact that the children should not be in the home.

I have spent considerable time going over this file and I would strongly suggest that you do so, since the conduct of both Mrs. Sarchioto and Miss Wunder in ignoring the constant complaints of abuse of Howard and Robert, is shocking indeed. On various occasions, it appears that Mrs. Sarchioto would indicate to Mrs. White and Mr. Pope that unless they treated the children better that Mr. White would take them back to Family Court. This obviously left the matter to Mr. White rather than the Department of Social Services taking action itself.

It appears clear that you haven't had the opportunity to read the file and I would suggest that you do so, since you may want to take some kind of diciplinary action against Miss Wunder and Mrs. Sarchioto. I do understand that Miss Wunder's department has been independent from the rest of the department, but I do also understand you intend to control this part of your department to make certain that their conduct is proper and that all abuse compaints are investigated and the necessary action taken. As Attorney McLenithan will advise you, throughout the police investigation, we have consistently cooperated with your department and given them statements which were taken from various witnesses, as well as a copy of the autopsy report and other information. On the other hand, no information was supplied to me and, as you know, I was told that I must go to Court to get a subpeona to examine this file. I am sure you are well aware of the fact that to prosecute a child abuse case is very difficult and is almost impossible without the cooperation of your department. I would, therefore, expect and assume that in the future you will make sure that Miss Wunder and Mrs. Sarchioto, if they still remain with your department, and any other

Wash. Co. Dept. Social Services   -7-   November 26, 1973

members of your department, cooperate with both the police and my office.

I am sure that you are upset and concerned with the death of Howard White and wish to take appropriate actions so that members of your department will not allow a situation to exist so that this may happen again, and so that members of your department will not in the future feel, as obviously they did in this case, that they are on trial rather than the person actually involved. It is by no means my intention to in any way become involved with the way your department is run. However, I would strongly urge that you exert a stronger control over Miss Wunder's department and become familiar with the results of their investigations and complaints filed with members of this department.

I am returning the above case file to you.

                                        Very truly yours,

                                        Philip A. Berke,
                                        District Attorney

PAB:rr

cc: Richard E. McLenithan, Esq.
    Attorney for Washington County Department
       of Social Services
    124 Main Street
    Hudson Falls, New York

    Hon. Laurence E. Andrews, Supervisor
    Town of Granville
    Town Rooms
    Granville, New York

    Hon. Keith Sweet, Chief of Police
    Granville, New York

Connie L. Aiken and Thomas M. Aiken

Letter from D.A. Berke to NYS Director Joseph Franco

March 27, 1973

Mr. Joseph DeFranco
Assistant Welfare Inspector General
1450 Western Avenue
Albany, New York

Re: Washington County Department of Social Services - Howard James White

Dear Mr. DeFranco:

Pursuant to our telephone conversation of this morning, I am writing you this letter, stating the facts concerning a child abuse case which occurred in this County.

On January 3, 1973, the January Term of the Washington County Grand Jury indicted David Pope for the crime of Assault in the Second Degree, in violation of § 120.05 of the Penal Law, concerning striking Howard James White, approximately 2 1/2 years of age, with a board with nails protruding from it, twice in the rear end, in the kitchen in the apartment where he was living with Howard's mother, Mae White, and at the same time striking Howard once in the back while he was going upstairs, with the same board, thereby causing his rear end and back to bleed, to be scraped, and to be red.

The Grand Jury also indicted this defendant for the crime of Reckless Endangerment in the First Degree in violation of § 120.25 of the Penal Law, wherein it was alleged that a few days later that David Pope took Howard James White and held him upside down and held his head in a baby's bathtub, under water, thereby causing him to gasp for breath, spit up water, and be unable to breathe.

On September 11, 1972, Howard James White died, under very suspicious circumstances. I have previously given your investigator, James Donohue, a copy of the pathologist's report, which among other things indicates multiple ecchymosis, recent and old superficial abrasions, a recent healing puncture wound of the scalp, recent fracture of the posterior segment of the tenth right rib, subpelvic hemorrhages, and hemorrages

Now They Lay me Down to Rest

Mr. Joseph DeFranco   - 2 -   March 27, 1973

of the left kidney and recent hemorrhages of the ileum and colon, possible early acute meningitis, and a large acute perforation of the anterior wall of the stomach.

The pathologist's report further indicates that thee was emaciation with serous atrophy of fat.

It is my understanding that Mrs. Anita Sarchioto was the case worker involved with this family, who were receiving assistance from the Washington County Department of Social Services.

No police agency, nor myself, were at any time contacted by the Washington County Department of Social Services concerning this matter. The first involvement of the Granville Police Department was on Sunday evening, September 3, 1972, when Patrolman Joseph Brindise was called to the Pope-Whte apartment by Miss Gladys Barker, and at that time Patrolman Brindise was advised that Howard White was continually mistreated, and physically abused. Patrolman Brindise immediately went down to see Dr. John E. Glennon, the Health Officer here in Granville.

After Howard White died, on September 11, 1973, Granville Chief of Police Keith E. Sweet investigated this matter and obtained statements from Gladys Barker and Linda Belden, that they were babysitting in the Pope-White apartment during the period from July 17 to July 19, 1972, and saw the board incident and that they were also babysitting in the apartment during the period from July 20 to July 25, 1972, and saw the dunking incident. Miss Barker and Miss Belden, as well as the other neighbors, gave the police various statements indicating other incidents of mistreatment, involving Pope kicking Howard White with steel-toed boots, and indicated that on various occasions, they saw Howard eating out of garbage cans and eating stale pieces of bread off the floor from the dog's dish, and taking bones away from dogs. I have personally talked to theneighbors concerning these matters in my office, and they have all verified these incidents to me.

One neighbor indicated that two to three weeks before Howard White died, that Howard had a bad cut over his eye, and she offered to take Howard to the doctor, and Mae White indicated that David Pope would kill her if she did so. This neighbor finally took Howard to Dr. Lynch with Mae White, and while they were in the office, she called Dr. Glennon and advised him of Howard's very poor condition, and Dr. Glennon indicated that it appeared that he was suffering from malnutrition. The police and myself waited for the coroner's report from Dr. Lynch, which we finally received on November 15, 1972, which indicated that there was some evidence of abuse of this child, but death was from natural causes. Dr. Lynch further went on to state, "regarding the other children, it probably would be in their best interests to be placed in a foster home." I gave a copy of this report to Mr. Donohue.

There was not enough evidence to charge anyone with murder or manslaughter, but there was enough to charge David Pope with assault and reckless endangerment, as indicated above. On November 17, 1972, this defendant was charged with assault and reckless endangerment.

Chief Sweet and myself were very concerned about the other three children, and based solely upon information provided by myself to the Department of Social Services Attorney, Richard E. McLenithan, Attorney McLenithan instituted a proceeding in the Washington County Family Court to have the other three children temporarily removed from the home. I discussed this with Commissioner Reynolds, and he advised me that the Department of Social Services was more concerned with the safety of Howard White's brother, Robert, than with the other two children in the Pope-White home, David Pope and Edward Pope, who are the children of both David Pope and Mae White. I advised Attorney McLenithan by my letter dated November 13, 1972, a copy of which I gave to Mr. Donohue, that I could not agree with Commissioner Reynold's position, and that I felt that the lives of all these children were in serious danger, and both Chief Sweet and myself would hope that all of these children were immediately taken from the Pope-White apartment.

Family Court Judge Julian V. D. Orton has temporarily taken these children from the Pope-White apartment, based, as indicated above, solely upon the information furnished by the police and myself, and to this date, it is my understanding that Attorney McLenithan has not received any information from the Department of Social Services, which would justify the removal.

Now They Lay me Down to Rest

Mr. Joseph DeFranco   - 4 -   March 27, 1973

This could be verified by contacting Attorney McLenithan, who has his office at 124 Main Street, Hudson Falls, New York.

It disturbs me that this matter will be held within a few weeks by Judge Orton, and it is my understanding that the Department of Social Services still has not presented any evidence of neglect and mistreatment of these other three children. The simple fact that the pathologist's report indicated so many injuries to Howard White at the time of his death would seem to have made it apparent to the case worker that Howard was being mistreated, when she made her visits.

It should also be noted that Mae White had charged David Pope on December 28, 1972, with striking her, in the apartment in the Village of Granville, and threatening to kill her "just like his brother William Pope had killed JoAnn." As you know, three or four months ago, David Pope's brother, William Pope, killed a woman in Whitehall and then committed suicide.

I keep a complete ledger record of every criminal case I handle, and my records indicate, as I showed Mr. Donohue, that on January 25, 1973, after David Pope had been indicted by the January 1973 Grand Jury, I contacted Mrs. Dorothy Randles, and indicated that Miss Gladys Barker had advised me that she had contacted the Department of Social Services by telephone after both incidents, and she advised me that she was not there until September of 1972, but she would check their records and advise me if they indicate any calls were made.

On January 30, 1973, I talked with the case worker, Mrs. Anita Sarchioto, who advised me their case file was CW2801, under the name of Robert and Mae White, and that their file contains information indicating that Miss Barker reported something about both of these incidents or one incident to the Department of Social Services. She further advised me that their files did not contain any more information concerning these incidents. I advised Mrs. Sarchioto that I would like to examine their file, and I was advised that a staff meeting would have to be held to see whether this information could be released to me. On January 31, 1973, I received a letter from Attorney McLenithan, a copy of which I gave to Mr. Donohue, indicating that this file could not be released to me. I wish to point out

Mr. Joseph DeFranco   - 5 -   March 27, 1973

at this time that prior to January of 1973, Department of Social Services fraud files have been furnished to me, and since the Pope trial, additional fraud files have been sent to me, including additional information concerning requests made by me in this regard.

I had been advised by Miss Barker that she had gone to Jurnak's Store, which is nearby, and called the Department of Social Services Granville Office after both of these incidents, somewhere around 3:45 p.m., and during one of these times she was accompanied by Mrs. Patricia Perry, whom I have not talked with.

At the trial, Mrs. Sarchioto, under oath, denied that the Department of Social Services had been contacted by Gladys Barker concerning the board incident and the dunking incident. This came as a complete shock to me, since, as indicated, Mrs. Sarchioto had previously told me on the telephone that she had a report of both or one of these incidents in their file. I have today called Mrs. Josephine Jurnak, who owns the store, and she advises me that she remembers distinctly Gladys Barker coming into the store and asking for the telephone directory to find the Department of Social Servides telephone number, and calling the Granville Office.

The trial of this case was held during March 14 and 15, 1973. At the trial both Miss Barker and Miss Belden testified as to witnessing both the board and dunking incidents, and the defendant testified that this did not happen, but I introduced into evidence his 22 criminal convictions, a copy of which I gave to Mr. Donohue, which I am sure the jury took into consideration in wieghing his testimony. Mae White also testified that these two incidents did not happen, but it was shown that during the board incident, she was at the Rutland Hospital delivering Edward.

Miss Margaret Wunder and Mrs. Sarchioto had been subpoenaed by the defense, and Miss Wunder testified that their records contained no information concerning a report of either incident by Gladys Barker. In response to my questioning, she denied that it was even possible that Gladys Barker could have reported this incident to the Department of Social Services, because it wasn't in their file.

Gladys Barker had testified that she did not know anyone at the Department,

Now They Lay me Down to Rest

Mr. Joseph DeFranco   - 6 -   March 27, 1973

and told the girl who answered the phone about these incidents. Mrs. Sarchioto also verified what Miss Wunder had testified to, and then went on to indicate that on July 21, 1972, she had gone to the Pope-White apartment to investigate an unrelated incident reported by Mr. Burch, and that she happened to notice Howard's rear end, which showed no sign of any type of physical injury, which was only about two days after the board incident.

Mr. Harold Burch had told me that one of the neighbors had offered crackers to Howard, and that Pope had gotten so mad that he threw him off the porch, and kicked him all the way back to the apartment, with big boots with steel toes, and Mr. Burch had become so upset that he had gone personally to the Social Services Office in Granville to report this.

Mrs. Sarchioto reluctantly admitted on the witness stand that Mr. Burch came personally to the office to report this incident. I was very surprised and shocked at the hostility shown to me at the trial by both Miss Wunder and Mrs. Sarchioto.

I wish to also make clear that at no time had I any intention of putting the Washington County Department of Social Services on trial, but it is clear to me that certain people in the Department felt this would be the case.

I have requested a copy of the testimony of both Miss Wunder and Mrs. Sarchioto, and as soon as I receive same, I will send you a photocopy.

What concerns me the most about this whole thing, is the fact that I am very concerned about child abuse cases, and because of the nature of the case, it is very difficult to prosecute this type of case, without the cooperation of the Department of Social Services, who have made it clear from this case, that they are reluctant to cooperate with me in a child abuse case.

They have also made it clear that they will cooperate with me in a Department of Social Services fraud case.

Mr. Joseph DeFranco   - 7 -   March 27, 1973

At no time has any child abuse case been reported to my office, or the police, and I would hope that it would be made clear to this Department what their responsibilities are in this regard, and that they should reveal any child abuse files to me in the future.

I am sending a copy of this letter to Commissioner Levine, with the hope that he will ORDER the Washington County Department of Social Services to cooperate and furnish ALL files to the Washington County District Attorney's Office, involving all child abuse cases, and all other cases involving possible criminal proceedings.

                                            Very truly yours,

                                            Philip A. Berke
                                            District Attorney

PAB:djc
CC: Commissioner Abe Levine
    New York State Department of
    Social Services

Now They Lay me Down to Rest

Social Service Document – "ADC3405

White,   Mae   V 1/7/71
                                                       V 1/22/71
ADC 3405   D 3/1/71
                                                       T 3/22/71 ws
92 Main Street, Granville, New York

Special Grant: $30.50 budget deficit 1/15/71 - 1/31/71
Special Grant: $61.00 budget deficit 2/1/71 - 2/28/71
Special Grant: $40.00 rent deficit 2/15/71 - 2/28/71
Special Grant: $25.00 utility deposit 2/25/71
Grant: $93.50 semi-monthly effective 3/1/71 - 6/30/71

<u>Application for ADC</u>
Mrs. White completed a WS-11 on 12/28/70 at the Whitehall TWO. The address given on application was 1 High St., Whitehall, N.Y. However, when the 1/7/71 visit was made, worker learned from Mrs. Beatrice Kelley, Mrs. White's mother, that she had left their household and was probably living with Wilma and Alex Van Guilder. Applicant finally telephoned the agency to give her new address, 32 Skene St., Whitehall, N.Y. Apparently, Mr. Pope was also residing at the Van Guilder address - Mrs. Van Guilder is man's sister. Another visit was scheduled for 1/22/71. Both Mrs. White and Mr. Pope were interviewed on this date. It was later learned that woman moved to the Granville address indicated above.

<u>Cause of Dependency</u>: Mrs. White is currently separated from her husband, Robert. She is most interested in obtaining a divorce so that she will be free to marry her boyfriend, David Pope. However, as she lacks funds to meet her family's needs, it is highly unlikely that she will be able to afford a divorce in the near future. The Washington County Family Court has ordered Mr. White to pay monthly support in the amount of $100.00 through the probation department. Apparently, he has been making these payments regularly. The agency has not received any information to indicate otherwise.

According to Dr. Rhode's written statement (filed in MA record), Mrs. White would be considered four months gestation by 3/1/71. Mrs. White claims that Mr. Pope is the father. Apparently, Mr. Pope acknowledges this - at least for the time being!

Applicant stated that she was not at all interested in reuniting with her husband but that she hoped, as noted above, she would soon be free to marry Mr. Pope. Man stated he would be willing to support Mrs. White and children once he secured employment. Worker reminded both that woman agreed to rent the new apartment for herself and the two children only. Mr. Pope was expected to reside elsewhere.

The case was opened effective 1/15/71 by special grant. The support income was credited. Apparently, this was her only resource at the time of opening. The Van Guilders were providing shelter and overhead items. When Mrs. White moved to Granville, the rent was verified as $80.00 monthly, including heat. A special grant was issued to cover rent for the last half of February. A grant was also issued to cover a $25.00 deposit required by the New York State Electric & Gas Corporation. The increase in the grant commencing 3/1/71 reflects an increase in number of dependent children as Mrs. White has completed the fourth month of pregnancy.

<u>Supplemental</u>:
                                                       V 2/11/71
                                                       D 3/1/71
                                                       T 3/22/71 ws

Mrs. Tobin, Whitehall TWO, telephoned the agency this day to advise that she had received a complaint from a man who would not identify himself. He claimed that Mr. Pope had hit the children and that Howard had black and blue marks and Robert had bruises on his back from being hit with a broom. Mrs. Sarchioto, Child Welfare worker, received this call. As it was also a public assistance case, both workers made the investigation.

The nature of the visit was explained to client (Mr. Pope was present). According to woman, the children had been napping in the bedroom - she awakened them. Robert appeared quite pale and almost frail - Mrs. White stated that he had been suffering from a cold. Mrs. Sarchioto examined the boy and discovered no bruises. Howard, though looking better nourished than Robert, did have bruises on his face - a large bump and bruise in the middle of his forehead and a black and blue mark on the right side of his face near his mouth. There was also a small cut near the corner of his left eye. Worker also noted a bruise on his left arm. Mrs. White attributed all of these marks to a fall from a rocking chair at the Van Guilder home. Both children were quite subdued. They seemed to wear troubled expressions.

Workers were not convinced there had been no abuse. However, there was no definite evidence.

<u>Defined Problem</u>: - identified as children in need of protection.

<u>Plan of Treatment</u>: It was hoped that additional contacts might give worker a better idea of what actually was happening in this home. The children would be watched for any further suspicious signs. In any event, Mr. Pope's presence in the household was considered to be anything but healthy.

MJC   L. Harrington
        3-24-71

Now They Lay me Down to Rest

White, Mae
ADC 3405

V 3/1/71
D 3/16/71
T 3/22/71 ws

92 Main Street, Granville, New York

Special Grant: $50.00 budget deficit 3/1/71 - 3/15/71
Grant: $143.50 semi-monthly effective 3/15/71 - 6/30/71

Supplemental Visit:
Client's landlord, Mr. Mattison, called to complain that Mrs. White spent her entire check on groceries and had nothing left over for rent. At the time of visit, worker finally learned that woman had not been receiving support payments. This was later verified by call to Whitehall Probation Department. Mrs. White failed to notify the agency. She claimed that she had forgotten to mention it. A special grant was issued to cover the budget deficit resulting from loss of support. It was authorized for regular rolls effective 3/15/71.

At this time, it was noted that Robert had a black and blue mark on his cheek. It appeared very much like a thumb mark. Howard still had the bump in the middle of his forehead.

Worker again urged Mrs. White to have a local doctor see the children. Not only was Robert's lingering cold cause for concern but the fact that Howard still had the pronounced bump was rather alarming.

MJC

Supplemental Visit:

V 3/4/71
D 3/16/71
T 3/22/71 ws

The condition of the children observed at the above visit was described to Case Supervisor, Lorraine Harrington. Both supervisor and worker made a home visit this date. The children seemed somewhat better - more active but the bruises were still visible (although slightly faded).

Mr. Pope was again present - both he and Mrs. White were cautioned against abusing the children. They continued to maintain Robert and Howard received all marks from a number of falls - from chairs downstairs, etc. Mrs. White did agree to have Dr. Lynch examine both boys. She had previously brought them to Dr. White.

Mr. Pope's presence in the home was again discussed. It was suggested that he reside with relatives until Mrs. White obtains her divorce. He continues to be unemployed and the question of how he supports himself was raised. It was stressed that the ADC grant is to be used for Mrs. White and her son's needs only. Man was advised to apply for Granville Home Relief if he required help. He stated he did not desire to do so.

MJC

Supplemental Visit:

V 3/16/71
D 3/16/71
T 3/22/71 ws

Mr. Kelly telephoned the agency to complain about the treatment her grandchildren are receiving. It seems a number of people had seen them in Whitehall yesterday - their faces again bruised. It was also reported that Mrs. White returned to her

Connie L. Aiken and Thomas M. Aiken

Social Service Document – Memo 3-18-71

MEMO

TO: Mrs. Anita Sarchioto
FROM: M. Joanne Carpenter
DATE: March 18, 1971
RE: Robert and Howard White

Mr. Robert White, father of these children, filed a neglect petition against his spouse, Mae White, on or about 2/25/71. The hearing was scheduled for 3/17/71 at 9:30 A.M. Since worker was aware of the hearing and had made home visits as the result of complaints regarding the possibility of child abuse, a telephone contact was made with the court on 3/16/71. Worker's most recent observations were reported and at that time the Judge requested that she appear at the hearing.

Testimony was based on the following summary. A total of five home visits were made. Mr. Pope was present at all times.

1/22/71: Mrs. White, children and Mr. Pope were residing at the home of man's sister, Mrs. Wilma VanGuilder, 32 Skene Street, Whitehall, New York. (number of household members was 13.)

Although Robert looked thin and pale, both children seemed healthy, no marks were apparent.

2/11/71: This investigation was made by child welfare worker, Mrs. Sarchioto, and public assistance caseworker upon receipt of an anonymous complaint that Mr. Pope had been seen abusing the children.

Robert again appeared pale, but upon examination, no bruises were found. Mrs. White stated that the boy had been suffering from a cold.

Howard, though looking better nourished, did have marks on his face: a large bump and bruise located in the middle of his forehead, a black and blue mark on right side of face near his mouth. There was also a small cut near the corner of his left eye. In addition, worker noted a small bruise on his left arm.

Both children were quite subdued and seemed to wear troubled expressions.

Mrs. White attributed all of these marks to a fall from a rocking chair at the VanGuilder home.

Although there was no definite evidence that Howard had been abused, both workers felt it would be necessary to keep in touch with the home and take careful note of any further signs.

3/1/71: Robert had a bruise the size of a nickel on his cheek. He still had a cold.

Howard still had the large bump on his forehead.

Mrs. White claimed she had had the doctor examine both boys.

Again the children seemed quite subdued. They rarely uttered a sound.

3/4/71: Case supervisor, Lorraine Harrington, and caseworker made a visit this day.

The children seemed somewhat better. They were more active and for the first time smiled (Howard).

The bruises described above were still visible, but considerably faded.

Mrs. White and Mr. Pope insisted that Robert and Howard received all marks from a number of falls, from chairs, downstairs etc.

Woman agreed to have a local doctor examine the children.

Mr. Pope's presence in the home was discussed. It was stressed that the ADC grant was to be used for Mrs. White and her son's needs only. Man was advised to find employment or apply for Granville Home Relief if he required help. He stated he did not desire to request assistance.

3/16/71: Mrs. Beatrice Kelly, client's mother, called the agency to state a number of people had seen the children in Whitehall on 3/15/71. Bruises were observed on their faces. This visit was made as a result.

Robert had a bruise on the left side of his face. He seemed to be shaking and wore a very painful expression. The boy was lying on a cot and did not move at all during visit.

Howard's bump was then covered with a new bruise. He did get up off the cot and walked across the floor.

Mrs. White explained that both children had fallen again and that Dr. White examined Howard yesterday. When worker telephoned the doctor and he described Howard's bump as a hematoma, worker then asked if he thought there was a possibility of abuse. The doctor answered he had no definite feeling one way or the other.

The judge ordered the children to be placed temporarily in the department's custody. He directed the transfer to foster care be made that day. He also appointed Mr. Francis D. W. DeCamilla of Hudson Falls as law guardian and ordered the agency to make a thorough investigation to be submitted to the court. Mrs. White stated that she would retain a lawyer. Mr. White will be represented by Mr. Kingsley of Whitehall. Please note that Mr. White's support payments will be directed to this agency.

Chapter 10
Hey, Jo Ann

Evil ran strongly through the Pope family. David Pope's brother William was no exception. What could have happened to both of them to become so mean, vicious, and evil…? By the end of their investigation, Tom and Frank still did not have all the answers to that question. They did ascertain that the Pope brothers were raised solely by their very cold and heavy-handed mother. No father. They were very poor growing up, but as we all know, money is needed, but not the main staple to care for and love your children. You do not need money to fill your home with love.

William Pope seemed to be breaking out of the mold that so enveloped David Pope. He was married with 6 children and seemed to be successful at running his own small farm. He seemed to beat the odds. There was hope he was going to lead a normal and productive life, supporting his wife and children. All of this hope went out the window when William Pope became infatuated with a then 16-year-old girl in the Village of Whitehall, New York. An infatuation that seemed insane. Her name was Jo Ann Zakeski and her meeting William Pope was the start of the end of her life. She had no idea who William Pope really was and the legacy he and his brother David would have. Jo Ann lived with her family on the outskirts of Whitehall. An area known for an elbow in the East Rutland Bay on West Haven Pike. She was a tiny and very young-looking girl when she had her first child with William Pope.

William Pope left his home. Left his wife and 6 kids for a 16-year-old naïve girl. He gave up everything and was forced to live out of his old station wagon after he impregnated her. It wasn't long before she was now an 18-year-old girl with a 2nd child. This was a daughter, 6 months old in July of 1972, when William lost his mind because she finally told him to stay away forever. The Pope brothers don't take orders from anyone, especially a now 18-year-old girl. In July of 1972 he stormed into her parents' small house on the edge of Whitehall, New York. Thank God she was not home in her West Haven Pike residence when he barged in and scooped up this infant girl named Stacey. He also took a diary that he knew Jo Ann kept. As he went outside with the kidnapped child, he warned the frightened family about what would happen if they called the police. He told them he was going nowhere until Jo Ann came home. He then locked himself in his station wagon with this baby and read the diary. What was in the diary enraged him even more. The family did not know what to do as he waited in that station wagon with that child for many hours. They did know that if Jo Ann came home, it would not have a good ending, so they sent a neighbor boy out the back door and through the woods to find her and warn her not to come home. Finally, after many hours and knowing he was not going to leave and the crying baby needed care, they found the courage to put a call into the police. As we state in other chapters about policing in 1972, this story was no different. Police Chief William Stewart was called and two police cars showed up with four officers. As they ordered William Pope out of the car, he glared at them defiantly. An officer tapped the window with his night stick and warned Pope that they would break the window if he did not unlock the door. He knew they were serious, so after one more angry and defiant glare to the group of officers, he finally unlocked the door and they yanked him out and rescued the baby. Fortunately, the baby was not hurt. So what did the police do in July of 1972…? Arrest William Pope on the serious charges of kidnapping…? No, they told him that he caused enough pain and problems for Jo Ann and her family and they gave him the standard 1972 TV movie warning of "Beat it and don't come back or we will arrest you!" This as they escorted him out of the village and had him head away from their small village. They did not realize that he kept the stolen diary. They did not realize that this stolen diary would enrage him into a frenzy that would eventually lead to the stalking death of Jo Ann on that late Saturday afternoon in August. As I tracked down and talked with Stacey in preparation of this book, I had a heart-to-heart talk with her and Stacey stated that she lives with the agony of constantly wondering if the police had arrested William Pope that night, would her mother still be alive?

William Pope knew the actions and routines of Jo Ann from dating her for a couple of years. He knew she would walk downtown on a Saturday afternoon and would have to walk back home on the only route leading to her house on the edge of town. She would have to walk by the infamous Skene Manor for which the town is known for and also named for at another time. The manor, which dates back to 1761, was built into the side of the mountain and she would have to walk by it. William Pope was a hunter and a patient man when he was hunting..! He was prepared to wait as long as necessary to take his revenge out on a girl that dared to rebuff him. He parked his old station wagon next to the Skene Manor with Jo Ann's diary left on the front seat with it opened to the last page where he wrote his words to Jo Ann and the world. Only he knew Jo Ann would never read it. He walked up to the ledges with his .30 carbine and waited. He was on the cliff where the downtown road comes out and Jo Ann would have to turn left to go home. She finally showed up as expected with two young children walking with her. When she was in the right place, he yelled out to her, "Hey, Jo Ann! Up here." As she looked into the sun and finally spotted this former lover on the ledge, William shouted to the kids to get away from her. She pushed them away heroically and then the first shot rang out. This one struck her in the stomach. He then fired three more times with one going through her wrist and into her side and the third also striking her and the fourth missing her. She immediately dropped to the ground and was dead before first arriving help could come. His final words as quoted from a national magazine article on this incident by Stafford Mann were "You didn't have to die, you bitch! I gave you the chance to live! With me! Now die!" He knew his way around and somehow managed to escape one of the largest manhunts to date in the northern New York area. He made it off those ledges and all the way to Granville without being caught. How did he do that when he left his station wagon and the diary for the world to find…?

I may have found the answer from Mae Pope. I befriended Mae while doing research for this book and was told that William Pope hid out in the large chimney area of their longhouses while the search was going on. They knew the police would come and interview David and her while trying to find William, and this was true. She said he was hiding in that chimney when these interviews were taking place. So how did he elude the largest manhunt ever on both sides of the New York-Vermont border…? Even correction officers with shotguns helped out immediately in this manhunt. Mae alluded that David Pope had something to do with this. If true, then David would have to have been in on this from the very beginning. He would have to be there when this murder took place and waited with his car to quickly drive William away from this scene, village, and quickly growing manhunt. There was no way William Pope could have escaped that mountain and village on foot and make it all the way to Granville. The final ending for William took place in a shack at a stone quarry in Vermont right off the New York border. Wiretaps were placed on many family phones and information came in to the police that he was hiding in this shack. William Pope had called on the phone to his mother. As we later learned, most of the abuse suffered as kids by William and

David Pope came from their callous mother. As Vermont and New York State Troopers closed in, they found William dead of a reported suicide by the .30 rifle. The official report by the Vermont State Police lists this as a suicide, but is it…? Mae alluded to one more very interesting story that can't be totally proven at this time. That William did not have the guts to do himself in, so David was there to help out again. She insinuated that David was the one to help William commit suicide. This was not known to Stafford Mann when he wrote this magazine story documenting all of this. To this day, I believe it is one of the best written true story articles I have read. Stafford Mann had a unique way of writing. Another interesting twist on this story occurred after Tom's father died suddenly in December of 1993. His father never got the chance to watch Tom open and close this case, but he did help Tom. Tom's father's parents' family ties are very strong in Whitehall, New York, so that village was always very dear to his father. After opening this case up in August of 1994, Tom's mother asked him to help her with moving things out of their family home before selling it. As he was helping her sort things from their bedroom cabinets and cedar chest, he found a well-preserved magazine article. The original article from Stafford Mann. Tom and I read it. We read it many times because it was such a well-written article. Then it hit Tom. This was the brother of David Pope and this occurred just prior to the murder of Hodgie. This article provided Tom and the District Attorney with great background information. **Thank you, Dad..!!**

I also tracked down the daughter of Jo Ann Zakeski. Her name is Stacy and she is the little girl William Pope kidnapped in July of 1972, just a few weeks before Jo Ann's murder. Stacy and I communicate a lot and she provided a picture of her mom from that time period, just before her death. This allowed us to put a person to this story. What struck us most was how young little Jo Ann looked at the time of her death. Young, pretty, and innocent. Another interesting twist was told in chapter 1 of this book. This was the homicide that I knew nothing about but that my friends told me they were concerned I was going to become the next Jo Ann Zakeski if I did not leave my now abusive relationship.

There were many newspaper articles written about this case from 1972. These articles detail the homicide and subsequent manhunt, including the reported suicide by William Pope. Some excerpts of these newspaper writings are *"Police said the killer was standing on a mountainside cliff that overlooks the road. Spent cartridges were found in the area of the ledge and these will be compared to those from the rifle found with Pope's body. Pope's car was found shortly after the shooting and a note found inside the vehicle indicated he intended to kill the girl, her six-month-old baby and then himself. Whitehall Police said they found the man's name in the girl's diary, and she indicated he was the father of her baby. Chief William J. Stewart said he had been familiar with the situation of Pope bothering the girl for some time. She didn't want anything to do with him, he said. We had a call on it just last week.*

"Early Monday Pope reportedly called his mother at the family home in Granville. He asked if the girl was dead, and when told she was, he hung up. Mrs. Nellie Pope told police her son had called from the Hilltop Quarry. A search of the quarry near Granville began at 5 A.M., but when no trace of the suspect was found, the search moved to the Hilltop Quarry at Wells, VT. State Police from New York and Vermont had just arrived at the quarry and were starting to search the buildings when a single shot was heard. Police traced the sound to a small, abandoned wooded shed on top of a slate pile and found the body of William Pope Jr., 30, of Granville inside on the floor. A suspect sought in the Saturday evening slaying of an 18-year-old Whitehall girl apparently shot and killed himself at 8 A.M. Monday as police closed in on him at the Hilltop Quarry at Wells."

The obituary page posted in the Tuesday, August 22, 1972, edition of the Post Star provides one more injustice to a young and innocent victim. This obituary page listed the obituaries of William E. Pope and

Now They Lay me Down to Rest

Jo Ann Zekeski directly side by side. Imagine the lack of respect for having their obituaries side by side for the people who loved Jo Ann.

Photo of Jo Ann Zekeski

CONNIE L. AIKEN AND THOMAS M. AIKEN

Falls Area Obituar[y]

William E. Pope

GRANVILLE — William E. Pope was found dead Monday morning in Wells, Vt.

Born July 22, 1942, in Granville, he was the son of William H. and Nellie Holcomb Pope.

In addition to his parents, survivors include his wife, Alice Bushman Pope; two sons, William and Charles of Granville; four daughters, Patricia, Michele and Linda of Granville and Stacy of Whitehall; a brother, David of Granville; two sisters, Mrs. Rose Cook of Granville and Mrs. Wilma Vanguilder of Whitehall; two half-brothers, Richard Hurlburt of Granville and George Hurlburt of Kingsbury, and several nieces and nephews.

Friends may call at the Robert M. King Funeral Home tonight from 7 to 9.

Funeral services will be conducted at 2 p.m. Wednesday at the funeral home by the Rev. Gordon Clark.

Interment will be in North Granville Cemetery.

Jo Ann Zakeski

WHITEHALL. — Funeral services for Miss Jo Ann Zakeski will be conducted at 9:30 a.m. today in Our Lady of Angels Church where a Mass of Resurrection will be celebrated.

Interment will be in Cedar Grove Cemetery, Fair Haven, Vt.

Wallace Carter

SARATOGA SPRINGS — Wallace Carter, 84, of 36 Vermont St., died Monday at the Littauer Nursing Home, Gloversville.

A veteran of World War I, he was a retired body and fender repairman.

He is survived by a daughter, Mrs. Ralph Clark of Saratoga Springs; a son, Wallace Carter Jr. of Wayland; six grandchildren, three great-grandchildren and a niece.

Friends may call at the Kark & Tunison Funeral Home today from 2 to 4 and 7 to 9 p.m.

The funeral service will be

Obituary Notice – Post Star William Pope & Jo Ann

Now They Lay me Down to Rest

Man Sought in Slaying At Whitehall Kills Self

By DON A. METIVIER

WELLS, Vt. — A suspect sought in the Saturday evening slaying of an 18-year-old Whitehall girl apparently shot and killed himself at 8 a.m. Monday as police closed in on him at the Hilltop quarry at Wells.

State Police from New York and Vermont had just arrived at the quarry and were starting to search the buildings when a single shot was heard.

Police traced the sound to a small, abandoned wooded shed on top of a slate pile and found the body of William Pope Jr., 30, of Granville inside on the floor.

Pope had been shot once police, members of the Border Patrol and correction officers from Great Meadow Correctional Facility at Comstock took part.

Early Monday Pope reportedly called his mother at the family home at Granville. He asked if the girl was dead, and when told she was, he hung up.

Mrs. Nellie Pope told police her son had called from the Hilltop quarry.

A search of the quarry near Granville began at 5 a.m., but when no trace of the suspect was found, the search moved to the Hilltop quarry at Wells, Vt.

Since the shooting of Pope took place in Vermont, state police from Rutland were in charge of the investigation. Rutland County State's Attorney Stephen Klein ordered the body removed to Mary Fletcher Hospital at Burlington for an autopsy.

The New York State Police and Whitehall police investigation of the shooting of Miss Zakeski was then all but closed, police indicated. When police in Vermont complete their investigation of the apparent suicide the rifle will be returned to New York investigators for ballistics tests to determine if it was the weapon used to kill the girl.

Funeral services for the girl will be at 9:30 a.m. today in Our Lady of Angels Church, Whitehall, where a Mass of the Resurrection will be celebrated.

Apollo 17 Trip to Moon

Monday, August 21, 1972

Girl, 18, Murdered

WHITEHALL — As darkness fell Sunday night, police had found no trace of a Vermont man suspected of being the killer of an 18-year-old Whitehall girl.

The girl, Jo Ann Zakeski of 150 N. Williams St., was killed by two rifle shots while walking along North Williams Street near her home at 5:50 p.m. Saturday. The shots struck Miss Zakeski in the stomach and left arm.

Police said she was shot by a man standing on a mountainside cliff overlooking the road in this village of 4,500 about six miles from the Vermont state line.

A manhunt was started soon after the shooting. Authorities refused to divulge the identity of the suspect, although they said he was named as the girl's lover in her diary.

His automobile was impounded soon after the shooting, and police found a photograph of him in the car.

Police said a note found in the suspect's car said he intended to kill Miss Zakeski, her one-year-old baby and himself. The home where the baby was being kept was placed under police guard.

The shooting took place at the foot of Skene Mountain.

New York and Vermont State Police, village police from Whitehall, Granville and Salem, and Washington County sheriff's deputies took part in the hunt Sunday. They were aided by bloodhounds in combing the cave-pocked mountainside.

Police bulletins described the suspect as 30 years old, 165 pounds and 5 feet 11, with brown hair. He was believed armed with a rifle and a pistol.

Early Sunday morning police said they believed they had the suspect cornered in a cave on Skene Mountain. That report later proved groundless. When the intensive search was begun at dawn Sunday, police were hampered by a heavy fog that lingered into late morning.

The slain girl lived with her parents at the Williams Street address, according to police.

Miss Zakeski is survived by her mother, Mrs. Leona Choppy; her step-father, Albert Choppy; three sisters, Mrs. Janet Latterell of Fort Edward, Mrs. Irene Dazzi of Rutland, Vt., and Miss Michele Choppy of Whitehall; two brothers, Henry Campbell and Albert Choppy Jr. of Whitehall and several nieces and nephews.

Friends may call at the Jillson Funeral Home, Whitehall, today from 2 to 4 and 7 to 9 p.m.

Funeral services will be conducted Tuesday at 9:30 a.m. in Our Lady of Angels Church, Whitehall, where a Mass of Resurrection will be celebrated.

Interment will be in Cedar Grove Cemetery, Fair-Haven, Vt.

Now They Lay me Down to Rest

The Line Of Fire — The bottom X in the photo is where 18-year-old Jo Ann Zakeski of Whitehall was felled by shots from a rifle while walking along Williams Street at Whitehall Saturday afternoon. The top X, to the left of the pole, is where police said the shots were fired.

Police said a note found in the suspect's car said he intended to kill Miss Zakeski, her one-year-old baby and himself. The home where the baby was being kept was placed under police guard.

The shooting took place at the foot of Skene Mountain.

New York and Vermont State Police, village police from Whitehall, Granville and Salem, and Washington County sheriff's deputies took part in the hunt Sunday. They were aided by bloodhounds in combing the cave-pocked

Now They Lay me Down to Rest

Pope had been shot once through the heart with a large caliber rifle. A .32 caliber rifle was found on the floor beside him.

Pope had been sought by as many as 100 officers following the fatal shooting of Jo Ann Zakeski, 18, of 159 N. Williams St., Whitehall, at 3:50 p.m. Saturday.

Miss Zakeski died instantly from two shots that struck her in the stomach and arm as she walked along North Williams Street in Whitehall.

Police said her killer was standing on a mountainside cliff that overlooks the road. Spent cartridges were found in the area of the ledge and these will be compared to those from the rifle found with Pope's body.

Pope's car was found shortly after the shooting and a note found inside the vehicle indicated he intended to kill the girl, her six-month old baby and then himself.

A guard was placed on the home where the baby was being kept, but police said Pope did not show up there despite his threat in the note.

Whitehall police said they found the man's name in the girl's diary, and she indicated he was the father of her baby.

Chief William J. Stewart said he had been familiar with the situation of Pope bothering the girl for some time. "She didn't want anything to do with him," he said. "We had a call on it just last week."

For a time police believed they had Pope surrounded on Skene Mountain at Whitehall, but he apparently got away in a heavy fog Sunday morning.

The search for the one-time carnival worker, who had been living out of his car for the past few months in the Granville-Whitehall area, continued all day Sunday. Officers from New York and Vermont state police, the Washington County Sheriff's Department, Whitehall, Salem and Granville

Chapter 11
911

The escape from a life of absolutely no love and daily starvation, torture, and abuse came on September 11, 1972, for little Howard "Hodgie" White. This was a day not much different than the 2 years, 10 months, and 13 days of life on this earth prior to that date. A life marked by unimaginable days. 1048 days to be exact. That poses a tremendous philosophical question. Why would a beautiful and healthy newborn baby be put on this earth only to experience no love and constant pain and suffering from those that were supposed to nurture and care for him the most…? We believe that every person has a purpose. Here we sit, just shy of 50 years later and 26 years since the beginning of what felt like an impossible start. Believing his life, although cut short, has a purpose. If just one police officer, one Social Service worker, one prosecutor, one relative, one neighbor, and keeping one mother from not allowing this to happen, then his life will not be in vain. Why was he one of 7 to be put into the care of Mae White and David Pope…? The only slight exposure to love and caring Hodgie found was when he was placed with a foster mom for a while. She read him stories, she fed him, she nurtured him, and she clearly stated that he and Robbie were not clumsy or aggressive toward each other. They were normal children. Normal children that long for love and proper care. She said they were very sweet boys when she got them to finally open up a bit.

She knew that they were battered and bruised, which was evident upon meeting them and taking them into her care. The longer she had them in her care, she saw the bruises fading and the emotional scars were fading also. They no longer were fearful of baths. They enjoyed story time. She saw how they could put their guard down and smile and play. Bonding had occurred. She was one of the people I felt I needed to talk to personally while researching more for this book. I asked her about her statement given to the investigators. She is still scarred from what eventually happened to Howard. She, like many others, talked as if it was yesterday, telling me how she had to report a situation that happened when Dave and Mae came for a visit to her home. She saw something that would never leave her mind. These little boys didn't run up and hug them like most children do when they have not seen their mommy and daddy. She saw the fear in their eyes as she had come to know them without that look and had to request Social Services to never allow David Pope in her home again. He kept repeatedly asking the boys as he clenched his fist described as made of stone, if they wanted to be punched in the nose and he would then break into an evil laugh. The smirk and the evil laugh was not only terrifying to her, but she realized how abused these boys were. I won't forget her telling me how devastated she was of learning of Hodgie's death when reading of his obituary in the local Post Star newspaper. Hodgie's last hours of life were not different than the rest he was forced to live with Mae and David. The contempt both of them had for Hodgie and their lack of caring at all for him comes through in the following callous descriptions obtained from excerpts from each of their statements as they describe the last moments of his life:

These are some excerpts from Mae Pope's statement:

> *"At some point when the kids were out playing, one of the other kids said that Hodgie was doing something wrong so David went over to discipline him and he took him into the house, but I don't know what he did. I put the kids to bed*

around 7:00 P.M. I just remembered that after dinner Hodgie went upstairs to go to the bathroom and he fell down the stairs. I heard him fall and I went to see if he was okay and his color was not right. Hodgie looked like he was sick all day anyways and acted as if he did not feel good.

"After we put the kids to bed around 7:00 P.M. the night Hodgie died, David and I went to bed around 9:00 P.M. We were in bed with the lights off and I heard moaning and groaning and I went in and it was Hodgie and he told me he did not feel good and that his stomach hurt. I went downstairs and got him a glass of ginger ale. Hodgie did not want this, he wanted a glass of water and David went and got the water I think, I know one of us got the water and gave it to Hodgie. Hodgie drank some water and his eyes got real big and he did not look good and I said that we should call the rescue squad, but David said that we shouldn't because of the bruises. Someone called the rescue squad and they came and took Hodgie. Dave and I went to the hospital and they were working on Hodgie and David looked in and asked the people if Hodgie was dead.

"I also remember that the night Hodgie died and we were calling for the rescue squad, Hodgie was throwing up and it was greenish yellow-like phlegm."

Remember the part about Mae offering Hodgie a glass of ginger ale and even at 2 years old and on his deathbed, Hodgie knew what ginger ale would do to him. You will truly understand this when you see the photos of his 1972 autopsy including a photo of his stomach.

This is from the statement of David Pope:

"The kids always went to bed at 7:00 P.M. Mae and I went upstairs to go to bed around 9:00 P.M. and as we were going into our room, we could hear Hodgie making a commotion and when I went in to his room he was standing up in his crib and he asked for a glass of water. I got him a glass of water and he took a couple of sips and I then told Mae to

call for an ambulance because something was wrong with him and his eyes were very big and his stomach was very hard. Mae said she couldn't because of all the bruises on Hodgie and I told her to call anyways and she did. The ambulance came and took Hodgie to the hospital and we went too, but Hodgie died quickly at the hospital."

These excerpts came from the statement of Robert Lewis Flower. He was the ambulance driver in 1972 that responded to the call to the Longhouses and cared for Hodgie:

"I drove and when we got to the apartment of David Pope and Mae White, David brought the small boy out and he gave him to Bud and said that the boy was acting like he was dying.

"We immediately left for the hospital. David Pope asked us to go to the Rutland Hospital, but I said no, that we were going to Granville Hospital which was only a couple of minutes away.

"Bud started mouth-to-mouth breathing. Dr. Glennon and a nurse worked on the boy for several minutes and during this time David stuck his head in a couple of times and asked if he was dead. Neither David or Mae showed much concern at all.

"Bud and I both felt that David and Mae waited until the last 5 minutes of this boy's life before they called for help. I was with the rescue squad for 8 years and this was the only child that I ever took to the hospital that died. The facts surrounding this boy's death have stuck in my mind very clearly ever since then because we did everything we could do very quickly and he still died and because I had a son that age myself."

Some irony about that son. He became a schoolteacher and coach and was one of our boys' favorite teachers and coach. This chapter will further document the death of Hodgie and the aftermath, including the fact that neither David Pope or Mae Pope shed one tear at the time Hodgie died or at the funeral. This was well documented in statements. The irony of the chapter title should not be missed. There was no 911 to dial back then, but it was a 911 call that occurred on 911. 09-11-72. One final stroke of evilness and contempt for an innocent child came screaming out when Mae and David were provided with a headstone for Hodgie. One that was donated to them and the evil David Pope would not allow it to be placed at his gravesite. We don't know exactly what happened to it other than to assume it was thrown out, because David Pope made it very clear that it was not going on the gravesite of Hodgie White. A gravesite where he was squeezed in between two family plots. A gravesite this little boy could never claim as his own.

The photographs of this little angel from his 1972 autopsy are included. We can tell you all day long how horrific the abuse was, but until you hear the excerpts from the statements of those that witnessed it or actually suffered from it, you can't fully understand how bad it was. Until you see the pictures of Hodgie from 1972, nothing will really bring that full extent of abuse to you. As you take the time to go over each well-preserved photograph taken of Hodgie at the start of his first autopsy, you can see that there are not many places on his little body not covered with cuts, punctures, scrapes, and bruises in various stages of healing. Tom has been through hundreds and hundreds of death cases and approximately 100 autopsies. He has seen bodies in any manner you could imagine. Still, no words could properly paint the accurate picture of how much abuse Hodgie suffered every day of his life with David Pope and with a mother who looked the other way and had no nurturing bones in her body as we have come to learn. No words could describe the horrors of abuse shown in these photographs. The words provided to Tom and Frank from so many witnesses around Hodgie in 1972 describing the emaciated state of his body are truly apparent in these photographs. Hodgie being compared to Ethiopian pictures on TV soliciting money donations for starving children is so apparent. The skin hanging off his shoulders and all bones. The gaunt look of his body and his eyes set back in his eye sockets. The distended stomach that David Pope later said was caused by overeating. All of this is haunting to look at. The photograph of his stomach with such a large hole blown out looking like a volcanic opening. Going over Mae's comments about Hodgie not wanting the Ginger Ale and wanting water instead is very telling. As you examine the photograph of his stomach with the gaping hole, you will understand. For this little boy on his deathbed to know that the ginger ale would hurt and burn his stomach is amazing. I can't imagine the pain he was going through, but to have ginger ale go down into his stomach and then spill out to his organs would have been beyond comprehending. This little boy instinctively knew that at 2 years old and on his deathbed. Mae never had this instinct at all, much less as a mother. This lack of motherly instinct was quoted many times in many statements and documents.

The autopsy of Dr. Walter Stern on September 12, 1972, at 10:30 A.M. was very telling of his horrific findings. These are some of the descriptions and findings he documents:

- Emaciation with serious atrophy of fat. (history of malnutrition noted in May 1972)
- Atrophy of thymus gland
- Fatty change of the liver, moderate
- Multiple ecchymosis, recent and old and superficial abrasions, recent and old, small
- Healing fracture of posterior segment of 10th right rib
- Recent healing puncture would of scalp in region of anterior fontanel of frontal bones, small
- Subgaleal hematoma below puncture wound, small
- Organizing peripelvic hematoma and pyramidal hemorrhage of left kidney, small

- Chronic inflammation, hemosiderin deposits and focal thrombosis in rectus muscles, slight
- Recent hemorrhage of segment of mesentery of ileum and descending colon, small
- Hyperplasia of bone marrow, slight
- Perforation of anterior wall of stomach, acute, large (history of large meal ingestion hours before death)
- Acute chemical peritonitis with undigested food particles (approximately 500 ml)
- Hydrohemothorax, bilateral
- Cerebral congestion and edema, moderate

A couple of quick observations from this list. I researched atrophy of the thymus gland and this is very indicative of severe stress. How much true stress should ever be noticed at all in a 2-year-old child…? The cause of brain congestion is primarily from traumatic brain injury.

In the section of Dr. Stern's autopsy report titled GROSS NOTE and / or ILLUSTRATIONS:

A large well-formed scab in the hairline of the frontal region is present approximately 7 cm. from the glabella; on removal of the scalp this is a through and through wound with a fairly recent sub-galeal hematoma measuring approximately 6 cm. in length and 2 cm. in depth. Scabs present in the region of the right superciliary prominence measuring 3 cm. and 1.5 cm. respectively. On the chin on both sides there are well healed linear scabs on the right measuring 2½ cm. in length and the left 1½ cm. in length. The neck is clean. Two circular rounded discolored ecchymotic areas are present on the thorax, one is 1½ cm. below the right nipple and measures 2 cm. in diameter. The other is 3 cm. below the left nipple and measures 1.8 cm. There is a 2.5 cm. abrasion below the right costal margin. The rectus muscles are bluish outlined which can be seen through a thin, transparent skin. There is a moderate hematoma of the left scrotal sac. There are multiple ecchymoses over the right and left knee and recent scabs over the lateral portion of the left knee. The hands and feet are dirty. There is a bluish discolored puncture wound covered by a scab over the knuckles of the left fourth finger. There are small abrasions in the midportion of the back and right flank. The body is moderately emaciated with sunken eyes. The abdomen is distended. On opening the abdomen air escapes. Stomach contents fill the abdomen with a grey-brown gruel-like fluid containing partially digested food identified as fragments of potatoes; in the small pelvis there is a 5½ cm. long undigested piece of meat with skin and some cartilaginous portions attached which has the appearance of portions of chicken leg. No bone is present. After removal of approximately 500 ml. of this material a round perforation of the anterior fundic portion of the stomach is seen with everted, intact mucosa. This perforation measures approximately 5 cm. in diameter. There is recent hemorrhage into the wall and subserosa. The remainder of the stomach externally is normal in appearance except for the discoloration caused by the chemical peritonitis. The liver is pale grey in appearance due to its action. There are no other significant findings in the abdomen except for small hemorrhages in the mesentery of the jejunum and colon. The opened stomach has normal rugal pattern throughout; there are in addition to the perforation several longitudinal linear hemorrhagic tears in the anterior fundic portion near the perforation. There is a fracture with surrounding hemorrhage of the right 10th rib in the region of the angle about 5 cm. from the costovertebral junction. The lesion measures 1.2 cm. in.

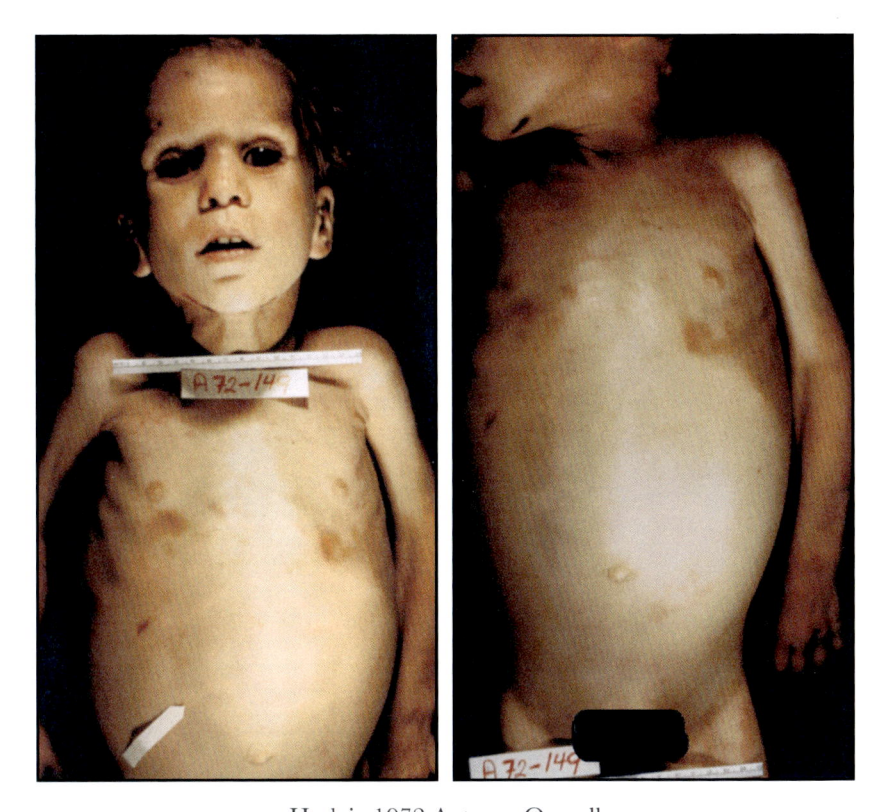

Hodgie 1972 Autopsy Overall

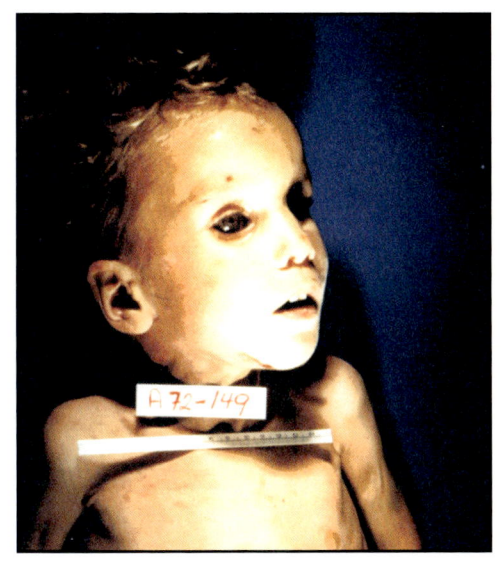

Hodgie 1972 Autopsy Head

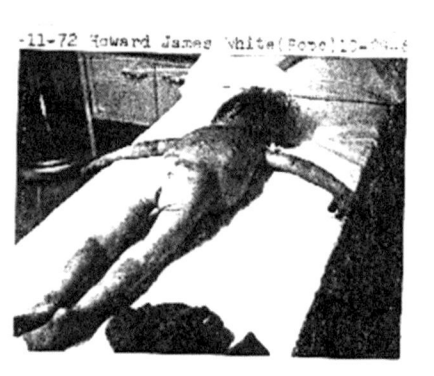

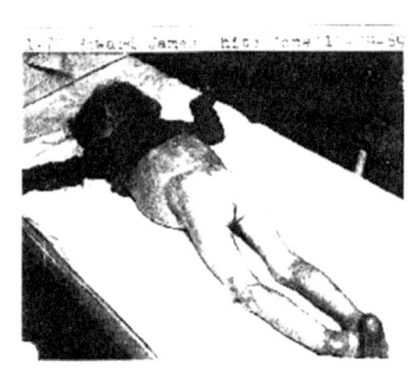

Hodgie Black & White 1972 Autopsy

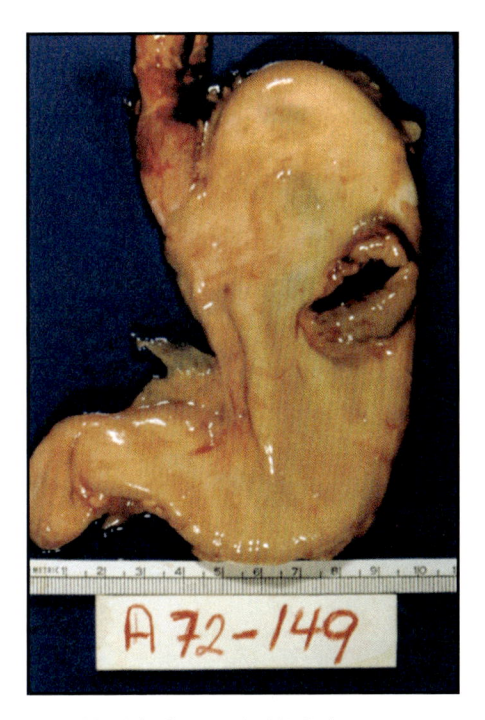

Hodgie Stomach 1972 Autopsy

CONNIE L. AIKEN AND THOMAS M. AIKEN

Dr. Stern 1972 Autopsy Report – Formal

```
                    Glens Falls Hospital
                    Glens Falls, New York  12801            Coroner Case
                    Department of Pathology

Name____Howard White_____Hosp No.___DOA____Autopsy No.__A-72-149____

Age__3__Sex_M__Race_W__Marital Status___-___Service_Micheal J. Lynch, M.D.

Date of Admission_____-_____Date and hour of Death__Sept. 11, 1972
                                                              A.M.
Date and hour of Autopsy_12 Sept.72/10:30__Pathologist__Walter R. Stern, M.D.

Clinical Diagnosis____Unexplained sudden death._____
```

Use of this protocol for publication or legal purposes without permission of the Department of Pathology is not authorized.

ANATOMICAL DIAGNOSIS

PRIMARY: Emaciation with serous atrophy of fat. (history of malnutrition noted in May 1972.)
Atrophy of thymus gland.
Fatty change of the liver, moderate
Multiple ecchymoses, recent and old and superficial abrasions, recent and old, small.
Healing fracture of posterior segment of 10th right rib.
Recent healing puncture wound of scalp in region of anterior fontanel of frontal bones, small.
Subgaleal hematoma below puncture wound, small.
Organizing peripelvic hematoma and pyramidal hemorrhage of left kidney, small.
Chronic inflammation, hemosiderin deposits and focal thrombosis in rectus muscles, slight.
Recent hemorrhage of segment of mesentery of ileium and descending colon, small.
Hyperplasia of bone marrow, slight.
Perforation of anterior wall of stomach, acute, large (history of large meal ingestion hours before death.)
Acute chemical peritonitis with undigested food particles, (approximately 500 ml.).
Hydrohemothorax, bilateral.
Cerebral congestion and edema, moderate.

ACCESSORY: Sinus reticulum hyperplasia of spleen with prominent fat storage, moderate.

GROSS ANATOMIC FINDINGS

NOTE: This protocol contains neither a gross nor a histologic description. In the Anatomical Diagnosis all abnormal findings are recorded.
The Primary Diagnoses are listed in pathogenetic sequence, i.e. The first diagnosis in this section represents the basic underlying process which leads to the terminal event. The Accessory Diagnoses are grouped by organ systems and are not directly related to the major disease processes.
A Gross Note and/or illustrations may summarize the major findings as a guide to the histologic evaluation. It will appear in those instances where single diagnostic terms are insufficiently descriptive. Descriptions are subjective and therefore we will rely on a listing of organs weights and/or measurements. The Block Record Sheet serves to record the histological sections prepared and will note Special Stains when performed.
The conclusion and the clinico-pathologic correlation by the prosector are recorded in the Summary and Interpretation.

DATA

I. EXTERNAL:
1. Length __34__ (N 36-38) inches
2. Estimated weight __25-28__ lbs
3. Rigor mortis Slight __Moderate__ Severe None
4. Liver mortis Slight __Moderate__ Severe None
5. Edema __none__
6. Skin See description Normal Jaundice Puncture Wounds
   Scars
7. Incision Y_____ U __X__ Limitations __None__
8. Subcutaneous fat at umbilicus __0.1__ cm.

II. HEAD:
1. Circumference: __19.5 in.__ (N 49.5 cm.)
2. Color of hair: __blond__ Amount: __normal__
3. Eyes: Color of Iris __grey__ Size of pupils: Left __3mm.__ Right __3 mm.__
4. Ears: __clear__
5. Nose: __dirty__
6. Mouth: __X__
7. Gums: __X__
8. Teeth: __X__
9. Tongue: __X__
10. Pharynx: __X__

III. NECK:
1. Thyroid: Left __3 x 1.5 x 0.5__ Right __2.5 x 1 x 0.5__ cm.
   or Weight __2.5__ gm.
2. Parathyroids: __Normal__ Enlarged Weight_____
3. Thymus: 2.5 gm. Fatty replacement Yes_____ No_____
   (20-28 gm)

A-72-129

IV: CHEST:
    X Breasts: Small   Medium   Large   Nodular
    2. Circumference level of nipples: __20.5 inches__
    3. Shape of Chest: Flat_____   Round X_____   Barrel_____
    4. Diaphragm   Normal_____   Low_____   Elevated x
    5. Pleural cavity: Left 40 ml.blood tinged   Right 50 ml. bloody
    6. Lungs: Left 90 (N77)   Right 90 (N89) gm.
    7. Heart: __80 (N 59-69 gm)__ Pericardial Fluid: __95 ml. straw__
        a. Wall left ventricle __0.7__   b. Wall right ventricle __0.2__
        c. Tricuspid valve __7.0__   d. Pulmonic valve __3.8__
        e. Mitral valve __5.4__   f. Aortic valve __3.5__
        g. Aorta 2 cm. above valve: __3.6__
        h. Congenital abnormalities: __none__

V: ABDOMEN: Adhesions
    1. Umbilicus Circumferance 21.5 inches - distended abdomen
    2. Fluid See note 500 ml. brownish gruely with particles of food.
    3. Liver 600 (N 420-510)
    4. Spleen 100 (N 37-48)
    5. Pancreas X
    6. Gallbladder X
    7. Biliary tree X
    8. Esophagus X
    9. Stomach See note   Lesser Curvature 11.5 cm.   Greater 23 cm. Curvature
    10. Duodenum X
    11. Jejunum X
    12. Ileum X
    13. Colon X
    14. Appendix: _____ Present X   Length 7.5 cm.   Absent_____

VI: GENITOURINARY TRACT:
    1. Adrenals: Left 2 gm.   Right 2 gm. (4.6)
    2. Kidneys: Left 65 (N49)ortex 0.2   Medulla 0.8
        Right 50(N58)Cortex 0.2   Medulla 0.8
    3. Bladder   Small   dilated   contracted
    4. Prostate X
    5. Testis X   Left   Right
    6. Penis   Circumcized   Not circumcized
    X. Uterus: Length   Cavity
        Endometrial thickness   Color: Tan   White
    X Tubes   Left   Right
    X Ovary   Left   Right

VII: GREAT VESSELS: Aneurysm   Yes   No_____
    1. Aorta   Elastic   Yes   No
        Atherosclerosis None   Mild   Moderate   Severe
    2. Vena Cava X
    3. Iliac veins X

VIII. MUSCULOSKELETAL SYSTEM:
  1. Bone   Soft   Hard   Normal   Fracture 10th rt.rib.
  2. Marrow   Pink   Red   Pale
  3. Lymph nodes: Enlarged   Site general

IX: CENTRAL AND PERIPHERAL NERVOUS SYSTEM:
  1. Brain   1180 (N1140)
  2. Pituitary 0.3
  3. Special none

X. GROSS NOTE and/or ILLUSTRATIONS

A large well-formed scab in the hairline of the frontal region is present approximately 7 cm. from the glabella; on removal of the scalp this is a through and through wound with a fairly recent sub-galeal hematoma measuring approximately 6 cm. in length and 2 cm. in depth. Scabs present in the region of the right superciliary prominence measuring 3 cm. and 1.5 cm. respectively. On the chin on both sides there are well healed linear scabs on the right measuring 2½ cm. in length and the left 1½ cm. in length. The neck is clean. Two circular rounded discolored ecchymotic areas are present on the thorax, one is 1½ cm. below the right nipple and measures 2 cm. in diameter. The other is 3 cm. below the left nipple and measures 1.8 cm. There is a 2.5 cm. abrasion below the right costal margin. The rectus muscles are bluish outlined which can be seen through a thin, transparent skin. There is a moderate hematoma of the left scrotal sac. There are multiple ecchymoses over the right and left knee and recent scabs over the lateral portion of the left knee. The hands and feet are dirty. There is a bluish discolored puncture wound covered by a scab over the knuckles of the left fourth finger. There are small abrasions in the midportion of the back and right flank. The body is moderately emaciated with sunken eyes.
The abdomen is distended. On opening the abdomen air escapes. Stomach contents fill the abdomen with a grey-brown gruel-like fluid containing partially digested food identified as fragments of potatoes; in the small pelvis there is a 5½ cm. long undigested piece of meat with skin and some cartilagenous portions attached which has the appearance of portions of chicken leg. No bone is present. After removal of approximately 500 ml. of this material a round perforation of the anterior fundic portion of the stomach is seen with everted, intact mucosa. This perforation measures approximately 5 cm. in diameter. There is recent hemorrhage into the wall and subserosa. The remainder of the stomach externally is normal in appearance except for the discoloration caused by the chemical peritonitis. The liver is pale grey in appearance due to its action. There are no other significant findings in the abdomen except for small hemorrhages in the mesentery of the jejunum and colon. The opened stomach has normal rugal pattern throughout; there are in addition to the perforation several longitudinal linear hemorrhagic tears in the anterior fundic portion near the perforation.
There is a fracture with surrounding hemorrhage of the right 10th rib in the region of the angle about 5 cm. from the costovertebral junction. The lesion measures 1.2 cm. in greatest dimension and is totally removed for further examination. There is no dislocation.

RECORD OF BLOCKS: 1st Sheet
To be filed with original protocol

Autopsy No. A72-149 WS

1 Left ventricle	11 Left kidney hemorrhage	21 Psoas muscle
2 Rt ventricle	12 Rt kidney Z	22 Slow heart
3 LLL	13 Thymus	23 Thyroid
4 RUL	14 Mesenteric Lymph nodes	24 Thymus
5 Pancreas	15 Lymph nodes Z	25 Lymph node pectoral muscle
6 Liver Z	16 Peyer's patch Terminal ileum 3 on edge Z	26 Thyroid + parathyroid
7 Liver formalin for fat stain	17 Intestine Z	27
8 Spleen Z	18 Small bowel	28
9 hemorrhage	19	29
10 L kidney Z	20	30

Now They Lay me Down to Rest

RECORD OF BLOCKS: 2nd Sheet
To be filed with original of protocol

Autopsy No. A72-149

31 Sternum marrow	41 more descai with	51 Dentate nucleus
32 Vertebra marrow	42 —"—	52 4th Vent.
33 Rib F	43 —"—	53 medulla & cord
34 Pituitary	44 Skin	54 Mx 73
35 Spinal cord	45 Liver (Fit) tHE F	55
36 Lt. frontal lobe	46 Spleen (Fit) tHE F	56
37 Lt. motor cortex	47 Kidney (Fat) tHE F	57
38 Hippocampus	48 Heart (Fat) tHE F	58
39 Thalamus	49	59
40 Occipital cortex	50	60

Autopsy A-72-149

SUMMARY AND INTERPRETATION

The historical information is scant, even at this time some months later after the autopsy. Apparently this child was considered malnourished, noted in May 1972 by a physician according to Dr. Lynch. On the day of death he allegedly had a large meal and went to bed moaning. From then on the story is hazy.

There is moderate emaciation with atrophy of the abdominal fat. In conjunction, the thymus is atrophic with multiple dystrophic calcifications probably as a consequence of necrosis of the thymic tissue. The lymph nodes show sinus reticulum hyperplasia and in some areas including the Pyer's patches germinal center hyperplasia.

The primary lesion is the perforation of the anterior fundic portion of the stomach with recent submucosal hemorrhage and intact glands without inflammatory reaction indicating that this is a very recent lesion. There is only slight serosal edema indicating that this is an acute chemical peritonitis without apparent reaction. The associated sections of stomach (Block 29) contain a sharp separation of the mucosa with submucosal hemorrhage extending laterally beneath the mucosa but no injury of muscle at this particular point. This lesion perhaps suggests a mechanism for perforation.

As an acute consequence of the peritonitis hydrothorax developed bilaterally and there is focal atelectasis, congestion and edema of the lungs. There is also osmotic nephrosis of the kidneys and marked fine fatty change in the liver. The small droplets suggest the findings seen in Reye's syndrome but are not substantiated in other sites.

The various sites of hemorrhage are of interest. The hemorrhagic appearance of the healing fracture (Block 33) was grossly misleading. There is callus formation indicating that this fracture has been there for sometime. The peripelvic hematoma of the left kidney has been there for several days because beginning organization at the periphery with fibroblasts growing into the hematoma are noted. Similar changes are also present in the hemorrhage noted in the descending colon while the hemorrhage of the mesentery is of an acute, recent nature without early organization. The location of these lesions does not fit a disease pattern and in my opinion are related to trauma. Chronic inflammation between rectus muscle bundles is unexplained.

An unusual lesion is that of marked sinusoidal macrophage reaction of the spleen. Diffuse fatty deposits are present.

Other special stains are non-contributory.

Name of deceased White, Howard   Age 3   Sex M   Marital Status S
Time of Death 9 PM   11   Sept   72
Place of Death Granville   Wash
                City   County

In accordance with Section 4210, Subdivision 2 Public Health Law and Article 17-A,
Section 673 Subdivision 1, County Law postmortem dissection of the body of the
above-named individual is authorized for the purpose of determining the cause of
death because of:

_____ a. A violent death, whether by criminal violence, suicide or casualty.

_____ b. A death caused by unlawful act or criminal neglect.

  ✓ c. A death occurring in a suspicious, unusual or unexplained manner.

_____ d. A death caused by suspected criminal abortion.

_____ e. A death while unattended by a physician, so far as can be
        discovered, or where no physician is able to certify the
        cause of death as provided in the public health law and
        in form as prescribed by the Commissioner of Health can
        be found.

_____ f. A death of a person confined in a public institution other
        than a hospital, infirmary or nursing home.

Coroner M. J. Lynch MD (642-2872)
County Wash
        9/11/72

Known circumstances of the death are: Child has been complaining of
stomach. Ate well tonight at evening meal. Put to bed
talked to "moms green" fell off bed appeared groggy —
rescue squad called. child died en route to
the hospital

Funeral Director Willson
                  White Hall

Chapter 12

The Chicken Bone

There are many reasons that David Pope was allowed to walk free for the 22 years prior to the reopening of this case. Each of these reasons, each of these people, all led to 22 more years of torturous and unbelievable abuse of 6 additional children. All of these will be discussed in the next chapter titled "Acquittal." This next chapter will go into detail on all the forces that came together to prevent justice and to save additional kids. I do want to touch on one very important factor that needs to be highlighted by itself: The Chicken Bone.

The biggest lie causing the injustice of this case came from the family physician, Dr. Michael Lynch. Dr. Lynch wore two hats at that time. His 2nd hat was as the county coroner. This position allowed him to get away with this lie. As a coroner, he is the one that investigates the circumstances surrounding deaths. The cause and manner of each death. They rely on the police investigation and the pathologist conducting a detailed autopsy to properly fill out the death certificate. The two most important lines on every death certificate are the cause of death and the manner of death. The cause of death is exactly what it says. What caused this death. Heart arrhythmia, gunshot wound, cirrhosis of the liver, blunt force trauma from a motor vehicle accident, etc.… The manner of the death will be one of five categories: suicide, accidental, homicide, natural causes, or undetermined. It will always be one of these five. In 1972, Dr. Michael Lynch was not neglectful in not filling out the manner of death, he was devious, deceitful, and dishonest. He intentionally did not do his elected and professional duty to fill out this death certificate properly because he was covering his butt. When finally questioned hard by Tom in 1994, he readily admitted why he did this. He was afraid of being sued for not doing his duty as the family physician and he was very physically afraid of David Pope. He let a baby down multiple times. First, by not doing his job and fulfilling his oath as a doctor and by not screaming out about what he saw when Hodgie was brought to his office by Mae or Social Services. Second, by lying. He lied when he did not fill out the manner of death. He lied when District Attorney Phil Berke pressured him for a manner of death and in a letter dated November 13, 1972, he wrote the following:

> *"There was some evidence of abuse of this child but death was from natural causes. Regarding other children, it probably would be in their best interests to be placed in a foster home. Yours truly, M.J. Lynch, M.D."*

Some evidence of abuse of this child…? Death from natural causes…? We showed you the photos of Hodgie the day after he died. Did this look like some abuse of this child…? NO…! This was as much abuse as one child could take. Actually more. He died from it. Death from natural causes was the biggest lie next to the statement about a chicken bone causing that tremendous hole in Hodgie's stomach.

For whatever reason, you decide, Dr. Michael Lynch wrote out a statement on his notepad a lie that became the statement of innocence for David Pope. He wrote the following:

> *"results of autopsy on Howard White. Chemical Peritonitis Secondary to Perforated Stomach by Chicken Bone. From Dr. Lynch 9-19-72."*

He even had the gall to have a Social Services supervisor notarize this note. A supervisor involved in the coverup! He did this even knowing the autopsy performed by Dr. Walter Stern indicated that there was NO bone found in Hodgie's stomach. In the original autopsy report by Dr. Walter Stern in 1972, he noted the following:

> *"Stomach contents fill the abdomen with a grey-brown gruel-like fluid containing partially digested food identified as fragments of potatoes; in the small pelvis there is a 5½ cm. long undigested piece of meat with skin and some cartilaginous portions attached which has the appearance of portions of chicken leg. No bone is present."*

David Pope was given a copy of this note and used it many times to convince people he was found innocent and he also used it to threaten people because of the power he had to control a physician and coroner. Imagine a physician who was also the coroner going out of his way to not just lie, but to cover up the murder of a 2-year-old boy. To make up a lie out of whole cloth. A boy so brutalized that it is hard to look at his death photos, only to envision the abuse and starvation he went through every day.

When interviewed by me just recently, Dr. Lynch was as pompous and unapologetic as ever. When I asked him why the manner of death was never filled out, his pompous reply was *"Well, you would have thought someone would have picked up on that by now."* He clearly knew what he was talking about and that he intentionally never filled out that manner of death. He let a tortured little boy down. He let a child murderer walk free.

Dr. Lynch Notarized Chicken Bone note

Chapter 13

Acquittal

In the spring of 1973, then District Attorney Phil Berke tried his best to hold David Pope accountable for starving, beating, torturing, and then murdering little 2-year-old Hodgie. His frustration with the lack of police and forensic resources came out strongly in all of his calls and letters to the New York State Legislature. His complaints were well founded when you had a police report consisting of a few pages on the starvation, abuse, torture, and then death of a 2-year-old boy. Only pages on a child homicide investigation. It was justified when he had a coroner, also the child's physician, corruptly and falsely not completing the death certificate on this little boy. The coroner lied. He made up more lies out of whole cloth to cover his lies. All of this and only to have the county Social Services department blocking every attempt he made to find the truth. The very people and agency on the frontline to protect children. To make sure they were not abused. To make sure they lived. If something positive came from all Hodgie went through, it was the changes in New York State Law that took place to help and protect kids. All of these calls and letters from D.A. Berke did catch their attention. Hodgie's death and case became an impetus to create the way Social Services handled child cases and how they trained. It also led to the creating and perfecting the modern-day New York State mandated hotline law.

When you question why a physician did not act on what he saw when examining Hodgie while he was alive, and why the physician coroner lied when completing the death certificate, and why that doctor would then again risk everything and lie when questioned on the stand in 1973, the answers came out in 1994. When Tom tracked him down in 1994 and questioned him, Dr. Lynch was quick to get this off his chest. He too had to be convinced that David Pope would now be held accountable. He stated that things were different in 1972 and he was afraid of being sued for not doing his job correctly. The other main reason was his tremendous fear of David Pope. If he, like all the other adults that came in contact with David Pope were that afraid of him, think of the fear all 7 of these kids had while being horrendously and unimaginably abused. Dr. Lynch knew because he was a doctor and the coroner that the two most important lines on a death certificate must be filled out. The cause of death and the manner of death. He intentionally left the manner of death blank. An incomplete death certificate. He knew that you could not prosecute this case as a homicide without the manner of death stating homicide. Also, how much of a conflict of interest was there when the family physician, specifically a family physician that did not report all the abuse of the child he saw, was also the coroner that is tasked with reporting how a child died…? This was a huge conflict of interest. Especially for Hodgie.

District Attorney Philip Berke was frustrated. He forced Dr. Lynch to provide a manner of death. Was Dr. Lynch honest…? No. In a return letter dated November 13, 1972, to the District Attorney, Dr. Lynch stated the following: *"There was some evidence of abuse of this child but death was from natural causes. Regarding other children, it probably would be in their best interests to be placed in a foster home. Yours truly, M.J. Lynch."*

Natural causes…?! Really…?! As you saw from looking at the photos of Hodgie preserved from the September 1972 autopsy, could this be natural causes…? Look at all the bruises, lacerations, and evidence of starvation. What about the gaping hole in Hodgie's stomach…? How could he possibly explain that…? Well, that is where his notarized notepad note came into play. He explained that hole by stating it was caused by eating a chicken bone. Does that gaping hole look like a laceration that could be caused by any chicken bone…?

District Attorney Berke could not file homicide charges against David Pope in the spring of 1973. He charged one count of assault for striking Hodgie with a board with nails sticking out of it and one charge of reckless endangerment for holding Hodgie underwater until his whole body turned blue. The prosecuting attorney was District Attorney Phil Berke and the Public Defender assigned was attorney Gordon Hemmett. Phil Berke was later elected as the County Court Judge (Superior Court) and Gordon Hemmett became district attorney. Hemmett later moved up to the 2nd County Court Judge position. When Tom reopened this case in 1994, Phil Berke and Gordon Hemmett were the two Washington County Judges. Tom knew them both well from his involvement in so many horrendous cases. Both judges had to recuse themselves. Berke because he prosecuted Pope in 1973 and Hemmett because he defended Pope. Why did David Pope get acquitted in 1973 when Phil Berke had two eyewitnesses to this abuse…? The answer is easy. Professional people lied. They lied in an official death certificate. They lied in child abuse cases filed with the State. They all lied when subpoenaed to testify on the stand at this trial. If you ask why, the reasons were actually simple. To cover up their failures in protecting Hodgie and their fear of David Pope. Social Service workers and supervisors lied to cover up the abuse they saw and did nothing about it. They lied about the number of people reporting this abuse to them and about the number of calls and walk-in reports made. The family physician and many Social Service workers have blood on their hands. Not just the blood of Hodgie, but the blood of 6 other innocent children that suffered unbelievable torture and abuse. When they lied and opened up the doors of freedom to David Pope, they opened the doors to 22 more years of abuse.

Another reason for the acquittal was the defense of David Pope by then Public Defender Gordon Hemmett. He fought hard to win the freedom of a child murderer. He worked with the coroner, Dr. Michael Lynch, to keep the truth from coming out. To keep the death certificate uncompleted with no manner of death. To obtain a notarized note from Dr. Lynch that the large laceration of Hodgie's stomach was caused by a chicken bone that never existed. Dr. Stern was very clear in his autopsy report. There was no bone in Hodgie's stomach. To pressure Dr. Lynch into stating that death was caused by natural causes despite the overwhelming evidence to the contrary. No medical degree needed. No special training needed. Just look at the roadmap of abuse written all over Hodgie's body. Defense Attorney Hemmett then went to work on his main defense. Attack the two main witnesses. These were young girls, around 16, from tough backgrounds that he used as his weapon to attack their credibility. These girls testified to what they observed. David Pope striking Hodgie with a board with nails sticking out of it. David Pope dunking Hodgie underwater and holding him under water until he turned blue. Attorney Hemmett did his job well. He convinced the jury more than District Attorney Berke could with limited police and forensic resources. He won the acquittal. In a strange twist of irony, I became very close to both Superior Court Judges Phil Berke and Gordon Hemmett. I was also assigned to investigate the 2004 suicide of Gordon Hemmett. Again, one of many investigations very difficult to conduct.

David Pope and Mae White then married and moved to Massachusetts. Along the way, they had 5 children of their own. Mae White married the man that murdered her baby and then had 5 additional children served up to him for continuing abuse and torture. In a quote from David Pope's own sister Rose St. Louis' statement, she wrote, *"When D.J. was about 2 ½ years old, I visited Mae and David where they lived in Massachusetts and I saw D.J. was missing two teeth and D.J. told me that Daddy hit him in the mouth with a hammer."* A quote from Mae

Pope's 1994 statement included, *"I have also seen Dave knock out DJ's two front teeth with a hammer in Massachusetts. I remember that David once went to a psychiatrist in Massachusetts because the welfare people made him go because of all the abuse."* The State of Massachusetts tried to do the right thing. They did mandate this psychiatrist visit. They did permanently remove Robbie, DJ, and Eddie from the custody of Mae and David Pope. At least this is what we were told. There are no records that could be obtained. When Tom and Frank did this investigation in 1994, they reached a dead end with DJ and Eddie. They did track down Robbie, but he was unable to assist them with their case because of all the abuse he suffered. David Pope made sure he could not testify. He has had assisted living his entire life. He was not adopted, but had a somewhat permanent foster care family that took good care of him. The acquittal of David Pope was not the end, but a new beginning of horror and torture.

Connie L. Aiken and Thomas M. Aiken

Letter from Dr. Lynch to D.A. Berke

MICHAEL J. LYNCH, M. D.
19 QUAKER STREET
GRANVILLE, N. Y.

November 13, 1972

Philip A. Berke, D.A.
43 Main Street
Granville, New York 12832

Dear Mr. Berke:

Re: Howard James White

There was some evidence of abuse of this child but death was from natural causes.

Regarding other children, it probably would be in their best interests to be placed in a foster home.

Yours truly,

M.J. Lynch, M.D.

MJL/bjs

Dulcolax®
bisacodyl NF

Geigy

October 6, 1972

Enclosed please find a copy of post mortem examination on Howard White.

M.J. Lynch, M.D.

Now They Lay me Down to Rest

Letter from Hemmett to Dr. Stern

GORDON M. HEMMETT, JR.
ATTORNEY AT LAW
214 MAIN STREET
HUDSON FALLS, NEW YORK
12839

TELEPHONE 518-747-3596

12 March 1973

Walter R. Stern, M.D.
Dept. of Pathology
Glens Falls Hospital
Glens Falls, N.Y. 12801

Dear Dr. Stern:

I have received yours of March 7th and I am enclosing for your review and signature a proposed affidavit which is required for authorization of payment for your services. If you find the statements in the affidavit acceptable to you, would you complete the affidavit in the presence of a notary public and return it to me in the enclosed envelope. I will then present the affidavit to the judge who will issue an order requesting the Washington County Treasurer to pay you the amount requested.

Thank you for your immediate attention to my inquiries. Your courtesy and assistance were greatly appreciated.

Very truly yours,

Gordon M. Hemmett, Jr.

H/cw

Encls.

Connie L. Aiken and Thomas M. Aiken

OFFICE OF THE TREASURER | HERMON BENJAMIN
(518)747-4113

WASHINGTON COUNTY

FORT EDWARD, NEW YORK 12828

March 21, 1973

Walter R. Stern, M.D.
c/o Glens Falls Hospital Laboratory
Park Street
Glens Falls, New York 12801

Dear Sir: Re: The People of the State of New York
against
David Pope, Defendant

    Enclosed please find our Check No. 6419, in the amount of $50.00, compensation for services rendered in the above named action.

Very truly yours,

HERMON BENJAMIN
Treasurer of Washington County

SC
Enc.

Chapter 14
Unmarked Grave

Upon the completion of our consultation with a couple of world-renowned experts at the State Police Forensic Science building and their determination that an exhumation and new autopsy would be required to move forward, Robert Winn and Tom did not waste any time. District Attorney Winn completed an application for a court order authorizing the exhumation and applied to Supreme Court Justice John Dier on September 9, 1994. This order was signed authorizing the exhumation for a complete physical and chemical analysis to ascertain the correct cause and manner of death of Howard "Hodgie" White. With this court order in hand, the process was still only beginning. Everything had to be completed in order and as professionally and completely as possible to later pass the scrutiny of court hearings and challenges. As Tom and Frank were advised by Dr. Michael Baden during the consultation, if Hodgie's body was not touched by water or critters and it was embalmed properly, then he could come out of the ground looking very similar as to when he was buried in September of 1972. They needed to complete two crucial and important steps and they worked on one of these while Rob was completing the exhumation order. The exact location of this grave must be determined to prove to a court that they exhumed the correct body and the correct site. They also had to prove identify of the body. Even if he came out and appeared to be Hodgie, they still had to work hard with Dr. Baden to prove the identity to satisfy the requirements of a superior court challenge. Interviews were conducted with the operators of the North Granville cemetery to determine this site through records and searches of graves. Like many times already, this became a huge challenge for Tom. Hodgie was never respected enough to be buried in his own site. It was determined that he was squeezed in between other family plots. The proprietors of this cemetery, like so many others, took on this cause with Tom and Frank. They wanted to help. They wanted justice for Hodgie after hearing the story presented to them. They agreed to work with the family records and a probing rod and find the correct site. They did as they promised and later contacted Tom with the good news. They probed with the sounding rod and found a vault buried between family members that matched the size as stated by family members and that would match up to the size needed for a 2-year-old child. This made the follow-up interviews with cooperating family members even more important. They needed to obtain all information possible to positively identify Hodgie. Numerous family members were interviewed including Mae Pope and Rose St. Louis. It was determined that Hodgie was buried in a type of blue navy sailor's suit with white trim, and he had a Catholic-type medallion pinned to his shirt. They stated he had on socks, but no shoes. They stated he was buried in a wooden casket with a grey-colored cloth. They also stated that he had flowers placed in the cheap wooden casket with "Son" on them.

When Tom communicated many times with the cemetery caretakers that knew this cemetery and would be assisting them, he had a ray of hope that he would see Hodgie as he was when he died. They told Tom the water table in that area, and specifically in the cemetery, was low and therefore they believed no water would have entered the vault or coffin. When Tom arrived very early on that September Saturday morning, he was hopeful things would go their way for the first time as he observed the four stakes and orange tape marking the outline of the gravesite. An outline that was cramped in between other family member plots. An outline that had no headstone. The two cemetery workers were already waiting with all of their equipment, excited to participate in something that would bring justice to a little boy that never had any. Something that would hold a monster accountable. Everyone was hopeful that day.

The exhumation began very early on Saturday, September 10, 1994. Once again, this was after a long week of working leads, Tom was taken away from his family on a Saturday. He and I knew this would be a very long day beginning with the exhumation and ending with the autopsy. This was an excerpt from Dr. Michael Baden's 1994 autopsy report:

CEMETERY

The disinterment is begun at 7:45 A.M. on September 10, 1994. The gravesite is unmarked within the Holcomb and Tanner family plot area and has been located by family members and by cemetery records. The soil is dry surrounding the cement vault within which is the casket. The top of the child-sized vault is 24 inches below soil surface and it is tightly attached to the remainder of the intact vault. However, upon removing the lid, the unlined vault is approximately 1/3 filled with dark gray water within which is an intact wooden casket. The water line extends two thirds (2/3) of the way up the sides of the casket. An intact wooden, child-size casket is removed and transported to Albany Medical Center in a white zippered plastic bag.

The New York State Police forensic identification team was present to properly document each step of this process. One evidence team member videotaped the entire process, while another took dozens and dozens of still photos. Others were there to record measurements and take evidence. Dr. Baden does not have the reputation worldwide for no reason. He is professional and detailed to a fault. He knows how to conduct a proper exhumation and autopsy, the value of a thorough examination of all evidence, and how to win cases in court. He had the evidence team collect soil and water samples to eliminate any and all possible defenses, and to find the truth. His goal, like all of the Police Officers and Investigators there, is simply to seek the truth. The reason for the water and soil samples are plentiful in his forensic investigative mind, but first and foremost is to check for any toxins or other substances that may have leaked from the body and coffin into the soil. Any that could have something to do with Hodgie's death. Much of this was to eliminate future arguments compared to thinking something would be found.

This was also an excerpt from Dr. Michael Baden's 1994 autopsy report:

> *Sr. Invs. Michael J. Kelleher, June M. Bradley, Inv. Thomas Aiken, Tprs. P.J. Hasson, M.F. Wells and S.J. Wetmore, Dr. Michael Baden, Lowell Levine, Mr. Gordon Oakes, NYSP; Ed Affinito, Richard Jillson, Jay Jillson, Jillson Funeral Home; Edward Parsons, Washington Co. Coroner; Robert Winn, NancyLynn Ferrini, Washington Co. DA's Office; Ronald Daigle, Granville PD; Bob Buxton, Matt Rathbun, Caretakers; Robert Graham, Ft. Miller Vault Service*

As investigators, they learn early what roles they play and what they should or should not do. Tom and Frank's roles as lead investigators at the cemetery was to monitor and learn while letting the experts do their job. Dr. Baden would diligently point out different observations he made and he thoroughly explained every step of the process. They stepped back at the beginning as the cemetery workers dug the hole, first using the small backhoe and then transitioning to shovels as they finished. They were given their instructions and knew they did not want to harm any evidence. This was now a full crime scene. You may not understand that because the coffin and vault were placed into that ground almost 22 years ago, but with this being an exhumation and evidentiary search, this was a full crime scene. Just like you would see a crime scene in general where you see the yellow tape. That day it was a full crime scene, but yellow tape was not needed because everyone there that day were police officers or had a reason for being there. The press was not invited that day. There were no onlookers that could enter or contaminate this scene. As the workers painstakingly, but quickly, worked to totally uncover the entire vault to raise it out of the ground, the Forensic Investigators would stop them, take measurements, and soil samples at different levels until finally the vault was ready to come up. The straps were put around it and the workers carefully raised it up to ground level and set it on protective boards. When the photographs were all taken, it was now time to raise the cover of the vault. As they worked to open it, the adhesive used to seal it appeared to Tom to be like beeswax. That impression has always stayed with him. The first disappointment came when the cover was lifted and there was water in the vault. Two thirds of the way up the casket. The investigators used a new blue tarp to place the casket on it. The entire casket was now 100% evidence and had to be treated that way. The casket was not opened at the scene, just preserved. The casket was first sealed in a large white zipper bag and then a blue tarp was securely wrapped around the entire casket and white bag and tied off, to protect any and all evidence that could possibly come from the casket or anything inside of it. This would be painstakingly examined at the Albany Medical Center. The Jillson Funeral Home was selected to assist in this exhumation and they provided the hearse to transport the casket to the capital city of Albany. A uniformed New York State Trooper was with that casket and hearse at all times and escorted it to the Albany Medical Center and walked with the casket until it was placed in the secure vault at the morgue. This casket and everything inside was evidence and the chain of custody must be preserved. What an epiphany Tom had. It wasn't your average crime scene, but it seemed like a small part of justice watching this forgotten poor child driving away in a hearse, escorted by the New York State Police, and given some type of dignity and knowing that the world renowned expert Dr. Michael Baden would be soon performing Hodgie's 2nd autopsy. If anyone could give this boy his dignity back, it would be this man. After Tom had done previous work and autopsies with Dr. Baden, he knew that this was going to be a long day and night because both Tom and Doc Baden had similar drives to find the truth and would never stop until all was uncovered. Once an autopsy is begun, you cannot stop until it is finished. A long night was to follow what started out very early as a long day. Final work was completed at the cemetery and then most of those in attendance took the little over an hour trip south to Albany for the next step. The re-autopsy. As Tom would reflect to me, all sorts of things were going through his mind. His ride was filled with mixed emotions. Would he look like the little boy that was buried in September of 1972? He was thinking about all the hours and days spent away from our family already. Calling home to update me. Having a sense of pride that he was doing the right thing seeking justice that Hodgie never obtained while alive. Thinking about our own three little boys and the life they were living and being so upset that Hodgie never had a chance at a life like that. Unconditional love and protection. He was still holding out hope that the water did not contaminate the inside of the casket and he would see Hodgie as he was in September of 1972.

Now They Lay Me Down to Rest

PRESS RELEASE

September 12, 1994

The New York State Police and the Granville Police Department are investigating the September 11, 1972 death of Howard James White. Howard, nicknamed "Hodgie", died just weeks before he would have been 3 years old. He died at the former Emma Laing Stevens Hospital in the Village of Granville after being transported there from his family's apartment located in the old Longhouses apartment building in the Village of Granville.

On September 10, 1994 the New York State Police Forensic Sciences Unit, Troop "G" ID Unit, Granville Police Department, New York State Police Bureau of Criminal Investigation Unit, the Washington County Coroners Office, and the Washington County District Attorney's Office were present at the North Granville Cemetery when the body of Howard James White was exhumed upon a court order which was issued by Supreme Court Justice John Dier on September 7th, 1994. The body was then transported to the Albany Medical Center Hospital where an autopsy was conducted by Forensic Pathologist Doctors Michael Baden, Lowell Levine, and Barbara Wolfe. Washington County Coroner Edward Parsons has issued an amended death certificate listing the manner of death as homicide based upon the pathologists' findings.

A joint investigation by the New York State Police, the Granville Police Department, and the Washington County District Attorney's Office is continuing and anyone having information concerning this case is encouraged to contact the police at the following phone numbers:

NEW YORK STATE POLICE - 518-583-7000 or 518-745-1033

GRANVILLE POLICE DEPARTMENT - 518-642-1414

Press Release – David Pope Investigation

CONNIE L. AIKEN AND THOMAS M. AIKEN

At a Regular Term of the Supreme Court held in and for the County of Washington on the 7th day of September, 1994 in Lake George, New York

PRESENT: HON. JOHN G. DIER, J. S. C.

In the Matter of the Application of Robert M. Winn, Washington County District Attorney for an Order pursuant to §4210 of the Public Health Law to Exhume the Body of Howard White, Deceased.

ORDER

On the reading the annexed application of Robert M. Winn, Esquire, District Attorney of Washington County, sworn to the 7th day of September, 1994, together with the annexed autopsy report relating to Howard White, age 2, the annexed deposition of Mae Kelly, the annexed deposition of Michael Pope, the annexed deposition of Harold Burch, and the annexed copy of Washington County Indictment No. I-73-94, and it appearing that an Order should be entered granting the application of the District Attorney to exhume the body of Howard White, pursuant to §4210 of the Public Health Law, it is

ORDERED, that, pursuant to the provisions of section 4210 of the Public Health Law, the District Attorney of Washington County may exhume, take possession of and remove the body of Howard White, a deceased person, to the Albany Medical Center, for a proper physical or chemical examination or analysis, to ascertain the cause of death of said Howard White.

Signed this _7_th day of September, 1994, at Lake George, New York.

Hon. John G. Dier
Supreme Court Justice

Exhumation Order

Now They Lay me Down to Rest

Exhumation Photo – Unmarked Grave

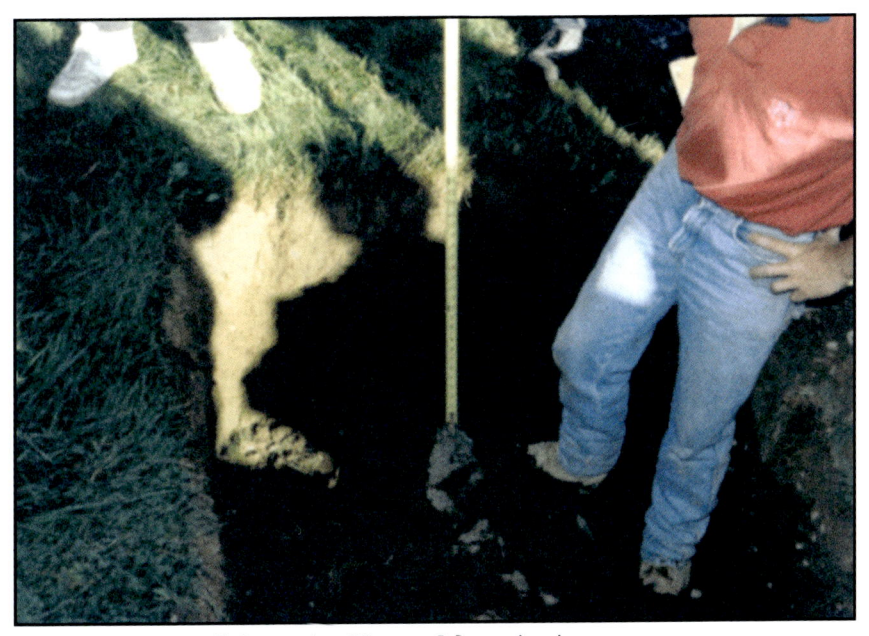

Exhumation Photo – Measuring into grave

Exhumation Photo – Lifting Vault from Grave

Exhumation Photo – Vault out of Grave

Now They Lay me Down to Rest

Exhumation Photo – Vault

Exhumation Photo – Opening Vault

Casket from Vault

Chapter 15
Forensic Soup

The enthusiasm Tom had on that September day, where summer turns to fall, beginning with a well-orchestrated exhumation continued into the forensic autopsy room at the Albany Medical Center. Tom was anxious to see this little boy and have him, through his body, tell the story of what happened to him. These were the things swirling through his mind as he was waiting to introduce himself to this beautiful little boy that no one loved. He kept the image from the photograph showing a healthy and almost happy smile on his face at 5 months of age. Doctors Michael Baden, Lowell Levine, and Barbara Wolfe were ready to begin. The New York State Police Forensic Team was in place to fully document the entire autopsy. Tom, Frank, and others were there to witness this process and learn from the experts. It is not every day that you find yourself in an autopsy room with the expertise of legends like doctors Michael Baden and Lowell Levine. By the end of his career, Tom has been to almost 100 autopsies from infants, to toddlers, and mainly adults. Tom knows that every autopsy brings some new learning of facts and this one was so necessary to hear what happened and to hopefully amend a death certificate to allow the prosecution of a homicide. Even though Tom has told me about numerous autopsies and what he has seen and learned, Tom was actually mesmerized by Dr. Baden's reaction when the casket was opened. He was not deterred one bit. His professionalism and ability did not miss a beat. As they meticulously opened the top of that cheap wooden box that became Hodgie's final resting place, Tom's enthusiasm quickly dissipated. The wooden casket was completely full of a very dark and murky water containing floating bones and items from his burial. A phrase to explain it came to Tom immediately, and has never left him to this day. Forensic soup. These expert doctors know that they must work with the facts they are dealt with. A decision was made to drill a hole into the bottom of the one side of this casket and everything coming from that box would be filtered and saved for examination. Everything. This took a lot of time, but forensically and as best evidence practice was completely necessary. Even though Tom lost hope of new evidence to help their case, the great doctors did not. Tom thought that any future prosecution was gone. No justice for a little boy. I'm not saying that Tom underestimated these great doctors, but he could not see the outcome coming out their way. They went to work. Each bone taken from that forensic soup was found and put on a table with a sterile sheet. Each was examined and then carefully cleaned of the black-and-green residue. Once examined and then cleaned, they were placed onto a second table with a new sterile sheet. Never did Tom imagine that a complete skeleton would come from the few floating bones he first observed. Tom could not believe his eyes when Dr. Michael Baden found every bone and put them all into their proper placement and a complete skeleton of Hodgie appeared to him on that final table. A complete skeleton. Every bone, every finger, toe, and rib. A forensic work of art. Once this skeleton was completed and photographs taken, the next step was to fully x-ray every bone for fractures and other signs of abuse. Once again, the expertise of Dr. Baden paid off. He discovered what appeared to be an undocumented skull fracture on the left side of Hodgie's face near his nasal opening. All the findings from Dr. Stern and his 1972 autopsy where he documented other fractures and abuse were identified by doctors Baden, Levine, and Wolfe. Dr. Baden knew he was looking at another undocumented facial fracture, but he needed to be completely sure. He consulted the expertise of another world-renowned doctor. Dr. William Maples. An acclaimed doctor and anthropologist from Florida. I will never forget how impressed Tom was with Dr. Maples. He described him as a very down-to-earth person, but by far one of the most intellectual persons he has ever talked to. Tom would say that he was so intelligent, he made his (Tom's) brain hurt. Dr. William Maples did his examination later and confirmed what Dr. Baden suspected. A facial fracture not documented in the original autopsy from 1972.

The magic of world-renowned doctors was not done yet. Dr. Lowell Levine found every tooth in that murky water and identified each one and correctly placed them into their proper place in Hodgie's mouth. When he was done completing this complete set of teeth, he then x-rayed each one and as a complete set. His examination, confirmed with x-rays, led to a finding of malnourishment, emaciation, and starvation. Severe emaciation which confirmed what witnesses told and what the 1972 photographs showed. Confirming the skin hanging from his bones and the large distended stomach. All came to life to Dr. Levine with his visual examination and confirmation x-rays. Tom and I both remember the television commercials from the 1970s asking for donations and showing photographs of starving and completely emaciated children from Ethiopia. Graphic images hard to see. This was Hodgie's life and now confirmed. Tom and Frank heard so many times doing interviews how Hodgie looked just like the kids they showed on television of the 3rd-world countries with starving and emaciated children.

The final task that had to be verified during this autopsy was the positive identification that this was Howard White "Hodgie" that this autopsy was being conducted on. A positive identification is a must in every autopsy and this one was no different, except it was more difficult because of the condition of the contents of the casket. Making matters worse was no DNA, fingerprints, or other normal identifying certainties. The main way most difficult positive identifications are made is through teeth and dental work. Hodgie only went to a doctor when ordered by Social Services or his injuries were so serious that they had to bring him. With that in mind, you know Hodgie was never brought to a dentist. Therefore, no chance of a positive identification through dental records. That left identifying Hodgie through any means they could. This goes back to the interviews Tom conducted with family members concerning how Hodgie was dressed and other identifying items. Dr. Baden located everything in that Forensic Soup that Tom came up with when Hodgie was buried. The flowers with the word "son" on the ribbon. A sailor-type suit. A religious medallion which was photographed with the body. A positive identification was made by Dr. Baden. One that would eventually withstand the scrutiny and satisfaction of a Superior Court examination. Now, Dr. Baden had enough evidence to properly amend the death certificate. He filed an amended death certificate with the Washington County clerk's office that listed the cause of death as "Multiple old and recent contusions of head, chest, and abdomen. Traumatic laceration of stomach with acute diffuse peritonitis, healing fracture of rib, malnutrition. Battered Child Syndrome." Now, there was a manner of death included. A correct manner of death. One that enabled the prosecution team to move forward. "Homicide."

Tom did not get his wish to see this little boy as he was when no one loved or helped him, but he did get the answers he was seeking and needed. He did get the green light to go forward with this investigation and prosecution.

NOW THEY LAY ME DOWN TO REST

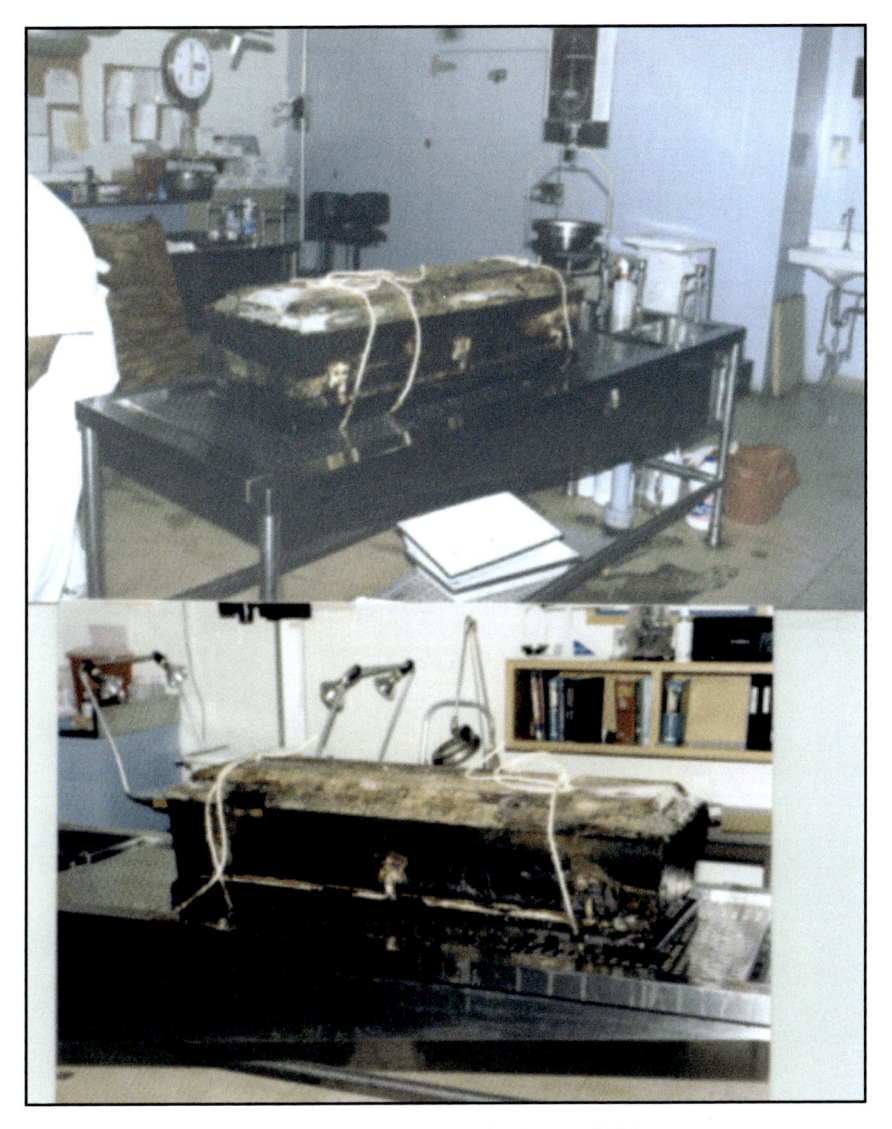

1994 Autopsy Photo – Casket on Table

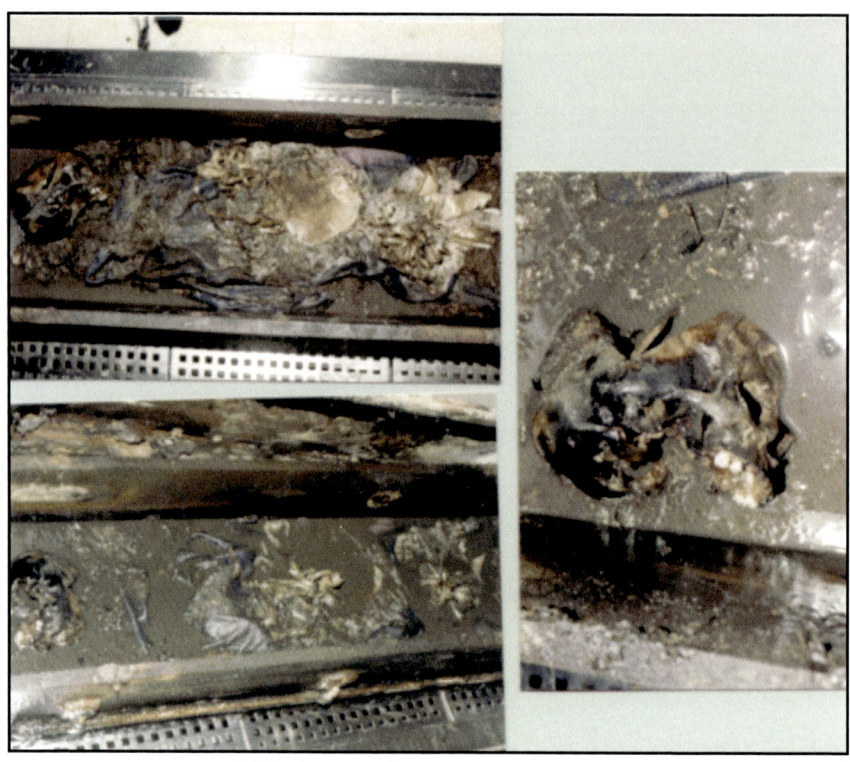

1994 Autopsy Photo – Forensic Soup

1994 Autopsy Photo – Body on Table to Start

Now They Lay me Down to Rest

1994 Autopsy Photo – Ribbon and Son

1994 Autopsy Photo – Saw Cut on Bone

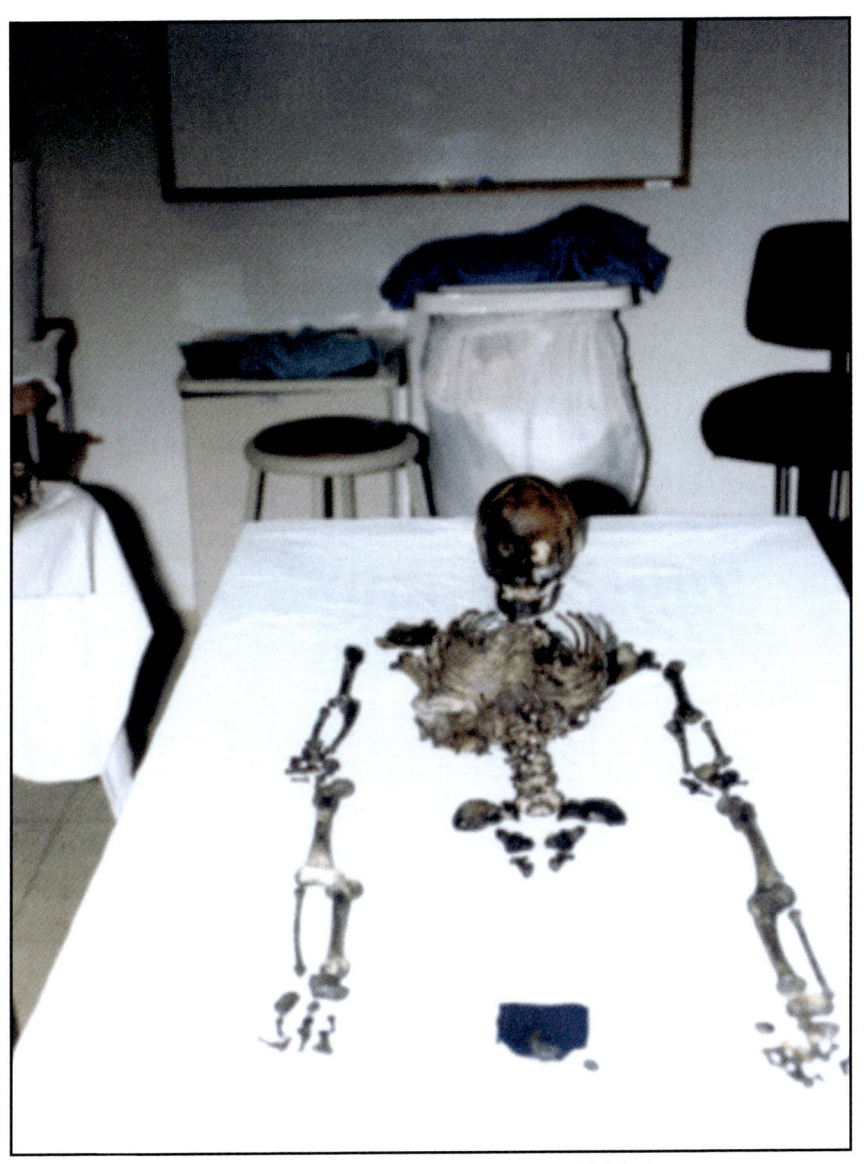

1994 Autopsy Photo – Skeleton on Table 1

1994 Autopsy Photo – Skeleton on Table 2

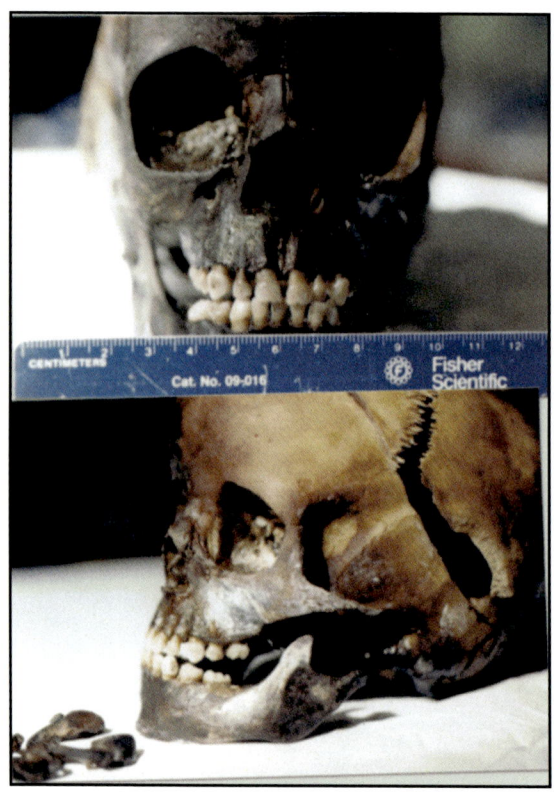

1994 Autopsy Photo – Skull with Teeth

Now They Lay me Down to Rest

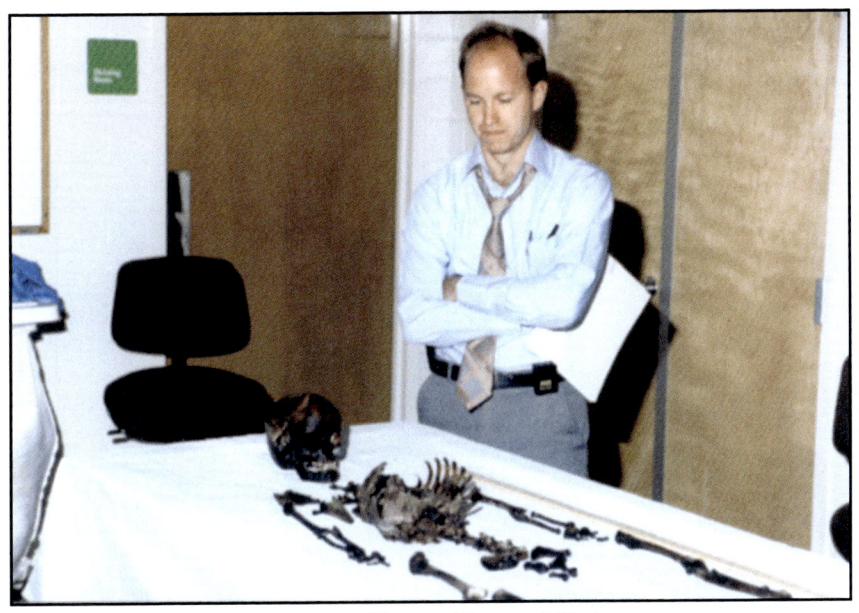

1994 Autopsy Photo – Tom and Skeleton

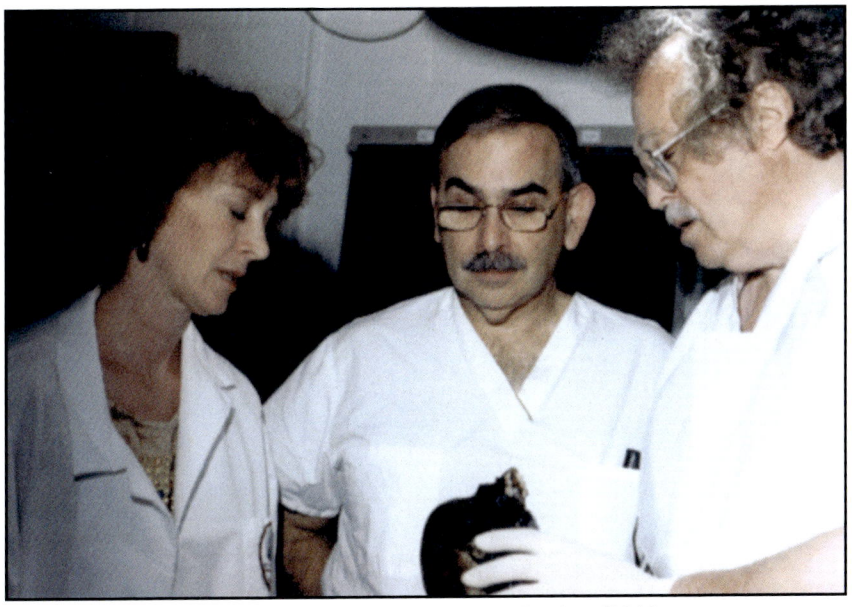

1994 Autopsy Photo – Baden, Levine, Wolf

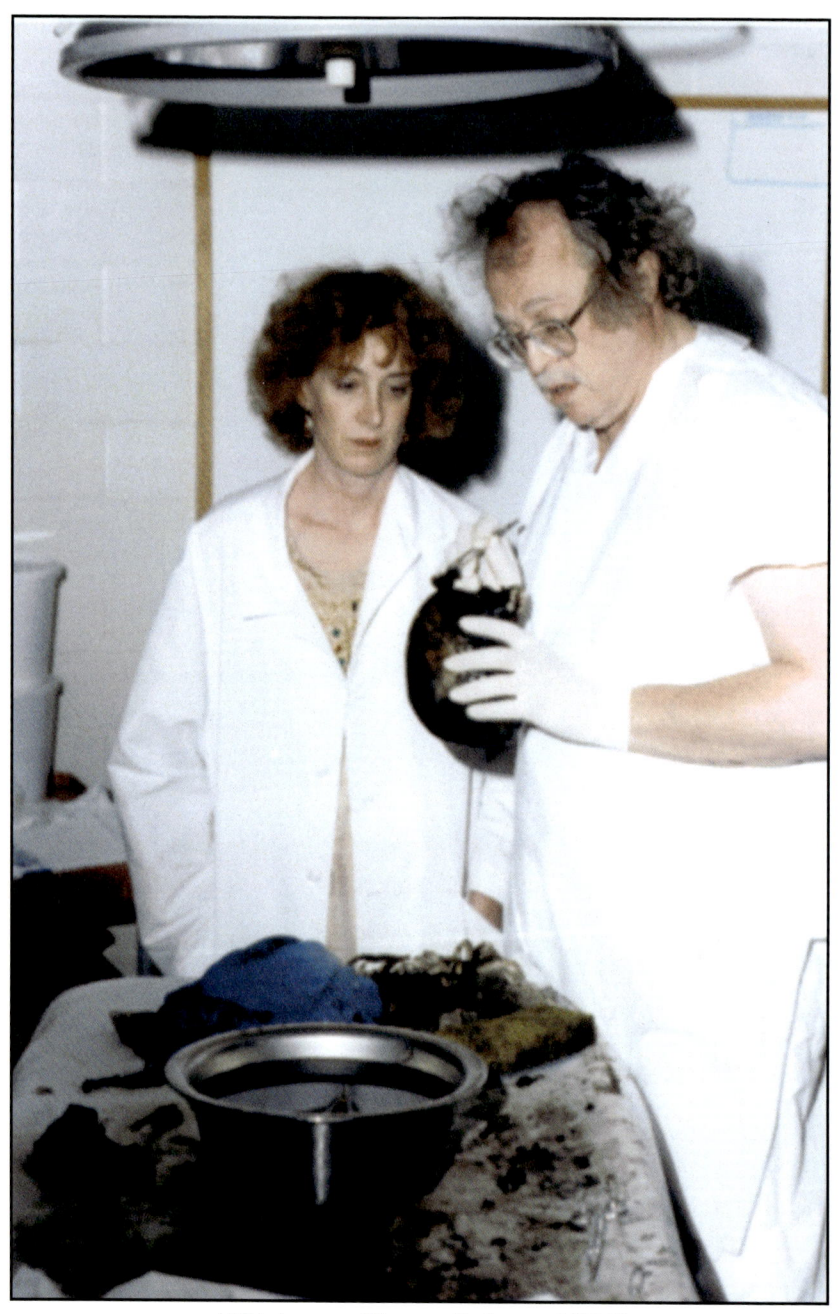

1994 Autopsy Photo – Baden and Wolf

Now They Lay me Down to Rest

1994 Autopsy Report of Dr. Michael Baden

DR. MICHAEL M. BADEN
DIRECTOR

DR. LOWELL J. LEVINE
DIRECTOR

NEW YORK STATE POLICE
FORENSIC SCIENCES UNIT
ALBANY, NEW YORK 12226
(518) 457-8678

REAUTOPSY REPORT

DECEDENT:	HOWARD JAMES WHITE
DATE OF DEATH:	September 11, 1972
DATE OF INITIAL AUTOPSY:	September 12, 1972
PROSECTOR:	Walter R. Stern, MD
PLACE OF INITIAL AUTOPSY:	Glens Falls Hospital, Glens Falls, New York
CORONER:	M. Lynch, MD
DATE OF REAUTOPSY:	September 10, 1994
PLACE OF DISINTERMENT:	North Granville Cemetery, Granville, New York
CORONER:	Edward Parsons
PROSECUTORS:	Michael M. Baden, MD Lowell J. Levine, MD Barbara C. Wolf, MD
PLACE OF REAUTOPSY:	Albany Medical Center, Albany, New York
PRESENT AT DISINTERMENT:	Sr. Invs. Michael J. Kelleher, June M. Bradley, Inv. Thomas Aiken, Tprs. P.J. Hasson, M.F. Wells and S.J. Wetmore, Dr. Michael Baden, Lowell Levine, Mr. Gordon Oakes, NYSP; Ed Affinito, Richard Jillson, Jay Jillson, Jillson Funeral Home; Edward Parsons, Washington Co. Coroner; Robert Winn, NancyLynn Ferrini, Washington Co. DA's Office; Ronald Daigle, Granville PD; Bob Buxton, Matt Rathbun, Caretakers; Robert Graham, Ft. Miller Vault Service
PRESENT AT REAUTOPSY:	Sr. Invs. Michael J. Kelleher, June M. Bradley, James Booth, Inv. Thomas Aiken, Tprs. M.F. Wells, S.J. Wetmore, Doctors Michael Baden, Lowell Levine, Mr. Gordon Oakes, NYSP; Ed Affinito, Jay Jillson, Jillson Funeral Home; NancyLynn Ferrini, Washington Co. DA's Office; Det. F. Hunt, Granville PD; Tim Komdat, Perry-Komdat Funeral Chapel; Dr. Barbara Wolf, Nancy Bulzek, Denise Rollin, Herman Thomas, Albany Medical Ctr.

CEMETERY

The disinterment is begun at 7:45 AM on September 10, 1994. The grave site is unmarked within the Holcomb and Tanner family plot area and has been located by family members and by cemetery records. The soil is dry surrounding the cement vault within which is the casket. The top of the child-sized vault is 24 inches below soil surface and it is tightly attached to the remainder of the intact vault. However, upon removing the lid, the unlined vault is approximately 1/3 filled with dark gray water within which is an intact wooden casket. The water line extends two thirds (2/3) of the way up the sides of the casket. An intact wooden, child-size casket is removed and transported to Albany Medical Center in a white zippered plastic bag.

ALBANY MEDICAL CENTER

The casket is received at the Albany Medical Center Mortuary at 11:05 AM. The casket is 40 inches long and 15 inches wide and is made of pine wood with metal trim. The hinges are rusted. The wooden lid is easily removed to reveal murky water filling 2/3 of the casket and extensive loss of soft tissue and skeletonization of the body. Upon removing the water, the disarticulated skeletal remains of an approximately three year old child are identified, dressed in a blue sailor-type jumpsuit with a "100% Acrylic" label attached. Dark socks are present on the feet. No shoes are present. A religious crusted oval metal medallion is affixed to the left upper chest pocket of the jumpsuit. Dried flowers and wet ribbons are present at the feet with "Son" inscribed on a heart-shaped fabric and the inscription in gold "Brother" on a crucifix-shaped design.

The opened skull lies separate from the spine with the calvarium incision from the first autopsy apparent. On removing the jumpsuit there is evidence of a prior thoracic autopsy incision with previously dissected formalin-fixed viscera returned to the thoracic and abdominal cavities. The small and large intestines have been previously opened in their entirety. Dissected portions of liver and lungs are also identified. The teeth, many loose in the casket, are recovered and are those of an approximately three year old child. The long bones are also those of a three year old child. There is soft tissue adherent to the back of the thorax but the extremities and skull are otherwise completely skeletonized. The outer surfaces of the bones have been colored black by the murky water. All of the skeleton is reconstructed but for a portion of the right tenth rib which was removed at the first autopsy. This area is described in that autopsy report as containing a healing fracture. There is an

White/Baden

autopsy saw cut of the adjacent eleventh rib. The skull is devoid of soft tissues but for the posterior aspect of the right eye which is in the orbit. Embalmer's tissue building material is present about the left maxillary bone just below the left orbit. The viscera are absent but for a portion of aorta adherent to the thoracic spine which is unremarkable.

The circumstances of death, first autopsy report and microscopic sections, and x-rays taken at reautopsy are reviewed.

CAUSE OF DEATH

Multiple old and recent contusions of head, chest and abdomen. Traumatic laceration of stomach with acute diffuse peritonitis. Healing fracture of rib. Malnutrition. Battered Child Syndrome.

MANNER OF DEATH

Homicide

Date: October 13, 1994

Michael M. Baden, MD

CONNIE L. AIKEN AND THOMAS M. AIKEN

STATE OF NEW YORK
DEPARTMENT OF HEALTH
VITAL RECORDS SECTION

MEDICAL/BURIAL DEATH CORRECTION REPORT

Name of Deceased: Howard James White
Date of Death: 9/11/72
Place of Death: V/O Granville

Cause of death: Multiple old and recent contusions of head, chest and abdomen. Traumatic laceration of stomach with acute diffuse peritonitis. Healing fracture of rib, malnutrition.

Battered child syndrome

Signed: Michael Baden MD, Consultant Forensic Pathologist, 9/12/94
NYS license # 85329

Registrar: Elizabeth M Truso, District Number 5725, 9/12/94

Amended 1994 Death Certificate

Chapter 16
A Mother's Worst Nightmare

I am writing this chapter myself for two reasons. I know, and never will forget the facts so intimately, and this case out of hundreds of horrendous cases, is at the very top of the list of cases bothering me and living with me the most. Evil comes from many directions, with many disguises, and without a schedule. I have been asked many times with doing major cases for 25 of my 30 years, including approximately 100 of the worse homicide cases and over 700 of the most heinous child abuse cases, how I kept my sanity and emotions in check. This included hundreds and hundreds of death cases and attending close to 100 autopsies. I learned to compartmentalize all I dealt with and my strong attachment and support from my family has helped tremendously. I will tell you that within months of retiring, it all came crashing down on me. My emotions are worse than a train wreck and I have cried and sobbed more times than I could ever detail here. Just talking about this case and others with my wife can create these moments all the time, so much so, that she no longer asks what is wrong.

Frank Hunt and I have worked many cases and are not only close in a working relationship, but as friends. We could literally write a book on just the cases he and his agency has asked us to assist with. When I was asked to reopen this case by District Attorney Robert Winn in August of 1994, we both agreed that we must bring in the Granville Police

Department since the jurisdiction for this case was in their village. It was an easy decision since I enjoyed working with Frank. He and I literally worked 12-hour days together until it was completed. We both still had other cases coming through the doors, but we devoted as much time as we could to solving the Hodgie case. Hodgie never received the attention and love he deserved, not once in his short 2 years and 10 months of life, so he certainly deserved it now. One of those cases that came through the door and took time away from Hodgie's case was the Stephanie Sady case.

Frank and I were so used to working up to 12+ hours every day on the David Pope case. It was a routine. We knew everything about each other, much less the case we were devoted to. We were totally on the same page. After working around five straight weeks and covering many, many leads, evil came knocking on our door again.

On Monday, September 19, 1994, Frank did what he normally would do. He went to his office for a quick lunch and to check his emails and cases coming in there. What made this day different was his call to me after lunch. He told me he needed to take the afternoon off from working with me because a case came in that he needed to look into. I didn't think much of it and said to call if he needed anything. I continued doing leads and interviews, but also talked to Frank and watched the news and learned why he left me that day. A 17-year-old mother of a 5-month-old boy was reported missing by her mom. It was a normal missing person complaint until you looked into it more and saw the outpouring of support and help. Television news crews from New York and Vermont descended the next day on the little border town of Granville, New York. Dozens, if not hundreds, of volunteers started coming to help the police and fire departments in their now coordinated search efforts. Missing person's flyers went up overnight and television and newspapers accounts were dominating all the news cycles. The family spokesman was an uncle named William Burdick. He was also the last person to see this girl, Stephanie Sady, before she went missing.

Tuesday morning the 20th, Frank called me and checked in very early. He said, "Tom, I'm going to spend this day working on Stephanie's case, so I can't join you." I again said the usual response. "Let me know if you need anything." Wednesday morning, the call came in really early. Frank called me and said it was not looking good, and he needed a lot of help. I called my supervisor and we brought in multiple State Police Troopers and Investigators. We did like we do on every major case, we set up a major case lead desk. Probably 20 investigators from the State Police and some other departments worked leads all day until late at night. I intentionally stayed out from doing anything but regular leads because of my pending David Pope investigation. This kept me from meeting or interviewing the main players, William Burdick or Stephanie's boyfriend. Late Wednesday, our first full day of conducting leads on this case, we went around the room and debriefed the leads and facts to date. We then went around the room and asked opinions of each officer. Everyone except one State Police Investigator went against what everyone in the public thought. They all thought that Stephanie's abusive live-in boyfriend killed her because she was truly leaving him this time. No, we all said it was Uncle Bill. The reason was because no matter how many leads we conducted and how hard we tried, we could not show Stephanie taking one step outside of Uncle Bill's house after making that call home to her mom. Also, any female, especially Stephanie, would never leave her baby and run away or run home. Another small but huge detail, no female would leave her purse behind and Stephanie's was still in her car parked in Uncle Bill's driveway. That one dissenting investigator said he thought Frank either killed her or he was trying to be optimistic in saying he thought she ran away to clear her head and straighten things out.

We continued working all day Thursday, but the next major event was to occur on Friday. An agreement was made with William Burdick to have him take a polygraph examination in Albany late Friday morning. Frank Hunt and I were assigned to bring him to this test. This was my first time meeting William Burdick and I drove from Granville. I love to talk to people and get a feel for their veracity in telling the truth. I have a very high confession rate that I perfected in all crimes, but especially homicide and horrendous child abuse cases. For those that know much about polygraph examinations in criminal cases, they are very long and you cannot stress out the person prior to the examination. They last an average of four hours from beginning to end and they are stressful enough by definition. I still wanted a chance to meet with Bill and plant seeds. The trip from Granville, NY, to the Troop "G" headquarters in Albany, NY, for the polygraph is about 1 hour and 15 minutes minimum. Along the way, I stopped with Frank and Bill at my office in North Granville. I sat down with Bill and I planted seeds. I planted them as methodical as I could, without stressing him out too much for a test. I continually told Bill that I was not accusing him of doing this, but things did point that way, and the family needed closure more than anything in this world. I explained to him that they would not immediately understand or forgive him, but if he cared about them and Stephanie, they deserved to know where she was and what happened to her. I could not minimize or downplay what happened too much, or I lose all credibility. I did plant many of these seeds by wording the same phrases in different ways and very repetitively. I explained to him that this was the greatest gift he could ever give to Stephanie and her family. I assumed, but did not fully know at this time, that he truly cared about Stephanie in more ways than we knew. I played on any conscience or feelings he may have for her and her family. Little did I know, he had very little conscience. He did have evil, perverted feelings for Stephanie, but he only cared about himself and his own selfish needs and wants.

After about 30-45 minutes of planting these seeds, I continued the drive to Albany. The New York State Police have many polygraph operators. Some better than others, but the one we were going to work with this date was at the top of the list of best State Police interviewers and polygraph operators. He was the coleader of our major case crime squad at the time and he was outstanding. The best. We arrived and the test began. Frank and I waited in a separate room, not knowing what was taking place. After what seemed like an eternity, this Senior Investigator came out to me and uttered words I never expected. He said, "Tom, I know you guys all believe this guy is good for this homicide, but I'm telling you he did not do this." He told me he had some final work to complete and he would put the results down as inconclusive, but he said he was stating this guy did not do this. Anyone with much experience with criminal case polygraph examinations knows that as a rule, a test will not falsely state an innocent person was guilty, but a guilty person could possibly beat a polygraph. There is a clinical term for these people. Sociopaths.

Just after he delivered this crushing news to me, I immediately heard a panicked transmission come over the radio in the room we were waiting in. A dangerous criminal had just escaped from the custody of two State Police investigators that were stopped at a red light in the area of Ballston Spa, New York. This was about 20 minutes straight up the Northway from our location. I immediately received a call from my supervisor advising me I needed to immediately respond to this escape and to also bring some needed supplies from our headquarters. I quickly made arrangements for Frank to get a ride from a uniformed Trooper back to Granville after the test was completed and I ran out of the office and quickly drove up the Northway. The escapee was a notorious bad man currently facing charges for burglary, rape, and other charges. This case became a major black eye for an elite agency.

This was my life. Working a cold case homicide 12 hours a day, getting another homicide in the middle, and then redirected to a major escape / manhunt. I remember working so many hours, even into the middle of the night doing interviews and surveillance. This escape took over 12 hours from my family for each of the following days until I broke free on Tuesday, September 27th, to continue following up on leads on the Stephanie Sady missing person case.

Stephanie Sady was a beautiful 17-year-old girl who devoted her life to her 5-month-old son and worked double shifts to support herself, her live-in boyfriend, and their son. Her boyfriend was known to be abusive to her. She finally reached her breaking point on September 19, 1994, when they had one more argument and he left the house with their newborn child and she took the car to the only person she knew and trusted in Granville, New York. Her Aunt Terri Burdick. They only lived blocks away from each other and were extremely close emotionally with each other. Cell phones were not around much in 1994 and when Stephanie decided she was leaving her boyfriend for good, she needed a phone to call her mother for a ride back home to Vermont. Stephanie drove those few blocks to her Aunt Terri's house. Terri was at her job at the Grand Union supermarket and her Uncle Bill Burdick was home getting ready for his job on the 2nd shift at the Native Textiles mill in the City of Glens Falls. When she arrived at the house, Bill was in the shower and she used the phone to call her mother in Vermont. It is very unfortunate that her mom was out and away from home when she called and left the voicemail. She left this message in which she asked her mom to come and get her and the baby to move back home, across the border to Vermont. She said she knew she told her mom these things before, but this time she truly meant it. She even told her mom in this message that she was going to reenter college and start her life in another direction. After leaving this voicemail, Uncle Bill came out and joined her. He was very concerned as he heard a lot of her message and came out to see her in tears. She told him that her and Frank fought again and she was leaving him for good. Uncle Bill asked if he hit or hurt her and she said no, it was only verbal. Uncle Bill knew that this time, she meant it. She was truly going back home to Vermont and he would not see her much in the future as he told her he was very fond of her. He offered to smoke a cigarette with her to which she agreed and then joined him in the basement. The basement, with its dirt hard pan floor, was the only place in the house he was allowed to smoke. He asked her if she wanted to smoke more to which she answered no, that she must get going. Uncle Bill then asked Stephanie if she would help him move a desk upstairs with him and of course she said yes and offered to help. When she went up there, he had plans other than moving furniture. Information came out from the investigation that Uncle Bill had put the moves on this pretty girl one other time and she, being strong willed but loving her Aunt Terri, gave him a pass with a strong warning. She told him that this stupid move was free because she loved her Aunt Terri and did not want to cause her problems, but if he ever tried putting the moves on her again, she would not only tell Aunt Terri, but she would have him arrested. Uncle Bill knew she meant what she said, but he also knew she was serious about moving back across the border. This would be his final chance. Instead of having her help him, he tried to put the moves on her. She resisted fiercely and he ended up strangling her. He then fondled her dead body while masturbating and he used a video camera to record this for his own sick and perverted use in the future.

I will never forget that Tuesday, late morning. It was September 27th, 1994. Myself and another State Police investigator were freed up from the major escaped prisoner search to continue following leads on the Stephanie Sady case. The Granville Police Department was a small department with only a main entrance room with a tall front desk area and two doors leading to the back offices. I was in the center room directly behind the front entrance going over leads when the old time Chief for Granville was conducting an on-camera interview with a Vermont television station. He conducted these on-camera interviews multiple times a day with New York and Vermont stations to update them on the status of the missing person investigation. As he was conducting this interview, he took a phone call from Aunt Terri. Whatever this old-time chief had accomplished prior to this call, this was a shining moment for him. In the middle of an on-air interview, Aunt Terri called in a loud, frantic tone saying that we needed to come over to her house immediately because she "thinks" she knows where Stephanie is. Remember the "I think" statement. The Chief did not miss a beat. He excused himself from the television reporters and ducked back into the area we were in. He said, "Tom, you need to get over to Terri's house. She just frantically called and she thinks she knows where Stephanie is." He said he had no additional information and he went back and continued his on-air interview as if nothing happened at all. He never missed a beat. We went out the 2nd door, the one leading into the front room, and were directly behind the reporter and cameraman. It was just about lunchtime, so to distract attention away from them, I told the chief that we were going to get a bite to eat and asked him if he wanted us to bring back anything for him. Again, without missing a beat while off air now and talking to the reporter, he said, "No, thank you, I brought my lunch today." He said this while holding up a brown lunch bag. As I slowly and deliberately walked out the front door, my heart was racing. As soon as the door fully shut, we ran out to my car parked on the street and made record time driving those 5-6 blocks to Aunt Terri's house. Upon arriving at her house, we now received the story from a very distraught Aunt Terri. She said she came home for lunch like she does every day, and this day she smelled a bad smell. She said she tried mopping a few floors, but she could not get rid of the smell. Remember, this is one week and one day since Stephanie went missing. Aunt Terri said she called a friend to come over and help her figure this out. She said her and this friend then followed the smell and it took them down the cellar stairs. She said the smell brought them to the area of a wooden workbench set up in the main room. She said there were rolls of pink insulation lined up under that bench. We now know that Bill put them there to not only hide her body, but to help keep the smell from coming out. Aunt Terri said that she found a plain white curtain rod and used it to pull out the first large roll of insulation. When she did, she said she then saw her beautiful niece in an awkward position stuffed under the bench and behind the insulation. As she walked me through each step and I used the same white curtain rod to fully pull out the insulation, I then saw this beautiful young girl with her knees up to her chin and blown up like a helium balloon from the buildup of body gases. I then did something that I teach investigators to never do. I got tunnel vision. The knowledge and acceptance that this was not going to have a good ending the past 8 days is still held at bay by the hope we will find her alive and doing well. That all came crashing down and I knew that Uncle Bill Burdick did this and I knew where he currently was. He was at work at the Native Textile factory on Warren Street in the City of Glens Falls. I am very familiar with Native Textiles. My father worked there his entire life until he died suddenly walking down the street with my mom. He had a massive undetected aortic aneurysm. He allowed me to work there summers while in college and then full time during my final year of college. I knew the plant manager very well. Phil Cassella. Ironically, my wife later ran a daycare out of our house and his two grandsons were in there and loved my wife.

I called Phil Cassella directly while starting my 40-minute drive there. I told him what was going on and asked him to meet me and to quietly walk Bill Burdick out when I arrived. I asked him to keep this information extremely quiet so no one was tipped off. I then made the smartest call in a long time. I called my immediate supervisor whom I had a very good relationship with. He was at the command center in Saratoga Springs for the escaped inmate manhunt. He knew me very well and had great confidence in me and my work. He also knew when he heard an alarming tone to my voice. He immediately told me he would join me at Native Textiles and not to do anything until he arrived. He could hear my tunnel vision. I thank God to this day he did stop me at that moment. It gave me a restart so I could now focus on what needed to be done and more importantly, it kept me from doing exactly what my tunnel vision wanted me to do and could have done. I arrived at Native Textiles before he did. Upon his arrival, I contacted Phil Cassella again and he went into the lace section of Native Textiles and walked Bill Burdick out to us. Now you must know, it is very unusual for a plant manager to ask an employee to walk out with them. Upon Bill coming out, I went up and shook hands with him as if nothing happened and it was just another beautiful fall day. I said to him, "Bill, you promised me that if we had additional questions, then you would sit down with us anytime." He acknowledged this was true. I told him we just had some routine follow up questions as I opened the back door to my supervisor's car and sat him in the back seat. The look on his face and shocked expression came out as we started to drive away. "Where are we going?" I told him that we needed to go over everything again from the beginning and it was too difficult to accomplish this in the car. I told him that we would go to our office, cover everything, and then bring him right back to work. I promised him that Phil Cassella was okay with this and would not charge him the time off. I told him it was very important because we needed to go over all the minute details in case we missed something that could be important. He seemed good with this explanation. We drove the 10 – 15 minutes up the Northway to the State Police Queensbury office. We went into the interview room and I sat him down in the appropriate chair. The setup of interview rooms and positioning of suspects is very important to a good outcome. The room should be small with a plain table and four plain chairs with no distractions in there. In this room, there was a two-way mirror, but this was long before the standard recording setups. I sat him on my side of the small table with me next to him and between him and the door. The symbolic escape route. My supervisor sat across the table from us. I led the entire interview. If it were my choice, I would have read the Miranda Warnings to Bill prior to starting this interview. It was not my call and my supervisor was afraid we would "spook" him, so we went right into the interview. For the first 45 minutes or so, I went over the same details of the case Bill related many times. Painstaking details and descriptions of everything. Over and over we went over every detail. After 45 minutes, I looked at Bill and told him that we found Stephanie.

It is hard to describe his body gestures in words. He showed no stress, no worry, no sign of deceit. He sat with his legs crossed and his chin comfortably cupped in his hand. His immediate reply was something like this: "Really, that's great. Where is she? How is she?" I looked right into his eyes to read them and said, "We found her body in your house, in your basement, under your workbench and you are the last person to see her. Tell us what happened." Without a hint of concern, guilt, or stress, he replied many times, "Look, I know you think I did this and it looks like I did, but I'm telling you I did not have anything to do with this." We went back and forth this same way with just a little different wording, and each time he calmly denied any guilt. At one point my supervisor across the table came down very hard slamming both hands on the table. I did not see it coming and I jumped up. Bill did the same thing, but with no effect. He continued to deny any involvement. Finally, I asked him to give us a plausible explanation as to how this could happen with him having no involvement after she was found in his house, in his basement, under his workbench, with him having nothing to do with this. He then proceeded to do just that. The explanation he provided would have been very easy to believe and accept, but something in me reading him today, and the day I planted those seeds, told me different. My gut feeling reading him was no, he did do this and you must get it out of him. His explanation was as follows:

> *When Stephanie decided to leave Frank for good, she had to come to our house to use the phone. She made the call and we smoked a cigarette and she left to get her baby and wait for her mom. Frank and everyone knew she made that call from our house. He knew this was the last place she was before he killed her. You know he has knocked her out before. When she went back to her apartment, Frank got mad when he found out she was leaving him for good and he killed her and then brought her back to my house and hid her in the basement to make it look like I did it because this was the last place she was when she made that phone call to her mom.*

While telling me this very believable story, he continued sitting there with his legs crossed and his chin cupped in his hand. He seemed very believable and like he did not have a concern in the world. After a few more minutes of going back and forth on this, my supervisor left out of frustration and maybe because he wanted me to go to work.

I have been to many trainings on interview and interrogation. Some good, some great, and some just okay. You take what you learn and you add these techniques to your own toolbox. Not all techniques will work for each interviewer. Over the past 20 years and continuing today, I now teach interview and interrogation. Part of this is my success in obtaining confessions. I have over an 80% confession rate in all cases, including major cases. I then went to work. I tried every technique I ever learned or invented myself. Most had no seeming effect on him. I continued working. My goal was to hit one of those seeds I planted that previous Friday when taking him down to the polygraph. I kept shooting and I kept missing. Or so it seemed. I continued anyway, relentlessly. I never give up. While doing this, I was using a truly successful technique in all cases. I was slowly breaking our body spacing. Little by little, while shooting and shooting to hit those planted seeds, I moved closer and closer to him. Finally, I was so close, our bodies were touching and I had my right arm around his shoulders and my left hand on his left knee. I kept frantically shooting. People have said many times over the years that people confess to me to get me to shut up and leave. I don't care as long as it works. Some things in life you will never forget. I will never in my life forget the moment that this sociopath's head dropped like a rock. It dropped with a noticeable sound down toward his lap. I will never forget his words as his head reached its lowest point. "Okay, I did it. I will tell you what happened." This sadistic murderer's head never came up again. Not once during the next few hours taking his horrendous confession and going over all the details. Although his head never came up again, his eyes did. Now I had to move quickly. I pulled out a Miranda form and read Bill his constitutional rights. He signed the waiver at 3:50 P.M. and proceeded to tell me a story that haunts me today. Never in all of my horrendous cases did I ever emotionally lose it later on to the point I truly wanted to check Bill back out of jail, drive him down a dirt road with no weapons, and proceed to exact justice from him. I will explain. After the Miranda was read, I went right into our conversation and soon wrote out his confession based on his words. He went over the background for that day, not knowing she would show up at his house to use the phone. Upon overhearing the phone call and talking to her, he was convinced she was serious about leaving Frank and going back to Vermont with her mom to start over. He knew this was going to be his last chance to have his way with her. He did invite her down to the cellar for a cigarette, but she only wanted one and said she had to get going. He made up an excuse about having her help him with moving a desk and when she went upstairs, he tried to take from her what he could not have. He started physically and sexually abusing her. She told him that this was it and she fought for her life. He related how she fought for her life, including using her knee repeatedly to try to kick him off from her. He proceeded to choke her until thinking she was dead. He then panicked because he realized it was time for his wife to come home on her lunch hour, so he quickly moved her body off the bed and hid her lifeless body under the bed. While doing this, her body made death-gurgling sounds of air escaping that sounded like breathing, so he grabbed stereo cable from his speakers and wrapped them around her neck as a ligature and choked her more. Shortly after hiding her body under the master bed, Terri did come through the front door. If the next part was not in his confession and coming directly from him, I would not expect you to believe it. Bill and his wife were not getting along that well for a long time and sex was almost nonexistent. Of all days for this to happen, when she came home for lunch, she wanted to surprise him and offered to have sex with him on her lunch hour. Try to imagine that scene. Unknowing to her, her beloved niece was dead and under her bed when she made this offer. Bill did not have time to think and told her he was not feeling very well and therefore he did not want to have sex. Of course he had to say that. She accepted his answer and said she was having a quick lunch because she had errands to do before going back to work. After she left for work, Bill went upstairs and pulled Stephanie's lifeless body out from under the bed and place her on the master bed. He then set up a video camera on a stereo speaker and looked through the lens until he had the perfect angle. He then went to Stephanie and pulled her sweatshirt up, exposing her very large breasts. He then straddled her body and proceeded to masturbate himself with her breasts. All this while taping it to save for later perverted pleasure. Not every word of this is included in his detailed statement below because he did not include everything, but they were part of what he told me. As I said earlier, his head never came up, but his eyes did. Going back, when Bill's head dropped and he started admitting to his actions, my supervisor and others were observing and listening through the two-way mirror.

About 10-15 minutes into his statement, my supervisor came back into the interview room and again sat down on the other side of the table. He was experienced enough that he knew to play off me. Every time Bill got to very bad and horrible details, his eyes rose up and he studied me and my supervisor to see if there was any reaction. Despite wanted to cringe, grab him, and scream out, we were both very disciplined to show no reaction and no facial expressions. Just one expression of disgust would have shut him and the remainder of the interview down forever. We were very disciplined. We were trained well. He said after he shut the video camera off, he had to figure out what to do with her. He knew their daughter was coming home soon from school. To buy time, he decided to drag her lifeless body down two flights of stairs and into the basement to hide her under the workbench until he could figure out a final solution for her body. I asked Bill what he did with the videotape he made. He explained that not long after he hid her body and his daughter came home, Stephanie's mother came there looking for her and immediately reported her as a missing person. He stated that there was never a time from that moment on that his house was empty. It was the extended family command post for the search for Stephanie. He knew he had to get those tapes out of the house for fear of them being discovered. I asked him where they currently were and he stated that this tape and others were put into a McDonald's food bag with garbage and put on the floor of the passenger side of his car which was currently parked at Native Textiles. He said the other tapes included him stalking Stephanie from his attic while she was swimming in their pool out back with Terri while wearing a bikini. He said other tapes were him and Teri having sex and him and other girlfriends having sex. My supervisor was disciplined too. Bill's eyes spied on us for any reaction as he described the tapes and their location. After about 10 more minutes, my supervisor excused himself to use the restroom and ran out and called the closest State Trooper and Glens Falls City detective to go to Native Textiles and locate Bill's car with Vermont plates. He gave them strict orders to not touch or search the car, but to look in the back window and see if there were McDonald's bags on the back seat floor. They arrived and observed the bags just as he described and their orders were to now guard those cars until a search warrant could be obtained and they could be thoroughly searched. He did obtain a search warrant while I finished the interview and statement and they did find all the tapes he described, exactly where and how he described them. During the interview, I asked Bill what he was going to do with her body. He again explained that there was never a time when their house did not have family members in it. He stated that his first attempt was to dig into the dirt floor to bury her. Anyone who has ever had a dirt cellar floor understands what hard pan is. You can't dig into it. Much like cement. He said he found that out and quickly gave up. His only other plan was to find a time to bring her body in his car to one of the many stone and granite quarries bordering the New York – Vermont border. These quarries go down hundreds of feet and are filled with ice-cold water. He said he planned on weighting her body down with stones and dumping her into a quarry body of water. Again he said he could never do this and he was out of ideas until his house someday emptied out.

After search warrants were executed on Bill's house and car and he was placed into jail, I had to drive to Albany to view that videotape to prepare for a preliminary hearing the next day to keep Bill in jail. Anyone who has spent hours on obtaining a confession knows it physically and mentally exhausts you. Like running a marathon. This, after the day starting with leads and viewing her lifeless body. It ended with having to view that disgusting and horrendous video. Now you know why my reaction of wanting to check Bill out of jail. The next day, I had a previously scheduled interview with a young 19- or 20-year-old guy that had a relationship with his 16-year-old girlfriend. Just under the age of consent in New York. They were actually dating and not just a sexual relationship, so most of the times we don't make arrests for this misdemeanor. Because her parents were insisting, I had to complete the investigation and arrest. He came into my office for this interview and arrest and unfortunately I was in the middle of coordinating with the two legal secretaries in the District Attorney's office. Now I am very close to both of these ladies from doing so many cases with them and they were both like sisters to me. I have never lost it on a phone like I did with them. It was not at them; it was the situation. I was figuratively eating the phone and saying things I can't even put into this book. They knew me well enough that both of them took turns finding reasons to check in with me by phone every 10 minutes or so. I can't explain how much I lost it that day other than the expression on this young man's face. After a few of these calls he listened to and seeing me, when I finally turned to him to deal with his interview, his face was ashen white and he raised his hands and said to me that he did it and he will tell me anything I wanted to know about his relationship with his girlfriend. The quickest and easiest confession I ever took. I never even had to work for it. Again, I can't explain what that entire case did to me other than to say that even now, while typing this out, my eyes are completely filled with tears.

Bill Burdick's family had money. Enough money that they were able to hire the best attorney in the entire capital district area. This attorney was so good, and we had other cases together, that he became my attorney for anything I ever needed like civil cases and I have referred him many times to friends and family. He was the first attorney to beat me in court. One of the only ones in my career. I did not have much of a chance in that case and the difference with him in court compared to other attorneys is night and day. I got my revenge in this case. He put me and my supervisor through a rigorous suppression hearing to quash the confession. Without the confession, we have no true evidence including the search warrant with the tapes. His best legal argument was delay in reading required Miranda Warnings to his client at the beginning of the interview. As I stated, have taught interview and interrogations for many years and I also teach law enforcement other legal issues. I actually enjoy testifying so I try to also teach officers how to testify properly. When my supervisor testified, I had no idea what he was asked or what he said. I did know the law though and it was on my side. We won this suppression hearing and this top attorney pled his client out to the maximum sentence allowed by law. He received a sentence of 25 years to life.

THE CONFESSION

>**Start Time: 3:50 P.M.**
>
>*I am at the Queensbury State Police station & I know that I am not under arrest. Investigator's Aiken & Kelleher came to my work today & asked me to answer some more questions about Stephanie Sady's dis-*

appearance and I agreed to go with them and answer their questions. I have worked at Native Textiles since March of 1993. On Monday morning 09-19-94, I got up before Jill went to school & I went downstairs & went to the bathroom. I wasn't feeling good so I went back up to bed. This was between 7:00 A.M. & 7:30 A.M. & my wife Terrie had already gone to work at the Grand Union. I got up again after 10:00 & went downstairs & still did not feel good & I threw up after drinking coffee. I then smoked a cigarette down in the basement & came upstairs into the living room & lay down on the couch & watched TV. I dozed on & off into sleep & at some point I took my temperature & it was 100.4 F. Around 10 minutes before noon I got in the shower because I wasn't sure if it was going to work. Around the end of my shower (downstairs shower) I heard the back door shut. I said hello & Stephanie said that she needed to use the phone. I heard her crying on the phone & I got dried off & got dressed & I came out into the living room to comb my hair because the bathroom mirror was fogged up. Stephanie was at the kitchen table holding her head in her hands & she looked like she was crying & her face was red & her hair was messed up. Stephanie told me that she had been fighting with Frank & he took off with their baby on foot. She just kept saying that this was it & she was leaving Frank & she was getting her baby & moving back to Rutland. She said she could still get in this semester for College, but I said that I didn't think she should be starting school right now. I asked her if Frank hit her today & she said no, that it was just a pushing & shoving match. I asked Stephanie if she wanted a hug & I put out my arms & she stood up & we hugged each other. I asked Stephanie if she wanted a cigarette & she said yes & we both went into the basement & smoked a cigarette. I asked her if she wanted another one & she said no. I asked her what time it was & she looked at her blue watch & said that it was about 12:30 P.M. She said that she had to get going & we went upstairs. She started to leave & I asked Stephanie if she wanted to help me move a desk upstairs. She said yes & we both went upstairs and into my bedroom. I grabbed her to hug her & she pushed me away & I pushed her & she fell on her stomach onto my bed. I jumped on top of her & turned her over & she said to me, "What are you doing?" I told her that I was helping her. I started choking Stephanie with my hands & she kept hitting me in my ass with her knee & she then passed out & I thought then that she was dead. I didn't know what to do then so I put Stephanie under my bed because I knew my wife Terrie was coming home for lunch. Terrie came home a little bit after 1:00 P.M. & she asked me where Stephanie was because she saw her car in our driveway. Terrie said that she wanted to surprise me & have sex on her lunch hour, but I told her that I didn't want to because I didn't feel good. Terry had a quick sandwich & left for the cleaners & bank. She came home for a few minutes & then left for work shortly before 2:00 P.M. I went back upstairs & pulled Stephanie back out. When I did this her sweatshirt pulled up & her breasts came out of her bra. I put her on my bed & fondled her bare breasts for a few minutes. I then got our Panasonic camcorder from under a blanket on a trunk. I set this up on a stereo speaker & turned it on. I then recorded myself while fondling Stephanie's breasts. I think I had sweats on & I took my penis out & fondled her breasts with my penis. I put the camcorder off & away & I took the videotape & put it in my strongbox by my desk in the bedroom. I then went downstairs & smoked some cigarettes while trying to figure out what to do with her body. I forgot to say that when I moved Stephanie off the bed & put her under the bed before Terrie got home, Stephanie's body made a gasp & I wasn't sure if she was alive so I took stereo speaker wire that was loose behind the stereo. It's grey & about 4' long & I choked Stephanie by tying it around her neck. I left it there & took it off before moving it back downstairs & I put it back behind the dresser. I knew Jill was coming home & I thought the neighbor next door would see me if I took her outside, so I dragged Stephanie downstairs by her arms. I dragged her all the way down the cellar & I hid her under the workbench. I moved stuff out to put her under there & I hid her behind insulation & a garbage bag full of stuff from hunting camp. I think that her sweatshirt was still over her head. At some point while moving her, Stephanie's sweatshirt came off & I tried putting it back over her head under the bench. I went back upstairs & smoked more cigarettes until Jill came home from school. I sent Jill over to Frank's to look for Stephanie so that I could cover my tracks & she came back & said that just Frank & the baby were there. From that point on, everything I said was the truth. I could never bring myself to move Stephanie & I was very nervous when Det. Hunt & Fred Washburn came over & I showed them where we smoked in the cellar. I also forgot to say that Monday I called in sick from work around 1:00 P.M. because I was sick & I was so upset with what I did. I didn't go back to work until Thursday & I took missing posters with me. I also remember now that at one point I twisted Stephanie's neck with my hands because I didn't know if she was dead. The next day, Tuesday, I took the videotape of me fondling Stephanie, and other tapes of me having sex with Terrie & another old girlfriend & a videotape of when I spied on Stephanie wearing a bathing suit; & I put all of them in my mother's car. I was driving it until my car got fixed & I put them all in my car on I think Thursday morning. There are 2 big tapes & I think 4 small videotapes & they are all at Native Textiles right now. It is the only car there with Vermont *plates – 336C5. The 4 tapes are in a McDonald's bag on the back floor behind the passenger seat. The 2 big tapes are under the front passenger seat. When I choked Stephanie, she was wearing a gray McDonald's sweatshirt with fancy stripes, a beige bra, blue jeans, a belt & boots. I feel that Stephanie's family should stomp me to death for killing Stephanie & may god bless my family. I loved Stephanie dearly & she deserved more than she had & I was angry when I knew she would go back to Frank again. I have been advised by Investigator Aiken of the State Police that it is a crime in New York State to knowingly make a false written statement.*

End Time: 5:20 P.M.

Epilogue:

Sometime around the summer of 2019, 25 years after Bill Burdick pled guilty and was sentenced to a state prison term of 25 years to life, Bill Burdick was eligible for parole. With the direction the state of New York has been trending to, most people are getting out on parole. Even evil, horrendous murderers. The retired Granville Police Chief, who later put himself through Law School, contacted me and the other police officers that worked this case. He also started a Facebook page requesting people to contact the parole board with letters in an attempt to convince them not to grant Bill Burdick parole. I wrote my heartfelt letter, through many more tears of writing, and submitted this to the New York State Police board. I also worked with the retired District Attorney that prosecuted that case, Robert Winn, and a copy of the tape was sent to the parole board. People of New York and this country in whole can now rest easier and safer knowing that our efforts worked and he will be held in prison for a few more years until his next parole hearing. We will write letters then too.

Final Epilogue:

On Wednesday, December 2nd, 2020, I received a VINE Link notification regarding William Burdick. I fully explain the meaning and value of registering for VINE Link in Chapter 21. Immediately upon receiving this notification and hearing that the custody status of William Burdick has changed, rage fill my every sense and cell of my body. How dare the parole board release this monster early after all he did and all we went through to keep him in. Early, because the next possible release date was not until June of 2021. I then continued listening and heard the best news I could. William Burdick's custody status had changed because he was deceased. I can't tell you how many monsters I have signed up for through VINE Link, but William Burdick was at the top of the list. Attached in this book is a Post Star article dated December 6th, 2020, detailing his death in prison. It starts out with *"The Granville man who killed his niece 26 years ago has died in prison, authorities said Friday. William A. Burdick, 54, was pronounced dead at about 6:50 A.M. on Wednesday. Burdick was incarcerated at the Coxsackie Regional Medical Unit, according to the state Department of Corrections and Community Supervision."*

Now They Lay Me Down to Rest

William Burdick Confession

GENL. 15 6/85

STATEMENT

STATE OF NEW YORK PAGE ONE OF 5 PAGES
COUNTY OF Washington DATED: 09/27/94
Village OF Granville
I, William Adin Burdick, AGE 28, BORN ON 04/12/66
AND RESIDING AT 3 Lincoln St Granville, NY 12832
HAVE BEEN ADVISED BY Investigator Thomas M. Aiken
OF THE New York State Police, OF THE FOLLOWING:

I HAVE THE RIGHT TO REMAIN SILENT, AND I DO NOT HAVE TO MAKE ANY STATEMENT IF I DON'T WANT TO.
IF I GIVE UP THAT RIGHT, ANYTHING I DO SAY CAN AND WILL BE USED AGAINST ME IN A COURT OF LAW.
I HAVE THE RIGHT TO HAVE A LAWYER PRESENT BEFORE MAKING ANY STATEMENT OR AT ANY TIME DURING THIS STATEMENT.
IF I SHOULD DECIDE I DO WANT A LAWYER, AND I CANNOT AFFORD TO HIRE ONE, A LAWYER WILL BE APPOINTED FOR ME FREE OF CHARGE AND I MAY HAVE THAT LAWYER PRESENT BEFORE MAKING ANY STATEMENT.
I ALSO UNDERSTAND THAT I HAVE THE RIGHT TO STOP AT ANY TIME DURING THIS STATEMENT AND REMAIN SILENT AND HAVE A LAWYER PRESENT.
I FULLY UNDERSTAND THESE RIGHTS, AND AT THIS TIME I AGREE TO GIVE UP MY RIGHTS AND MAKE THE FOLLOWING STATEMENT:

SIGNATURE — William A Burdick 3:50 PM
WITNESS — Inv. Thomas M A

I am at the Queensbury State Police Station & I know that I am not under arrest. Investigators Aiken & Kelleher came to my work today & asked me to answer some more questions about Stephanie Snay's disappearance and I agreed to go with them and answer their questions. I have worked at Native Textiles since March of 1993. On Monday morning 09/19/94, I got up before Jill went to school & I went downstairs & went to the bathroom. I wasn't feeling good so I went back up to bed. This was between 7:00AM & 7:30AM & my wife Terrye had already gone to work at the Grand Union. I got up again after 10:00AM & went downstairs & still did not feel good & I threw up after

GENL. 19A 6/85
STATEMENT CONTINUATION SHEET   PAGE 2 OF 5 PAGES
NAME: William A. Burdick   DATE 09/27/94

drinking coffee. I then smoked a cigarette down in the basement & came upstairs into the livingroom & layed down on the couch & watched TV. I dozed on & off into sleep & at some point I took my temperature & it was 100.4 F. Around 10 minutes before noon I got in the shower because I wasn't sure if I was going to work. Around the end of my shower (downstairs shower) I heard the back door shut. I said hello & Stephanie said that she needed to use the phone. I heard her crying on the phone & I got dried off & got dressed & I came out into the livingroom to comb my hair because the bathroom mirror was fogged up. Stephanie was at the kitchen table holding her head in her hands & she looked like she was crying & her face was red & her hair was messed up. Stephanie told me that she had been fighting with Frank & he took off with their baby on foot. She just kept saying that this was it & she was leaving Frank & she was getting her baby & moving to Rutland. She said she could still get in this semester for college, but I said that I didn't think she should be starting school right now. I asked her if Frank hit her today & she said no, that it was just a pushing & shoving match. I asked Stephanie if she wanted a hug & I put out my arms & she stood up & we hugged each other. I asked Stephanie if she wanted a cigarette & she said yes & we both went into the basement & smoked a cigarette. I asked her if she wanted another one & she said no. We talked some more & asked her again if Frank hit her & she said no. I asked her what time it was & she looked at her blue watch & said that it

Now They Lay Me Down to Rest

GENL. 19A 6/85

STATEMENT CONTINUATION SHEET   PAGE 3 OF 5 PAGES

NAME: William A. Burdick   DATE 09/27/94

was about 12:30 pm. She said that she had to get going & we went upstairs. She started to leave & I asked Stephanie if she wanted to help me move a desk upstairs. She said yes & we both went upstairs into my bedroom. I grabbed her to hug her & she pushed me away & she I pushed her & she fell on her stomach onto my bed. I jumped on top of her & turned her over & she said to me, "What are you doing?" I told her that I was helping her. I started choking Stephanie with my hands & she kept hitting me in my ass with her knee & she then passed out & I thought then that she was dead. I didn't know what to do then so I put Stephanie under my bed because I knew my wife Terrie was coming home for lunch. Terrie came home a little bit after 1:00 pm & she asked me where Stephanie was because she saw her car in our driveway. Terrie said that she wanted to surprise me & have sex on her lunch hour, but I told her that I didn't want to because I didn't feel good. Terry had a quick sandwich & left for the cleaners & bank. She came home for a few minutes & then left for work shortly before 2:00 pm. I went back upstairs & pulled Stephanie back out. When I did this her sweatshirt pulled up & her breasts came out of her bra. I put her on my bed & fondled her bare breasts for a few minutes. I then got our Panasonic camcorder from under a blanket on a trunk. I set this up on a stereo speaker & turned it on. I then recorded myself while fondling Stephanie's breasts. I think I had sweats on & I took my penis out & fondled her breasts with my penis. I put the camcorder off & away & I took the

CONNIE L. AIKEN AND THOMAS M. AIKEN

GENL. 19A 6/85
STATEMENT CONTINUATION SHEET   PAGE 4 OF 5 PAGES
NAME: William A. Burdick   DATE 09/27/94

Video tape & put it in my strongbox by my desk in the bedroom. I then went downstairs & smoked some cigarettes while trying to figure out what to do with her body. I forgot to say that when I moved Stephanie off the bed & put her under the bed before Terrie got home, Stephanie's body made a gasp & I wasn't sure if she was alive so I took stereo speaker wire that was loose behind stereo. It's grey & about 4' long & I choked Stephanie by tying it around her neck. I left it there & took it off before moving it back downstairs & I put it back behind the dresser.

I knew Jill was coming home & I thought the neighbor next door would see me if I took her outside, so I dragged Stephanie downstairs by her arms. I dragged her all the way down cellar & I hid her under the work bench. I moved stuff out to put her under there & I hid her behind insulation & a garbage bag full of stuff from hunting camp. I think that her sweatshirt was still over her head. At some point while moving her, Stephanie's sweatshirt came off & I tried putting it back over her head under the bench. I went back upstairs & smoked more cigarettes until Jill came home from school. I sent Jill over to Frank's to look for Stephanie so that I could cover my tracks & she came back & said that just Frank & the baby were there. From that point on, everything I said was the truth. I could never bring myself to move Stephanie & I was very nervous when Det. Hunt & Fred Washburn came over & I showed them where he smoked in the cellar. I also forgot

Now They Lay me Down to Rest

GENL. 19A 6/85

STATEMENT CONTINUATION SHEET   PAGE 5 OF 5 PAGES

NAME: William D. Burdick   DATE 09/27/94

To say that Monday I called in sick from work around 1pm because I was sick & I was so upset with what I did. I didn't go back to work until Thursday & I took missing posters with me. I also remember now that at one point I twisted Stephanie's neck with my hands because I didn't know if she was dead. The next day, Tuesday, I took the video tape of me fondling Stephanie, and other tapes of me having sex with Terrie & another old girlfriend & a video tape of when I spied on Stephanie wearing a bathing suit, & I put all of them in my mother's car. I was driving it until my car got fixed & I put them all in my car on I think Thursday morning. There are 2 big tapes & I think 4 small video tapes & they are all still in my car. My car is a 1989 Olds Calais (black) & it is parked at Native Textiles right now. It is the only car there with Vermont plates - 336C5c. The 4 tapes are in a McDonalds bag on the back floor behind the passenger seat. The 2 big tapes are under the front passenger seat. When I choked Stephanie, she was wearing a Grey McDonald's Sweatshirt with fancy stripes, a beige bra, blue jeans, a belt & boots. I feel that Stephanie's family should stomp me to death for killing Stephanie & may God bless my family. I loved Stephanie dearly & she deserved more than she had & I was angry when I knew she would go back to Frank again. I have been advised by Investigator Aiken of the State Police that it is a crime in New York State to knowingly make a false written statement.

Statement of: William A Burdick 5:20pm
Witness: Inv. Thomas M Cl
Witness: SIT _____

CONNIE L. AIKEN AND THOMAS M. AIKEN

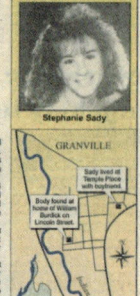

Now They Lay Me Down to Rest

Parole Appeal Letter – Connie Aiken

February 25, 2019

SORC
Woodbourne Correctional Facility
99 Prison Road
P.O. Box 1000
Woodbourne, NY 12788

Inmate William Burdick
Indictment # I-89-94
DIN # 95B0600

Parole Board Members,

    I am the wife of the State Police Investigator that took the confession of William Burdick. We have been married this July for 34 years. We have six children, three grown sons and three adopted daughters. People hear about how stressful it is to be married to police officers, but I can attest to this very true reality! I have lived through all of these 100's & 100's of horrendous crimes side by side with my husband. I know each case had an impact on him but a few are very vivid in my mind. William Burdick is one of those. A person who could pass a polygraph has no conscience. I truly believe that the expert police work and investigation could have possibly stopped a serial killer in the making. I will never forget my husband coming home after his confession. He had to somehow act like he didn't just hear the horrific, sadistic, perverted details that made his stomach turn, his head spin, and his heart ache knowing what Stephanie had endured at the hands of William Burdick. The sight of her decomposing body and horrific scene will always be a part of him now. He not only mourned Stephanie's death, but his heart ached for her son left behind. William Burdick never gave any of this a thought and how his actions would affect and haunt many people for a life time. He only thought about his own sadistic self. I can not stress enough that after living through this, that there is no place in society for William Burdick.

    I want to thank you for helping society and keeping William Burdick behind bars so there will never be a Stephanie Sady type case again at the hands of a true killer, William Burdick.

Respectfully,

Connie L. Aiken

CONNIE L. AIKEN AND THOMAS M. AIKEN

Parole Appeal Letter – Thomas Aiken

February 22, 2019

SORC
Woodbourne Correctional Facility
99 Prison Road
P.O. Box 1000
Woodbourne, NY 12788

        <u>Re:</u>   Inmate William Burdick
               Indictment # I-89-94
               DIN # 95B0600

Parole Board Members,

     My name is Thomas M. Aiken. I worked for the New York State Police for 30 years, retiring on December 30, 2013. In my 30 years, I worked major cases for 25 of those years, including approximately 100 horrendous homicide cases, robbery cases, major burglary cases, kidnapping cases, and over 700 of the most horrendous child abuse cases you could ever envision. I also supervised criminal units most of those 25 years that worked on these crimes. I taught Law Enforcement in New York and I am now certified to teach Law Enforcement in South Carolina where I live and currently continue to work in Law Enforcement.

     In my 30 years in New York, and total of 35 years in Law Enforcement to date, I have never felt the need to write to a parole board on any of my hundreds and hundreds of horrendous cases until I heard that William Burdick was up for parole. I was one of the lead investigators in that case and I ended up obtaining the confession from William Burdick that helped to obtain justice for beautiful Stephanie Sady and to help keep society safe from Burdick. This case was so horrendous and evil, that 25 years later I not only include it in lectures I do, but I can still recite his confession almost word for word. I still maintain a majority of the original case file since September of 1994. In all my homicide cases, I do not use the term evil lightly. Most of my homicides I investigated did not involve evil as people kill for a variety of reasons. I did walk with, sit down with, and talk to evil a handful of times, and William Burdick is at the top of this list.

     The clinical name associated with someone that is so cold they can beat a polygraph administered by one of the best New York State Police Senior Investigators and polygraph operators ever, is a sociopath. William Burdick is not only an evil murderer of a beautiful young lady that had her entire life ahead of her, he is a sociopath. He beat the best New York State Police interviewer and polygraph operator in a polygraph because he is evil and he is a sociopath. When Stephanie's beloved aunt, Williams's wife, went through the horror of discovering this beautiful young lady stuffed under a workbench in his basement after he viciously murdered her and then sexually abused and fondled her body after death, it started the final process of my interview with William Burdick. Aunt Terri was very close to her beloved Stephanie and she will have to live forever with the vision of this beautiful girl stuffed in an awkward position under this workbench surrounded by rolled pink house insulation to keep the smell from emanating to the rest of the house. Unfortunately for William, after eight days, the smell of her decomposing body came through and alerted her aunt to her final dumping spot. A beautiful little boy never experienced a life being loved and taught by his mother, who worked overtime at McDonald's to support herself and him the best she could. Her dreams of returning home to her mom in Vermont and finishing college to better her life for her and her baby will never be fulfilled.

1

Now They Lay me Down to Rest

As you make your decision, and I submit that the William Burdick's in this world should never breathe a breath of free air, please remember that he not only did these despicable acts, but after doing so, he led the tremendous professional and volunteer searches done to find Stephanie's body. He was the family spokesman and kept this up for a week, knowing where he dumped the body of this beautiful young lady as if she were trash to be disposed of. All of this because this evil sociopathic murdered, could not control his urges, and took what he could never get.

Stephanie was a beautiful and honorable young lady and put up, one time, with her Uncle Bill Burdick trying to put the moves on her. She immediately rebuffed him and because she loved her Aunt Teri so much, she left him with only a warning. "If you ever try anything like that again, I will tell Aunt Terri and have you arrested". Little did she know, that by his own admissions, William Burdick was stalking her and secretly talking photographs and videos of her from a small attic window while she was innocently swimming in a bikini in a small backyard pool with her beloved Aunt Terri.

One of the investigative techniques we do is to complete detailed interviews to ascertain that the suspect knew right from wrong to combat any future mental disease or defect defenses. With William Burdick, it was continuous. He knew how wrong it was to murder Stephanie because after fondling her dead body and knowing his wife Terri was coming home for lunch, he quickly hid her body under the master bed until she left to go back to work. He knew because he then carried this lifeless beautiful young lady down two flights of stairs and attempted to conceal her body under his workbench in his dirt floor basement and surrounding her body with rolled pink insulation to keep her from being found and to keep her decomposing body from alerting people until he could find a final and permanent dumping location for her body. He knew because he took the VHS and smaller videotapes of him secretly filming and stalking Stephanie and then fondling her dead body with his penis and he hid these tapes with garbage in McDonald bags under the seat of his car so no one would discover them. He knew because he attempted to dig into his hardpan dirt basement floor to dispose of her body. He knew because when he could not dig into this floor, his goal was to take her body and weight it down and dump it into one of the quarry ponds that are hundreds of feet deep on the Vermont / New York border.

Stephanie's fate began that day when she only went to her beloved Aunt Teri's house to use the telephone to call her mom across the border in Vermont to come and pick her and the baby up so she could start her life over and get back in college. William Burdick overheard this and knew this was his last chance to take what his urges wanted. As Stephanie was getting ready to leave, he asked her to go upstairs and move a piece of furniture with him. Of course, Stephanie suspected nothing and would help anyone, so she went upstairs and he again put the moves on her. She screamed and he threw her on the bed and choked her to death. As he was hiding her under the bed knowing Teri was coming home, he heard death gurgles and then took stereo speaker cord and continued choking her to make sure she was dead. When Terri left to go back to work, he took her lifeless body from under the bed and placed it on the master bed and set up a video recorder on a stereo speaker and proceeded to film himself sexually pleasing himself by fondling her lifeless body with his penis. Is this the type of man or person you want walking free in society with your family, loved ones, and other innocent people..?

In closing, I am strongly asking you to continue making society safe from the likes of sadistic murderers like William Burdick. He deserves no less than Stephanie, her baby, her mom, her Aunt Terri, and everyone else that loved her so much permanently received from William Burdick on September 19, 1994. He deserves a real life sentence of never walking free in society again. I know I will live forever with these events, his statement, and the viewing of this videotape etched in my psyche, but I can't imagine the pain that her baby lived with everyday for the past 24+ years without his mom holding his hand, watching his first steps, watching him graduate, watching him date, and watching him grow up to be a fine man and person.

Respectfully,

_____

Thomas M. Aiken

Now They Lay me Down to Rest

BREAKING   UPDATED: Fire tears through apartment building in Hudson Falls

https://poststar.com/news/local/granville-murderer-denied-parole/article_c9e5be54-ce65-5671-ab1e-c9d652a2b0e4.html

Granville murderer denied parole

DON LEHMAN dlehman@poststar.com   1 hr ago

William A. Burdick, right, is led into court for sentencing in March 1995 for the murder of his teenage niece in 1994. The former Granville man was eligible for parole from state prison this year.
Post-Star file photo

The Granville man who killed his niece 25 years ago has been denied parole, and will have to wait two more years before getting another shot at release from prison.

The state Parole Board decided earlier this month that William A. Burdick should remain behind bars until at least June 2021.

Burdick was eligible for parole next month, less than three months shy of 25 years from when he killed 17-year-old Stephanie Sady in his village of Granville home.

He admitted choking her to death, and police said he sexually assaulted her after killing her and videotaped the act of necrophilia. He hid her body in his basement, then took part in a search for her in Granville before police found Sady's remains.

Burdick pleaded guilty to second-degree murder and was sentenced to 25 years to life in state prison. His first chance at parole came this spring.

The parole board heard Burdick's case May 20. In a ruling released late last week, the board found that, even though Burdick had completed therapeutic programs in prison, release was not appropriate under the circumstances of the case.

"Your actions demonstrated a callous disregard for human life and remain a concern to this panel, especially when considering the aggravating factors involved in the instant offense," the board's decision reads.

Numerous family members, police officers, Granville area residents and the judge who sentenced him, former county Judge Philip Berke of Granville, weighed in against his parole after his eligibility got media attention in February.

Ronald Daigle, who was Granville's police chief at the time, helped organize the comments to the Parole Board, and he said he was glad to hear Burdick was denied parole.

"It is a great day for the whole community that this predator is denied parole," he said "I made sure that our community's voice was heard and I will continue, as long as I am alive, to fight any release for this monster."

Burdick, 53, is serving his sentence at medium security Woodbourne Correctional Facility in Sullivan County.

Don Lehman
reporter - crimes & courts, public safety and Warren County government

Don Lehman covers crime and Warren County government for The Post-Star. His work can be found on Twitter @PS_CrimeCourts and on poststar.com/app/blogs.

Now They Lay Me Down to Rest

https://poststar.com/news/local/crime-and-courts/granville-man-who-killed-17-year-old-niece-in-1994-dies-in-prison/article_4d2b2e5a-2f58-547c-a563-1e775233ad18.html

Granville man who killed 17-year-old niece in 1994 dies in prison

Michael Goot
Dec 6, 2020

SALE! Subscribe for $1/mo.

William A. Burdick, right, is led into court for sentencing in March 1995 for the murder of his teenage niece in 1994. The former Granville man died on Wednesday.

Connie L. Aiken and Thomas M. Aiken

Post-Star file photo

Michael Goot

The Granville man who killed his niece 26 years ago has died in prison, authorities said Friday.

William A. Burdick, 54, was pronounced dead at about 6:50 a.m. on Wednesday. Burdick was incarcerated at the Coxsackie Regional Medical Unit, according to the state Department of Corrections and Community Supervision.

Corrections officials did not disclose the cause or manner of death. An autopsy will be conducted by the Greene County Medical Examiner's Office. The Coxsackie Regional Medical Unit is a 60-bed long-term care facility for inmates.

Burdick was serving a sentence of 25 years to life in prison after pleading guilty to second-degree murder in February 1995.

Burdick admitted that he choked 17-year-old Stephanie Sady to death in his village of Granville home. He then sexually assaulted her after killing her and videotaped the act of necrophilia.

The case shook the local community. Sady was reported missing by her mother, Gloria Davis, on Sept. 19, 1994. Sady had been living with Davis in Rutland, Vermont, while she was pregnant and gave birth to her son Patrick.

A group of 75 residents, including Burdick, searched yards, homes, businesses, rivers and woods, according to *Post-Star* archives.

Family members believed that she did not run away because she was a good mother and responsible person. She was working at McDonald's on the morning of her disappearance. She came home sick.

Now They Lay me Down to Rest

Relatives said she had an argument with her boyfriend and father of her child on the morning of her disappearance.

Police said Sady went to a neighbor's apartment to place a collect call to her mother because they had no phone in her apartment. Then, she took the car to the Lincoln Street home of the Burdicks. Her plan was to walk home to get her son, return with him to get the car and then drive to her mother's home in Rutland.

However, the car stayed parked in the Burdick's driveway.

There was no sign of Sady until on Sept. 27, 1994, when Burdick's wife and sister found her under a workbench in the basement of the Burdick home.

William Burdick told police that he had lured Sady into his bedroom under the pretense of helping him move furniture. He then made sexual advances toward her, which she rebuffed, and he strangled her during a struggle on the bed.

Burdick's defense had attempted to suppress the evidence seized at Burdick's home and car, which had the videotape of his necrophilia. After that was unsuccessful, Burdick pleaded guilty before his trial was set to begin in March 1995.

Burdick was denied parole in his first opportunity in June 2019. The parole board determined that he had completed therapeutic programs in prison, but his release was not appropriate under the circumstances.

He would have been eligible for parole again in June 2021.

Burdick was serving his sentence at Woodbourne Correctional Facility in Sullivan County at the time of his parole hearing, but was moved at some point since then.

Reach Michael Goot at 518-742-3320 or **mgoot@poststar.com** and follow his blog poststar.com/blogs/michael_goot/.

💬 0 comments

Sign up for our Crime & Courts newsletter

CONNIE L. AIKEN AND THOMAS M. AIKEN

CHAPTER 17
TIME OUT

This chapter will again be written by Tom. The Grand Jury presentation, like everything else about this case, was not normal or free from the David Pope anger and control. Before we start that, what exactly is a Grand Jury...? The short answer is: A Grand Jury is the mechanism or vehicle that takes a case from a local court to a superior court for the final adjudication. I have testified hundreds and hundreds of times in front of Grand Jury panels in many counties throughout New York and now South Carolina. My longest testimony involving one case involved a house explosion where 6 people were killed, including a 3-month-old girl. I testified over three different days for a total of 5-6 hours. Most all states have the same set up for a Grand Jury, but they do not all present the same way. A Grand Jury consists of 16-23 citizens from the community that sit for a designated period of time like 6 months, and meet on a regular schedule to hear cases continuously. Their job is to decide if there is enough evidence to advance the case to Superior Court (called a true bill) or that there is not enough evidence to advance (a no bill). It takes 12 or more votes to approve an indictment. Their job is not to decide guilt or innocence, just to decide if there is enough evidence to hold the case over to a Superior Court. I am now working in South Carolina and a Grand Jury presentation down there is much different than in New York. In New York, a Grand

Jury presentation is almost like a mini trial. The presentation is usually run by the District Attorney or one of his assistants, and the 16-23 grand jurors sit and hear the testimony. The District Attorney's office will not present their entire case, or even most of it, just enough to satisfy the legal requirements of proving enough evidence to advance the case. A stenographer is taking down all testimony. The District Attorney will ask the questions of each witness and at the end, Grand Jurors can ask questions, but usually with permission from the prosecutor presenting the case. The rules that apply to a trial also apply to Grand Jury including the fact that no hearsay evidence is allowed. This is not the same in South Carolina. One officer presents the entire case, so obviously hearsay is allowed. In New York, the witnesses must come and testify themselves. This can be a problem with very young child abuse victims. A defendant has the right and choice to testify before the Grand Jury. If they chose to testify, they must sign a waiver of immunity prior to any questions or testimony. The reason for this is that all witnesses who testify have immunity to what they testify about unless they sign a waiver in advance. A defendant has the right to have an attorney with them, but that attorney cannot speak or answer any questions. If a prosecutor fails to allow them to testify or even give them notice, an appeals court will throw out the indictment. This came to play in this case. David Pope showed his usual contempt and he wanted to be in control. He went back and forth with his decision to testify, causing the District Attorney's office to hold off on voting and delaying this case in Grand Jury for a couple of weeks. This almost two-week delay means there could be evidence and testimony forgotten by the Grand Jurors as they hear dozens of major cases every week they sit. Not this Grand Jury. Like the actual trial jury, they would never forget this case, the testimony they heard, or the images they had to endure seeing. When we present a case to the Grand Jury, we do not put most of the evidence or testimony in. Only enough to prove that a felony was committed and that there is enough evidence to "true bill" the case. We don't tip our entire hand. In the David Pope case, we only subpoenaed 18 witnesses to achieve our goal. Something happened that has never happened before. After only 12 witnesses, the Grand Jury, through the jury foreperson, requested or should I say begged the District Attorney to stop. They called a timeout. They said they did not need anymore and that they could not handle anymore. These are Grand Jurors that hear death, major cases, and homicide cases every week. They actually pleaded with us to stop, that they heard enough. This does not and has not ever happened in my career or the District Attorney's career. There is something else special about this Grand Jury. Little Washington County, New York, used to average a homicide every year or two. This Grand Jury had to sit through 5 of the most horrendous murder cases ever. I testified in every one of them. This was one right after another for them. One was a very sad case of a volunteer fireman leaving his daughter's birthday party at his home with many friends and relatives for a fire call in Hudson Falls at the Kingsbury Hotel. This was a very nice older-style hotel in the middle of this small village. This hotel, which was a total loss, was built in 1899 and had character you don't see anymore. It was three stories high with 45 rooms. As he was fighting this fire, the fire overtook the roof and upper floors with him and others trapped and ordered to get out. This is called a flashover. The others made it out, but he did not. As if this could not get any more tragic, the fire did not have to be. It was set by a male suspect who did it just to set the hotel on fire. He obviously had issues, but the fire was intentionally set taking the life of this dad away from a loving family. A dad who left his daughter's happy birthday party. This daughter and his entire family will never be the same. He left behind three young daughters that were 10, 7, and 4 years old. Another was an evil drug user that needed his fix and when he was told no by the drug dealer, he took the hammer to the head of her, her 7-year-old daughter, and her 17-year-old sister that was due to give birth at the same time. She lived as did her 7-year-old daughter, but this daughter is paralyzed on the entire left side of her body. Her sister died but was kept on life support long enough to have her baby boy successfully delivered. This case is talked about in another chapter. Another case was a guy who was upset with his wife and took a full-size axe to her face, head, and body as she slept in her bed. She obviously did not live, but her 7-year-old niece did after he used the axe on her. She survived, but with no life. She is in a wheelchair and cannot move any part of her body and is kept alive with a forced breathing and feeding tube.

The fifth case is fully documented in an entire chapter of this book. It is the Bill Burdick case. A case where he tried to sexually abuse a beautiful 17-year-old girl and when she fought him, he murdered her and sexually abused her after death while videotaping this abuse. This tragic case is fully documented because it took a week away from me investigating the David Pope case. These cases all took time away when it came to adjudicating them until their plea bargains or trials. I will never forget watching Grand Jurors coming out from all of these cases and watching them use the restroom on breaks and hearing that many were vomiting. Even with this, they all stuck it out through all of these and came back with true bills on each case. They all wanted to fulfill their duties. They were true Troopers. Many of us involved in these cases said that we truly believed these Grand Jurors needed counselling after just these five cases alone.

When it came to presenting this case, the District Attorney and I used a unique strategy. We knew David Pope's contempt toward children, but he had the same contempt for females. When it came to David Pope actually testifying, we used the First Assistant District Attorney, Nancy Lynn Ferrini, to question him. It did not take long with Nancy Lynn asking tough and pointed questions of David that he blew up in front of the very startled Grand Jury. The District Attorney, Rob Winn, said you could see the fear in their faces. He rose from his chair and went to the exhibit table and grabbed his signed waiver of immunity and tore it up in front of a very scared panel of Grand Jurors. They actually had the chance to see and feel the same fear that Hodgie felt every day of his very short 2 years of life. As I document in the chapter about the trial, these two halves of his Grand Jury immunity waiver became exhibits at the trial. His testimony did finish and the Grand Jurors unanimously voted to send this case to superior court with a true bill indictment. There was a comment overheard after where a Grand Juror questioned why he even bothered to testify.

GRAND JURY SUBPOENA

IN THE NAME OF THE PEOPLE OF THE STATE OF NEW YORK

TO: Mae Evelyn Kelley
R.R. 2, Box 2009A
Route 4
Fort Ann, New York 12827

You are commanded to appear before the Grand Jury of the County of Washington, at the Grand Jury Room located on the Second Floor of the County Courthouse Building, Route 4, Fort Edward, New York, on October 20, 1994, at 9:00 o'clock in the forenoon of that day, as a witness in a criminal action prosecuted by the People of the State of New York against

DAVID POPE

This you are not to omit under the penalties provided by law.

Dated at Fort Edward, New York,
on October 7, 1994

Robert M. Winn
District Attorney

Grand Jury Subpoena – Mae Evelyn Kelley

Chapter 18
Battered Child Syndrome (The Trial)

The trial of David Pope began on a spring day in May of 1995. This was a much different trial than the one first held in the spring of 1973 when District Attorney Phil Berke tried his best to hold this evil man responsible for beating, torturing, starving, and eventually murdering this little unloved boy. This time, the District Attorney Robert Winn had the full police investigation he needed and this time he had a world-renowned forensic pathologist that filled out the correct death certificate and was more than willing to testify. Justice delayed 22 years was hopefully now coming forward. Unfortunately, the justice denied in 1973 allowed horrific abuse of 6 additional children that did not need to happen. If Social Services and a doctor coroner did their job in 1972, then a little boy may still be alive today. If Social Services and a doctor coroner did not lie in the 1973 trial, then all of that additional abuse and all the work put into this 1994-1995 investigation would not have been necessary. Unfortunately, we cannot change the past, we can only move forward and right the scales of justice in 1994.

In New York, Tom cannot attend most of the trial because he is a main witness. He can only attend the closing arguments, jury charge, and deliberations. Because of this, he assisted Rob Winn with coordinating the witnesses and evidence. On the day Dr. Baden was scheduled to testify, it was planned for him to meet with Tom for over an hour to go over the case facts and evidence that he had not seen since the fall of 1994. Dr. Baden had his main residence in New York City, so it was a 3½-hour ride to the Washington County Courthouse. Tom was set up in the District Attorney's library awaiting Dr. Baden's arrival so he could go over the case file with him. When Dr. Baden arrived late, it did not leave a lot of time for review. On top of that, he came in talking on a cell phone and then he switched to the hard line phone in the library. Cell phones were not very common in the spring of 1995, so it was unusual to see someone come in talking that much on one. Who was he talking to…? What was going on in the U.S. in May of 1995…? He was on the phone continuously with the Dream Team. O.J. Simpson's powerful dream team of attorneys in Los Angeles, California. Tom will never forget Dr. Baden showing him the gold American Express card Dr. Baden displayed to him with basically unlimited spending from the dream team. After being on the two phones for a long time, he finally gave Tom his attention, but time was now limited as Tom knew he would be going downstairs and into the courtroom soon. Tom had the case file spread out on the conference table with photos from both autopsies. Dr. Baden looked them over and to this day, Tom will never forget him saying, "Oh, that poor little black girl." Tom quickly reminded him that this was a little white boy. Tom has always referred to Doc as the absentminded professor at times. His mind was in Los Angeles as much as it was in Washington County, New York. Any worries Tom may have had, and he really did not have any, soon dissipated in that courtroom. Doc Baden made his entrance through the main back doors of the courtroom when summoned by the Court Officer. He has an air about him in courtrooms. He is very comfortable and confident. Although Tom could not hear this firsthand, he was updated by many people. Dr. Baden commands respect with his demeanor and delivery. Tom was told that it was at least 45 minutes for Dr. Baden to go over his experience and professional expertise. His resumé. Tom was told that he owned that jury before the first main question was asked by Rob

Winn. A world-renowned witness can do that. Defense Attorney Patrick Barber could not lay a hand on him and any attempts he made only backfired worse and gave more benefit to the prosecution. There is a well-known concept in the world of attorneys and questioning. You never ask a question that you don't know an answer to. Remember the main turning point of the O.J. Simpson case when Chris Darden asked O.J. Simpson to try on the infamous glove…? That is your example. There was no recovering from that point on. Dr. Baden explained "Battered Child Syndrome" to the jury in a very down-to-earth way that needed no further explanation. That was the cause of death. When he was done with his testimony and documented every step taken and fully explained every reason that Hodgie died and all the bruising and injuries documented in 1972 and 1994, it was very easy for the jury to understand why he was able to amend the death certificate to homicide. When Dr. Baden was asked by District Attorney Winn to explain to the jury the amount of force necessary to cause that gaping hole in Hodgie's stomach, Tom will never forget the analogy used by Dr. Baden. He explained to the jury that they needed to imagine watching a Sunday NFL football game and seeing the running back heading full speed into the line with a linebacker running full speed at the running back. He explained the force needed was equal to the closing force at impact when both are running full speed into each other. They told Tom that he pounded his fist into his other palm while describing that impact.

Tom was called to testify for a long time. He fully detailed the investigation and all the steps taken. Tom is unique in the world of police officers. He not only is not afraid of testifying; he actually enjoys it. There is a technique to testifying as Tom teaches to other police officers. Listen carefully and intently to the question asked, whether it is from the District Attorney or cross-examination from the defense attorney, and then turn completely to the jury and provide them with your answer. There are usually two full rows of jurors and the answer should be given to all of them with eye contact made with each one going up and down both rows. The answers provided by Tom or any witness are not for the benefit of the attorneys or even the judge. They are for the jurors who decide the facts of the case. Tom has a way of relating to juries. They actually can feel his passion for the case and especially for victims. I have never heard of any jury that has not totally believed Tom and his answers. A normal major case jury is made up of 12 regular jurors and a minimum of 4 alternates. A juror can read people just like you read people in everyday life. If they feel you are not sure of your case or testimony, then how can you expect them to come back with a guilty verdict that actually takes freedom away from someone? Tom's passion is never hidden. He believes in his cases. He believes in his victims and the case they are presenting. Tom usually plays cleanup as Rob calls it. He fills in all the blanks. The collecting of paperwork, interviews conducted, evidence, and various other legal issues are covered through his testimony. The detailing of a case that is 22 years old and with over 100 interviews and investigative leads conducted takes time. Tom cannot testify as to what the witness says. They must do that themselves. No hearsay is allowed. The only exception to this law in this trial was the statements made by David Pope himself. Statements made by suspects are an exception to the hearsay rule. Tom was able to first read the entire 5-page statement to the jury and then they played the tape recording read back to the jury. This allowed the jury to hear David Pope's statement twice. Tom went through the very graphic photos with the jurors. The gasps from the jurors was so real and damning to David Pope. He watched the looks on their faces go between shock, sadness, and complete anger and contempt.

 Dozens and dozens of witnesses were called to explain what they saw, heard, and felt back in 1972. These were witnesses, family members, neighbors, and others. One after another came and took that stand. This was different as most witnesses come because they are subpoenaed and have no choice. Most if not all of these witnesses came in because they wanted to. They have been muzzled by fear and inept work of police and Social Services for too many years, and now was their time for justice. It was very clear to the jury that they believed and needed justice. The jurors could also read their passion and watched each one relate their observations as if they occurred last week. One after another relating so much abuse, torture, and starvation of Hodgie and his brother. Then, David Pope's biological children came in. Kevin, Nellie, and Michael. Each related their own experiences and then what they saw happen to each other. Their testimony documenting years of abuse, injuries, and all the weapons and devices that caused these injuries. Each talked about their lack of love and their permanent injuries, including PTSD. Their testimony was graphic and compelling. Very hard to listen to. Unnatural with any child much less an abuser's own children. Actually so horrific that if the jurors did not hear it directly from each child, then hard to believe because it was that bad.

There were two other witnesses they called to create pain and discomfort more than to obtain useful information to assist the jury. One was a Social Services supervisor from 1972. She was long since retired when Tom tracked her down during the investigation. She was living in Fort Edward and Tom said he knocked loudly on her door. He said she was still pompous, arrogant, and defending of their actions from 1972. Tom related to me, and I know him well enough to know he was very truthful, that he cut her no slack when questioning her and how she and her agency had blood on their hands and not only allowed a little boy to be beaten and tortured, but then opened the door to David Pope abusing 6 other children. Tom and Rob wanted to make her uncomfortable and forced her to sit there and explain her actions or inactions. Tom said he enjoyed serving that subpoena forcing her appearance at the trial. She did show up and she was called to testify. She tried to explain to the jury how different things are today compared to 1972. How different…? Protecting children never changes. Those that watched her testify, gave Tom the pleasure of knowing how uncomfortable this woman was on the stand. The other witness was Dr. Lynch. He did have needed testimony, but he was also forced to explain his inactions. He was forced to explain himself. Why…? Why did you allow a child to be beaten and tortured without screaming out for help…? Why did you not properly complete the death certificate…? Why did you make up a lie out of whole cloth about a chicken bone that never existed…? On the stand, he was very uncomfortable. He was forced to acknowledge and admit to all the abuse he saw. Tom and Rob wanted him to be uncomfortable on that stand. They wanted him to feel just a small amount of pain compared to the amount of pain that Hodgie and other children felt every day of their lives. He did tell the jury of his overwhelming fear of David Pope in 1972.

NOW THEY LAY ME DOWN TO REST

THE POST-

Home Newspaper of The Adirondack Region   Gle

Monty Calvert
Forensic pathologist Dr. Michael Baden testifies Monday during the murder trial of David J. Pope Sr. of Kingsbury.

Baden testified that Hodgie's death was a homicide. He said that the boy suffered a ruptured stomach some 8-10 hours before he died, leading to an infection known as peritonitis.

Baden said he found various old and new injuries when examining the boy's remains, such as a broken rib, old and new bruises and cuts.

He also said it was his opinion the tear in the toddler's stomach wouldn't have been caused by a fall

saw her punch the boy in the stomach while giving him a bath.

Washington County District Attorney Robert M. Winn, though, pointed out that Pope had never given that account to investigators or anyone involved in the case before Monday.

The prosecutor also produced a death certificate from 1972 in which it was noted by the coroner that Pope had told authorities shortly after Hodgie's death that the child fell from bed.

And he also testified that his ex-wife told him

Chapter 19
The Closing

As we write this chapter, we realize this will be the easiest chapter to write because Rob Winn threw every bit of his heart and soul into writing his closing statement to the jury. Rob, like us, not only lived this case, he felt it. With Tom attending many trials, and myself not attending every trial he ever did, I do remember Tom saying how well Rob's closing statements were. This one was like he was fighting for justice and not wanting to see David Pope walk out of that courtroom like he did in 1973. This made David Pope more of a monster and gave him more power to abuse these kids as he felt invincible and that no one could ever hold him accountable. It is a perfect example for any District Attorney to follow and learn from. Most don't realize how emotionally draining it is to be presenting these types of cases and the emotional roller-coaster of doubt wondering if you covered everything. No matter how many cases you present, this case is a perfect example of not knowing how to read the jurors. With the long process from the opening of these cases to presenting them at a trial, there comes a point where you get a sense of relief of being able to express your emotions in your closing statements, not being dictated to as to how you word every question or comment. It can be actually therapeutic where it is usually unheard of to have an objection or limiting order from the court. Rob clearly knew the statute of limitations and that no one else would be held responsible. Rob took this opportunity to get the point across that this was a failure of the system. He knew he would not get the opportunity to prosecute anyone who was part of the wrongdoings that led to this toddler's death and the failure of this system. He was able to express it through his closing statement. This leads us back to a conversation that was documented between the Public Defender for David Pope and the District Attorney at the time in the 70s stating that if this went to trial, it would be very embarrassing to Doctor Lynch. We knew then and now what the meaning of that statement was. The failure of a doctor to protect his vulnerable and helpless patient. As we said before, why would a doctor put his reputation and license on the line for a monster like David Pope, other than he, during a telephone call, stated that he was afraid of him but never gave a 2nd thought to how much fear a child had? This leads us to again mentioning the hold David Pope had on people that he would agree to write on a prescription pad that the child died from a chicken bone perforating his stomach and having the audacity to go as far as to have the CPS Supervisor, Miss Margaret Wunder, to notarize it. Who does this? Someone who knows they are guilty. Someone who did not do the right thing, and knows they can be sued. Someone who delayed multiple requests by the District Attorney for the autopsy report and death certificate and who never put a manner of death on it. The lack of any manner of death, much less one that truly said homicide, is what prevented the District Attorney from charging murder. It was not just the fact they were afraid of David Pope. Who better to have notarize it than the one who was involved in the massive coverup and knew very well that the county could have been sued for millions if discovered. Dr. Lynch could have had anyone notarize this prescription pad lie, but who better than the CPS supervisor involved in the coverup. Other CPS workers who were just beginning their career when this case happened told me that the commissioner himself warned and threatened every worker that any inquiries pertaining to the Pope children or the

Pope case were not to be discussed and were to come to him immediately. They all knew it was their job or go up against the system. As much as some of these Social Service workers wanted to do the right thing, they knew the threat was real. Why even write this lie on a "prescription pad"? Why have this note on a prescription pad even notarized? No reason other than to have David Pope use this to show anyone that dared to question him that it was a "chicken bone" that caused this major stomach laceration. It empowered Pope. He had this phony explanation on a note with Dr. Lynch's heading and signature and it was notarized to give a lie credibility. As I was dissecting everything we came across in those protected storage totes, boxes we protected more than Hodgie's mother protected him, I happened to ask Michael, the youngest who remembers everything very well, if he had ever seen this chicken bone note before. I took a picture of it and sent it to him. I was floored and shocked when he answered yes. That is when I knew that his controlling and abusive father used this note to convince everyone that a chicken bone caused the death of Hodgie. Michael was convinced himself all those years that this was the truth because of this notarized doctor's note. Even though Michael knew the beatings they all suffered from could have killed anyone of them at any time, he still thought to that day the chicken bone caused the death of his brother that he never knew. The only other person that knew there was no chicken bone in Hodgie's stomach beside Dr. Lynch, David Pope, and the pathologist was Mae. She knew what Hodgie ate for his last meal, but with all her lies, she forgot that her statement indicated the last meal was canned meat with no bones. This told me again that Mae completely knew Dr. Lynch's signed and notarized chicken bone statement was a complete made-up lie. They both did this knowing all along that this was not possible. As you have seen, there is no possible way a chicken bone could cause that type of stomach laceration. On top of that, the pathologist, Dr. Walter Stern, fully documented that there was NO bone found in Hodgie's stomach during the autopsy. Lynch knew this.

We see all the bruises, cuts, abrasions, lacerations and injuries to Hodgie. David Pope saw them happen. David Pope heard his screams firsthand. David Pope saw all the tears. David Pope saw the fear in his eyes. Hodgie felt every one of them. Hodgie screamed with every one of them. Hodgie felt the fear every day with every kick, punch, hit, and assault. How difficult did every person or agency involved that did not do the right thing make it for then District Attorney Philip Berke to charge the appropriate charges and for the jury to even convict David Pope of anything in 1973? Rob Winn is exceptional at what he did during his career and this case, but all of the things that Philip Berke was denied access to which made it impossible for him to incarcerate David Pope. Rob on the other hand had everything he needed due to the very thorough investigation completed. He had every medical record, every statement, an exhumation and new autopsy which led to a correct death certificate with a manner of death reading homicide. Rob didn't have the frustrations and roadblocks of not having what he needed to present this case, he just need to put it all together like a real-life puzzle. As you will learn, you never know what a jury will do. As you continue to read his full closing statement, imagine yourself sitting in the jury box and seeing everything we have presented to you. His full closing will allow you to position yourself in that jury box and have the entire case brought together and will stay with you for the rest of your life. Read every word intently.

Now They Lay Me Down to Rest

Entire Written Closing – D.A. Robert Winn

May it please the Court and may it please you ladies and gentlemen of the jury:

It is my-privilege to now deliver the closing statement of the People of the State of New York in this trial. Each time I am given this opportunity, but particularly in cases of homicide, I think about my client, the People of the State of New York. The People of the State of New York is all of us. The People of the State of New York seek justice. It desires and needs justice. By your verdict, you too will speak for the People of the State of New York and your verdict must give the People justice. The People of the State of New York need and require all persons who are guilty of such crimes to be convicted of these crimes, without regard to issues of sympathy, social status, age, sex, class, race, or reputation. Justice, decency, and public concerns require murderers and child abusers be convicted of their crimes and the evidence of this case requires that this murderer and child abuser David Pope be convicted of murder in the second degree for causing the death of Howard White. Anything less would be an injustice to the People of the State of New York and, while participation in this case means examining and hearing about the worst in human nature, I am privileged to have this opportunity to participate in bringing a child abuser to justice after twenty two years of freedom..

At this juncture, I like to express my thanks to you, the jury, for agreeing to participate in this search for the truth. I

Page 1

think that your agreement to sit on a case involving a child abuse murder with us is a testimony to your character. You agreed to serve and it is appreciated. In the typical case, I submit to you that the words of Judge Moynihan that finding someone guilty of a crime is generally a disagreeable duty are true. In only a few cases do I fail to feel some compassion for the defendant who is before the court. In this case, however, in view of the obvious nature of the evidence, in view of the demonstrated cruelty of this defendant toward a defenseless child, I would submit to you that the announcement of a guilty verdict in this case would not be a disagreeable duty, but will be an act of justice which you will take pride in. Under our procedures, your foreman, Mr. Hall, will announce your verdict after your deliberations are completed. I submit to you that, because of the evidence of this case, the announcement of the verdict, which represents justice after twenty two years of justice being delayed and denied, that the annoucement of that verdict will be an act that all of you can take pride in. In this last opportunity which I have to talk with you, I would like to share with you some of the memories of this case which will stay with me for the remainder of my life and which may affect you in the same way:

- I will always remember the extraordinary testimony of Lena David and Rose St. Louis. Two women, perhaps of humble circumstances, but of extraordinary character, who testified against their own relative in a child murder case for one reason and one reason alone: it was the right thing to do. This was a case of child abuse so bad, so heinous that even the defendant's own relatives testified against him.

- I will always remember the shocking autopsy report of Howard White with the list and itemization of the various injuries and bruises and conditions on this two year old's body and can only state that I find such report, after reflection, to be about as sad and depressing of a document which could be offered in a court proceedings. It truly is an

- I will always remember the professionalism of the State Police who worked this case, not only with the excellent forensic science personnel, but also remember with pride that I had the opportunity to work with Investigator Aiken who professionally interviewed a murderer and gained important admissions in a homicide case. After he had completed his work, reason and logic compel a guilty verdict.

- All of us will always remember the tragic photographs which we saw of Howard White as he laid on a hospital guerney and in the morgue of the Glens Hospital with number A72-149 next to him. I will sometimes see a photograph in the Post-Star in which a face of a smiling child enjoying life is shown and it picks our spirits up for a moment. The haunting look on Howard White's face will be a constant reminder as to the depths of criminal activity, the cruelty of this man. These photographs are a silent reminder of the pain which this child suffered prior to his death.

In analyzing the evidence, I would request that you closely listen to the final instructions of Judge Moynihan. While I am not certain of the precise and exact language that Judge Moynihan will use, I would expect that he will, generally, refer to a trial as a procedure by which we quietly, rationally and objectively attempt to ascertain the truth. I believe that you will receive instructions to the effect that "It is the duty of each juror carefully to review, weigh and consider all of the evidence in the case." By following this instruction, that you must carefully review, weigh and consider all of the evidence in the case, collectively, with the god given common sense of twelve reasonable people, twelve people which the prosecution agreed to accept after a long voir dire process, you will know in your hearts and minds that this defendant's guilt has been established beyond a reasonable doubt.

Let us together, carefully consider, weigh, and review the evidence of this case and what it means. We have to review the evidence carefully because a young child has been deprived of his life. His childhood, his adolescence, his adult years. I know

Page 4

Now They Lay me Down to Rest

that it could be stated that he may have been better off dead than to have continued to have received the abuse, the whippings, the bruisings, the beatings, the deprivation of food, we know that this boy should have had a chance at life. That there is a great injustice which has to be rectified. The evidence of this case, carefully considered, weighed and review will lead you all to the conclusion that Howard White was abused and battered causing him to suffer from Battered Child Syndrome and to die and that David Pope was responsible for this death and must be held accountable.

We begin our analysis of the facts with the autopsy report of Howard White. You will have a chance to examine **People Exhibit's** 2 and you will see the long list of symptoms and that the fact this abused child died of a perforation of his abdomen. To make your job as jurors easier, to give you life-time confidence in your decision, we have had this autopsy report examined and analyzed by Doctor Baden, who is, as you have heard, a leading forensic pathologist in the country and world. Doctor Baden's testimony is consistent with all of our lives and understandings. Two year old boys do not rupture their stomachs from falls and tumbles off beds or down stairways. If they did, the human race would be extinct as no two year old boy would ever survive to age three. Doctor Baden merely tells us what we all know when we consider the facts carefully and analyze them carefully. A ruptured stomach is going to occur as a result of severe trauma. It occurs as a result of severe blunt trauma. A stomach will not rupture as a result of falling off from beds,

Page 5

273

etc. Doctor Baden's carefully considered opinion is that this death was the result of intentionally inflicted trauma, a localized blow caused by a foot or a fist. It was not an accidental injury. As a result of a severe blow to the abdomen, peritonitis set in. The medical cause of death, as described by Doctor Baden's death certificate, is Battered Child Syndrome. The final blow to the abdomen was the fatal blow--the last of a long lines of beatings before death ensued. You know, we hear these medical terms such as Battered Child Syndrome and then we compare it to the medical criteria, the diagnostic criteria. The diagnostic criteria for Battered Child Syndrome as including malnutrition, multiple fractures, multiple ecchymosis, perforated abdomens, etc. Those critieria were not developed especially for this case. They were not uniqure medical theories developed for this case. These were diagnostic criteria which were formulated by national experts in this field. These criteria fit this case exactly. This is an obvious case of battered child syndrome. The battered child will be malnourished. Doctor Stern's report notes Howard White was emacitiated. His relatives and neighbors talked about his distended belly and how skinny he was. The pictures which were received for evidence demonstrate this as well. The battered child will have bruises and black and blues in various stages of healing. This is because the battered child is essentially always being knocked around and beaten by his abuser. Howard White had bruises and black and blues in various healing stages. A battered child will have multiple fractures in various forms of healing. Howard White had a healing fracture of a nose

Now They Lay Me Down to Rest

and a healing fracture rib. There were no histories or explanations for these injuries. Think of your own childhood, think of your own children. If you ever broke a bone, it could be related to a specific event. A child might say that he broke his arm playing football, or in a car accident. The battered child has no such history. His bones are just broken without histories, waiting, in the case of Hodgie White, to be diagnosed by an expert such as Doctor Maples. A battered child's bones are examined by forensic pathologist while in the normal household they are treated by an orthopedist. A battered child will have injuries such as a perforated abdomen caused by severe blunt trauma and that it the final blow which caused the death of Hodgie. Little Hodgie was a textbook case of a battered child from simply the examination of the autopsy report. No one is trying to put a square hole in a round peg. This is simply a fact that Hodgie was a victim of Battered Child Syndrome and he died from such affliction, which was not genetic, but only because he was a member of the household of David Pope.

Doctor Baden's expert opinion was that the fatal injury could only have resulted from a severe blunt trauma. A kick or stomping or some other fatal type of localized blow. It had to be a severe blunt trauma. It would not be a simple fall. I submit that the opinion of Doctor Baden was fairly obvious. The photographs and the autopsy report make it clear in 1995 to persons of common sense that this child was murdered. However, the testimony of Doctor Baden, as much as for your benefit as Hodgie's was simply

275

to give you the life-long confidence in your verdict that this child was murdered.

When you carefully analyze, review and consider the testimony of Doctor Baden in connection with the other evidence of this case, now and later in your lives, you will know that there is no reason to doubt his finding of homicide, which he certified and signed as set forth in **People Exhibit #3**. Doctor Baden is a highly regarded forensic scientist. I submit to you that his testimony, which was straightforward and consistent with the physical exhibits such as the photographs, together with his conclusions should be accepted by you. I note that the only witness who examined those photographs who indicated that Hodgie White was not an abused child was the defendant himself. But I submit to you that Doctor Baden is no different than an average person. He understands the importance of a certification and he certainly knows the consequences of ruling a death a homicide. He knows that there will be a criminal prosecution and, with that knowledge, he signed People's Exhibit #3, unlike the original death certificate. In weighing and considering the evidence of this case, you have a certification from a leading forensic pathologist that this child was abused and battered to death. That this is a homicide.

I would like to turn to the map which has been received for evidence as **People's Exhibit 4**. This map generally depicts the Village of Granville. On September 11, 1972, a little boy, not

Page 8

NOW THEY LAY ME DOWN TO REST

even three feet tall, was brought into an emergency room. It would be determined, twenty two years later, that the infant was killed as a result of battered child syndrome. If Lena David, Rose St. Louis, Patricia Longley and the others had been told, there is a child from the Village who is up at the hospital with a perforated abdomen from being a battered child and he is dead, you would not even have to tell them that it was Hodgie. They would have known. In the Village of Granville, in our society, children are not normally brought into emergency rooms with bruised bodies and broken bones suffering from malnutrition with perforated abdomens as a result of natural causes. This is why decent law-abiding citizens like Bud Davies, the rescue squad attendant remember events from 22 years ago. They do not come from just anyone's homes in that condition. They come from the homes of child abusers. When you think about this map, think about the fact that an abused child was brought into the hospital. Where would it come from. Without question this poor abused child would come from the home of a child abuser. There was no coincidence that the battered and abused child who died as a result of battered child syndrome found in the Granville Hospital came from the apartment of David Pope. It was inevitable that, at some point, these vicious beatings would cause the death of Howard White. The map is also a sad commentary on how indifferent the children's services department was to the abuse of Howard White. On cross-examination of Mrs. Sarchioto, you heard how she first saw Hodgie in February of 1971 with cuts and bruises on his face. He was only sixteen months old. This same child is seen five days

Page 9

277

before his death after being in foster care periodically. Judging from the photographs, he had to be starved and yet Mrs. Sarchioto failed to make that short ride to turn down Park Street. But she is not on trial in this case and we are here because Hodgie was deprived of his life.

We examine together the horrible photographs which were received for evidence as **People's Exhibit 13 and People's exhibits 5 onward**, allowed as evidence by Judge Moynihan over the objection of the defense and it is understandable why these photographs were objected to. They are vivid, irrefutable proof that Hodgie was an abused and battered child who was simply beaten to death. They say that one picture is worth a thousand words, but in this case, it could be said that one picture will generate a thousand tears. We could see the hurt. But in our analysis of the evidence, we must consider that Hodgie felt the pain necessary to cause each and every bruise and black and blue mark. This is important when you consider the elements of the reckless depraved murder count. We saw the aftereffects. David Pope saw the immediate response. Hodgie got bruised in the buttocks from a kick presumably. We see the bruise. David Pope saw his foot go into the body of Hodgie. David Pope would see Hodgie's little body fall off its feet. He would hear the scream and the tears and see the fear in the eyes. We heard testimony of the screams of children coming from the apartment at the Long Houses of David Pope. You would expect a child who was receiving the beatings necessary to cause these injuries to scream. You would expect a

Page 10

child who was being whipped with an antenna cord to scream in pain and fear. How could any man who heard these screams ever beat a child again? But David Pope testified that he heard no cries, heard no tears. That Hodgie did not cry when whipped or kicked. We are here to review, analyze and consider and ask you to do this with these photographs. We see the bruises in so many different body parts. His head, his chin, his arms, his legs, his chest, his buttocks, his starved condition. There are literally bruises all over his body in varying colors, varying degrees of healing, which means that he was abused on different occasions.

We consider the testimony of Doctor Maples. If nothing else, he shows the extreme professionalism of the New York State Forensic Sciences Unit which works on these cases. The most experienced experts in their fields have been called to this case. Doctor Maples' testimony may have appeared over-kill. Certainly, all of you knew that this child was abused and, while perhaps this testimony was more than was required, we do wish for you to have confidence in your verdict. This testimony simply show how better equipped the police are to deal with forensic issues.

Obviously Doctor Maples and Doctor Baden, with their great expertise, have a great deal of forensic experience, which means that they apply their science to criminal and legal matters. We consider briefly the testimony of Doctor Lynch and I would simply submit that, God forbid, any family member of mine was murdered, I would certainly pray that experts like Doctor Maples and Doctor

Baden were consulted and not Doctor Lynch. Doctor Lynch was simply ill-equipped to handle such an important criminal matter. It is simply so obvious that Hodgie White was murdered and I do not mean to harshly criticize Doctor Lynch, but he was wrong in not examining Hodgie's photograph, he was wrong in not attending this autopsy, and he was wrong in not telling it like it was even back in 1972. Although his direct testimony was confusing, on cross-exmination, you heard that he told the grand jury that this case was homicide. After hearing from Doctor Glennon and Doctor Baden, it is obvious that their shared opinion that Hodgie was the victim of blunt trauma was correct. During the voir dire, I asked some of you if you could return a verdict even if it meant, in practical effect, that a local coroner was wrong. You all assured me that you could. I accepted you as jurors on that basis and I submit to you that the opinion of Doctor Lynch, which has changed, which was formed without even examining the autopsy photographs, is valueless. This is not the type of examination which we would have expected for one of the children of our county. You know, things work sometimes in mysterious ways. The prosecution of this case was delayed because the failure to designate this case as a homicide back in 1972. But had the prosecution back then relied upon Doctor Lynch for his expertise, the jury would have been floundering no doubt.

When I think about any criminal case, I first and foremost think about motive for the crime. It is difficult to consider motive in a child abuse case. There is no reasonable motivation

Page 12

Now They Lay Me Down to Rest

to abuse a 34 inch, 25 pound child. I submit to you that the motive for child abuse could be anger, could be just plain meanness, could be that the abuser is simply rotten. But we can say this, simply because there is no motive, there is no reason to beat and pummel a child, this is really the key to this case. There is no motive to beat little Hodgie White. We then turn to find out who would beat this particular child even though he had no legitimate motive to do so. No credible witness testified that Mae Kelly White ever abused this child or any child. Even the defendant himself admitted that there was no such abuse by Mae Kelly White. But while this defendant had no motive, we have evidence as to how he would whip and kick and brutalize Hodgie, how he would not only brutalize him physically, but mentally as well by feeding meat to dogs while the starving child looked on. The average person loses his apetite when he is confronted with those terrible pictures from Africa or other impoverished countries. The defendant lived in a household with a starving child. What did he do? He feeds the dogs meat in front of the starving child. I am not going to try to explain a motive for doing this other than simple meanness. I am not goint to try to explain a motive for his whipping this child with an antenna wire other than just plain meanness. It was the defendant and the defendant alone who had the fortunately rare and pathetic mean streak which would let him inflict the injuries which we saw on the body of Howard White at the time of his death. The injuries on Howard White show a unique savageness and the reported conduct of David Pope show the same kind of unique savageness necessary to beat a child to death. If you do not believe the prosecution witnesses, then I would direct your attention to Mrs. Sarchioto's testimony who was asked by Mr. Barber a question to which he did not know the answer. Whether any of these reports related to Hodgie's mother and he heard Mrs. Sarchioto's reply that the reports related to his client and he then retreated.

The testimony of Lena David and Rose St. Louis was, I submit to you, extraordinary evidence in a homicide trial. Looking at this trial as an outside observer, think how extraordinary it is that two close relatives would offer testimony, very damning testimony, against their brother in a child abuse murder case. Their own family name is, to some extent, diminished by a conviction. No one would normally want a family member in jail. However, when they testified, we saw their emotion and their desire to remedy an injustice which they knew had occurred to young Hodgie White, who is not a blood relative of theirs. Think of the abusive conduct which they must have observed which compelled them to testify. I submit that their testimony, without motive to lie, should be accepted. They knew this was a murder trial and they still testified against their own flesh and blood and their testimony was consistent with all of the other testimony in this case. I submit that the testimony of Wilma Van Guilder, who was not a credible witness and whose testimony stood alone against an entire parade of prosecution witnesses, must be rejected as being not credible.

NOW THEY LAY ME DOWN TO REST

You know, ladies and gentlemen, when you think about these beatings, bruises, etc. for a minute, think about what an acquittal would mean. An acquittal would mean that this defendant finally got away with this murder once and for all. That he brutalized his child, that he bruised his face, his chest, his arms, his legs and his buttockes, that he broke this child's bones, that he whipped this child like a dog, that he kicked this child and booted this child like a dog, that he just turned this bruised and battered child over to the rescue squad workers only asking if he was dead like it was nothing and to him it was nothing and telling his sister Rose St. Louis that they could never prove anything. An acquittal means that he pulled it off. He pulled it off notwithstanding the fact that a leading forensic pathologist testifies to the obvious fact that this child died as a result of abuse. Notwithstanding the fact that he admitted to Investigator Aiken that he had kicked and slapped this child and was aggressive in his punishment and that he knew there was no reason for a grown man like him to kick this young infant. He pulled it off and there would be nothing the State Police, Doctor Baden, Lena David, Rose St.Louis or the District Attorney's Office could do about it. You know, there are some members of society who admire persons who get away with crimes. People write books about "The Great Bank Robbery," The World's Largest Diamond Heist", but they has never ever been a book or movie made which admires a child abuser who brutalizes a child and finally beats him to death. Do not let this defendant pull off this crime. Do not allow this defendant get away with his crime. Give the People of the State of New York the justice which it seeks.

I want to talk for a minute about the statement which this defendant made to Investigator Aiken and Detecive Hunt and the defendant's testimony in this courtoom. The professionalism of Investigator Aiken is readily apparent and is amply demonstrated in the playing of the audio tape which has been received into evidence. The written statement contains very damaging admissions as to aggressive punishment, kicking and knocking the 34 inch infant off its feet, feeling heavy hearted in that the punishment may have had something to do with Hodgie's death. These admissions are even more extraordinary in that this defendant will not cooperate with authorities generally. But we hear David Pope explain his version of the statement taking process. He is, to say the least, on the witness stand, extremely critical of Investigator Aiken. You heard his accusations, a word was changed, the meaning was shifted, etc., etc. I re-played the tape to show simply how ludicrous those allegations were. You heard Investigator Aiken very slowly and deliberately read the defendant's statement and you heard no argument from the defendant during the process. He admitted that he could read the statement, that his hearing difficulty did not present problem, because Investigator Aiken repeated himself whenever necessary. There was no sense of any argument. When David Pope criticizes Investigator Aiken, I refer you to this tape and I also refer you to the

Page 16

Now They Lay Me Down to Rest

photograph of Howard White, which was Grand Jury Exhibit 6. Certainly, all of us know who are now familiar with what Hodgie looks like can identify him as being depicted in this photograph. This photograph is not blurry, is not distorted. It is simply a fairly well-taken autopsy photograph which is very clear. No reasonable person who knew Hodgie White could deny that this was Hodgie. I recall showing, I believe Rose St. Louis, one of the photographs and then decided not to do it for further witnesses as it would only upset them. How did David Pope respond to this photograph at the Grand Jury? That is not Hodgie. I don't believe that is Hodgie. There is no emotion...There is denial of the obvious. The tape shows you, proves to all of you that David Pope's reality is different than our reality. All of us hear the tape and we know that this is a competent investigator who is simply confirming a statement which was given to him. David Pope denies this reality even though his reality is disproven by the tape. David Pope denies the reality of Grand Jury Exhibit 6 being Hodgie because it does not fit into his version of reality.

This audio tape demonstrated that the defendant's constitutional rights were protected and honored. As you reflect back on this case, you will not ever have to worry about any possibility of whether this defendant's constitutional rights were protected. You heard on the tape that the defendant was told these rights. But more than the professionalism, you heard the intelligence of Investigator Aiken and his knowledge and understanding of child abuse cases. In a case such as this, the

Page 17

defendant is not going to admit that he struck Hodgie White in the abdomen with a blunt object before his death which led to his demise. But, as a matter of logic and common sense, something which Investigator Aiken knows and has, as an investigator of child abuse cases, Investigator Aiken knows that, at the beginning of this case, there were only two possible members of this household who could have caused this severe blunt trauma injury, the mother or the mother's boyfriend, which was David Pope, Investigator Aiken knew that all of the witnesses, including David Pope's own aunt and sister, identified the defendant as the abuser in this household and testified that Mae Kelley White, to whom they were not related, did not abuse the children at all. Under these circumstances, there was really no great need for any statement from the defendant. There was more than enough evidence to convict him, but, again, to give you greater confidence in your decision, a statement was obtained. Investigator Aiken is surely slight in build and stature, but he might be what you could call a modern law enforcement officer. He does not shout. He carefully advises the suspect of his Miranda rights. He understands the case. He does not bully the suspect. He is cordial and polite to the suspect and listens and takes down everything the suspect has to say and I submit that is what we are paying him to do. He holds in his emotions and gains the information necessary to prove to even the most hesitant mind that the defendant is guilty of this terrible crime beyond any doubt. Keep in mind, once the forensic team established that Hodgie was a victim of Battered Child Syndrome, the only question to be resolved is who was the

NOW THEY LAY ME DOWN TO REST

batterer. Period. Once Mae White is ruled out, then the defendant, as a matter of logic and rational analysis, must be guilty.

The most damning part of this statement, besides his admission as to his aggressive punishment of a toddler, which is despicable, aggressive punishment which includes booting him, knocking him off his feet, visualize that in (you) mind for a minute, a grown man knocking a toddler off his feet in an aggressive manner, but equally important in our careful review, consideration and analysis of the evidence is the admission by David Pope that Mae Kelley White did not abuse the children. An admission which was confirmed by his own relatives and his Grand Jury testimony.

Of course, now the defendant, whose credibility is worthless, now suggests that Mae White, who he said never abused this child, may have caused (her) death by hitting the child in the abdomen. I note that this suggestion was never made during the three hour interview with Investigator Aiken. I would submit that the defendant has simply an overwhelming motive to deceive and, since he knows that no third party can be blamed, he offers up this last-minute theory about Mae White, even though he never mentioned it to Investigator Aiken. It should be given no weight by you. Quite simply he has heard the testimony of Doctor Baden about a localized blow and now must offer up an explanation and Mae White is the only logical target for his desperate finger pointing.

Before I leave the written statement, I submit that the most ludicrous statement of David Pope, his greatest insult to your collective intelligence, is his explanation for feeling heavy hearted about Hodgie's death. The statement, which he signed, which was read back to him, reads that he was heavy hearted about the punishment. I saw this statement. I heard it on the tape read without objection by David Pope. Unless I heard his testimony wrong, and it is your collective recollection which counts, David Pope indicated that he was heavy hearted because he thought he left a chicken bone around. The evidence proved beyond all doubt that this child was abused repeatedly by the defendant, that he died from this abuse, in a starved, bruised condition, with multiple fractures, a ruptured stomach, that he whipped the child in the presence of relatives, that he kicked this child off his feet, and this defendant has the audacity to tell you, a jury of twelve carefully selected citizens, that he is heavy hearted because he left a chicken bone around.

After the written statement was completed, the defendant did orally admit that Hodgie died from being abused and that Hodgie's bruises made it look like he was kicked and abused the length of a football field. He admitted that there was no reason for a grown man to hit a boy that size like he did. He admitted that the child died of abuse, but could not come up with the name of any possible suspect.

Page 20

Now They Lay me Down to Rest

As I mentioned during the opening, the shocking portion of this statement is that David Pope is talking about a toddler who never got taller than 34 inches, who weighed between 25 and 28 pounds. I note that the model used by Doctor Baden is only slight smaller than Hodgie. I measured the diagram and it is 27 inches tall. In any event, We hear briefly the voice of David Pope on the tape recording which has been received for evidence. The calm voice of David Pope is somewhat amazing. He admitted in this statement that hitting a child with an antenna cord sounds like something he might do. He said that he put his boots to his backside and slapped or hit Hodgie causing him to fall off his feet. There is no shame in this voice. But then, we would not expect that a person who whips a child would be remorseful. He is without conscience.

Likewise, the Grand Jury testimony of David Pope simply makes the job of deliberations that much easier. His admissions with his attorney sitting next to him that he kicked and booted this poor child, who was only 34 inches tall, was likewise unprecedented All of these admissions that his rights were read to him prior to his statement to Investigator Aiken were amazing. The defendant admitted to hitting the child with sticks, kicking, etc., and finally led a Grand Jury to ask him why he came to the Grand Jury to testify.

For some reason, the defense called Anita Sarchioto and asked her about a particular date in July, 1972, in which she observed only fading bruises. It is an outrage that a child services worker, even a retired one, would allow herself to be a called as a witness in this case. Mrs. Sarchioto said that she was there in July of 1972. On direct, she did not recall being back there before Hodgie died. Fortunately, the records were found, delivered to the District Attorney's Office after we were told that Mrs.Sarchioto would be testifying and we were able to demonstrate that she was there less than a week before this child died. Mrs. Sarchioto had to admit that the child shown in the autopsy photographs was a textbook case of battered child syndrome. She also had to admit that there were other times, beginning in February of 1971 when this child had bruises on him. He was only 16 months old. Far younger and smaller than even the two year old toddler which was killed before his third birthday. Mrs. Sarchioto drove by Hodgie's street every day to and from work. She let him down and there is no excuse for her. But she is not on trial. In your verdict, do not let justice down.

During the course of this trial, various people were shown the photographs of Hodgie. Only one person who saw those photographs testified that he was not abused child. The defendant. You have seen the photographs and can form your own conclusions.

During his instructions, Judge Moynihan will instruct as to the law and definitions of murder in the second degree and lesser included offenses. Under the law, it is his obligation to charge requested lesser included offenses. However, I submit to you that

Page 22

this is murder case. The People absolutely are seeking a verdict of guilty of murder and not the lesser included offenses. When a person acts with depraved indifference to human life and recklessly he can be held accountable the same as if the death was caused intentionally. **To be murder, a defendant must, under circumstances evincing a depraved indifference to human life, recklessly engage in conduct which creates a grave risk of death and thereby cause the death of another person.** During his questions during jury selection, Judge Moynihan indicated that twelve jurors seldom immediately agree on a verdict. It is a rare case that they do, although I submit that this may be such a case. Be that as it may, should one or two jurors not immediately see the evidence the way that the rest of you do, please work with that juror and carefully review, weigh and consider the evidence with that juror. On behalf of the People of the State of New York, do not compromise justice which has been delayed. Do not let this defendant off on manslaughter charges to reach a compromise. Work with any juror which does not share your view of the evidence.

First, when you consider whether the defendant was reckless in his actions, the court will generally instruct you that the defendant's conduct must constitute a gross deviation from the standard of care that a reasonable person would observe in the circumstances. I submit to you that the reasonable person, the reasonable member of society, the average person, does treat children with kindness and appropriately. The average person does love children and does nothing deliberately to harm them. The actions of the defendant in his treatment of Hodgie, by battering and abusing him, whipping him, feeding food to the dogs while he was starving, was such a gross deviation from the standard of care that it is really beyond dispute. Decent people, reasonable people put children first. They do not abuse and batter children. His actions recklessly created a grave risk of death. You simply cannot abuse and batter a small, emaciated child without creating a grave risk of death.

The Court will instruct you that such conduct must demonstrate a depraved indifference to human life. It is for this reason that the size of Hodgie is so important. He was just really a baby. Thirty four inches. 25 pounds. He was suffering from malnutrition. This defendant was in his twenties at the time. At the prime of his physical strength. It is a depraved indifference to human life, human life consisting of an emaciated two year old, which would abuse such a small infant. To intentionally inflict severe blunt trauma on the body of a two year is as depraved of an act as can be imagined. People's Exhibit 13, the autopsy photographs, are the handi-work of a depraved mind. Plain and simple.

The Court will instruct that the battering and abusing of the defendant must have caused the death of Hodgie. There will be no requirement for the People to prove a specific act, a specific kick or blow which caused the death. The People do not have to prove that he kicked this child with his left foot, or his right foot, in the living room, or the bedroom. Child abuse is a crime which occurs in the privacy of a person's home. It does not occur with witnesses generally, although the defendant had such little regard for society that he would abuse this child when others were around. If it was necessary to prove a specific kick or punch, then it would basically be a repeal of the child abuse laws. It would basically be legal to kill a child by battering and abusing, as long as you do it in the privacy of your own home. Don't do it on the street. Do it in the privacy of your own home and even if you bring the child into the emergency room with a perforated abdomen, with multiple bruises, starving, multiple broken bones, etc., according to the defense, it is not murder because the prosecution has not proved the specific kick or blow. We only have to prove that the defendant caused this death by battering and abusing Hodgie. We do not have to provide even a theory as to the exact mechanism and the judge will not instruct you that we do have to provide such a precise cause of death. The fatal beating was unwitnessed by other adults because it occurred within the privacy of David Pope's home. That does not make it any less of a murder case. We have proven that this death was caused by child abuse and that the defendant was the only possible abuser that lived in the

Page 25

household. That fully satisfies our burden of proof. Do not make the straight-forward complicated. This infant was murdered. The People proved this through photographs, records and the testimony of a leading forensic pathologist. We prove that the defendant was the abuser from his own statement, his own relatives and a parade of other witnesses. There is no reasonable doubt as to the fact that this defendant and no one else was Hodgie's murderer. People have compared trials in the past to jigsaw puzzles. Each piece of the puzzle is not intended to portray the entire picture. With any jigsaw puzzle, you can tell the truth of what the picture is even if a piece or pieces are missing. You may be putting together a jigsaw puzzle of a boy fishing near a stream. Before the puzzle is completed, you know beyond a reasonable doubt what the picture is before all pieces are inserted. When you start putting a jigsaw puzzle together, the pieces are in disarray and you cannot tell what the picture is. After the pieces are put together, you know what the truth of the picture is long before the final piece is inserted and you know what the truth of the picture is even if a piece or two is missing.

Listen carefully to the judge's instructions on reasonable doubt. Beyond a reasonable doubt does not mean, however, beyond

Page 26

NOW THEY LAY ME DOWN TO REST

all doubt. It does not mean without a doubt. It does not mean that the people has to prove its case to a mathematical certainty, which can never be done in human affairs. It means a doubt for which you can assign a reason. It is not based upon speculation or whim and is not a subterfuge to avoid a disagreeable duty. If you feel certain and fully convinced that the defendant is guilty, then you do not have a reasonable doubt. You have now heard the evidence. At this time, you know that Hodgie White was abused and died as a result of the abuse which was cruel and sadistic. It was abnormally bad abuse. You know that Hodgie White was abused sadistically by this defendant and this defendant was the only person who abused Hodgie. As you sit here today, you all know that the defendant was the person who caused Hodgie's death. It is now your duty to hold him accountable for his actions.

You will soon have an opportunity to begin your deliberations after the court charge by Judge Moynihan. I would like to end my summation with echoing a question which Judge Moynihan asked you during jury selections. Have you ever sat a jury before? Some day, a friend or a neighbor or a relative will ask you if you ever sat on a jury and you will say yes. They will ask you what the case was about and you will tell them that it was about a child who was murdered. They will say that it must have been hard to sit on that case and you will tell them that a great number of people did, in fact, ask not to serve because of the subject matter, but you felt that it was your duty to serve. They will ask you about the evidence and you will tell them that you saw terrible pictures showing how abused the child was. You will tell that the autopsy clearly showed that the child was abused. They will ask you about the witness and you will tell them that the prosecution called a leading forensic pathologist who was involved in the O. J. Simpson case and that this expert confirmed the obvious, that the child was murdered. You will tell them that the defendant's own relatives testified as to how he beat, kicked and abused the toddler, and that the State Police had an excellent young investigator who handled the case. They will ask you what proof the defendant presented and you will tell them not much. He didn't even contest that the child was murdered. Didn't call any experts to rebut the testimony of Doctor Baden. There is one question that they will not ask you and that is what your verdict was because they will know that your verdict was guilty and you will know in your hearts and minds that the evidence required this verdict and you will always know that one of the most important things that you ever did was to return a guilty verdict against this defendant.

In closing, in the name of the People of the State of New York, when your verdict is announced by Mr. Hall, I ask that your foreman announce a verdict of guilty of murder in the second degree and hold this defendant accountable for the death of Howard White. For Hodgie and the People of the State of New York, justice has been delayed, but don't deny them justice now.

Page 28

Thank you.

Now They Lay me Down to Rest

D.A. Robert Winn

Chapter 20
Avenging Angel

Tom was very close to the two Superior Court judges that would normally hear this case. As stated earlier, both were forced to recuse themselves from hearing this now high-profile case. Judge Phillip Berke because he was the prosecutor in the 1973 trial and Gordon Hemmett because he was the public defender for David Pope. A very stern and strict, but fair judge, G. Thomas Moynihan, was assigned to preside over this case. He is the Superior Court Judge in neighboring Warren County. He is a very intelligent and experienced judge with many years in the courtroom. Observing in his courtroom does not take long to understand he commands respect. He would never put up with anything out of place from the prosecutor, defense, defendant, police, or any witness. A tough judge. A fair judge. Tom has stated he would not ever step out of line in his courtroom. Judge Moynihan presided over this case no differently.

The case went in very well from Rob and Tom's perspective. It lasted approximately one week with many witnesses and much evidence to talk about. So different from 1973. Media coverage was large. With Washington County only 40 minutes straight up the Northway from the Capital City of Albany, every major news outlet covered this case from the first press release of the reopening of this 22-year-old homicide case to the trial, sentencing, and beyond. It captured the attention of television and newspaper audiences. The trial and sentencing was no different. Many newspaper reporters attending every minute of the trial. Many articles were written opining the failures in our systems and the horror that these children all went through. Many relatives, witnesses, neighbors, and Pope children attended this trial. The large courtroom was at capacity every day. Tom has been involved in hundreds and hundreds of major cases and he has participated in so many major trials. Each time, he nervously waits with the District Attorney while the jury deliberates and requests readbacks from the trial testimony. They always speculate about what the jurors are thinking about, arguing about, and doing in that well-guarded deliberation room. They try to read them by their expressions when they come back each time to hear crucial testimony read back, the definition of the charges, or the actual jury instructions read to them by the judge advising them what they could or could not do. Most of the time, they were wrong trying to guess what they were thinking or doing in the jury deliberation room. They know this because they have interviewed jurors so many times after verdicts were read. Most jurors are willing to sit down and talk to them because they let the jurors know they wanted to know what they did right or wrong. They want to know how they can improve how they do their jobs and present better cases.

The David Pope case was no different with one exception. They did not have time for much speculation or guessing. In a case that was 22 years old with no witnesses that could state they saw the fatal blow or was there when Hodgie died. A case where even the world-famous forensic pathologist Dr. Michael Baden could not tell the jury whether the fatal blow was caused by his steel-toed boots to Hodgie's stomach, or his fists described by his living children as being made out of stone. A case where the defense could argue they could not definitively state that David Pope was the one to cause the fatal blow. No, they did not have time because even with all the above said, this jury took only two hours to come back with a verdict. There are things that you can bank on with trials and juries most of the time. A very quick verdict is usually bad for the prosecution. A trial with days of deliberation means that at least one juror is held up on convicting. This was a two-hour verdict. They were prepared for the worse. Another given is this. When a jury walks into the courtroom with their heads down as they find their seats for the reading of the verdict, this almost always spells out a very bad day for the defendant. They don't look at him or her before they know a long prison term is coming. When the jury walks in talking or looking around the room or making eye contact with the defendant, this is usually a bad sign for the prosecution. The David Pope jury walked in and all of them made direct eye contact with David Pope. For all of these reasons, Rob and Tom were prepared for the worse. They were both elated when the clerk of the court read from the verdict sheet. GUILTY…!!! The defense then has a right to poll the jury. This means they can request to have each juror stand and read their individual verdict. The hope from the defense is that one or more juror will hesitate or not say guilty for whatever reason when asked what their verdict is directly by the judge. In this case, another first happened. Each juror, all 12, stood up proudly one at a time and glared at David Pope. Each juror shouted out their verdict of guilty directly at David Pope as they glared at him as if they wanted him to know how much they despised him and wanted him to die in prison. They wanted to show they were not afraid of the monster, David Pope. His days of complete control and intimidation were over.

When the jurors left the courtroom, Rob and Tom sent in a request to sit down with the jurors. All said yes and all were eager to talk to them. The jurors were very proud of the work by Tom and Rob and all were very thankful that they brought this case to justice after 22 years. Then, a statement by all jurors to Tom and Rob took them by surprise, but not really. They all wanted to know why they could not deliberate and convict Mae Pope. Tom and Rob both explained to them that the statute of limitations in New York prevented any charges against Mae

Pope. The only charge they could file after 22 years was murder, and as bad as Mae was, her actions did not rise to the definition of murder in the Penal Law. This was now the 2nd time Rob and Tom heard this. The first time was from the Grand Jurors hearing the case.

Another incident happened after the verdict was read and the jurors were leaving the courtroom. Michael Pope rose from his seat next to Tom and literally ran out of the back of the courtroom. This surprised Tom then, but actually made sense to Tom and I after we had time to rationalize it. Michael was totally on board with the prosecution of his father and wanted him to spend the rest of his life in prison. He would tell Tom often that he wanted his father to "rot in hell for all he did to me and my siblings." There was now a competing emotion inside of Michael. Now that he was over 18 years old and an adult, this was the first time in his life he did not take any more abuse from his father. He was now big enough to fight back. He was taught well by his father. He was not afraid to go as far as to kill his father if he tried to inflict more pain and injury on him and David actually knew this at 48 years old. Michael told Tom how this was the first time in his life that he had a relationship with his father. One moment he hated him and wanted him to rot in jail, and the next he wanted to have a father-son relationship that he and every child longs for. These mixed emotions came raging out of him as he ran from the courtroom knowing his father was soon to get that life sentence and this relationship would never happen. As he ran into the lobby of the brand-new multi-million-dollar courthouse, he ran through the heavy front doors and shoved them so hard, he actually sprung the heavy-duty hinges and broke the doors. Two courthouse security police officers immediately ran after Michael and arrested him in the parking lot for criminal mischief. So sad, but nothing could be done at that time to help him.

In New York, sentencing after a trial verdict or a guilty plea takes a minimum of 30 days. This is because a PSI or Pre-Sentence Investigation has to be conducted by the probation department and presented to the court detailing everything about the defendant prior to sentencing. The day of David Pope's sentencing was no different than the trial. The courtroom was packed with live media, police, and spectators. Tom again sat next to Michael Pope. Victim impact statements were read by many including Michael's sister and his Aunt Rose St. Louis. Both asked Judge Moynihan to impose the maximum sentence possible. I talked at the beginning of this chapter about how Judge G. Thomas Moynihan was a very tough judge. He can eviscerate people with words alone. He so believed in this case and the verdict, he eviscerated David Pope with his sentencing. This is a quote from the Post Star detailing the sentencing of David Pope:

> *"Calling himself the 2-year-old victim's 'Avenging Angel,' a judge Tuesday sentenced a grinning David J. Pope Sr. to the maximum term of 25 years to life in prison for killing his infant stepson more than 20 years ago.*
> *"Afterward, Judge G. Thomas Moynihan, apparently taking exception to Pope's smile, which persisted throughout the 20-minute proceeding, warned him, 'I don't think you'll have that grin in about a month,' once he arrives in state prison.*
> *"'Yes, I will,' the lanky, bespectacled Kingsbury man replied."*

The contempt David Pope had for people, the system, the world, and even the judge came out loud and clear. He did not care. The evil in him came out for the world to see, especially the people in that courtroom.

There was another good that righted an evil act. It came at the end of sentencing and was not in the courtroom or the media. In 1972, Mae and David were given a headstone to mark this unloved little boy's final resting place. In typical David fashion, he took the headstone and said it was a waste and threw it away. Destining an unloved boy to an eternity of unknown existence, even after death. When the trial and sentencing was completed, family, friends, neighbors and police all got together and collected enough money to purchase a new headstone for Hodgie. Finally, his eternal resting place was now known and properly marked. Tom and I have been by this gravesite many times since then and there has not been a time where flowers, toys, decorations, or trinkets were not adorned on this site so sacred to those that wished they could have been there to help Hodgie in life. To show him love, compassion, and family. No matter how much we wish we could go back, we can't. What he can do now is to help him now forever rest in peace. If he could talk to Tom, Rob, and all who so supported him after death, his words would be thank you. Now, they lay me down to rest.

'Avenging angel' gives Pope the max

By Don Lehman
Staff Writer

FORT EDWARD — Calling himself the 2-year-old victim's "avenging angel," a judge Tuesday sentenced a grinning David J. Pope Sr. to the maximum term of 25 years to life in prison for killing his infant stepson more than 20 years ago.

Afterward, Judge G. Thomas Moynihan, apparently taking exception to Pope's smile, which persisted throughout the 20-minute proceeding, warned him "I don't think you'll have that grin on your face in about a month, once he arrives in state prison."

"Yes I will," the lanky, bespectacled Kingsbury man replied.

The exchange between judge and defendant concluded an emotional hearing during which Pope's daughter and sister berated him and asked Moynihan to impose the maximum sentence for murdering Howard "Hodgie" White.

Reading a victim's impact statement, his sister, Rose St. Louis of Granville, told him he deserves the same punishment he gave Hodgie.

"We all feel you should be

'We all feel you should be kicked, punched, whipped and starved until you die a horrible death just like he (Hodgie) did.'

Rose St. Louis
Pope's Sister

receiving new information. Last fall, the boy's body exhumed from an unmarked g in North Granville and a fore pathologist reclassified the d as homicide. The cause of d was labeled as peritonitis cau by Battered Child Syndrome.

During the week-long t about a dozen relatives and for neighbors testified ab witnessing Pope brutalizing toddler. They told of incide where, unprovoked, he whip the boy with stereo wire, kic him off the ground and punc him in the stomach, among oth

His lawyer, Patrick J. Bar

Now They Lay me Down to Rest

Hodgie's Grave

CONNIE L. AIKEN AND THOMAS M. AIKEN

Victim Impact Statement

David James Pope

From Rose Mary St Louis - 05/30/95

David James Pope - we all love you as a brother and a relative, but no one can let love stand in the way of the truth!!!

Hodgie did not ask to come into this world and I am sure he never asked for what he got. Punching, kicking, beatings, whippings, and even being starved until his little life was robbed from him because of you.

For 22 years we have had nothing in our hearts and minds except sorrow for all the abuse Hodgie received. We all tried to get him help and we did get involved, what little bit of good it did us or Hodgie.

Yes he did lay for 22 years in an unmarked grave. Why, I can't answer this question - maybe you can. As for a stone for our cousin - truth again, he had one long before Hodgie was murdered. We say this because you tried to claim at the trial that relatives, especially your Aunt Lena David who helped raise you, testified against you because we were mad about you not providing a head stone years ago for another relative. David, you know that none of us testified out of spite and none of us wanted to go against a family member, but we testified and told the truth because it was the truth and it was the right thing to do and because we owed it to Hodgie. He deserved to grow up and enjoy life - not to have his very young life robbed from him and have to spend every day of his short life in pain, fear, and starvation.

-page 1 of 2 pages-

Now They Lay me Down to Rest

Rose Mary St Louis - May 30, 1995

Now our hearts and minds are relieved and lighter. Hodgie's murderer has been found and convicted. Hodgie can now rest in peace with his head stone that the whole world can be proud of and remember him by. Even though Hodgie is gone, he is not forgotten. Some of us go to visit his grave site regularly and let him know he is **loved** and that justice will now be served.

My request, as well as those of all of our family members, is a request that you receive a punishment that we know you will not get. We all feel that you should be kicked, punched, beat, whipped, and starved until you also die a horrible, tragic death, just like Hodgie suffered.

Because we know that this is not possible in a civilized world, except from monsters like you, and we know that this should not happen to anyone, especially a beautiful, defenseless, smiling two year old boy - we are all requesting that the judge sentence you to spend the rest of your life in prison with no possibility of ever again living another day as a free person.

Chapter 21
Closure

So many talk about closure when it comes to deaths, criminal cases, obtaining justice, or finding a body that you have been looking for to provide your loved one with a proper burial. Does someone ever truly obtain closure…? Tom has had to give death notifications so many times and he has had to hold the hands of moms, dads, kids, friends, and relatives of so many people that have tragically lost loved ones. He knows what not to say. He knows you don't provide patronizing insincere remarks, but instead provide honesty. That is what a person truly needs when going through something tragic or very difficult. They need sincere empathy with honesty. You don't know what someone else feels or is going through. You are not truly in their shoes. Even if it is a suicide and you went through a suicide, the experience and the dynamics are not the same. Tom has learned for many years to be honest and tell them that he doesn't know and can't know what they are feeling or going through. He tells them the only thing he can promise, that the pain will dull however slightly each day to the point it becomes a little more bearable each day. It does not go away, it does not get better, it just becomes a little bit less painful each day. This was true for Nellie Pope and Michael Pope on October 7, 2012.

Tom and I were on our annual beautiful Columbus Day weekend trip to the coast of Maine with our two young daughters when the news came in. Tom does not normally sleep in at all but it must have been close to 7:00 A.M. when his phone went off and woke him up. It was a recorded message. "This call is to inform you that the custody status of inmate David Pope has changed." A simple sentence. As Tom shook the cobwebs out from just waking up, he tried to make sense out of that simple sentence. What did that message mean that the custody status of David Pope has changed…? He thought to himself, he is never getting out of jail. Then he tried to focus and his next thought was that David Pope had escaped. Finally, in that very short amount of time, the message finished playing the remainder of the recorded notification. "David Pope was deceased." That is what changed his custody status. Tom was right, that David Pope would never step foot out of prison alive.

Tom received this automated call from a system known as VineLink. He teaches people about VineLink and the benefits of signing up for notifications. VineLink is used in all states and almost all counties in each state. It is a system where you can sign up to be notified by text and/or phone call when an inmate's custody status changes. The main benefit is to know when a defendant you are concerned about is released from jail. You must take the initiative to sign up, but it is very easy and quick, and the notification is almost instant. Anyone can sign up; you don't have to be the victim. Tom has put many, many really bad people in jail and because of this he has signed up for notifications on some of the worse ones. This would include David Pope. He has over 38 years in Law Enforcement now, so defendants sentenced to even 25 years are starting to get out. David Pope served his life sentence. This consisted of 17 years, 4 months, and 7 days. A total of 6,340 days from the day he was sentenced until the day his sentence ended. Not nearly enough considering a beautiful little boy was only allowed to live 1048 days on this earth, and almost all of those days consisted of starvations, torture, abuse, and tremendous fear. Two years, 10 months, 13 days, with no love, no support, no help, and no mother that cared enough to save him.

Now They Lay Me Down to Rest

It was not long on that Sunday morning in Maine before Tom called Mike Pope and advised him that his father was now dead and they could rest easier. At some point that day or Columbus Day Monday, Tom was told by Mike that the hospital in Westchester County would not let them come down to view their father's body so they could get the closure they so desperately needed. This may seem like a small point, but to people that have gone through the amount of bone-chilling abuse that Nellie and Mike went through, it is not even close. It doesn't matter that Tom told them their father was dead. It doesn't matter that the Westchester County Medical Examiner's office told them their father was dead. It did not even matter when they read that he was dead in a Post Start article or saw it on the 6:00 news. When someone goes through the amount of torture, pain, and suffering that they did, the only belief is with their own eyes. They needed this in-person confirmation. They needed that so desperately. Tom could feel it from their words. Tom promised Mike that he would do everything he could to help them get this closure. Tom tried to pull in a favor from the man who helped so much on this case and had worldwide connections, Dr. Michael Baden. Tom called Doc Baden and asked for this favor. He was very surprised at the answer he got. Doctor Baden was more than happy to help, but he knew what the people in Westchester County were like and his relationship with them was not good. Westchester County is a very wealthy bedroom community for New York City. The impression they give off is that they are better than the rest of New York State. Doctor Baden knew this was one of the few places in the country he could not pull in a favor. Tom was not deterred.

The next day, Tuesday, October 9th, Tom called directly to the Westchester County Medical Examiner's office and asked for a personal favor. No, he actually pleaded with them for a favor. He was told that since David Pope died in the prison system at the infamous Sing Sing prison, it was not necessary for a positive identification and therefore it was against their policy to let anyone view the body. Tom kept pleading for a professional favor. He once again told the unbelievable story of the David Pope case and once again, it struck a chord. When they finally gave in a little and agreed to let the body be viewed, it came with strict rules. Only Mike and Nellie could go in, no one else. There was no touching of the body. There would be no outbursts. The time in there was also limited. Tom said yes for Mike and Nellie not knowing what their response would be, but they did agree to these terms when I immediately called them up. Mike and Nellie, with their spouses and support people, piled into an older car and made the 3+-hour drive down. They had no idea what their reactions or emotions would be. They knew they had to follow the rules and they did. After, they profusely thanked Tom and explained how important actually viewing his body was to them. You can tell them all day long the devil is dead, but they need this closure themselves.

Now They Lay Me Down to Rest

Toddler-killer from Granville dies in prison

DON LEHMAN - Oct 9, 2012 Updated Oct 5, 2017

A Granville man whose 1972 killing of his son played a part in the state's creation of a child abuse hotline died Sunday in a state prison, 17 years after finally being brought to justice.

David J. Pope Sr., 67, was serving a life sentence in state prison for the murder of his 2-year-old son when he died Sunday of natural causes in Sing Sing Correctional Facility, according to the state Department of Correctional Services.

Pope had been in state prison since 1995 for the 1972 beating death of his 2-year-old son, Howard "Hodgie" White, in the family's home in the village of Granville.

The 1972 death had led to Pope's prosecution and acquittal on lesser charges as family members withheld information about what happened to the boy.

State Police Senior Investigator Thomas Aiken, who along with then-Granville Police Detective Frank Hunt led the investigation, said the case also played a part in the changing of state policies and laws regarding child abuse reports.

Upset at the apparent failures in the child welfare system, then-Washington County District Attorney Philip Berke's lobbying campaign played a part in the creation of laws that require mandatory reporting of child abuse by certain

CONNIE L. AIKEN AND THOMAS M. AIKEN

PostStar

Family seeks to heal after convicted father dies in prison

OCTOBER 20, 2012 5:26 PM • DON LEHMAN--
DLEHMAN@POSTSTAR.COM

Nellie Younger likes to think of her work as a foster parent as something good that came from the horrific abuse she suffered at the hands of her father, convicted murderer David J. Pope Sr.

Younger, 37, of Whitehall has adopted two of the foster children she has watched, and is in the process of adopting a third. Those three are in addition to her two biological children.

"It's definitely helped me to help these children," she said. "By helping others, I help myself."

Younger was one of six children of Pope, the former Granville resident who died in prison earlier this month while serving a sentence for second-degree murder in the 1972 beating death of one of his children, Howard "Hodgie" White.

Testimony during Pope's 1995 trial showed Pope viciously beat the 2-year-old and deprived him of food, but systemic failures of child welfare agencies at the time allowed him to not only abuse and neglect his children for years, but get away with killing one of them until a renewed police investigation led to his prosecution and conviction.

The fact Pope was not held accountable in the 1970s allowed him to abuse his other children for years, abuse detailed in Pope's 1995 trial in Hodgie's death.

That abuse prompted Younger and brother Michael Pope to reach out to State Police with a request to see their father's body after he died Oct. 7, to serve as a sort of closure to what they had endured. He died in Sing Sing Correctional Facility, and his body was taken to Westchester Medical Center.

State Police Senior Investigator Thomas Aiken, who headed the murder investigation of their father, was able to arrange for them to visit the downstate hospital to see for themselves that their tormentor was dead.

314

Now They Lay me Down to Rest

"He was still psychologically controlling us in a way," Michael Pope, 36, said. "This man controlled us from the day we were born until the day he died. To put this to rest we had to see the body."

Michael Pope said the visit was emotional, but served its purpose. Both he and his sister decided to attend their father's funeral Wednesday in Granville. (He was cremated after their visit to Westchester.)

"He had a lot of demons of his own, and he paid the price for what he did," Younger said.

Both Michael Pope and Younger continue to harbor anger toward their mother, from whom they are estranged and who they believed should have done a better job protecting them from Pope when they were children.

Testimony at Pope's trial showed Pope was abusive toward her as well, but Michael Pope and Younger said they've long felt their mother could have removed them from the situation or cooperated with the Department of Social Services to spare her children.

"I went to her and told her what my father was doing. She told him and I got the life beat out of me," Younger said.

"I was beaten every day of my life as a kid," Michael Pope said. "The system failed us for the hell we've gone through."

Michael Pope has dealt with significant emotional problems he believes stem from the physical and psychological abuse he suffered, resulting in his diagnosis with post-traumatic stress disorder.

Michael Pope said he finally mustered up the courage to go to the Granville cemetery where Hodgie's remains were buried earlier this year, a visit that also helped him get some closure.

"People will never know what we've been through," Michael Pope said. "We've been to hell and back."

Chapter 22
The Forgotten

We know the things that you have seen and heard in the previous chapters are not easy to imagine. This chapter will be about the forgotten. They are the ones who are left here to carry on. Ones that have been victimized and if they are lucky and in a perfect world will receive justice in the courtroom when they hear the word guilty. Imagine being victimized and not getting justice. Every person needs to know they are cared about, loved, and protected. There were many victims involved in this case. We call them the forgotten. Mae and David had one child dead and another with severe brain damage from his beatings and lack of care which stunted his growth who will never live a normal life and has the mentality of an elementary child. After the first trial in the early 70s, these two wonderful parents moved on to the state of Massachusetts. The only thing the Social Service worker involved in this case had to say in her final report was "CASE CLOSED." The next five children were just as severely victimized as the first two. As they started their new life in Massachusetts, the monster became even more enraged. He was like he was untouchable. As a few of the kids became school-aged, the state of Massachusetts removed three, never to be returned. We have had a hard time tracking down a couple of the children that were removed. We have always hoped that they had a better life. Before the last three children of Mae and David were removed, they hightailed it out of Massachusetts and back to New York. After they returned to New York, these remaining children were abused on a daily basis. They had one daughter and it was her act of courage after many years of the system in New York failing again, she and her siblings, no matter how many times they tried crying out for help, were forgotten. Each time they had the courage to reach out for help, no one came forward and helped them. The whole system failed miserably again. The youngest Pope child is Michael. These are the writings of the war within, not only being a victim of his parents, but a victim of the system. Feeling extremely hopeless, extremely helpless, and crying out with nobody hearing him, he had lasting damage. He has mixed emotions. The reopening of this investigation was like ripping a large bandage off a gaping wound trying to heal. He wanted his father to pay for everything he had done, but yet something inside of him yearned for a father / son relationship. At this time in his life, he was physically able to protect himself, so the violence subsided. He was trying to just move forward, but can you really? When you are realizing as a young adult that your father murdered your baby brother. How do you move forward and be a part of society that did not protect or listen to you? How do you trust? You can't even trust your own mother who never protected you. When a mother fails to protect a child, the hatred you feel is sometimes worse than the one victimizing you because moms are supposed to always protect them. When the case was now being reopened because of the courage of the only female Pope child who came forward, but the boys had no trust that the system would ever work and they felt the system would actually make them pay and hold him accountable. Why now? A few good men vowed to put a stop to it. There was something about my husband that Michael felt a connection to like a father. What a real father would act like. Through the years he has learned that not everyone in the system will fail or leave him. This has created a bond between them that will never be broken. There will never be a Father's Day, Christmas, or holiday that will go by without him always reaching out to my husband and telling him how much he means to him. As I have seen this relationship evolve through the years, and coming from a young man who came from a completely different world than my husband, I witnessed how they have both helped each other heal. In some ways they both suffer from post-traumatic stress, just in different ways. Michael from his early life and my husband from the career choice he chose. He will be forever grateful, even while fighting this war within himself, that actually started his healing whether he realized this or not. Is it perfect, absolutely not. Will he still have nightmares, yes. You read the closing, you read the verdict, now we want you to read the writings of the youngest and how it affected him and still affects his mental wellbeing. While everyone seems to go on with their lives, he is stuck wondering, could he have had a normal relationship with this man as an adult? Yet he knew this was not possible. He would have never been able to trust him after everything he saw and endured. He will never trust his mother to protect him. The false hope of ever being able to have this relationship, if you can call it that, which never seems like it would be possible because his father was a true monster and her mother was just as liable for all of the abuse and suffering. Even though he knew it would never be a normal functioning family, you always hold on to hope. The healing started even though he had mixed emotions of his father going to prison for the rest of his life, he knew deep down that this is where his father needed to be. The hope of ever having any type of normalcy was gone. We now want to bring you inside the mind, heart, and soul of the youngest victim and the demons he still fights every day.

From Michael Pope:

#1

War Wounds of war and unseen scars.
As a child abuse victim, you always seem to have mixed thoughts and feelings. Which causes a war within yourself. You think one way in your mind, but

you also feel another way in your heart. There is a constant battle with a very thin line between right and wrong. There lies the battleground. The war is not of being right or wrong, but a battle between love and hate. I know what my father has done to myself, my siblings, and others was very wrong, but in my heart I love him to death.

Many people ask, how can you love someone who has done these horrible things to you? It's not quite that easy. Thoughts and feelings are not something we can control. You cannot control what you think or feel, and there is the perfect setting for war.

I remember one instance where I did not make my bed one morning. I was about 6 years old. Due to not making my bed that morning, I was made to sleep on the floor with no blankets that night. It was cold outside. I got cold and uncomfortable, so I got in my bed hoping I would wake up before anyone else so I wouldn't get caught in my bed. My father had gotten up during the night. He checked to see if I was on the floor. Well, I wasn't. He yanked me out of my bed. He threw me on the floor, and he told me I was to sleep on the floor. He started stomping on me. Eventually he stomped me literally through my bedroom floor. I fell through to the first floor and landed on the kitchen table. I remember coming to with him running water on my face to wake me up as I became unconscious from the beating of falling. I don't remember which. Another instance, we had lots of animals when I grew up. Ducks were one of the many we had. My mother had bought a swimming pool for the ducks to play in. Well, my father figured it would be easier for the ducks to get in and out of the pool if it was ground level, so I was told to dig a hole big enough for the pool to be put into. The pool was 18 inches deep and 12 feet around. I started to dig the hole with a round pointed shovel and a bar to cut through the rooms and break up *stones. Shortly after I started digging, my father had left to go hunting. When he returned from the woods, I thought I was moving right along with my hole. Well, he didn't think so. He thought maybe I stopped and went and played while he was gone so he beat me once again unconscious. This time with his hunting rifle. Another time, we had gotten a snowstorm. Was over 2 feet of fresh snow. School was cancelled. We had to go shovel snow from our driveway. There was a 4-foot-high post rail fence on both sides of our driveway. We had to make sure we kept the snow on the back side of the fence. I was maybe 6-7 years old. Not a very big kid. The snow was wet and very heavy. I was scooping up a shovel full of snow and carrying it to the fence and throwing it over. My father asked, "What, are you too weak to stand here and throw the snow over the fence?" I said yes, it's too heavy, so he then said maybe I need to toughen you up a little. So he smashed me in the face with his shovel. I tried not to fall over because I knew if I fell I would get stomped on, but he hit me again with the shovel and eventually I fell and yes, I did get stomped. I woke up covered with snow and freezing. After that I started snoring pretty loud at night. I also would have trouble breathing through my nose. When I was about 10-11, I went to the doctor to see what was wrong with my nose. They said it had been broken once or twice which caused a piece of cartilage to shift and block most of my nasal passage. I eventually had surgery to cut the piece of cartilage. It was about 6 weeks after surgery the doctor had taken the packing out of my nose so he could check inside. Everything looked pretty good, I guess. Still had stitches but the packing was left out at that time. A few days later, back at home, we were building a horse barn. I dropped a board I was handing up to my father. He got mad cuz I dropped it. He got down off the ladder and grabbed the 2 x 4 and smashed me in the face with it for dropping it. So much for the nose surgery. Was once again busted. I was not taken to the doctor, of course.*

These are just a very small few of some of the stories I can tell you. I went through several beatings daily for almost 16 years. At times, 2-3 times a day. I was 3 years old and had to hunt and fish to eat while my father would feed our dogs steak. My mother would feed her pet skunk shrimp. I had to fend for myself. If I didn't catch any fish or find something in the woods to shoot and eat, I would eat berries or whatever I could find. Probably a few things I shouldn't have eaten not knowing if it was poisonous or would make me sick or even kill me. In my mind (thoughts) I know my parents were 100% wrong, but in my heart, I loved my father unconditionally. You may ask, how is that even possible? When my dad was finally brought to justice for murdering my brother, it tore my whole world apart. People told me I was wrong to love him. To care about him. To feel bad for him. To want to help him. Call him and go see him, to write to him. What right did I have to do all those things for him? Well, I ask, what right did these people have to judge me and tell me I'm wrong? They have no idea how this feels. No idea what I went through emotionally. They don't know that for about the last two years before my dad went to prison. That I had finally got what I fought for my whole life. The love and acceptance of my father. I was finally a person to him and when he was arrested and found guilty of murder, not only did it put him away and take the rest of his so-called normal life away, it also destroyed mine. People turned me away and looked upon me as him. These same people are people I tried to get help from as a child when I was being beaten and starved. People who turned their back on me when I was a child for asking for help and protection from my father. Because they were adults and afraid of my father, they refused to help, but now that he is locked up, they all talk big and frown on me. So now most of my family has cast me out because I stood beside my abuser through his court trial and even after the fact. So now here lies the perfect battleground for the inner war which creates unseen scars. In your mind and your thoughts, you know he was 100% wrong for the things he did to you, but in your heart and feelings, you love him unconditionally. So now you have a constant battle within your body. Between your mind and heart. At times, these battles explode into full-fledged WAR.

#2

Due to negligence from the very people whom are sworn to protect the innocent, the remaining 6 siblings were once again abused by the legal system resurfacing the horror and terror they had to live through. Because no wanted to listen to these children when they were physically living it. Now the 6 have to mentally live through this terror through questioning, trial and court appearances, news broadcasts and local newspapers. All of the terror they once lived through and somehow were able to put behind them was now front and center and smashing them in the face yet again. The father, David J. Pope, was eventually convicted of murder. He was sentenced to 25 years to life in prison. The mother, Mae E. Pope, was never charged with her part in any of it, but now these 6 children had to do what they could to fight through the pain and horror being forced to relive the terror they grew up in. Not physically, but mentally. This time things wouldn't be so easy for these children as adults to put behind them and move on in life. The 3 youngest that grew up with these horrid parents and were forced to deal with the abuse were now forced to deal with the mental issues of having to relive it all. With all the terror being fresh on the minds of these young adults. Neither of the 3 were able to put things behind them now. The 2 boys have had several jobs over the years, but dealing with the mental issues has made it impossible for them to keep a steady job for any period of time. The girl has not been able to work, mainly due to her fear of men. The prior tale is true to life as I am the youngest of these 7 siblings. I am no longer able to support myself nor my family. Due to the terror I was forced to live through, not once, but twice. Due to the local and state legal officials not doing their job to serve and protect. They instead elected to protect the evil people. I was forced to live through physical abuse as a child. As an adult I was forced to relive the abuse mentally. I now get social security and live on $876.00 a month. That's what the government says I'm eligible to receive. A government who chose to protect my abusers instead of me so therefore I am not able to support myself or family. I have contacted lawyers for legal advice. I strongly believe as long as the government chose not to do their job and protect my siblings and myself, they should be responsible for supporting us. The lawyers say there is no way. Too much time has passed. A little legal term called statute of limitations. When the law decided to exhume my brother's body and charge my father with murder, they say there is no statute of limitations on murder. Well, I say in that case, the legal system murdered me mentally for I have severe mental issues which make it impossible to live a healthy, normal life. Impossible for me to go to work every day and be able to work a normal life and support myself and family. Murder is murder. Physical murder or mental murder.

Sorry.

23+ years of abuse and torture. We as children depend on our parents to keep us safe and provide for us. Give their lives to protect us. Well, unfortunately, not every child has that luxury. Myself and my 6 siblings had to fend for ourselves, for personal safety and food and comfort, and to protect ourselves from our parents. Our dangers were not playing outside or having to worry about strangers. Not about eating or drinking things that might hurt us or make us ill. Our danger was our own parents. Our 2-year-old brother was beaten and starved to death. The other 6 were also beaten and starved, but for whatever reason, we survived the brutal terror. I'm not so sure who was the lucky on in the end. My little 2-year-old brother who was laid to rest and did not have to endure the pain and suffering any longer? Or the rest of us 6 who had to put through all the beatings and starvation? The mental or sexual abuse. Then as time passes, left to deal with a lifetime of mental anguish, hidden scars, and pain. We hide these things so as to continue to protect ourselves and others from the pain and suffering we were forced to deal with. Still do. There is no way to put into context or words to explain the pain and torment. The suffering. Some people use the words, I'm sorry, way too frequently and think everything will be okay. For some, it's a Band-Aid. It might help, but no completely heal. Well, I myself have waited and waited to hear those two words from the two people that have destroyed my life. One of the two people is now gone and I'm still waiting. I will never hear those two words from the people who needed to use them the most. It would have by far not healed the wounds or make the scars, pain, hate, or fear, go away. But those two little words coming from those two people would have meant the world to hear either of them say. It (I'm sorry) would have at least made myself or siblings start to think they were finally admitting to being or doing wrong. So I guess in the end, we have to be sorry. Not for ourselves, but for the people who have imposed the hell upon us. The living hell they have put us through for many years. We will all someday have peace. Those two people will have to face an eternity of hell. So no, I will never hear I'm sorry from them, so I'll have to settle for being sorry for them.

#4

History Does NOT Repeat
Some say they do things they do because that is how they grew up. What they were taught. That is all they know. They learned it was okay. Young children are very impressionable. Yes, indeed. A parent can only raise a child so far, and after a certain point in life, they begin to think for themselves. I learned right from wrong. Myself, as a survivor of one of the worst cases of child abuse in New York State. I could very easily abuse my children and others. I chose not to. I know how it feels. I know I wouldn't want to put anyone through the pain and suffering I went through. I have five biological children, three stepchildren and one I adopted. I am very strict with my kids, but I never have abused them in any way. I do however have many lasting issues from the abuse I suffered, but by no means do I use those issues as an excuse to abuse children or anyone else. The whole history repeating itself is such a terrible cliché and an excuse. One of the worst ever. We do not only learn from our own mistakes, but from mistakes others make as well. However, to blame others for our mistakes is so far wrong in so many ways. We need to take credit for our own actions and

not lay blame where it does not belong. It is too easy to make excuses and blaming others, which is yet again another excuse. Making excuses will never help the healing process. Blaming others will no help either. We need to take credit for the things we do and learn from our mistakes. Own up to your choices. Admit your wrongdoings. If you have an issue or problem dealing with something or someone, find the root of the problem and fix it. If you look inside yourself you will find the source of the problem. Don't make an excuse or lay blame. Admit the problem is within you and then you can find a solution to fix it. Once you start to fix the problems within yourself, that is when the healing process will start. Healing will never happen overnight, but to continue to blame others or blame your past and what you were taught or how you were raised is an excuse. Until we learn to take credit for our own actions, we will never be able to start healing and let go of the past. Don't blame others. Don't blame your past. History does NOT repeat.

The forgotten in this story is twofold. First was the inept and corrupt system. The system put into place to protect children at all costs, let all 7 of them down. One dead, one severely mentally challenged, two adopted out and unknown, and three left to fight their forever demons. Alone. They reached out for help so many times. In the 70s and the 90s and beyond. No one helped. No one listened to them. Teachers, Social Service workers, judges, police, courts, no one. They were forgotten. Not until a prosecutor took it upon himself to know this case screamed out for justice. Finally, but always remember, the terror lives within the forgotten ones forever.

The second way involved human reactions and life.

When all was done, the investigation, trial, verdict, and sentencing, all of us went about living our normal lives. The Pope children could not. They were forgotten. Their demons were still there. A guilty verdict did not take these internal wars away. Did many involved remember this and continue helping them? Does society understand this concept? We need to continue reaching out and helping those who have suffered so much.

Post Star reporter Tamara Dietrich wrote a succinct opinion article on May 7, 1995. A copy of this article is attached in this book.

A Thursday, May 11, 1995, letter to the editor published in the Post Star writing by a Glens Falls woman is attached in this book, but we feel we should publish it here too. It sums up inaction and the feelings people will have to live with for doing nothing. *Twenty years ago, I lived in a little house on Bay Road. In the evenings, during nice weather, I would sit on my front porch or in the living room, with the front door open. The house directly across the road was being rented by a couple who had small children. Many evenings the young boy would cry and not want to stay in bed. The boy would cry, the father would yell, the boy continued crying, the father continued yelling—until he got up! Not being able to see what was really happening, I can only tell you what I heard. The father would scream, "Get back into bed and go to sleep." Then when for whatever reason, he wouldn't, the screaming would start again. This time, though, it was the boy pleading, "Please, Daddy, don't hit me anymore." Then he would cry out in pain. Why the mother didn't try to protect her son, I'll never understand. All I ever heard her say was "Please stop." I knew something terrible was going on in that house, so I called the authorities. They told me that "unless I could actually see the abuse taking place, there was nothing they could do." If this were to happen today, I would never let someone tell me, "There is nothing that can be done." I would make such a nuisance of myself, someone would have to look into my complaints. After all of these years, I still feel guilty that I was unable to help this little boy. More so when I read in the Saturday, April 29, Post Star, how "a parade of relatives and former neighbors" testified* they saw David Pope's stepson "Hodgie." Even the doctor on duty, at the hospital, told the jury, "The boy exhibited numerous signs of Battered Child Syndrome the day he died, such as old and new bruises, healing fractures and malnutrition." Where were these people 22 years ago when Hodgie needed them so desperately? How could they see it, know it and do nothing? It makes me sick to think of the terror an pain this baby endured. It's true, Hodgie's death was no accident. Known he had no one to protect him. God just sent his angels down to bring him back home. Now that these witnesses have cleared their consciences, I certainly hope it's not a better night's sleep they're looking for. Finally now, with the conviction of this wicked man, Hodgie can have the peace he deserves. Hodgie can now "rest with the angels."

The forgotten, unloved, and never helped, children of the Longhouses.

CONNIE L. AIKEN AND THOMAS M. AIKEN

Thursday, May 11, 1995 The Post-Star, Glens Falls, N.Y. — A7

Letters

working at jobs for minimum wages, no benefits and paying our own high priced health insurance. Mr. Long, you must feel it is all right for Mr. and Mrs. New to make millions and not to allow the working class to have the little extras in life.

To all the Encore union workers — hold your heads high and don't give in to those greedy, scab-hiring people.

Robert Randall
Glens Falls

Hodgie can now rest with angels

Editor:

Twenty years ago, I lived in a little house on Bay Road. In the evenings, during nice weather, I would sit on my front porch or in the livingroom, with the front door open. The house directly across the road was being rented by a couple who had small children. Many evenings the young boy would cry and not want to stay in bed. The boy would cry, the father would yell, the boy continued crying, the father continued yelling — until he got up!

Not being able to see what was really happening, I can only tell you what I heard. The father would scream, "Get back into bed and go to sleep." Then when, for whatever reason, he wouldn't, the screaming would start again. This time though, it was the boy pleading, "Please daddy, don't hit me anymore," then he would cry out in pain. Why the mother didn't try to protect her son, I'll never understand. All I ever heard her say was, "Please stop."

I knew something terrible was going on in that house, so I called the authorities. They told me that "Unless I could actually see the abuse taking place, there was nothing they could do." If this were to happen today, I would have never let someone tell me, "There is nothing that can be done." I would make such a nuisance of myself, someone would have to look into my complaints.

After all these years, I still feel guilty that I was unable to help this little boy. More so when I read in the Saturday, April 29, Post-Star, how "a parade of relatives and former neighbors" testified they saw David Pope beat and kick Pope's stepson "Hodgie." Even the doctor on duty, at the hospital, told the jury "the boy exhibited numerous signs of Battered Child Syndrome the day he died, such fractures and malnutrition."

Where were these people 22 years ago when Hodgie needed them so desperately? How could they see it, know it and do nothing? It makes me sick to think of the terror and pain this baby endured. It's true, Hodgie's death was no accident. Knowing he had no one to protect him, God just sent his angels down to bring him back home.

Now that these witnesses have cleared their consciences, I certainly hope it's not a better night's sleep they're looking for. Finally now, with the conviction of this wicked man, Hodgie can have the peace he deserves. Hodgie can now "rest with the angels."

Donna M. Smith
Glens Falls

Teachers voted tenure by board

Editor:

The Bolton Teachers' Association would like to clarify the article (April 10) concerning the tenure recommendations of two of our members. Although it was stated by the Bolton Board of Education president, Bill Morehouse, that the teachers were to receive tenure by default as a protest against the tenure law, this was not the case, as was noted in one local weekly paper's article of April 27-May 3. The Bolton Board of Education voted unanimously to grant tenure to both teachers. It is unfortunate that The Post-Star did not follow up on the Bolton Board of Education's meeting to ascertain the results. We hope this corrects the impression left by your previous article.

Thomas Muscatello
President
The Bolton Teachers' Association

Today in History

Today is Thursday, May 11, the 131st day of 1995. There are 234 days left in the year.

Today's Highlight in History:

On May 11, 1946, the relief agency CARE (Cooperative for American Remittances to Europe) had its start as the first CARE package arrived in Europe.

On this date:

In 1647, Peter Stuyvesant arrived in New Amsterdam to become governor.

In 1858, Minnesota became the 32nd state of the Union.

In 1888, songwriter Irving Berlin was born Israel Baline in Temun, Russia.

In 1894, workers at the Pullman Palace Car Co. in Illinois went on strike. The American Railway Union, led by Eugene Debs, subsequently began a boycott of Pullman that blocked freight traffic in and out of Chicago.

In 1910, Glacier National Park in Montana was established.

In 1943, during World War II, American forces landed on Japanese-held Attu island in the Aleutians. (The territory was retaken in three weeks.)

In 1944, Allied forces launched a major offensive in central Italy.

In 1947, the B.F. Goodrich Company of Akron, Ohio, announced the development of a tubeless tire.

In 1949, Israel was admitted to the United Nations as the world body's 59th member.

In 1949, Siam changed its name to Thailand.

In 1973, charges against Daniel Ellsberg for his role in the Pentagon Papers case were dismissed by Judge William M. Byrne, who cited government misconduct.

In 1981, reggae artist Bob Marley died at age 36 in a Miami hospital.

In 1987, in a medical first, doctors in Baltimore transplanted the heart and lungs of an auto accident victim to a patient who gave up his own heart to a second recipient. (Clinton House, the nation's first living heart donor, died 14 months later.)

Ten years ago: More than 50 people died when a flash fire swept a jam-packed soccer stadium in Bradford, England.

Five years ago: President Bush, on a two-day trip of college commencement speeches, told reporters aboard Air Force One that there were "no conditions" going into a budget summit with Congress.

One year ago: Arkansas put to death two convicted murderers; it was the first time a state executed two people on the same day since the U.S. Supreme Court allowed states to restore the death penalty in 1976.

Today's Birthdays: Actor-comedian Foster Brooks is 83. Actor Denver Pyle is 75. Comedian Mort Sahl is 68.

Thought for Today: "We carry our nemesis within us: Yesterday's self-admiration is the legitimate father of today's feeling of guilt." — Dag Hammarskjold, U.N. Secretary-General (1905-1961).

Now They Lay me Down to Rest

DAVE BARRY
Dave gives most excellent fashion tips to his fellow males. **F3**

Sunday, May 7, 1995

Tamara Dietrich

The Here and Now

Nobody bothers to save them

This is People's Exhibit 6.

The small child is lying flat on a white sheet, so small his head falls short of the white pillow.

The dark eyes, glassy as marbles, stare at the ceiling. The mouth is slack. It lolls open. The cheeks sink back into the concave mouth. The eyebrows are raised in a state of perpetual surprise.

From this angle you can see dark scrapes along the curve of the chin and jawline, the taut, thin cords of muscle running lengthwise down the reedy neck.

The shirt is bunched up around a bony ribcage. The swollen belly is exposed to the top of the baggy trousers.

Someone has written beside the photographs in black pen: Howard James White. 10-29-69. 9-11-72.

People's Exhibit 7, 8 and 9 are more police photos of Howard James "Hodgie" White. This time he's lying naked on his stomach on the same gurney, the better to expose to the bloodless eye of the camera the countless cuts and bruises — the old ones and the fresh ones — that were the hallmarks of his short, brutal life. The spindly arms stretch out as if he were embracing the bed. The thin legs were just getting some growth to them. The vertebrae punch through his bare back like bony knuckles.

There's much these pictures don't show.

The ruptured stomach. The bleeding kidney, the bleeding small intestine. The punctured scalp. The broken rib. The broken bone in the face. The beatings with stereo wire, hammers, boards, shovels and belts. The steel-toed boot to the backside that once sent him flying through the air. The kick or punch to the stomach that finally killed him.

Twenty-two years after little Hodgie was stripped and posed for these forensic photographs, the man who put him in an unmarked grave in Granville has finally been convicted.

David S. Pope Sr. faces up to 25 years to life when he's sentenced later this month for murder.

Who's ca[

The child care system is being overwhelmed by more kids at risk

Associated Press

Jean Adnopoz, a psychologist at the Yale Child Study Center, said children who spend years drifting between foster care homes "can't be expected to come out in any way that would appear to be healthy."

"If you have a child with no psychological parents, essentially adrift in the world, you are headed toward all sorts of bad outcomes," she said. "And we as a society are going to pay and pay and pay for it."

States became the parent of last resort for these children in the last four decades, assuming the role from private and church charities. From the beginning, the solution often was to put the child in foster care.

"The system always functioned poorly, but it wasn't as noticeable when it was dealing with fewer kids. It became much more evident when there was stress on the system," said Marcia Lowry, director of the Children's Rights Project at the American Civil Liberties Union.

But by the mid-1980s, those few kids became many.

Fueled by drugs, teen-age pregnancy, AIDS and other crises, the number of children at risk has exploded. The American Humane Association says there were 1.7 million reports of neglect and abuse in 1985. The number reached 3 million last year. About 40 percent of all reports are substantiated.

"There's a giant spigot out there that lots of kids come rolling out of," said David Liederman, executive director of the Child Welfare League of America. "It has its source in poverty, drugs, lousy neighborhoods and inadequate affordable housing."

Crack cocaine devastated existing families and created a new urban term: boarder babies, newborns abandoned in hospitals by their addict mothers. Federal researchers estimated 22,000 babies were left in the nation's hospitals during 1991 alone.

Sheer numbers overpowered already

331

Everyone agrees that justice for Hodgie White was a long time coming. What took the system two decades to bring to trial, a jury decided in about two hours. The evidence, said the judge after the verdict was rendered, was overwhelming.

Just as overwhelming is the fact that a child can be brutalized to the extent that Hodgie was brutalized, and not be saved somewhere along the way. By somebody. By anybody.

Witness after witness testified at Pope's trial that they saw either the physical abuse outright or the bruises and cuts it left behind. But nobody — nobody — stopped it.

Not Hodgie's mother, Mae White. Not the relatives. Not the neighbors. Not the family friends. Not even the Social Services caseworker who visited the home just five days before Hodgie died. The caseworker who duly noted cuts and bruises on his body. Who had reports of child abuse from Hodgie's grandmother but labeled them "debatable." Who admitted in court that the signs of abuse she overlooked 22 years ago would be considered textbook today.

Even the doctor who examined Hodgie's body in 1972, who recognized the awful extent of injury, who considered the boy's death "suspicious" and the result of an "intentional act," still failed to classify it as a homicide. Indeed, he didn't classify it as anything at all on the death certificate.

Not until Hodgie's body was exhumed last fall and re-examined was his death determined a homicide, enabling police investigators — finally — to step in.

The family's former caseworker, Anita M. Sarchioto, said on the stand last week that "the mindset was different" back then. Apparently that means that in 1972 bruises weren't bruises, a starved child wasn't a starved child, reports of abuse weren't reports of abuse.

If so, the mindset hasn't changed much since then, because when it came time to file charges against Pope for Hodgie's murder, he wasn't hard to find — he was cooling his heels in Washington County Jail, charged with felony incest.

Health experts who like to package and label things have rubber-stamped what happened to Hodgie — and thousands and thousands like him — as Battered Child Syndrome. It has a tidy medical sound to it. By now it's probably shortened it to its initials — BCS. Even better.

But it does justice to no one, least of all Hodgie. The boy in the photographs lying on the white sheet — not quite reaching the pillow, not quite 3 years old — didn't die from a syndrome.

He died because his stepfather, in what the legal system classifies as a "depraved act of indifference," kicked or punched him so hard he ripped open his stomach. Because the system let him know he could.

He died because, in multiple, tangled acts of indifference, nobody else bothered to save him.

Tamara Dietrich is Sunday/Projects Editor at The Post-Star.

wobbly systems. New York City saw the number of children in foster care swell from 18,000 to 46,000 in the past five years; the rolls in Illinois' Cook County spiraled from nearly 24,000 to more than 46,000.

This explosion of numbers carries tremendous costs. Spending on child welfare has tripled in the urban areas of New York, California and Texas, as well as rural states like Vermont and Nebraska. Pennsylvania spends over $800 million on child welfare alone.

The Congressional Budget Office estimated the federal government will spend more than $9.2 billion between fiscal year 1991 and 1996 for foster care.

The Republicans want to change the formula. They've proposed block grants to the states for all child welfare efforts, arguing it's best to let the states establish programs that best fit their needs.

But critics say foster care would have to compete with other programs. States would no longer be accountable to the federal government if they aren't measuring up.

Even now, courts and agencies are showing increasing signs of poverty. Social workers are underpaid; vital computer systems are antiquated or nonexistent. Washington, D.C., beset by budget crises, recently had most of its caseworkers' cars repossessed.

From her vantage point of Manhattan family court, Judge Judith Sheindlin, sees funds that could be used to repair families

the $20,000 a year it costs to keep a child in foster care.

"The kids are being shortchanged. The taxpayers are being shortchanged," she sa

The system is cracking under caseloa Social workers often tend to 50, even 10 children; professional standards talk of r more than 20 cases per worker. Courts a so crowded that only a few minutes can afforded each case to clear the day's calendar.

"What if that case comes up only on a year and you're only spending three minutes? That's horrifying," said Nancy Sidote Salyers, a Chicago judge who handles as many as 150 children a day.

While the complexity of cases grow, with mothers on drugs and children witl special needs, the number of skilled soc workers is falling.

American Public Welfare Association surveys find agencies so desperate to fill spots they are reducing qualifications. On quarter of states surveyed now don't requ a college degree as a prerequisite; less tha half train workers before they take on cas

"You need a skilled professional to d what is a very complicated job," said M Hardin, director of foster care and famil preservation for the American Bar Association. "There should be competiti testing and training, like you'd see at a police academy."

Instead, undertrained and hard-press workers make tough decisions, pressure

Contributions of the

Justice Howard Levine, associate justice of the New York Court of Appeals, delivered the following speech at the Law Day ceremonies of the Warren County Bar Association on May 1. Before his appointment to the Court of Appeals in 1993, Justice Levine served as a justice of the Appellate Division of the state Supreme Court's Third Department since 1982.

Law Day gives us all an opportunity to pause and reflect on the contributions of the American legal system to the well-being, prosperity and stability of our society. This year's Law Day theme, E Pluribus Unum — Out of Many, One, is especially timely. We are the most diverse society in the world. We are a rich mosaic of different races, religious and ethnic backgrounds. Yet, although not always without difficulty and tension, we have managed somehow to live together — and actually come together in times of national crises. How have we avoided the bloodshed of cultural and ethnic religious warfare in less diverse societies, what was once Yugoslavia and between the Hutus and Tutsis of Rwanda, to take the most recent examples? Only once did we fail to avoid it — the Civil War.

I believe the explanation for our unique ability to live as one in diversity goes back to an equally unique and novel theory expressed in the Declaration of Independence, drafted by a young, then fairly recent law school graduate, Thomas Jefferson — the commitment to the proposition that

Howard Levine

Gues

all men are created equa each person was thereby concern, equal dignity. I will remember that that constitution adopted abc among the compromis sufficient approval of the

But it was eloquently great lawyer, 4 score an Address in which he refer liberty and dedicated, all men are created equal'

332

Now They Lay Me Down to Rest

Information on the Granville Longhouses

BUILDING-STRUCTURE INVENTORY FORM
DIVISION FOR HISTORIC PRESERVATION
NEW YORK STATE PARKS AND RECREATION
ALBANY, NEW YORK (518) 474-0479

FOR OFFICE USE ONLY
UNIQUE SITE NO. 115/44
QUAD _____
SERIES _____
NEG. NO. _____

V-442-?

YOUR NAME: WASHINGTON COUNTY INFORMATION - TOURISM AND HISTORIC PRESERVATION   DATE: 1/78
YOUR ADDRESS: COUNTY OFFICE BUILDING, PORT EDWARD, NEW YORK 12828   TELEPHONE: _____
ORGANIZATION (if any): _____

IDENTIFICATION
1. BUILDING NAME(S): _____
2. COUNTY: Washington   TOWN/CITY: Granville   VILLAGE: Granville
3. STREET LOCATION: 2/24/26/36 Park St.
4. OWNERSHIP: a. public ☐   b. private ☑
5. PRESENT OWNER: Hugh G. Williams   ADDRESS: 8 Maple St. Granville
6. USE: Original: tenement   Present: tenement
7. ACCESSIBILITY TO PUBLIC: Exterior visible from public road: Yes ☑   No ☐
   Interior accessible: Explain _____

DESCRIPTION
8. BUILDING MATERIAL:
   a. clapboard ☑   b. stone ☐   c. brick ☐   d. board and batten ☐
   e. cobblestone ☐   f. shingles ☐   g. stucco ☐   other: _____
9. STRUCTURAL SYSTEM (if known):
   a. wood frame with interlocking joints ☐
   b. wood frame with light members ☑
   c. masonry load bearing walls ☐
   d. metal (explain) _____
   e. other _____
10. CONDITION: a. excellent ☐   b. good ☐   c. fair ☐   d. deteriorated ☐
11. INTEGRITY: a. original site ☑   b. moved ☐   if so, when? _____
    c. list major alterations and dates (if known): _____

12. PHOTO: p.29-3   13. MAP:

CONNIE L. AIKEN AND THOMAS M. AIKEN

4/14/22, 2:05 PM   Park Street Building 1_0001.jpg

BUILDING-STRUCTURE INVENTORY FORM
DIVISION FOR HISTORIC PRESERVATION
NEW YORK STATE PARKS AND RECREATION
ALBANY, NEW YORK (518) 474-0479

FOR OFFICE USE ONLY
UNIQUE SITE NO. 115/44
QUAD
SERIES
NEG. NO.

V-44 1-2

YOUR NAME: WASHINGTON COUNTY INFORMATION DATE: 6/78
TOURISM AND HISTORIC PRESERVATION
YOUR ADDRESS: COUNTY OFFICE BUILDING   TELEPHONE:
FORT EDWARD, NEW YORK 12828

ORGANIZATION (if any):

IDENTIFICATION
1. BUILDING NAME(S):
2. COUNTY: WASHINGTON   TOWN/CITY: GRANVILLE   VILLAGE: GRANVILLE
3. STREET LOCATION: PARK ST.
4. OWNERSHIP: a. public ☐   b. private ☑
5. PRESENT OWNER: Hugh Williams   ADDRESS: 8 S. Maple St.
6. USE: Original: Tenement   Present: Tenement
7. ACCESSIBILITY TO PUBLIC: Exterior visible from public road: Yes ☑   No ☐
     Interior accessible: Explain

DESCRIPTION
8. BUILDING   a. clapboard ☑   b. stone ☐   c. brick ☐   d. board and batten ☐
    MATERIAL: e. cobblestone ☐   f. shingles ☐   g. stucco ☐   other:

9. STRUCTURAL   a. wood frame with interlocking joints ☐
    SYSTEM: b. wood frame with light members ☑
    (if known)   c. masonry load bearing walls ☐
                   d. metal (explain)
                   e. other

10. CONDITION: a. excellent ☐   b. good ☐   c. fair ☐   d. deteriorated ☐
11. INTEGRITY: a. original site ☑   b. moved ☐   if so, when?
                c. list major alterations and dates (if known):

12. PHOTO: P.29-4   13. MAP:

HP-1

Now They Lay me Down to Rest

14. THREATS TO BUILDING: a. none known ☑ b. zoning ☐ c. roads ☐
    d. developers ☐ e. deterioration ☐
    f. other: _____

15. RELATED OUTBUILDINGS AND PROPERTY:
    a. barn ☐ b. carriage house ☐ c. garage ☐
    d. privy ☐ e. shed ☐ f. greenhouse ☐
    g. shop ☐ h. gardens ☐
    i. landscape features: _____
    j. other: _____

16. SURROUNDINGS OF THE BUILDING (check more than one if necessary):
    a. open land ☐ b. woodland ☐
    c. scattered buildings ☐
    d. densely built-up ☐ e. commercial ☐
    f. industrial ☐ g. residential ☑
    h. other: _____

17. INTERRELATIONSHIP OF BUILDING AND SURROUNDINGS:
    (Indicate if building or structure is in an historic district)

18. OTHER NOTABLE FEATURES OF BUILDING AND SITE (including interior features if known):

SIGNIFICANCE

19. DATE OF INITIAL CONSTRUCTION: C 1905

    ARCHITECT: _____

    BUILDER: Alonzo Norton

20. HISTORICAL AND ARCHITECTURAL IMPORTANCE:

    built for slate workers - possibly a
    (Austrian, Polish, Hungarian, Chez.) slate operator or
    slate operators recruited slavic   a family named
    peoples from the Carpathian and High Divya had it built
    Tatra mountain area of Eastern Europe

21. SOURCES: they had quarried granite, etc. and
    mined silver and other ore there
    they were brought to Granville

22. THEME: Res. to work in the slate quarries.
    they lived here also.

335

CONNIE L. AIKEN AND THOMAS M. AIKEN

14. THREATS TO BUILDING: a. none known ☑ b. zoning ☐ c. roads ☐
    d. developers ☐   e. deterioration ☐
    f. other: _____
15. RELATED OUTBUILDINGS AND PROPERTY:
    a. barn ☐   b. carriage house ☐   c. garage ☐
    d. privy ☐   e. shed ☐   f. greenhouse ☐
    g. shop ☐   h. gardens ☐
    i. landscape features: _____
    j. other: _____
16. SURROUNDINGS OF THE BUILDING (check more than one if necessary):
    a. open land ☑   b. woodland ☐
    c. scattered buildings ☐
    d. densely built-up ☐   e. commercial ☐
    f. industrial ☐   g. residential ☑
    h. other: _____
17. INTERRELATIONSHIP OF BUILDING AND SURROUNDINGS:
    (Indicate if building or structure is in an historic district)

18. OTHER NOTABLE FEATURES OF BUILDING AND SITE (including interior features if known):

Park St. was part of Mary A. Organ Development of 1904 — in fact the only street mapped out that was actually put in. Park St. was offered as a street in 1905.

SIGNIFICANCE
19. DATE OF INITIAL CONSTRUCTION: __C. 1905__

ARCHITECT: _____

BUILDER: __Alonzo Norton__

20. HISTORICAL AND ARCHITECTURAL IMPORTANCE: Slate operator or Dirga's had it built

Tenement home for Polish, Austrian, Hungarian, Chez slate workers. & Slavic peoples. Slate operators recruited Slavic people from the Carpathian and High Tatra mountain areas of Eastern Europe three they had quarried

21. SOURCES: granite and mined silver and other ore, they were brought to Granville to work in the slate quarries

22. THEME:

Chapter 23
True Reflections of a Police Investigator

The story you just read outlining a true love story and the affects horrendous crimes have not only on the police officer, but their family as well, is our story. My venture into law enforcement began at the request of my brother to accompany him with taking an upcoming New York State Police entrance exam. I was in my 2nd year of college and quickly signed up for the test. Little did I know that there were well over 35,000 people throughout the state that took the test at the same time. The lines to enter the Glens Falls Civic Center were lined up and down and around blocks. By the grace of God, I scored a 96 which was just high enough to gain entry in the 2nd class to be offered. I attribute this to the fact I was in college and used to thinking and taking tests, I did not drink the night before, and I had plenty of rest. This opened the door to a 30-year career with the privilege of working with the best officers and investigators you could ever ask for. It was a very elite agency with unbelievable resources at our fingertips. All of these people and resources allowed me to look good at doing my job. I could not have done this without them. It took 30 years and final reflections entering retirement to realize why I entered law enforcement. I hated bullies. I was never afraid of getting a black eye or bloody lip growing up as I always stood up to bullies against me or especially against others. In 30 years, most all of my cases, especially my major cases, were against horrendous bullies. Child abusers, domestic violence, murders, they were all forms of bullying.

I used to teach various elements of law enforcement in New York and I gave lectures on two of my most horrific cases, including this one. I still lecture today and I am certified in South Carolina to teach law enforcement for continuing credit. A long time ago I was asked for a biography for introduction purposes. I quickly put one together, but after, I thought this might come in useful for the future as I continue teaching and lecturing. This was how I created my current 10-page biography which is attached at the end of this book. I would like to point out that you will not see the hundred homicide cases detailed with the highlights of cases. This is because those were almost always a tremendous team effort. As you read through some of the cases I highlighted in my biography, remember that these were ones I did myself.

As I sit down to write this, I struggle with many things after 30 years of Law Enforcement in New York State. 25 years were spent investigating major cases including homicides, other death cases including suicides, accidental deaths, natural deaths, car accidents, industrial accidents and many others, including kidnappings and horrendous child abuse. I have 38 years in Law Enforcement total today. My struggles include a term I resist being labeled with. PTSD. I am too tough for this term. How ironic I see myself as tough when I am currently crying like a baby just typing these first few innocuous lines. This is my first struggle. I am not a very big guy, only 5'7.5" and currently about 165 pounds. I will never give up that .5" even though my last physical has me down to no more than 5'07". I do not have the "little man syndrome" and I have no misconceptions that there are many fights I cannot win and many people that could kick my butt. I will tell you that there has never been a house I was afraid of running into, or a situation I have not taken head on, no matter what is on the other side of the door. This is still true today. I have fears like everyone, but I have learned to overcome these fears. I don't fear my own life or pain, only the thought of not being with my family or loved ones. There are many things I have not shared with anyone until recently, including the events of March 5th, 1990, when I lost a true hero. My Academy roommate named Joey Aversa. That is one of those situations I ran straight into, but not as heroic as he did. He gave the ultimate sacrifice. He gave up his life to aid a police officer in need. He ran straight into this situation with no fear or hesitation for his own life. He was shot entering the doorway where a police officer needed help.

Joey was my roommate throughout the Academy, starting when we were sworn in on March 12, 1984, until our graduation in August. He grew up in the Bronx and taught a naïve kid all about drugs while I helped him study for our college-level exams. We were very close for two young men from a world apart. He was a mixture of Hispanic and Italian, and was a golden gloves boxer. This was evident when we reached the boxing section of the Academy. Even though we were in two distant parts of New York State from each other, Joey and I were promoted to Investigator on the same day. October 12, 1989. We were both assigned to the same upper-level Federal Drug task force in New York City. This task force investigated the cartels through mainly major Federal Title III (Wiretap) cases. He was assigned to our sister group. This meant he was not with us on day-to-day activities, but each group would assist the others if extra bodies were needed. How ironic I know this, but a thought that will haunt me forever is that I forgot he was assisting us that day doing a high end "buy-bust," and when I ran straight in the middle of a shootout just as the last shots were fired, I looked over and saw a male subject lying in a large pool of blood next to the door and my first thought was "Good, we at least got one of them." The pain I deal with on an almost daily basis began when some screamed in agony that this was my friend Joey. His face was away from me and I never realized it was Joey as I saw one New York City Detective in a prone position on the ground, shot through both legs. As I saw a suspect lying on the other side of a wrought-iron fence shot through the wrist and stomach. As an undercover New York City detective came walking out of that "bad" doorway holding his forehead and obviously shot through the leg. As we ran to him and pulled his hand away, we were convinced he was shot in the forehead, only to learn later that the fight he was in for his life included a very large Dominican male biting his forehead to the point it looked like a gunshot wound. The large male suspect came walking out of that bad door and I assisted with handcuffing him, effectively ending this shootout that left my friend dead, two NYC detectives permanently disabled and two suspects serving life in prison. Another thought from that day is one of only two times in my life and career that I had to physically force myself to overcome any fears and look into and clear that bad door. My fears were holding me back for a split second, but it was one of only two times I had to actually force myself to push into bad danger. All the other times, I had no issues with running into apartments, houses, and situations where even the most hardened police officers from other departments shook their heads after and questioned my sanity. Another thought from that day is when the last shot was fired, the last suspect handcuffed, and the last bad door cleared, another experience occurred that I will never forget. In NY City, when an officer down call goes out, people come from anywhere and everywhere within minutes. I was wearing old worn clothing and had a scraggly beard to fit in better, so I and all my partners around me instantly realized that officers were coming out of trees and everywhere with armor and guns I have never even seen before. I have been around guns all my life. It seemed like an eternity, but in reality, it was only minutes at most. All of us instantly grabbed the badges hanging around our necks, put under our shirts, and put them out for display so the incoming heroes knew we were part of the good guys. I will never forget that this moment felt like a movie scene where you pan in a complete 360 continuously, and I felt completely outside of my body.

Going back to this first struggle, people have asked me all my career how I can survive mentally and emotionally every day dealing with at least a hundred homicides, over 700 of the worse child abuse cases you can possibly imagine, and hundreds and hundreds of death cases in total. I have attended almost 100 autopsies. I kept saying it was because I had to in order to help the victims, especially the kids. I reasoned that I learned to compartmentalize all of these nightmares that still wake me up at night. Here is the dirty little secret. I was successful at working through all of this, until a few months after I actually retired from New York. Then it all came crashing down. I live each day an emotional wreck. I cry while giving lectures, talking to my wife, or especially when thinking about victims. I can't help it anymore. It is just something I will learn to live with. I hate seeing people physically or emotionally suffer and I have been deeply scarred.

When Connie wrote about how Rob and I changed the way these cases were investigated and prosecuted, we did not go into enough detail. Back in our Upstate New York area, like most everywhere in the country still is today, when someone did report child abuse to the police and it was investigated, the outcome never amounted to much more than a slap on the wrist. Families hardly ever went to the police and kept things within the family. Even if a plea bargain or conviction after trial happened, which was not often then, it amounted to very little jail time. I can tell you after 38 years of law enforcement and conducting hundreds to thousands of sexual abuse and major case investigations and being in the minds of hundreds of horrendous child abusers to understand the way they think to obtain the confessions, my philosophy and statement is strong. NO ADULT ABUSER OF A CHILD WILL EVER BE SAFE AROUND CHILDREN..!!! Child abuse, like the forcible rape of an adult, is as much or more about power and control as it is sex. Even castration will not work because they will still find ways to exert their power and control and sexually abuse that child. We changed the way we investigated and prosecuted these cases. Children don't understand the sexual aspect of their abuse, they just know it feels wrong and they want it to stop. They don't want their loved one to go to jail, they want it to stop. They don't even know that all daddies don't do this with their kids. We started handling the kids in an entirely different way and we learned how to put these cases together and how to obtain legal confessions. If I tell you my confession rate in child abuse and major case crimes was around 80%, you would never believe me, but it was. We then took these better investigations to the District Attorney and together we changed the way we prosecuted them. This is why you will read so many lengthy sentences on my biography. We then also did public service announcements by holding many press conferences and issuing many press releases as we told about these horrendous cases and how we held these evil people responsible. You don't see many homicide cases pleading out to 20-25 years, but yet, we had child abusers pleading to this many years. A lot of times with no testimony from the child. In the rare cases we could not prosecute the suspects, we still handled the children or even adults, in such a way that they felt empowered and were able to heal. The first part of improving these investigations was the way we investigated and were able to obtain horrendous soul-shattering confessions. The second part was the way we handled victims. There is a certain way you need to interview victims, especially child victims, to allow their testimony to be accepted in court. You can't ask leading questions. Officers go through extensive training in today's world to be certified to do these interviews. We also empowered the victims to allow them to better understand the process and start the healing process. Remember, the goal is not just to arrest and convict, but to heal the victim. The third part was the way we partnered up with the prosecution. We took ownership with the District Attorney's part. We learned the law and the process. When you hand over a victim that was properly handled, that makes for a much better prosecution witness. The final statement on handling victims is this. When a victim gets to the point of being able to openly talk about the abuse they went through and their feelings without shame or guilt, they are truly on their way to healing.

If Connie and I could accomplish anything with this book other than to provide you with an interesting study of a cold case homicide that allowed an evil man to walk free for 22 years, it would be to teach one police officer, one CPS worker, one teacher, just one person the importance of doing their job right no matter how difficult or frustrating it is. When we are upset that we feel a relative, neighbor, friend, or other close person does not make that call or intervene, please never let that be a professional tasked with caring for and helping our most precious commodity, our children.

CONNIE L. AIKEN AND THOMAS M. AIKEN

Thomas M. Aiken

as of ~ August 10, 2022

Personal:

    Born: January 01, 1962

    Family: Married 37+ years ~ 6 children - 3 sons {Army, Air Force & Marines} and three young daughters.

Education:

    High School: Hudson Falls High School - Washington County
                    Graduated in June of 1980

    College: Adirondack Community College
                  Associate Degree - Business Administration
                  Graduated in 1989

                  Empire State College
                  Bachelor Degree - Criminal Justice / Management
                  Graduated in 1992

Furman Police Department: March 11, 2018 to the present ~ Currently a Lieutenant

USCB – Bluffton Campus: January, 2014 to March 11, 2018 ~ Left as Assistant Police Chief

New York State Police: March, 1984 to December 2013 ~ Retired as Senior Investigator

Now They Lay me Down to Rest

Academy: March 12, 1984
Graduated in August of 1984

Promotions: Investigator - October 12, 1989
Senior Investigator - February 27, 1997

Assignments:

1. SP Hadley — August 1984
2. SP South Glens Falls — Fall of 1984
3. SP Whitehall — Winter of 1984
4. SP Fultonville {Thruway} — June of 1985
5. SP South Glens Falls {Interstate} — Fall of 1986
6. New York City Drug Task Force {Investigator} — 10-12-89
7. SP Clifton Park {Investigator} — Spring 1991
8. SP Wilton {Investigator} — Winter 1992
9. SP Queensbury {Investigator} — 1993
10. Division Headquarters - Internal Affairs Section {Senior Investigator} — 02-27-97
11. SP Brunswick {Senior Investigator} — 02-04-99
12. SP Queensbury {Senior Investigator} — 08-30-01
13. SP Greenwich {Senior Investigator} — 02-05-04

Training:

- New York State Police Academy
- Basic Investigator's School
- Narcotic Investigator's School
- Dealing with Emotionally Disturbed Persons
- Homicide & Death Investigations School
- Hostage / Critical Incident Investigations
- Awareness during arrest Survival I
- Accidental Death / Body after death
- Child Molestation I & II
- Victim Oriented Sex Crime Investigations
- Handling / Cross Examinations / Court Tactics
- BCI Major Crime Seminar - 1993
- Investigation & Evaluation of Sexual Abuse Allegations
- Domestic Violence Training
- BCI Investigators In-Service Training
- Basic Leadership School {Supervisor Training}
- Child Fatality & Domestic Violence Conference
- Numerous other training courses on police investigations and specifically child abuse investigation training.
- Henry William Homicide Seminar
- Stalking in Schools: Learning to Identify & Respond
- New York State Police Sex Offense Seminar May 25, 2007

CONNIE L. AIKEN AND THOMAS M. AIKEN

| Senior Investigator Thomas M. Aiken | Biography |

- Beslan School Shooting - Terrorist Training - October 2007
- New York State Police Child Physical Abuse Seminar
- New York State Police Basic Leadership School - June 7 - 25, 1999
- "Mouse Trap" The Sexual Victimization of Children & Adults Online & Off - October 19-20, 2000
- Sexual Assault Reform Act Training - January 26, 2001
- Warren / Washington Counties Child Fatality & Domestic Violence Conference - June 8-9, 2000
- Numerous Animal Cruelty training Seminars – latest on 10-02-08 in Warren County
- Human Trafficking Training Seminar – December 17, 2008
- Firearms Qualification – Handgun & Shotgun – two (2) times per year for 28 years
- "Expert Bar" – 249 / 250; "Distinguished Bar" – 250 / 250
- Animal Cruelty Investigations: Beyond the Basics – DOCS Training Center in Albany on 09-30-09 sponsored by ASPCA and DCJS.
- Victim's Rights: Emerging Issues in the Criminal Justice System – this was a U.S. Attorney sponsored training in New York City from April 07th to April 08th, 2010.
- Interview Techniques & Deception Detection – NYSP Academy – October 05, 2010
- Child Fatality & Serious Physical Injury Abuse Investigations – October 18, 2010

Commendations:

- **September 17, 1992** - Plaque - Glens Falls Mayor Francis X. O'Keefe. Investigation and arrest of numerous members of a ½ million dollar silver theft case.
- **July 14, 1995** - Superintendent's Letter of Commendation - Superintendent James W. McMahon - David Pope investigation and arrest.
- **April 18, 2000** - Letter - Saratoga County D.A. James Murphy - regarding comments from a stalking victim that was assisted in an investigation.
- **September 19, 2000** - Letter - Rensselaer County CPS - regarding assistance with training of CPS workers.
- **October 12, 2000** - Letter - Det. Sgt. Paul A. Barci, Vermont State Police - assistance with Richard Borden Sexual Abuse investigation & arrest.
- **March 19, 2001** - Letter - Cambridge Police Chief George Bell - assistance with investigation and arrest of church burglary suspect.
- **April 22, 2001** - Plaque - U.S. Department of Justice - Daniel J. French - U.S.Attorney's Office - Department of Justice Award for Public Service.
- **April 30, 2001** - Letter - Rensselaer County District Attorney Kenneth Bruno - investigation & arrest of two twin 19 year old brothers in an attempted forcible rape & sodomy case.
- **November 28, 2002** - Letter - Warren County Sheriff Larry Cleveland - Dorothy Finelli homicide investigation & arrest.
- **December 17, 2002** - Letters - Warren County D.A. Kate Hogan / Warren County First Assistant Ted Wilson / Glens Falls Police Chief Richard Carey - Fred A. Beagle investigation & arrest - child fatality.
- **February 20, 2003** - Letter - Rachel Gartner, Director of Catholic Charities - regarding

Now They Lay me Down to Rest

| Senior Investigator Thomas M. Aiken | Biography |

- training provided to staff members.
- **June 20, 2003** - Letter - Mark & Catherine Klebbe - Rape investigation and arrest - former Police Chief Thomas Levandowski.
- **March 08, 2004** - Salem Central School Superintendent Richard G. Wheeler - investigation and arrests of school burglaries.
- **February 11, 2005** - Vermont State Police Lt. Edward J. Ledo - assistance with escaped prisoner from a Vermont State Hospital - Mary Ellen Gottlieb.
- **May 20, 2005** - Fort Edward Police Chief Walter Sandford - assistance with teaching at the Fort Edward Police Academy.
- **July 2005** - Federal Bureau of Investigation {FBI} - Plaque - Director Robert S. Mueller III - Joint investigation of two subjects that committed two murders and then carjacked an older woman and drove her south and viciously murdered her.
- **April 27, 2006** - Letter - D.A. Kevin Kortright - 2nd Letter from Sheriff Roger LeClaire. Assistance in investigation, arrest & prosecution of Sean Doyle. Missing person / homicide.
- **July 17, 2007** - Letter - Katherine Henley - Ray A. Blake investigation & arrest
- **November 14, 2007** - Letter - Plattsburgh Police Chief Desmond J. Racicot - Assisted with arrest of armed suspects from a robbery. Arrest was at the Budget Inn T/Queensbury.
- **April 14, 2008** - Plaque from Washington County District Attorney's Office - Crime Victims' Week
- **April 19, 2008** - Plaque - U.S. Department of Justice - "Spirit of Justice Law Enforcement Award". "The Eagle Award".
- **June 13, 2008** – Letter – Attorney John Patterson – Re: handling his client's investigation.
- **July 20, 2009** – Thank you card from Marilyn Sanders, grandmother of child rape victim Alexis Sanders.
- **July 13, 2012** – Commendation Letter from Sheriff Jeff Murphy – Re: Triple Homicide / Arson investigation, Arrest, and conviction.
- **December 11, 2012** – Major William Sprague – Letter of Commendation – Re: House Explosion with 6 deceased and 5 injured. Investigation, arrest, and conviction with a state prison sentence.

Community Fellowship:

1. Former member of Child Abuse Task Force Advisory Group in Washington County from approximately 1995 to 1997.

2. Former member of Child Abuse Task Force with the START Children's Center in Rensselaer County.

3. Former member of a Child Fatality Review Team in Rensselaer County.

4. Former member and Co-Chair of a multi-county Domestic Violence / Stalking Task Force.

Connie L. Aiken and Thomas M. Aiken

Senior Investigator Thomas M. Aiken	Biography

5. Former member of Child Abuse Task Force in Warren & Washington Counties {CARE Center}.

6. Former member of the Board of Directors – Warren / Washington County CARE Center. Vice President since June 2011.

7. Member of Washington County Child advisory team.

Notables:

1. Involved in the investigation of more than 100 Homicide / Major Crime cases.
2. Involved in the investigation of hundreds of Child Abuse cases - both sexual and physical abuse. Last testimony in court was over 700 Child Abuse cases.
3. Provided testimony hundreds of times including:
    - Preliminary Hearings
    - Grand Jury
    - Suppression Hearings - Mapp, Huntley, Wade, etc...
    - Local Court Trials
    - Superior Court Trials
    - Federal Court Trials
    - Family Court Trials
        - This would include testimony at various hearings & trials in Homicide Cases.
4. **David Pope Homicide Case** - an investigation opened 22 years after the Homicide of a then 2 year old boy which resulted in a murder conviction after trial and a sentence of 25 years to life.
5. Superintendent's Commendation on July 14th, 1995.
6. Presentation of the David Pope case to the Henry Williams Homicide Seminar in September of 1995.
7. Investigation of former **Police Chief Thomas Levandowski** - 50 year sentence after trial - later reversed on appeal. Multi year sentence on Child Pornography upheld.
8. **David A. Jansson** - Child Sex Abuser - 20 year plea bargain.
9. **Chad & Todd Swartout** - twin brothers - Forcible Rape & Sodomy - 20 year plea bargains

Now They Lay me Down to Rest

| Senior Investigator Thomas M. Aiken | Biography |

each.
10. **William Burdick** - Murdered his niece - 25 year plea bargain.
11. **David A. Bentley** - Registered Sex Offender - Rape & Sodomy - 20 year plea bargain.
12. **Gary Colvin** - School Janitor - Rape & Sodomy - 8 1/3 to 25 year plea bargain.
13. **Robert Mercado** - State Prison Guard - Rape & Sodomy - 8 1/3 to 25 year plea bargain.
14. **Burton Campney** - Burglaries in three states - 3 2/3 to 11 years.
15. **Randy Campney** - brother of Burton - trials - 7 to 14 years.
16. **Brian "Alphie" McLaughlin** - Cocaine Dealer - 7.5 to 15 year plea bargain.
17. **Sylvain C. Turcotte** - Double Homicide {wife & mother in law} - trial 50 years to life.
18. **Arnold Brock** - "Shaken Baby" case - 10 year plea bargain.
19. **Elmond S. Winchell** - Domestic Violence / Burglary 1st - trial - 20 years to life.
20. **Eddy L. Duncan** - Manslaughter 1st - 15 year plea bargain.
21. **Peter Manfredi** - Sexual Performance by a Child & Weapons - 7.5 to 15 year plea bargain.
22. **Eugene Coleman** - Child Abuse {daughter} - 10 to 20 years.
23. **Brian Tofte** - Course of Sexual Conduct - 10 to 20 years.
24. **Tony Longtin** - Rape - 3rd - 3.5 to 10 years.
25. **Juan Ortiz** - Course of Sexual Conduct - Trial 17 years to 20 years.
26. **Jason T. Shepard** - 16 year old child rapist - trial - 8.5 years to 17 years.
27. **Benjamin Hoy** - Sodomy 1st - 7 2/3 to 12 years.
28. **Richard Schwarz** - Rape 1st - 5 to 10 years.
29. **Rodney Bates** - Sexual Abuse 1st - 2 to 4 years.
30. **Zind H. Nutting** - Sodomy 1st - 6 to 18 years.
31. **Michael J. Gutkaiss** - Sodomy 1st - trial 21 & 1/3 to 64 years. Later amended to 13 to 39 years.
32. **Timothy J. Gutkaiss** - Sodomy 1st - trial 8 1/3 to 25 years.
33. **Nicole Dunn** - Sodomy 1st - trial 39 & 2/3 to 89 years. Later amended to 10 - 20 years.
34. **Mary Beth Anslow** - Daycare / Infant Death - investigation, arrest & trial - 1 year.
35. **David J. Nutting** - Child Abuse - 12 year plea bargain.
36. **Fred A. Beagle** - Manslaughter 2nd - Child Death by suffocation - trial 5 to 15 years.

349

Senior Investigator Thomas M. Aiken	Biography

37. **John C. Mastrangelo** - Sodomy & Sexual Abuse - 15 year plea bargain.
38. **Allen C. Sebast** - Rape & Criminal Sexual Act - 20 year plea bargain.
39. Many other plea bargains and trials with sentences of 10 years or more.
40. Affiant of over 150 Search Warrants. Taught Search Warrant training to other police officers and departments.
41. Presented & lectured numerous times for many multi-disciplined groups. This includes lecturing for other police agencies in Rensselaer County on Search Warrants, Interview & Interrogation, Major Case investigations & preparation and many other topics.
42. Designed two Power Point presentations on Major Case investigations. This includes a Homicide Case and a Rape / Sodomy / Sexual Abuse Investigation. These presentations have been presented to many different multi-discipline groups in the past few years, including representatives from prosecutors' offices in numerous counties, members of the U.S. Attorney's Office, Federal Agents, Crime Victim Advocates, Mental Health providers and Law Enforcement officers from State, County & Local Levels.
43. Teacher at a Police Basic School sponsored by the Fort Edward Police Department.
44. **Raymond Dilorenzo** - Murder Case - Warren County.
45. **Shawn Doyle** - Murder Case - Washington County.
46. **Trust Co Bank Robbery** - Happ, Abadia & Fortier - Fall of 2005 in Washington County. All pled guilty to Bank Robbery and sentenced to Federal Prison. Also, indicted in Washington County & Vermont on numerous burglaries.
47. **Fort Edward School Arson Fire** - investigation & arrests - Washington County.
48. **Arthur Russell** - Child Abuse investigation / arrest / indictment - 15 year plea bargain.
49. **Ray A. Blake** - Child Sexual Abuse - T/Greenwich - Trial in April of 2007. Sentenced to 34 & 1/3 to 53 years on 06-19-07.
50. **Donnie Fell & Bobby Lee** – they murdered their mom in Rutland, Vermont & then car-jacked an older woman at the Price Chopper in Rutland. They drove this mother / grandmother south toward NYC and viciously murdered her in a field as she begged for her life. I took recorded confessions from both as I interviewed them by phone in an attempt to locate this woman's body. She was located and one defendant committed suicide in jail and the other went through a Federal Trial in Vermont and is now awaiting a Federal Death

Now They Lay me Down to Rest

Senior Investigator Thomas M. Aiken — Biography

Sentence.

51. Murder / Suicide - Village of Granville - fall of 2006. **Dawn & Kelly Roberts**.

52. **Thomas Patrick** - Child Abuse {daughter} - arrest / indictment / plea - sentenced to 7 years determinate prison sentence with 5 years post-release supervision.

53. **Jared P. Bromley** - teacher at Fort Ann School. Sexual Abuse of students. Guilty Plea.

54. **William Clear** - Rape & Sexual Abuse - Town of Fort Ann. Pled guilty on 03-27-08 and sentenced to a six (6) year determinate prison sentence.

55. **Kason O'Neil** - Hudson Falls Teacher / Coach - Rape & Sexual Abuse of a 14 yr old student. Trial in September of 2008 – convicted of two misdemeanors of Sexual Abuse 3rd and Endangering the Welfare of a Child – loss of teaching certificate & registering as a sex offender. Reversed on appeal.

56. **Marcus A. Breault** – Murdered a 4 month old boy in January of 2006. Confessed on 09-11-08 to murdering this infant. Arrested & then indicted for two counts of Attempted Murder and one count of Murder. Pled guilty to Murder on 12-12-08 and sentenced to 20 to life prison term & waived his right to appeal.

57. **Todd M. Gregory** – Rape and Criminal Sexual Act involving a girl during the time she was 6 yrs old to 9 yrs old. Village of Fort Edward. Arrested on 01-07-09. Convicted after trial on 07-16-09. Sentence on August 26th to 32 years in State Prison with 30 years of post-release supervision. Child pornography charges still pending.

58. **Morgan Harrington** Overdose / Death Investigation – 17 year old male. Indictment handed up on 10-08-09. On 02-11-10 Joshua Seidel Pled guilty in Wash Co. Court. Sentenced on 04-16-10 to 4 years in State Prison.

59. Numerous other child abuse, assault, burglary and other investigations that have culminated in State Prison sentences.

60. Founder and organizer of a Washington County School Safety Task Force. This is a group of all Principals and other school personnel from every school in Washington County along with all Police Chiefs and Investigators from every police agency in Washington County working together on various school safety issues.

61. Case agent and Affiant of a Federal Wiretap in New York City. .Affiant of two State Wiretaps in Washington County.

CONNIE L. AIKEN AND THOMAS M. AIKEN

Senior Investigator Thomas M. Aiken	Biography

62. **David L. Cox** – Arrested Feb 16, 2011 for Predatory Sexual Abuse of a Child. Pled guilt 2 weeks and 1 day later on March 10th to Criminal Sexual Act 1st, a class "B" Felony. Sentenced on April 08th to 25 years in State Prison and 20 years post release supervision.

63. **Crystal L. Crandall** – Arrested with David Cox for Criminal Sexual Act – 3rd, a class "E" felony for abusing a separate 15 year old girl together. Pled guilty on 08-04-11 and sentenced to serve 1.5 years in prison and 10 years post released supervision on 08-31-11.

64. **Jill M. Ludwig 09-18-81 & John Maynard 03-16-81** – Five (5) Bank Robberies between Vermont and Granville, NY. Helped solve these cases and make the arrests.

65. **Salem House Propane Explosion July 13, 2011** – 11 occupants with 6 deaths including a 3 month old girl. 10 month investigation with well over 100 interviews leading to four week Grand Jury presentment. A sealed indictment charging Steven M. McComsey with 6 counts of Manslaughter 2nd and 2 counts of Reckless Endangerment 1st was handed up and McComsey was arrested and remanded to the Washington County Jail on June 14, 2012 in lieu of $75,000 / $250,000 cash / bond. On 11-15-12 Steven McComsey pled guilty in the Washington County Court to Criminally Negligent Homicide. He waived any right to appeal. On 12-13-12 Steven McComsey was sentenced by Washington County Court Judge Kelly McKeighan to serve a state prison sentence of 1 to 3 years.

66. **Leann M. Coon 08-14-79 & Frank F. Ruggles 11-03-68** – Arson 2nd {class B Felony}, Insurance Fraud 2nd {class C Felony}, Reckless Endangerment 1st and Endangering the Welfare of a Child. They started a fire in their mobile home with their 3 year old son sleep on the couch in the living room. Did this for $102,000 in insurance money. Grand Jury Indictment & Arrested on Thursday, September 20, 2012. Leann Coon pled guilty and was sentenced to a state prison term of 1-3 years.

67. **Robbery / Shooting – April 2013** – Investigation into the armed robbery of Puerto Rican drug dealers by Blood gang drug dealers in Whitehall, NY. Two Puerto Rican drug dealers then retaliated by shooting into multiple mobile homes in Whitehall. Eight arrests to date with prison sentences ranging up to 15 years on plea bargains.

68. **Ora L. Roaix – July 20, 2013** – multiple car fatal accident on Route 22 in the Town of Hebron, Washington County. Investigation revealed that Roaix intentionally drove into the opposite lane in a suicide attempt. He was indicted for multiple counts including

| Senior Investigator Thomas M. Aiken | Biography |

Manslaughter, Criminally Negligent Homicide and assault charges.

CHAPTER 24
MY LIFE

It certainly wasn't easy getting here. It almost became instinctual to hide what I endured as a child. The hard times during our marriage. You can't work those kinds of cases and see the things my husband has seen and have them described to you and not have difficulties. That is why the divorce rate is so high in different types of careers. The ironic part of it is, I am really truly like an open book. That is my personality. I have learned through the years that I must have hidden it really well, because most people when they hear brief parts about my childhood say things like "I would have never guessed." References to my marriage like, how do you do this every day? Let me tell you again, it wasn't easy. Through the years I've learned that I am a very approachable person. That is why I have had many people confide in me their secrets and things that were bothering and hurting them, with me telling them I could truly understand, only to see and hear that same expression, "I would have never guessed." The one that pertains to this book as an example is the last and youngest child of Mae and David. He said the same thing. He would have never realized this because he thought I was completely different than what he thought and was in his mind. The police investigator's wife, looking like she had it all together and looking like she had everything she ever wanted and needed. Someone he thought he could never confide in and he learned over time that he could. He tried several times to shock me, but I could sympathize, understand, and relate to what he was saying. I think he was testing me and he realized that because of what I endured, I could relate to him. Did he bring me to tears a few times telling me some of the things he endured and lived through? Sure did. I knew it was the same type of pattern his father had done to the children in the past. The other children grew to be adults and could articulate what had happened to them. Hodgie was never able to articulate this in his short life. Neither could Robbie because he was severely brain damaged and never developed enough to articulate everything that they endured. Through the years and hearing this so many times, I must present myself in such a way that people feel at ease talking to me and confiding in me, only to be surprised at our similarities. This is where our marriage wasn't always perfect. How could it have been when you are trying to raise 6 kids through the years and having demons haunt us? Not only my childhood, but my husband's cases as well have haunted him. I am a very strong-willed person for all the right reasons and so is my husband. Sometimes these personalities collide. I believe that is one of the reasons for such a high divorce rate in certain professions. The cases he has endured, the things I have seen and can relate to that he couldn't understand because he didn't have this beginning of his life. I hated injustice as much as he did. We learned to manage our life without allowing the numerous cases to destroy us. I truly believe this was God's plan. My life helped him to understand some of the things he was seeing through his career and I learned that not all fathers give up on or hurt their children. I always joked for the past 20 years, "Who adopts from Cambodia other than Angelina Jolie?" I will tell you who. The poor little girl from 25A Kenworthy Avenue in Glens Falls, NY, who nobody loved and who raised their baby sister and had a motherly instinct. I was as stubborn as he was when I first approached him after raising three very active boys who were not sat in front of a TV screen or a computer game. Boys who grew up playing ball, building forts, fishing, hunting, and getting into mischief that they shouldn't have. Boys that were being rambunctious with their father after he came home from work carrying the burden of these cases, where all I wanted was quiet. I soon learned that this was not only healthy for our boys, but for their father also. Our boys were sheltered to an extent and allowed to be carefree and it was easier when they were younger to go to the local IGA whenever their dad was working one of these horrible cases and late hours. I was able to let them pick out a few things a piece and come home and snuggle in and enjoy our treats and take our minds off his absence. This helped me to cope and not worry so much. It became more difficult to hide it as they got older. Although they did not completely understand it, they knew what was going on because so many of these horrific cases were broadcasted in local newspaper stories and on TV newscasts. In the back of my mind, I always knew that there were kids that couldn't wait for dads and moms to come home from work. That is all I ever wanted for my kids because I knew this was so important. I know I spread myself very thin after having three biological children, adopting our Cambodian daughter and then to go on and adopt two more special needs Asian daughters. We both have the philosophy of being well rounded. This case that this book is written about, I knew and my husband knew, that this child deserved as much love as we gave to our children and that someday we would make that known. Not just from the gruesome pictures you have seen, not just from reading the graphic autopsy reports, but documenting that his life was preserved in boxes and went wherever we went. He was always safely brought with us for the past 26 years. He should have been doing the things that my husband was doing when everyone asked him where he was for the past 22 years. We believe in proper discipline. Without it, a child does not have a sense of control. Every child needs and wants discipline. We knew that this little boy, among others that we do and some we don't know about, did not have discipline. They were battered. We knew over the years that there were many children being abused, but we also knew this little boy had a story to tell. That is why we have made him a part of our life. That little poor boy from the longhouses. We will be damned if he is ever forgotten. It was one of the most horrific cases in my husband's career. To say that I could understand some of his abuse allowed me to heal. I was no longer ashamed of where I came from. I was also not ashamed anymore of the fact that my father took his life violently, which was intertwined at the time this case was being investigated. I was proud. It has allowed me to help my husband, it has allowed me to be an approachable person, and it has allowed me to be a better mother. One who has traveled to the other side of the world and back again. One who fed a little girl with an eye dropper who came from the other side of that world. A place where I saw children who were described as what they saw when they spoke about Hodgie. The bones protruding with skin sagging down and distended stomachs. Kids that were truly starving. I wanted to take them all under my wings, not shoe them away and not protect them emotionally or physically like Hodgie's mother. I still just don't understand how some moms like me have such a strong motherly instinct to protect their children and others like Mae don't have it at all. Even daughters that were not born to me. Even though I didn't carry my daughters physically, the moment I met them, or even before, my instincts to love and protect were there. Why do some moms let their children be victimized? My husband and I also realized through our adoptions that a child does not have to be born to you to be your child. We have both told so many people that nothing could convince us after having three biological children, that our three adopted daughters were not born to us. As we told them all of their lives, some kids are born in the mommy's stomach, and others are born in the mom and dad's heart. They were all three born in our heart. A battered child learns early on, the arm motion of shoeing a child away when they look to you for protection. With a mom that has a true instinct to protect, her arms are like wings that will scoop them in and protect them. Not all moms do this. It is a swooping motion to pull those children into you to protect and keep them safe. Our jobs are not done here. We won't give up. We will continue the fight. I hope you learned something from my life, but I also pray you will not only see the battered Hodgie in your mind, but this will forever change you to not look the other way.

I sincerely and thank you for reading about my life.